BINYA

NEIL KIRBY

Neil Kirby
Binya

Copyright © 2025 by Neil Kirby
First Edition

Softcover ISBN 978-1-7640812-0-7
eBook ISBN 978-1-7640812-1-4

Book Design | Petya Tsankova
Editor | Tara McGuire
Editor and Proofreader | Justin Chevrier
Cover Art | Mary McKee
Publishing Management | TSPA The Self Publishing Agency, Inc.

Sitting lonely in the silence, come the phantoms of the past,
And across my heated fancy are their shadows swiftly cast,
Till the ghosts of buried mem'ries in the chamber silent tread,
And I seem to hold communion with the spirits of the dead.

Kenneth Mackay
1887

PROLOGUE

The farm, Binya, had been established by Edmund James in 1919. Long before then, Edmund's father and mother had sold their modest few acres in Tipperary, Ireland, and in 1883, set sail for a life as free settlers in Australia. They arrived in Botany Bay on the ship the *Illawarra* on 29 July 1883. Edmund was conceived on the journey and born later that year. The family was given a small grant of land just outside Harden.

In 1897, Australian troops were gathering to fight in the Boer War, otherwise known as the Second South African War. Word passed quickly that James Mackay would be riding into town to raise an army, ready to fight in the war. James Mackay came from nearby Wallendbeen. Edmund's father had been friends with the Mackay family and would often go to the races to watch James, for he was a talented jockey. Edmund would marvel at James's ability to handle a horse. Edmund's father had two books of poetry written by James Mackay.

Great excitement spread throughout the town when news broke that the very first muster to raise the troops of the Australian Light Horse would be held in Murrumburrah. Edmund joined the celebration, full of excited wonder. He pinned the advertisement, that appeared in the Harden-Murrumburrah Express, to the back of his bedroom door. The thrill of signing up for the calvary troop overwhelmed him. Edmund's enthusiasm was driven even further by the friendship between Mackay and Edmund's father. He boasted of his father's friendship with this famous soldier, jockey and poet (a description crafted by Edmund). Edmund only had a couple of days to wait for 30 August 1897 to dawn, but for him, the morning took an eternity to arrive. Everyone in town knew his age—he was fourteen years old. At the muster, when asked for his age, he proudly declared sixteen, and not an eyelid fluttered, only a hint of a grin on the faces of the ladies present.

Edmund's excitement could not be contained, and a smile lit his face for days. He threw everything into his new role as a cavalryman in the 1st Australian Horse. Edmund had not realised at the time the part he was playing in history—being in the first batch of recruits for the Australian Light Horse—a lasting iconic symbol of Australia's war time efforts and etched forever into Australian history.

Edmund's horse skills impressed his seniors. He always said his proudest moment in his life was when he first wore his khaki uniform. He proudly viewed the reflection in the mirror—face-to-face with an Australian cavalryman—keen to go to war. Disappointed not to be in the first group to go overseas in November 1899, he didn't have to wait long for the opportunity he longed for. On 17 January 1900, three weeks before his seventeenth birthday, he and 101 other soldiers, five officers and 121 horses set sail on the transport ship, *Surry*, for Cape Town.

Edmund first faced battle at Poplar Cove, then Pretoria. A fierce battle raged on 10 March, in the Battle of the Zand River. Two men were killed, one of them riding only two horses to Edmund's left.

Battles continued over the next month. He witnessed the day that Lord Roberts led a victory parade through the church square in Pretoria. The war rolled on and two days later, Edmund rode into the Battle of Diamond Hill. Surrounded by bloody battle, he felt the real presence of impending death. Multiple forces charged from many directions. The Boers had already successfully counterattacked. Edmund rode into battle and answered the order: "Charge!" Without hesitation, he whipped his horse into a gallop and, whilst under heavy fire, charged toward the Boer line.

Two of Edmund's comrades fell in the battle. He had formed a close bond with Percy Drage after meeting him in the battle at Pretoria, and they became good mates. As the last Boers retreated and the gunfire eased, he stumbled over Percy's body. Edmund picked him up, heaved him over his shoulder and carried him back to the bottom of the hill. When he found their horses, Edmund laid Percy's body across his own, mounted up and led Percy and his horse back to the British line.

Edmund lost count of the battles. In Cape Town, March 1901, he and his unit boarded the transport ship, *Tongariro,* arriving back in Sydney on 2 May 1901. The small contingent from Murrumburrah–Harden arrived home to a rousing reception at the train station. Their efforts in the Boer War had not gone unnoticed, both in Australia and England. The townspeople were proud of their heroes and let them know it, cheering them as they marched from the railway station, down the main street, showering them in streamers. Strangers hugging and kissing strangers.

The joy and celebration shocked Edmund. He had nothing good to remember or share about his time at war. The final days of battle had been tough. A year ago, he had never seen a dead body. Death had now become common, almost routine. He had not given any thought as to what may be waiting for him, other than the excitement of seeing his mum and dad. He longed for a quiet place without the smell of death.

On the contrary, a wild celebration greeted Edmund and his comrades when they disembarked from the train at Harden Railway Station. To his surprise, they were the centre of attention of many admiring young girls. After recovering from the initial shock, he embraced the festivities, hugging and kissing many people—his parents, family friends and many young women—some he recognised, some he didn't.

His eyes were drawn to Heather. He particularly remembered her kiss. They had attended school together and worshipped at the same church. At the station, she wrapped her arms around him and gave the biggest kiss he had ever experienced—lip on lip. He flushed at the attention.

At the welcome-home party held in the Harden Mechanics Institute Hall in Neill Street, they danced together most of the night. Later, in the bushes behind the hall, they made love. Both lost their virginity that night.

At the end of the week, Edmund proposed to Heather. He didn't know if he loved her. He was sure he didn't know what love was. Having never made love to a girl before, his thoughts were more concerned about what would happen if she were to fall pregnant. By marrying her, their secret would go with them to their graves. His parents were excited. Heather's father proudly welcomed a war hero into the family—a man of honour and integrity, or so he said at the wedding reception.

Heather was not pregnant. They were a happy couple and if not in love when they married, they were soon after intensely devoted to each other.

In 1914, Edmund, along with his comrades, set sail again to fight in the Great War. In late August, Heather lined Neill Street to farewell the men of the Murrumburrah Light Horse as they marched to the railway station. They were led by Bertie Reid, a neighbouring farmer to Edmund's parents. Edmund marched with his two mates, John Pope and Russell Gibson, "Gibbo" they called him.

They all fought together with the 1st Light Horse Regiment at Gallipoli. Both John and Gibbo were killed—first John, then Gibbo. They never found Gibbo, but Edmund stumbled upon his dog tags. Edmund continued, but the loss of his mates weighed heavily on him. He remained focused on his job and alert, but not with the invincible shield he once wore.

In October 1917, he and Bertie Reid, their leader out of Murrumburrah, were transferred to the 4th Light Horse Regiment B Squadron. On 31 October, Bertie led a successful cavalry charge against the Turkish trenches in Beersheba. Whilst the charge secured a water supply for the men and horses, Edmund laid wounded. He suffered a gunshot wound to the right shoulder and a broken ankle from when he fell from his horse, convalescing in a hospital in Egypt before being returned to Australia. This time, no fanfare welcomed his arrival, just his parents, Heather, with her loving embrace, and the proud father-in-law.

Once recovered, Edmund bought the farm. He called it Binya because that meant rest, and he sought rest. Very soon after his return, Heather became pregnant. In total, they had four children: Cameron's grandmother, Amy; two brothers, who were both killed in the Second World War; and Amy's sister, Agnes, who is still alive at the age of ninety-eight.

Edmund had inherited his father's sheep farming expertise. In no time, he had a healthy mob and a profitable shear in his second year. He also established a healthy but small herd of milking cows.

Agnes got married, at the age of eighteen, to the son of the owner of the local farming store. They first lived in the house attached to the store. Her husband demonstrated a successful entrepreneurial expertise. Early into their marriage, he established a store in nearby Cootamundra, then a second in Young, then a third in Bowral. Over several years, they moved from town to town, eventually settling in Bowral. Her husband died, and Agnes now lives in an aged care home in Bowral.

Edmund died a couple of months after receiving the telegram that his second son had been killed in the Second World War. He regretted that both of his sons had enlisted and blamed himself for their deaths in that they had followed his lead to join the army. Edmund died from a tetanus infection following an injury on the farm. Heather remained on the farm and died at the age of ninety.

Cameron's grandmother, Amy, never left Binya and became a nurse. Born on the farm, she said that she would die on the farm—and she did. When she married her husband, William

White, he moved in with her on Binya. Amy's nursing career lasted her entire working life. She was on duty at the hospital the night Cameron was born and managed the birth as the midwife. She worked at several hospitals in the area, including Young and Cootamundra. She retired as a matron of the Harden District Hospital.

Grandmother's bedroom had never changed. Even when his great-grandmother died, Cameron's grandmother had not moved from the room she had occupied since birth.

Amy and William had only one child, Cameron's mother, Rosemary. Cameron's mother had shared her family history with him and his sister many times. Family folklore says an understanding had been agreed that Rosemary would marry, and her husband would carry on the farm. But Rosemary married the clerk at the bank, Stanley Blanche, who went on to be the bank manager, living in the bank manager's house in Harden. Cameron and his sister Heidi were raised in that house. Stanley died in a car accident. Cameron often remembered the day the principal came to his classroom to take him back to the office to break the news. Whenever he heard of anyone going to the principal's office, his memory flashed back to that moment. A few years later, his mother remarried and later relocated to Melbourne, after Cameron had moved to Sydney to attend university. Cameron's sister, Heidi, a schoolteacher, married a fellow teacher and currently teaches on the NSW South Coast.

That left Grandma running Binya. Something she did very successfully, with the aid of the son of a long-time family friend, Billy, affectionately called Young Billy. Now in older years, though, everyone still refers to him as Young Billy.

CHAPTER ONE

It was the smell. A distinctly earthy sickly-sweet smell he hadn't encountered elsewhere. Since arriving back on the farm late last night, after an absence of many years, he had found the surrounds familiar, but different—not quite matching his childhood memory. Except for this smell. It smelt exactly as he remembered. Engulfed in white morning fog, the smell alone led him precisely to where he wanted to go, and at the same time, drawing him back into his past.

He'd returned to the farm, but not by his choice. Old people die at the most inconvenient times. There were other places he wanted to be—other places he needed to be. Frustration and anger burned within him.

Despite his anger and frustration, Cameron had awoken that morning with a feeling of comfort and security in a place he had always felt safe. He had always slept in his great-grandmother's bed when he visited the farm. It felt good. He suddenly had a thought of something he wanted to do—not later, but now.

He hadn't unpacked his bag last night, opting to sleep naked, as he often did. He quickly pulled on the clothes that lay discarded on the floor, where he had cast them off as he made a direct path toward the bed, to relieve his exhaustion. He had been in those clothes since arriving at Dubai Airport forever ago. He'd endured several hours of delay at the airport, a fourteen-hour flight, an exhausting day in the Sydney office, a one-hour visit that evolved into nine hours of tedious debate and discussion, followed by a four-hour journey in the rent-a-car to get to where he now stood. The stale, sweaty smell and crushed appearance of his shirt and trousers reflected how he felt, but something beckoned him, and fresh clothes could be found later. Cameron made one concession and ignored his suit coat.

He had a sudden desire to visit the dairy. Despite the dense morning fog, he exited the house yard, turned left, heading in its direction. He wanted to deny any desire to be here, but something ignited in his brain, and he let that spark lead him. He strode with conviction toward the dairy some 400 metres from the farmhouse, shrouded from view by the dense white fog.

Cameron's frustrations were being replaced by the stimulation of childhood memories as he got closer to the dairy. He continued to resist these comforting feelings. He still didn't understand why he awoke with a desire to visit the old dairy, but his anticipation increased with every step. The smell told him he was getting closer.

The chilly morning air freshened his face. Wet grass saturated his shoes and socks. His toes were numb. His trousers heavy with dew. Thistles pierced through his trousers, scratching his legs, but he almost welcomed it. As a child, he would prance through thistles to avoid the sharp pricks. His grandmother told him he walked through them like a ballerina. He smiled as he strode directly, with purpose—just like his grandmother always had.

And then it appeared. The smell had led him directly to the point where he wanted to be. As a child, he sometimes accompanied his grandfather to the morning milking, but he had never been an early riser, so his visits were infrequent. Cameron much preferred the shearing shed or the rock paddock as places to explore. His grandfather had placed the dairy out of bounds, along with the old quarry. Its unstable walls made it prone to landslides. He had seen dead sheep and sometimes cattle in the quarry that had fallen foul of its crumbling walls.

The dairy harboured snakes that were attracted by the waste milk overflow, according to his grandfather. One day, his grandfather found Cameron and his mate, Ian, playing in the back of the dairy and reacted with an anger that Cameron had rarely seen in his grandfather. Later that day, his grandfather arrived back at the farmhouse with a two-metre-long red-bellied black snake that he had killed, only a breath away from where they had been playing. For the first time, he had felt the reality of potential death. Cameron rarely returned to the dairy and never to the back room.

Now, many years later, he stood again at the fence surrounding the dairy. In its day, it had been a bold, three-tier wooden railway sleeper fence that he would scramble up and over, but he had been too scared to jump off the top, fearing he would hurt himself. Today, it lay in a sad state of disrepair—in some places, the old, decayed sleepers had all but collapsed, others were completely missing. With little effort, he walked through the once fortress.

Despite the state of disrepair, cows would wander to the dairy for the daily milking ritual. No longer the commercial milk producing venture it had been, however, his grandmother had insisted on keeping a few cows to supply her with milk and cream, from which she would make her own butter and ice cream, as well as supplying a few neighbours, for there was always ample milk to spare. The sale of a calf now and then would supplement the farm's income. Cameron recalled standing on a chair turning the handle of the milk separator to produce the cream from which his grandmother would produce butter and ice cream.

Standing in the holding yard, Cameron's Julius Marlow black leather shoes sunk in the wet muddy slush. Excess milk and water run-off from the hosing of the stalls mixed with urine and dung created the unique dairy smell. An old, rusted gate hung almost without purpose from a tired-looking fence-post, the bottom hinge completely broken and unattached, the chain latch doing more to prop the gate partially upright than keeping it shut. At the top of the yard stood the old dairy shed, a simple corrugated iron structure, now rusted and worn with a distinct lean to the east—a testament to the prevailing westerly winds.

At the top of the yard stood the milking stalls. To the right of the milking stalls were the machinery and storage rooms, enclosed in galvanized iron walls with one small window. A structure that somehow defied every summer storm. The main room contained the remnants of the old milking machine that had not been used since the farm stopped producing milk commercially. Over time, the room had become a storeroom for everything that couldn't find another home on the farm. Cameron always admired that on the farm, you disposed of nothing that had any potential of being reused. Grandma could have written the bible of recycling.

An assortment of old household goods, from TVs to kitchen sinks, occupied the entire room. When a handle broke in the farmhouse, Grandmother would say, "There is one in the dairy." An old piece of furniture would be harvested to fix the problem. When the shearers demanded a place to rinse their cups in the shearing shed, the dairy surrendered a disused porcelain basin. The dairy held a bottle or box suitable for any occasion.

Bridles and straps hung to the right, untouched for many years, now cracked and dried with age. Horses had not been on the farm for many years, but decayed saddles hung on the walls. Along the back wall, several old push bikes dangled from the rafters, including his mother's. Cameron could not believe they once rode bicycles through these paddocks, full of this-tles and thorns. Beside the bikes stood a big old wooden box, crammed full of bike frames, wheels and bike parts. He dared not go any closer, remembering the huge red-bellied black snake his grandfather had caught in that very box.

He stood there for some time, leaning on the rail of a milk-ing stall, taking the time to scan the entire dairy, absorbing the playground of his youth. A spring sun quickly established its dominance, burning off the morning fog. Beyond the farmhouse, he could now see the rusted galvanized roof of the shearing shed. He would need to allow time to visit it on his short stay.

He flared his nostrils to inhale a final intake of the sickly-sweet earthy smell unique to this place—his mind fleeting back to a time when the farm had been a place he enjoyed. A time before he pursued a career and life that offered more than the farm ever could. For the first time since his trip began, a little of his anger faded.

Strolling back toward the farmhouse, his mind attempted to reconcile the whirlwind of the last couple of days and his journey that brought him here—a continuum of frustration and sleeplessness. Cameron now lived in Dubai. He liked his busy and sometimes challenging job as a forensic accountant, while very much enjoying the vibrant and cosmopolitan social life that Dubai offered.

Upon hearing the news of his grandmother's death, he had quickly decided that he would not attend the funeral. Work demands didn't allow the time. However, Cameron soon discovered that no one shared his sentiment—not his mother, his sister, his great aunt or even his close workmates. He had been told more than once that there are just some things you simply must do. His mother made it very clear that she didn't approve, reminding him of his responsibilities as the only grandson. "Stand-up to your duties, Cameron," she told him. Cameron had just completed the phone call with his mother when his supervisor, Annand, entered his office. Annand allowed Cameron to vent about the lack of understanding, the disregard for the other priorities in his life and the waste of time this would be, let alone the expense.

When Cameron finally stopped, Annand paused briefly before speaking in a quiet tone, "Cameron, your mother sounds like a wise woman. I cannot say I understand what you're going through, or feeling, because I never knew my grandparents. They were murdered in the 1942 tribal revolt in Koraput in my home country of India. My father and mother almost lost their lives trying to give them a proper burial. They never succeeded and my grandparent's bodies were never retrieved. Sometimes, it is not always about you, Cameron."

With that, Annand left the office. Cameron began making the arrangements to travel to Australia.

Whilst accepting a moral responsibility to attend the funeral, he remained focused on balancing all the other priorities he perceived. The compromise would be to combine a work-focused trip with a funeral. That could be accommodated. His grandmother had lived in a small town of 1,000 residents, some 340 kilometres south-west of Sydney—not too far from his company's Australian office.

However, Cameron knew time and distance were not the real issues. He simply had no desire to return to his town of birth. Small country towns were becoming smaller country towns. Populations were reducing, school enrolments were declining and meaningful work didn't exist. But most of all, for Cameron, the prospect of boredom, the absence of a vibrant social life and lack of choice repulsed him. He accepted that he had to fly back to Australia for a funeral, but the thought of one night, or God forbid two, in his childhood town exceeded his level of tolerance. He would stay in Sydney, drive to the funeral and come back the same day.

But he soon found out the arrangements were not that simple. The funeral had been scheduled for 9 am Thursday. He realised he would need to travel from Sydney the night before. His mother insisted he stay on the farm. So would she. Cameron would need to be in town for the reading of the will sometime after the funeral. His mother had expressed her desire for a family dinner on the farm, making a Saturday return, at the earliest.

At least he could be back in Sydney on Saturday evening in time for the flight back to Dubai to work on Sunday, the first day of the working week.

He arrived at Dubai Airport with the plan to get into Sydney early Wednesday morning, visit the Sydney office for an hour or so and then make his way to his grandmother's home. But before he could settle in at the airport, a delayed departure of several hours threatened that plan. He washed away his immediate frustration courtesy of the business class lounge. He even took the time to indulge in a couple of Bacardi and Cokes whilst he sat in the courtesy seat and had his shoes polished. Despite the delay, his plan would still work.

His frustration intensified when he landed in Sydney yesterday to find that his great aunt, his grandmother's sister, had taken ill. The funeral had been delayed so that she could recover, hopefully early the following week. *How bloody inconsiderate.* At the age of ninety-eight, he wondered how she could even make it to the funeral. He adjusted his plan yet again. He could work in the Sydney office for a couple of days, spend a weekend in Sydney—having a good time, catching up with past university mates—attend the funeral and travel back the same evening for his return trip to Dubai.

That plan also soon went astray. Speaking with his mother, there were some matters with the funeral and farm that she insisted he attend to on Thursday and Friday. He realised that there would be no easy compromise, resolving that he would visit the Sydney office, spend an hour or so attending to work matters, drive to his hometown, attend the funeral and be back in Sydney as soon as possible, after all the other business had been attended to, sometime next week.

Frustration grew into anger as Cameron's one-hour work meeting crept into the afternoon and then into the evening. He had been working on a major forensic accounting examination of a multi-national company in the Pacific region suspected of tax evasion. Nothing of substance had been found yet and management wanted to close the analysis. But Cameron wanted to dig deeper into the activities of some offshore supply companies. He finally convinced them to give him some additional time. *That's what I should be doing instead of attending a funeral in some forgotten town in the middle of nowhere.*

Cameron did not leave his old Sydney office until 8 pm. He drove in silence, preoccupied with the file he had been researching. *I know there is something there, but I can't see it. I must find it.* He visualised the spreadsheets in his head as he drove. He agreed with management on one point—he had already put an exhaustive effort into the review, for no outcome. *But it's not over yet.* Cameron clearly understood a breakthrough had to be made soon. *In Dubai, I would be all over this.*

The twenty-four-hour truck stop at Marulan offered some relief. Normally with the choice between Hungry Jack's or Subway, he would take Subway, but the night called for an upsized burger and fries. He didn't rush, ordering ice cream and a further drink before leaving. For a while, he just sat and watched the Hume Highway travellers going to and fro on their journeys.

The upgraded highway impressed him—double lane and minimal intersections—bypassing numerous small towns that had once only served to delay the journey. *Did those small towns still even exist?* He hoped not. *Everything reaches its use by date.*

He finally reached the exit he had been longing for on the Hume Highway, signalling the last stretch of his journey. As he turned off, the small town of Binalong emerged before him—Population 500, according to a faded sign that hadn't been updated in years. Breaking the silence, Cameron exhaled in disbelief.

"My God," he murmured.

The past wasn't just a memory. It still existed, surrounding him in every detail. Nothing had changed since the last time he passed through this seemingly frozen streetscape. He felt as if he had stepped back in time.

On the outskirts of town, he passed the sign for John Gilbert's grave. He recognised the sign—it hadn't changed. Bushranger John Gilbert had been shot dead at that spot in 1865 by police. His dad had stopped there for a walk to the grave many times. *Not again, Dad, we've been here again and again and again.* Folklore said that fresh flowers would appear on the grave regularly, the identity of the mourner unknown. He rolled his eyes at the recollection. Only thirty kilometres to go.

At last, a speed sign to slow for Harden, his place of birth. A sign announcing a population of 1200 made him smile or grimace, he wasn't sure which. The "town," in fact, consisted of two towns, Harden and Murrumburrah. Harden at the top of the hill, Murrumburrah at the bottom. For the passing traveller, it had long since morphed into one small country town. For residents, they lived in Harden or they lived in Murrumburrah. For everyone else, no one knew where one finished and the other started.

The dashboard clock indicated midnight had come and gone without him noticing. No people. No cars. Nothing had changed. He passed by the old Harden Motel on the left, followed by the memorial swimming pool, then Rudge's Garage. He'd bought his first car from Rudge's. Nothing had changed: not the police station, not the tennis courts, not St Anthony's Catholic Church and not St Paul's Church Hall. They all seemed the same as his earliest recollection.

Binya, the family farm, straddled Currawong Creek a few kilometres out of town. He reached the gate that invited him onto the final 700 m track that led to the farmhouse. His mum had planned to be here, but with the last-minute postponement of the funeral, she had remained in Melbourne.

Cameron shook his head to bring him back to the present. He always found it difficult to let go of things that annoyed him, but his excursion to the dairy and its childhood memories helped dampen the irritations of the last couple of days, at least for now.

With his early morning walk and reminisce complete, he stood back to reorientate himself to the farmhouse.

He desperately needed a shower, but he remembered the farmhouse only had a bath, an original deep porcelain-coated cast iron bath—so deep that Cameron recalled that in his early years, he needed to be lifted in and out. He recalled how hot and steamy the water would be, but also how quickly it would cool because of the deep cold sides of the bath. They never seemed to get warm. Despite the depth of the bath, you were only ever allowed minimal water. Being fed only by tank, use of water was strictly controlled. The ancient water heater would dribble hot water into the bath, taking forever to reach the allowed level.

To conserve water, the bath would be run and then shared by everyone needing a wash, with a little top up allowed between each person. If you bathed last, you got the bonus of the deepest bath and no pressure of someone waiting to get in. Cameron appreciated the bonus of going first—hot water, clean water and the reassurance no one else had peed in the bath. He always did. This morning, Cameron ran it long and deep and hot.

Back in his great-grandmother's bedroom, Cameron absorbed the room and its memories. From his earliest memory, he loved this room and the bed. His great-grandmother slept in this room her entire life, literally from birth to death. Nothing had been altered in the room since her death and it became the family guest room. The four-posted bed, a wedding present, filled the small room. Many people, including his sister Heidi, never liked the very old straw mattress and chose not to use the room. Most people's first encounter with a straw mattress is like sleeping on uneven rocks, but Cameron found it would soon mould to his body shape and keep the memory.

Two items shared the room, a matching wardrobe and duchess—still laid with his great-grandmother's hairbrush, comb and jewellery box. Cameron had always liked the jewellery box—a hard plastic chocolate box produced by Hoadley's Chocolates in the 1950s. Pink and black in colour, with an embossed flower design, it had originally contained two pounds of assorted Hoadley's Chocolate. His favourite chocolate has always been—and remains so today—the Violet Crumble bar, originally made by Abel Hoadley in 1913. His grandmother kept Violet Crumble bars in that box, and she would often restock it when he visited. He opened the lid—empty. *I understand, Grandma, you weren't expecting me.*

Cameron made his way to the kitchen in search of breakfast. Coffee beckoned, so first he needed to boil some water. Two large black kettles full of water sat on the very cold wood-burning stove. He could see the stove had been prepared, as it had always been, as the last chore before going to bed, ready for lighting the next morning. A small pile of kindling wood and kerosene-soaked coals lay prepared in the fire box. A box of matches sat on the top of the stove. The smell of kerosene filled the air, as it had every morning.

He had no intent of lighting the fire today. A heavy ceramic bare-element electric jug, white and motley blue in colour, sat on the bench adjacent to the sink. It had one purpose: to boil water before the wooden stove reached operating temperature. That would do nicely. He hadn't seen a bare-element jug for a long time. They were a unique Australian invention, not used elsewhere in the world and discontinued in Australia in the 1970s. Bare-element jugs differed from electric kettles in that the water was actually electrified. *Grandma, how do you still have this?*

Cameron had moved to Sydney to commence university, setting himself on a journey of exploration, taking him well beyond Harden and the farm and discovering a life of excitement, fun and opportunity. He loved it. The past had passed and would stay in the past—according to Cameron. He believed the present is all that mattered. But standing in the farm kitchen that morning, memories of that life once lived rekindled.

Boiling water spitting from the electric jug brought Cameron back to the present. The old jug predated the whistle and automatic cut off. Cameron next made a most disturbing discovery: no coffee. *I forgot you don't drink coffee, Grandma.* It would have to be tea, then he recalled his grandmother never liked tea bags. He could not recall the last time he made a pot of tea. He settled for a teacup, unable to find a mug.

His reminisce of Binya prompted something he had not considered. *What will become of the farm? What would the new owners do? Could it be subdivided? Who is going to do all this?* He assumed it would be left to his mother in the will. He also expected that the proceeds would, or should, be somehow split between his mother, his sister and him. He made a note to himself to contact some people in his accounting firm who operated in the real estate market to get the current value. For the first time, he realised a financial windfall would come his way.

Putting his accountant hat on, he said out loud, "Thanks, Grandma."

Options for breakfast were limited. His grandmother had been gone for some days. He did some quick calculations. Today is Thursday. She had died on Sunday. Young Billy, the farmhand, had delivered the milk can to the back door on Saturday to find that the previous milk, delivered on Wednesday, still stood at the back door. Young Billy found Grandma unconscious in bed, and she died in hospital on Sunday. Everyone seemed surprised at her being ninety-three years old. "Not a day over eighty," they would say. An autopsy had determined that she suffered a stroke. The doctor had reassured Cameron's mum that nothing could have been done, even if someone had been there—a major stroke and a non-reversible, non-operable bleed. It surprised Cameron that the funeral would be held within the week, but in Harden, someone dying wasn't a common event—bookings not required.

The milk didn't smell good. The fruit in the fruit bowl on the bench did not look fresh. Fortunately for Cameron, his grandmother kept the bread in the freezer. The eggs in the fridge didn't float, so he settled for a couple of poached eggs on toast, followed by some expired Vegemite. He enjoyed the farm-made butter.

After breakfast, Cameron decided to go into town to buy some supplies and attend to the tasks his mother had given him. He would continue exploring the farmhouse later. Going back to his great-grandmother's room, he passed Grandma's bedroom, and for the first time, he felt sadness. He had passed by it several times since arriving last night and had never once thought of her. Cameron knew Grandma as a lovely lady and had much respect and admiration for her. He paused. The realisation that she had died in this room, only days ago, chilled him. He thought of Annand and his family and felt sad for them. For the first time, he felt the closeness of her death. He focused on the shut door, grasping the door-knob, turning it slightly, then decided no. It surprised him somewhat that he couldn't bring himself to enter. He would do it later. *Sorry Grandma. Miss you. I've been a bit of a prick. Sorry.*

As he sorted through his bag, Cameron concluded that the clothes he had brought were somewhat overdressed for Harden. Suitable for a walk through Dubai Mall, even Sydney, but he was not sure if he would blend into the crowd in Harden. RM Williams maybe, but not Gucci. He settled for a smart pair of navy slacks and an expensive but casual white Burj Al Arab golf shirt. No one in Harden would know of the Burj Al Arab, and he certainly would not need to tell anyone that he once stayed there in a suite that cost more per night than most farmers earned in a month or even two.

The drive into town invigorated him. Last night, he arrived in a vacuum of darkness. This morning, he had been blinded by fog. Now both were gone, and he found himself as the centrepiece of a picture-perfect postcard. The rich blue sky contrasted with the colourless dust-filled skies of Dubai. The paddocks were a lush green and bright yellow, full of canola, finished off with touches of purple, courtesy of the Paterson's curse weed. A stark contrast to the sand dunes of Dubai.

"Wow, wow, wow," he said, punching the steering wheel.

He travelled up Albury Street, left into Station Street, then left into a little no through road, Whitton Street, running along the back of the Neill Street shops. This is where his grandmother and mother would always park to go shopping, in front of the Ume Food Products sign. The entire brick wall had been painted with a yellow sign advertising butter, bacon, small goods, cold meat, sausages and frankfurts, all bearing the Quality Ume Certificate of Approval. Four happy cartoon characters of a dad, mum, son and daughter completed the picture. It hadn't changed. He smiled. A narrow laneway between shops led into Neill Street, the main street. A corrugated iron gate now guarded the entrance to the laneway, suggesting it may no longer be a public thoroughfare. Cameron accepted the absence of a lock as permission to enter. He navigated his way along the path as if he had the authority to do so. *Tradition demanded it.*

He first made his way to the familiar news agency, greeted by the news agent immediately upon his arrival. "Ah, Cameron.

Good to see you. Sorry to hear about your grandmother. A lovely lady. We will all miss her."

So much for the expected anonymity.

"Uh, thank you. Much appreciated," Cameron replied to the vaguely familiar man behind the counter and hoping that he would not be asked to address the man by name.

"I suppose you're here for your grandmother's papers?"

"Ahh, yes, that would be great," Cameron replied, not knowing what papers Grandma read.

"I've bundled them altogether from when she last picked them up. She always insisted on getting any papers that she hadn't collected."

The news agent went to the wall of boxed shelving, taking the papers from the hole marked "Amy White," then went to the back of the store and brought out an additional pile of papers.

"Can you remind me what papers she gets?" asked Cameron.

"Always got the same: Sydney Morning Herald, Country Life and the Harden-Murrumburrah Express."

"Can you give me the Financial Review as well, please?"

"For sure, do you want back copies of that?"

"No, no," Cameron replied with a start.

"I'll throw in yesterday's," as he bundled them together.

Whatever. No actually means no, but thanks. I'd read yesterday's in Sydney.

"You don't want them stuffing up your finances while you're away," quipped the news agent.

What the hell? The remark startled Cameron, and before he could think or respond, a lady approached him.

"Oh, Cameron, my dear, so good to see you again and so sorry to hear about your grandmother," said the frail short lady.

"Thank you so much. Yes, the news you always hope never comes," he responded.

What the hell? How come everyone knows who I am, and who are you?

He felt increasingly uncomfortable—trapped—needing air. He wanted to go and go quickly. He felt his neck and face getting hot and sweaty. *I'm not going red, am I?*

"Ruth sends her regards. She is married and teaching in Wollongong these days," continued the old woman.

Ruth? Ruth? He quickly scrambled through his mind. He recalled a Ruth in his class but could not remember her last name. *What was it? It was a Mac something. McDonald? McDougall?*

"Good morning, Mrs McIntyre, your papers," the news agent said.

As calmly as ever, Cameron replied, "Thank you so much, Mrs McIntyre, you're so kind. Please pass on my regards to Ruth."

Smooth work. You've got this.

"We are all so proud of you over there managing the Arabs."

Cameron didn't respond. He didn't know what to reply. *First, the man behind the counter, now Mrs What's-Her-Name? Fixing up my finances? Managing Arabs? What had Grandma been saying?*

"Cameron, do you want me to stop your grandmother's papers?"

"Will sort all that out next week. How much do I owe you?"

"It just goes onto your grandmother's account. We bill at the end of the month."

"Thanks, we'll get it all fixed," Cameron said, comfortable that he would not be here to settle the account. *Someone else's problem.*

"Nice shirt. Great place. Bet you got to stay there often with royalty," the news agent said, as he moved to give his attention to the next customer.

How the hell does he know what the Burj Al Arab is? What stories had Grandma been telling? Now he just wanted to get back to the farm—or better still, back to Dubai, where he could pass with anonymity.

Outside, on the footpath, he paused and took a breath. There were a few more things he needed. With some trepidation, Cameron walked to the Harden Butchery, a few doors up. He swung open the wooden gauze door, the same rusty gauze door he had swung open as a young kid for his mother. *Is that the original gauze?* He recognised the butcher, the same guy that came with the door, apparently, just about a decade older with white messy hair and silver-rimmed glasses balancing on the end of his purple-red, swollen, lumpy nose. *Why wear glasses if you're not going to look through them? Again, no idea of a name. Here we go again.*

"What would you like today, mate?" asked the butcher.

Mate, that's right, this guy calls all the men mate. Cameron tried to play it cool. He ordered some sausages, bacon and lamb chops. The butcher's routine had not changed since Cameron's last visit. Firstly, the meat got thrown onto the mechanical scale, the hands spinning around to indicate the weight. Weight and price were then written with a pencil on the white butcher's paper being used to wrap the meat. Tapping his head with the pencil, he calculated the price for each item, adding them together, all without a calculator or cash register. The wrapping paper became your handwritten receipt. With his meat bundled and wrapped in good old-fashioned butcher's paper, Cameron suddenly realised he had no Australian cash, just his credit card. No problem, the butcher manually entered the total amount into the EFTPOS machine, and he had his bag of meat.

"You're the Blanche boy, aren't you? Sorry to hear about your Nan. Been a customer here since I was a kid."

"Thanks. I appreciate it."

"Send my regards to your mum. Your dad and I used to play tennis together."

"I will," Cameron replied, and then he turned and left. *That's how it should be. Pity its driven him to drink, seeing his nose. Nice guy.*

He approached the grocery store, ready to run the gauntlet of recognition again. To his pleasant surprise, he passed anonymously. All the shop assistants were much Cameron's junior, and he tried not to make eye contact with any shoppers. He had one more stop; he wanted to buy some Harden attire so that he would camouflage better. A pair of jeans, a few casual shirts and a pair of boots. He drove around to the George Sewell's store and managed to buy clothes from a very helpful salesperson who appeared fresh out of school. Then a quick stop at the Hot Bake for fresh bread, a custard tart and a vanilla slice.

And with that done, he set off for Binya. He passed the Harden Town & Country Club, igniting memories of many visits as a child with his parents. He had aways enjoyed the family dinner at the Town & Country. He had been there on many occasions to christen a friend's first legal drink of alcohol on their eighteenth birthday. Return home visits from university, albeit infrequently, regularly included a gathering of old school friends at the club. Cameron glanced at the time on the car dashboard. Late morning. Perfect timing to drop the groceries back at the farmhouse and return for lunch. The last two stops had shown he could survive here with some anonymity.

Walking up to the front of the club, Cameron had the same observation he'd had elsewhere—nothing had changed. Two people were in the dining room. A young man sat at the end of the bar. A woman in a bright red dress with long black hair sat on a stool at the first bench table, facing the opposite direction. What he could see were two very attractive legs. Her dress-standard, making him feel more comfortable in his Burj Al Arab golf shirt. Obviously not from Harden.

Cameron walked to the bar and soon heard that familiar request: "What will it be, matey?"

"A Tooheys, thanks mate," he replied. First time he had used the term "mate" for a while and pleased he could remember the local beer. He enjoyed his Amstel Lager in Dubai, but nothing ever beat the home beer.

"Schooner or middy mate?" Slight panic. Which is which? He hadn't ordered a schooner or a middy for some time.

"Been a busy morning mate, go all the way."

"One schooner coming up."

Out of jail on that one. He wrapped his hand around the icy wet glass, beer froth running down the side. He took his first drink. *Yep, a good call.* Behind the bar, a sign read: Welcome Back. Cameron thought whether to appreciate it or not.

"So, the boy who made it big is back in town?"

He turned to the guy at the end of the bar. His schooner almost empty—a full one waiting, standing next to another empty glass.

"What?" Cameron asked, while at the same time trying to see if he recognised the person who had asked the question. He appeared young, but thin, sad and unhappy, not recently shaven and untidy hair that hadn't been cut for some time. But he looked familiar.

"Park your private jet at the airport, did yah?"

Cameron didn't know how to respond. *What the bloody hell has Grandma been saying?*

Cameron examined the guy more closely. "Gary?"

Cameron remembered Gary, a classmate. They weren't close friends, but they had got on at school. His father owned a sheep and wheat property just out of town, on the road to Boorowa.

"Come back here to rub our arses in your cash, eh?"

"Sorry mate, just after a drink," Cameron replied, turning to the barman, "Here's my card, you got a menu for lunch?"

"On the board above you, mate," the barman replied.

"Thanks. Put the beer on that, and one for my mate."

"I don't want your bloody beer," Gary spat. "And we don't use plastic around here. That is what cash is for."

Cameron picked up his beer and turned to head for a table far from the bar. As he passed by, the lady sitting at the bench table spoke, "Don't take it to heart, Cameron. Gary's had it pretty tough."

He turned to see the person behind the voice. Her beauty stunned him. He took a closer look.

"Jacqui?"

"What, you don't remember me?" she said softly with a grin.

He remembered her alright, but as a very plain girl, not what he would have called attractive. Before him now stood a stunning woman. Her face dominated by the most engaging smile, with the most perfect white teeth. Her eyes shone large and bright. They were the brownest eyes he had ever seen.

He stumbled for words. "Umm, sorry, umm, a bit disorientated, just got in last night and Gary over there scrambled me a bit."

Thanks, Gary, for helping me get out of that one.

"Don't worry about Gary. He has had it tough. His father didn't manage the property at all well. Went bust. Bank took it over. They still live on it, but any money goes to the bank. If you ever want him, just come to that stool."

As she spoke, he couldn't take his eyes off her. His Dubai mates would often mock Cameron for his lack of interest in recognising beautiful women. He was rarely sexually aroused or attracted to a woman or a man. If he didn't have sex, he didn't worry. He just wasn't a sexually active person.

His thoughts went back to the Jacqui with whom he grew up. Their family owned the neighbouring property to Binya, Currawong, but they had lived in town not far from where Cameron and his family lived in the bank manager's house. As families, they would frequently picnic together. One memory flashed into his head. He wished it hadn't. Pimples. Once, Jacqui had a large pimple outbreak on her cheek, only present for a few days, as pimples are, but the image had now jumped into to his mind. He wished it hadn't. His eyes glanced at her right cheek. He could have been mistaken, but he thought he saw her make a subconscious move to pull at her hair to cover her cheek—*Oh God, I hope she didn't notice that.*

"My grandmother died. I'm back for the funeral."

She smiled, "I know, Cameron, I'm actually the one managing the will and estate settlement. We have a reading next week," she said.

What a dumb thing to say. His thoughts were scrambled. Of course, Jacqui, the solicitor. He remembered now. Her father had been a solicitor in Harden for as long as he could remember. Not only were they family friends, but his father as the bank manager and her father a solicitor would frequently do business.

She filled the silent vacuum, "I've come back to Harden for a while to help Dad out."

He now recalled his grandmother telling him that Jacqui had returned to Harden to assist her father and that we should catch up. He had nonchalantly told his grandmother to tell her to come to Dubai.

A couple passed by, heading for a table for lunch. "Hello, Jacqueline."

She returned the greeting with her stunning smile and perfect brown eyes.

"Jacqueline. I haven't heard that for years. Where did they dig that up from?"

"I go by Jacqueline now."

He didn't respond. He simply didn't know what to say. He was in awe of the mature, beautiful and sophisticated person Jacqueline had become. He suddenly felt inadequate and helpless. He wanted to tell her he no longer went by the name Cameron. In Dubai, he responded only to Ronnie. He hadn't been called Cameron since leaving Harden. He dropped that at university to Cam. But he put that thought away, not wanting to fracture this first meeting anymore. The move from Jacqui to Jacqueline fitted her metamorphosis. Hans Christian Anderson was right, the ugly duckling truly had blossomed into a most majestic swan.

Jacqueline broke the silence, "Nice shirt, by the way. Bet you stayed there," she quipped. He quickly concluded that he would have to ditch the shirt. *Fancy everyone in Harden knowing the Burj Al Arab, the world's only seven-star hotel, self-ranked, of course.*

"Hey, I just came in here to grab a counter meal for lunch. Have you eaten?" he asked.

They moved to a table away from Gary and enjoyed lunch, chatting for quite some time. She filled him in on her solicitor career—she enjoyed it and was very happy with her choice of profession. She lived and worked on the north shore of Sydney and didn't have a partner. As she detailed her work and profession, Cameron could see she had an astute understanding of the legal profession and would not be easily intimidated. He sensed she liked being in control. Cameron wondered if Jacqueline had come back to help her father, or to control her father.

Cameron spoke of his accounting work and a little about his work in Dubai. She keenly listened to Cameron's description of his job and life. Her engaging shining eyes never left his. She enjoyed her grilled fish and salad, accompanied by a Sauvignon Blanc, whilst he very much enjoyed his steak, fries and salad, with a follow-up schooner. Finally, she excused herself to get back to the office—work waiting. They walked out together.

For the rest of the day, his thoughts were distracted by Jacqueline. He could not recall when he'd been affected like this before. He remembered the times they shared as kids and through school. He recalled her as being best friends with his sister, Heidi. In Sydney, while they attended university, their paths crossed, but he had never been aroused by her, not like he was now. He struggled to reconcile the girl from his past and the woman he met today.

He moulded into the mattress of his favourite bed. He laid there, eyes staring into the blackness of the night. His mind only saw Jacqueline—that magnetic smile drawing him in, her styled black hair, her engaging eyes, the stunning red dress perfectly complementing her physique. He slipped into a deep sleep without disruption until morning.

CHAPTER TWO

Cameron was awakened by the ringing of his phone.

"Hi Mum."

"Did you see the minister yesterday?"

"No Mum."

"Why not?"

"He wasn't available," *Should I lie about a minister?* "I've arranged to see him today." *Second lie.*

"Is the hall organised for the wake?"

"No one's there."

He had not given a thought to visit the Harden Mechanic Institute Hall although he'd shopped at the grocers right next to it.

"You have to contact Mrs Laddimore on the number I gave you. Did you confirm the will reading with Robert Forbes?"

"I spoke with Jacqui, ah Jacqueline. She confirmed Thursday 10 am," Cameron didn't add that they had not actually discussed the will at all other than her comment that she would be organising it for her dad and had mentioned the meeting.

"I didn't know Jacqui was back. I thought Robert would be doing everything."

"Jacqueline says he is very busy and she has come back to help him out a bit. She says she asked to do it out of respect for our family." He made that bit up. "Mum, why are we waiting so long after the funeral to read the will? I do need to get back to Dubai."

"That's what your grandmother wanted. Grieving and business don't go together, she would say. Maybe she thought it might be the only way to get you to at least stay in Harden for more than the length of a funeral."

Ouch. No response required.

"And also, don't forget to check on the flowers. I've ordered mine, and your sister says they're bringing theirs. Don't forget yours. And don't forget the funeral director. If there's anything else, you can take care of it. And you're giving the eulogy on behalf of the family."

"You hadn't told me that," he responded with shock, "Why can't Heidi do some of this?"

"Heidi is six months pregnant and, besides that, she has been at your grandmother's beck and call for the last decade. Do you want to start listing your visits? And may I add that you are your grandmother's only grandson, and you were always the apple of her eye. Let me know if there are any problems you can't solve.

"Love you, Mum," he said to a call already terminated.

Hate it when she's right. He hadn't been to see his grandmother for a decade or more. But he talked to her once a month on the phone. It would give his grandmother a buzz to receive an international call from the other side of the world. And she was always proud of her only grandson. "He's no ordinary accountant, you know!" she would tell many people. And the comments he'd heard in one day suggested she had been the proud grandmother to the day she died.

He scanned the emails on his mobile phone. His job didn't attract a lot of emails—a job done solo behind a closed door. He found the anomalies; others did the detective work. In fact, anonymity was a great asset. External emails were rarely sent to him directly other than one-on-one contacts with fellow accountants or investigators, normally with an instruction to examine something specific. His email didn't appear on a business card. In fact, he didn't have a business card. This morning, however, an email had arrived from his Sydney office. His superiors had agreed that further analysis of subsidiary companies would be worthwhile, given the amount of time already invested in this investigation. They wanted a summary of the activity he intended to undertake and time frames. Quite a conciliatory tone, given his meetings only two days prior.

Cameron identified a new problem—no internet connectivity on the farm. Thankfully, he could access his emails on his phone but reading and responding to emails on his mobile phone didn't appeal to him, particularly when it involved reading complex data sheets. The farm had only one landline telephone. At least it had a touchphone keypad, but it amused him that his grandmother's old rotary dial telephone still sat on the bottom shelf of the telephone table.

He typed a short response on his phone explaining his heavy involvement in supporting his mourning family and preparing the funeral. As the only grandson, he would need to give that priority. He offered a brief, high-level outline of what he intended to do for the analysis. He received a warm reply, apologising for disturbing him at this deeply moving and personal time, passing on respects for his grandmother, and telling him to touch base after the funeral and family needs were attended to.

He called Telstra to solve his internet problem, and after the normal routine of pressing one for this, two for that, he wormed his way through several layers of options to finally get a response. NBN was available to his line, but it would take several weeks. Did he want to book it? All too hard and not resolvable before he left. At least he had a lot of downloaded spreadsheets that he could work on offline.

He made a hearty breakfast—fresh orange juice, a bowl of Sustain cereal, bacon and eggs on multigrain toast and an ordinary cup of coffee, the best of what the local grocery store had to offer. *Harden needs a drive-thru barista.* He had seen a decent coffee machine behind the bar at the country club, putting it in a memory file for future reference, provided he could dodge Gary.

Recalling that the process for preparing the bath greatly outweighed the time spent in it, Cameron pre-ran his bath water whilst enjoying breakfast—hot and deep and he very much enjoyed the moment.

Cameron chose to first go to St Paul's Anglican Church. He had fond memories of when he would go regularly with his family. He recalled his confirmation classes as a young boy of fourteen and taking his first communion—the first time he was challenged to consider, inwardly, what he believed. He recalled that it raised more questions than answers for him. He had regularly attended church, but had not been back, other than for weddings and funerals, since he left Harden.

A large metal bolt and padlock prevented entry to the church, but the welcome sign gave a contact telephone number for the minister, and within a few minutes, Reverend Scott Bennett approached, with a broad smile, reaching out his large hand for a welcoming handshake. They were soon chatting under the old pine trees at the door of the church. Cameron found out that St Paul's was Scott's second posting since being ordained. He had grown up in the regional town of Goulburn, less than two hours away, seeming to have a genuine affinity for the area. Married with two young children, he played on the local cricket and rugby league teams, with cricket being his greatest passion. Cameron listened keenly to Scott sharing his sporting interests, including being captain of the cricket team and his prowess as a spin bowler. He told Cameron that the cricket club had a long-standing tradition that every bowler had to declare a wish that the team had to honour if the bowler was to bowl a hat-trick. Scott had wished that if he were to bowl a hat-trick, the whole team would come to a gospel service. He had bowled two hat-tricks, and the team honoured their commitment both times. Now many regularly attended the church. Scott joked that the Catholics snuck in over the back fence.

Like many country churches, the congregation had shrunk significantly, but Scott Bennett appeared to be breathing new life into the parish. He had become well-known and well-liked around town. Cameron took an instant liking to Scott. He found him a likeable guy, who also had a genuine, passionate interest in his parishioners.

"But Cameron, I'm sure you have come to me to talk about your grandmother, not to hear all about the life of St Paul's."

"No, truly, I found that very interesting and exciting. It's changed a lot. None of it sounds like the good old confirmation classes."

"We do move on."

They both laughed.

"Your grandmother embraced the changes. Of course, not all did. But your grandmother said, 'Make it for the young people, God is already going to take us.'" More chuckles.

"She once scored for us at a cricket match, you know," Scott continued.

"I can't believe that! Grandma scoring when she was over ninety years old?"

"Fair dinkum, she did—not long after I started. You may remember the lady's guild would often put on a cake stall at the cricket games and your grandmother always baked at least one cake, most often more, for every stall the church had. Well, Young Billy would bring her in and on this day, she arrived in the middle of a great kerfuffle because the scorer had not yet arrived. 'We can't start, we can't start,' some were crying, particularly those supporting the visiting team who were demanding that they be given the game on forfeit. She walked into the middle of the fracas, snatched the scorebook, obviously knowing what to do and directed everyone: 'Get on with the game, these cakes will go stale!' We won the game. The opposition scrutinised every entry she made and could not find a single fault."

Cameron gave a short laugh, but it quickly faded. In the silence, his eyes welled with tears as the reality of Grandma's passing settled in.

After a pause, Scott continued. "Your grandmother never missed a service. One bitterly cold and wet morning she braved the elements to be the only person present for church, other than my wife. She insisted I still give the sermon, and she sang every hymn."

Cameron absorbed the tribute being made to his grandmother and listened intently.

"And, of course, she is known and well regarded not only here in Harden and Murrumburrah, but throughout the district. Yes, she has Young Billy on the farm, but she has kept an eagle eye on everything that happens. They say she never missed a day in the shed at shearing time."

Scott studied Cameron, "So you are the grandson she is so proud of?"

"I'm getting a little concerned about what my grandmother has been saying. I think she's taken a few liberties. I'm simply doing my job as an accountant, well, a forensic accountant."

"Not according to your grandmother," Scott said with his huge grin. "Not every accountant gets invited to financially manage Dubai!"

"Is that what my grandmother has been saying?" Cameron asked with alarm, burying his face in his open palms, "I don't manage any finances of Dubai. I have nothing to do with the Dubai Government or authorities. I work for a private finance company, doing private accounting. Yes, some of that involves providing information to authorities when fraudulent activity is detected, but nothing more."

"Well, maybe not in so many words, but she thought your expertise and experience were well sought after across the world. 'One of Harden's finest exports.' And those were her words."

"Oh my God," Cameron exclaimed, "Sorry father, um, reverend, um pastor."

Scott laughed. "It's Scott, no need to apologise. You should be very honoured your grandmother thought so highly of you. Putting all that aside, I can tell you, your grandmother loved you very deeply. She spoke of you every week. Not just about your job, but about you. She told me so many stories about you—since the day you wore nappies. I know about the musicals, I know about your university days, I know about your band. I know about your love for the farm. I feel I know you. She always said to me, "He will come back.""

Cameron wanted to say something, but no words would come. He had always cherished his grandmother. He eagerly anticipated their monthly calls. He always left the call knowing someone loved him—truly loved him. As for the farm, yes, as a kid, he loved every visit, particularly weekend sleepovers. But he had moved on from that. He now loved the vibrance and diversity of a city. He loved singing with his guitar, not that he had done that much since Sydney. He loved finding something new and different around the next street corner. He loved everything Harden could not give him but now regretted that he had not found time to come back to visit more often. *Should have kept up the sleepovers.* Cameron knew in his heart he had the time and opportunity to do it but had simply failed to do it—*I'm not the best at making good choices.*

"Come inside, Cameron, and we can put the service together," Scott said, putting his hand on Cameron's shoulder and leading him into the church. Scott suggested some hymns that he knew were his grandmother's favourites, to which Cameron agreed. Next was the Bible reading.

"Do you have any in mind?" asked Scott.

Cameron tried to recall his church-going days but struggled. *A Bible reading? Could I quote one verse from the Bible?* Psalm

23 came to mind—he had heard it at funerals. Then there is the Lord's Prayer, but that's probably already included. And there is that one about many rooms in heaven.

Scott reached out to help, "Can I pass onto you some thoughts from your grandmother? I recall her once saying to me, following a funeral here at the church: *"Don't read the 23rd Psalm at my funeral and don't talk about the rooms in that motel up there. They are done to death."*

Cameron agreed. *Close call. Sorry Grandma.*

"There are a couple of scripture passages I've heard her quote if that's any help. Ecclesiastes 3:1–13 and Romans 8:31–39," Scott said has he reached for the Bible lying in the back of the pew in front of him.

Cameron found the Ecclesiastes passage and immediately recognised it. He could recall Grandma quoting it as he read it to himself: *There is a time for everything, and a season for every activity under heaven … a time to be born and a time to die … a time to plant and a time to uproot … a time to scatter stones and a time to gather them … a time to search and a time to give up.* Cameron softly read the final verse out loud, "That everyone may eat and drink, and find satisfaction in all their toil—this is the gift of God." *Perfect.*

Scott opened a second Bible to find the second reading. Cameron scanned, "If God is for us, who can be against us?"

"Yep. I can hear Grandma reading both. She had a record on her record player of *A Time for Everything*. Let's run with both."

It disappointed Cameron that he had not remembered these things about Grandma, until prompted by Scott.

"And who will do the Bible readings?"

His sister must make some contribution. "Heidi, my sister," Cameron volunteered and paused for a minute, "Perhaps Billy?"

"Billy can't read that well," Scott observed.

"Okay, how about my grandma's sister, Agnes? She's ninety-eight but that hasn't slowed her talking, from what I hear. And she will attend as if she is royalty. She may not be that mobile; she'll probably be in a wheelchair."

"Amy talked a lot about her sister Agnes, but I have never met her," Scott replied. "But a wheelchair is no problem. We have them here often. And we can always take the microphone to her; they are wireless. Contact her and see if there will be any problem. Remember, the service got postponed because she has been unwell, so make sure she is up to it."

"Great, thanks," Cameron's relief was obvious by the large sigh he exhaled.

"Now, your mum told me in an email you would be giving the family eulogy?"

"Yes, no problem," Cameron replied immediately. He hadn't been happy about it when his mum said it this morning, but with what he had been hearing over the last couple of days, he felt he owed that to his grandmother, and he wanted to do it. What he would say, he had no idea.

"I know your mother had a close friend in Mabel Ferry who still attends the church here. She is keen to speak on behalf of her church family. Is that okay?"

"Of course."

"Well, that's about it. There will be a small interment at the grave-side, but I will take care of all of that. The family will be asked to come forward and throw a spade of soil into the grave. And I understand you will be going to the Harden Mechanics Institute for a wake. Have you got any more questions or requests?"

Cameron had gone to the church with some trepidation, never having had planned a funeral. He now felt a satisfaction that he had honoured his grandmother, thanks to Scott. He also felt confident his mum would be happy. Grandma would agree. He slowly walked back to the car and sat. He felt remorse for ever considering not coming to the funeral. He felt embarrassed and disappointed he didn't know his grandmother better. He felt guilty that he had not visited. He missed her. He also knew he wanted to get back to his work in Dubai.

He drove to the Hot Bake, purchased a vanilla slice and Coke and then found a picnic table in the park opposite Rudge's Garage. Cameron rang his mother and briefed her on the funeral arrangements. He sensed his mother's relief. She commented, "I'm glad I wasn't there; I wouldn't know any of that stuff about hymns and Bible readings."

That made Cameron sad. *Did anyone know Grandma? Does anyone think to talk to old people about these things before they die?* Cameron's mum agreed to contact Aunt Agnes, phoning back soon after to say that she "would be truly honoured to do the Bible reading for her sister."

He rang Mrs Laddimore. No need to come to the hall—she had been talking to the minister and Percy, the funeral director. Between them, they estimated around thirty to forty attendees. Mainly the church congregation, along with the old-time farmers and shop owners who were left, as well as a representation from the hospital nursing staff. Mrs Laddimore assured Cameron that no one estimated numbers better than Percy. But Cameron had to select the refreshment package. For four dollars and fifty cents a head, he could have a selection of three variety of teas, coffee, water and dried biscuits. For eight dollars, he could add scones and two varieties of slices and/or cakes, and for twelve dollars, he would get an additional slice or cake, along with a variety of hot finger food.

"Go for the lot," Cameron responded. He organised the bill to be sent directly to him.

It surprised Cameron, but then again not, to find that the funeral director's staff consisted only of Percy. His wife and a few friends would help as ushers when needed. Funerals in

Harden were not normally that big. Percy had everything under control. Cameron's mum had already emailed a photo. Scott would send through a copy of the order of service and supply all the family names.

"There is only one more thing I need from you, Cameron," Percy said. "Your mum has only supplied the names of four pall-bearers: you, your brother-in-law Bruce, your stepdad Paul and Young Billy. Firstly, I recommend six. Four is barely enough—a coffin with a corpse is not that lightweight. Secondly, your stepdad should be free to escort your mum when they follow the coffin out. It can be a lonely walk, so having someone for support helps. Can you find another three pallbearers?"

Cameron thought for a few minutes. Another question he had no immediate answer for. Jacqui's father would do it. *That's one.* If he contacted Scott, surely there would be someone who could represent the church. One more. *Ian? Perhaps.* Ian had been Cameron's best mate. But that friendship had cooled over the last few years. It had been a long time since they'd had any contact. Since arriving back in Harden, he had thought about contacting Ian, but he thought more about not contacting him.

"Okay, I'll get back to you on that," Cameron replied.

"Well, I print on Monday afternoon, so let me know no later than Monday morning," Percy said.

Cameron suspected that "to print" meant placing it on the photocopier, selecting thirty copies and pushing start. "Of course, I'll have it to you on time."

One more task on the list: the flowers. Mother insisted that each family member give their personal wreath of flowers to display around the coffin in the church and later to lay on the grave. Apparently, flower wreaths were still the tradition in Harden. That would be easy to organise, he hoped. Cameron wished his sister Heidi had ordered her flowers at the same shop because he wanted to be sure that his was at least slightly bigger than hers. *It would be better if her husband had bought them, then they definitely would need to be a lot bigger. Sibling rivalry, you've got to love it.* But they hadn't and he could only assume they were bringing flowers with them. Not to overdo it, he ordered the same size wreath as his mum. On inspection, he concluded they were too small, so he upgraded both. The florist informed him that his mum had not mentioned casket flowers to grace the top of the coffin. Cameron conveyed with confidence that his mother had left that to him.

"What flowers do you want?" the florist asked, pointing to the pictures on the wall. His grandmother grew roses and daffodils when in season. He pictured the pretty fields of green and yellow that he had seen the last two days surrounding Harden. "Yellow roses in a bed of green, with a touch of purple," he said.

That's a real touch of Binya.

"That arrangement for the coffin will be $385. Do you want to pay separately or all together?" the florist asked.

What? It had been a long time since he'd bought flowers for anyone—in fact he could not recall ever ordering flowers. The bill totalled nearly $600. *And I'm going to bury these things in a couple of days?*

"That's fine, altogether, thanks," he smiled. *Grandma would like it.*

Back at the farm, after a homemade sandwich and a cup of supermarket coffee, he focused on what he does best—drilling down deep into the abyss of spreadsheets and financial statements to find the missing, or more accurately, hidden links that lead to black holes. He had no internet access on his laptop, but he had an ample amount of data downloaded to keep him occupied for some time.

But he knew that he had one final task to attend to before he immersed himself in the data interrogation: finding pallbearers.

He thought of consulting his mother, but she had been clear this morning that he had to fulfill his responsibilities. *Be careful what you wish for, Mum.* He rang Robert Forbes, Jacqueline's dad. No problem at all. He would be honoured. He rang Scott. Scott knew the ideal person to ask: Don, a widowed, retired man from the church. Don's mother and Cameron's grandmother had been soulmates all their lives. They even went to school together. Don had continued to support Cameron's grandmother by taking her shopping, picking her up for church and even having the odd picnic. Scott rang back to confirm Don had willingly accepted the request.

That left one pallbearer remaining.

Saturday dawned into another beautiful day—no fog. Cameron caught eye of the beautiful sunrise out of the bedroom window. Perfect day to explore the farm further. Another bacon and egg breakfast washed down with his supermarket coffee. *Must find that drive-thru barista.*

Decked out in his new Harden attire and an old brim hat he found in the laundry, Cameron could have been mistaken for a farmer—brown leather RM boots, a must for an Aussie man on the land, obligatory Levi's denim jeans and a long-sleeved work shirt for sun protection. He had purchased a few shirts: some plain, some bright and chequered, some short-sleeved and some long-sleeved. Today, Cameron would be a pale blue farmer.

First on the agenda was the shearing shed. It stood 150 metres from the homestead on the other side of a gully that fed one of the property dams. Swinging open the doors, he was immediately enveloped with the unique smell of a shearing shed. He could only describe the smell as the taste of blue vein cheese. The smell and taste of blue vein cheese comes from the combination of *penicillium roquefort* and sheep's milk. And that's the smell of a shearing shed. This was another smell that smelt exactly the same as he had remembered it. The taste of blue vein cheese always brought Cameron's emotions directly back to the shearing shed.

He once read that you can smell a shearing shed for years after the place had fallen silent. As a kid, many a shearer had told Cameron different explanations for the smell, including the lanoline oil in the wool, the sheep themselves and even the sheep dung that would pile up under the open slatted floors. But the belief held by every shearer he knew was that the final ingredient to the smell came from the sweat of the shearers themselves.

But his grandmother gave him the best advice. As a young child, as she walked him to the shearing shed one morning, Cameron asked, "What is that smell?" She replied, "That is the smell of the wool cheque Cameron. Never forget it."

Cameron walked through the holding pens where, as a very young boy, he would help, *or hinder*, the shearing hands, moving the sheep from pen to pen, finally reaching the fetching pens for the shearers. The shearer would push through the swinging doors, grab a sheep, throw it onto its back and pull it by its front legs to the shearing stand. First, he would shear off the rubbish wool around its belly and backside. Then systematically shear off the fleece, being sure to maintain it in one complete piece. Shearers would repeat this routine about 150 times a day.

Whilst the shearer collected the next sheep, the shearing hand would pick up the fleece and with art and skill, in one swoop, fling the fleece flat on the wool table, a round flat table made of rails that spun. The wool classer would go through the fleece, picking out inferior pieces such as the neck, belly and skirting around the edge of the fleece, and bin it separately.

The wool classer would then grade the fleece based on fibre diameter, yield, staple length and staple strength before throwing the graded fleece into marked bins dependent on its classification. The wool presser would then compress the wool into bales using a wool press, each bale weighing about 120 kgs. Finally, the bale had to be properly branded with the owner's brand, description of the wool, bale number and registered classer's number.

Shearing on Binya would occur around April and May. It would stop all other activity on the farm and the whole family was expected to be involved. It would be a major disruption for Cameron and his family. As a young child, Cameron could recall his father raising his voice at Grandma. *"What, you want me to close the bank and come shearing?"* The bank never closed, his father never came, except if they worked weekends when he had no excuse.

But Cameron never missed it. As a young child, he recalled sweeping the shearing stand between each shear. He only had the few seconds it took the shearer to fetch another sheep to have the floor clean. He advanced to working the holding pens, to ensure the fetching pen always had the desired number of sheep. Too few and the shearer would lose vital seconds chasing the sheep. In his later school years, he took on a very responsible position of bale branding: a very critical role, Cameron came to find out.

Strict regulations ruled many aspects of a bale of wool, including fastening, length, weight and the specific requirements of branding. Compliance was non-negotiable. A disallowed bale had major financial ramifications. Cameron mastered it and, despite his school year age, he was not backward in rejecting a bale despite the protests of the seasoned shearers and shearing hands. At an early age, Cameron demonstrated astute skills in quality assurance and the ability to identify any error or a non-compliance.

One famous piece of shearing shed folklore, told every year, recalled the time "when that little kid rejected a bale his father, the bank manager, had branded." Shearing had been extended into Saturday due to wet weather delays. Being Saturday, the banks were closed, giving Cameron's dad no excuse. He had the responsibility of correctly branding and labelling each bale, a logical job for a bank manager, it was thought. Cameron played the quality control role. Cameron rejected a bale his father had prepared for poor quality branding and incorrect location of the label. His father protested loudly, even threatening to send Cameron home, but to no avail, and he suffered the embarrassment of seeing the bale stripped for repacking.

Later in the afternoon, witnessed by no one, Grandma quietly sidled up to Cameron and said, "I have nothing to worry about, knowing you are in the wings."

Cameron recalled those words with pride as he surveyed the shed.

As Cameron closed the shed door, he visioned the bales stacked, ready for dispatch, recalling his job managing the quality of the bales, ensuring all the wool would get to market sales and be correctly presented. For the first time, he pondered upon a connection to his current job of forensic accounting, to the skills of quality control he learnt in the shearing shed. He had wondered where that interest and skill came from. It had been assumed that it had been passed through his father's finance and accounting DNA, but just maybe, those seeds may have been planted on the floor of the shearing shed.

He also recalled that on one of his regular phone calls, not that long ago, his grandmother boasted that, with some of their bales were fetching near $2,000, it would be a record year. With a final whiff, he could smell payday.

Along the western wall of the shearing shed stood an open machinery shed. The old farm truck, tractor, plough and crop planter stood silently along the wall. A nearby stand-alone shed with an extended high roof housed the harvester. None of the machinery had moved for a long time. Cameron saw it as a picture of the past—no longer a resource for the farm. His grandfather had moved away from cropping and commercial milking to concentrate on wool production. Small crops were planted to maintain a supply of grain for feeding the sheep mobs in times of drought. His grandfather's previous truck occupied the last bay in the machinery shed. As a young boy, Cameron had ridden in this truck—a light blue 1954 International R160—firstly with this grandfather, and later with Young Billy. He recalled sitting on his grandfather's lap and holding the steering wheel whist his grandfather drove into town. *Why would you keep it?* But you could ask that about everything on the farm. At least for every year the truck sat there, its value for antique collectors would increase.

For Cameron, the farm was a relic of the past, not a vision of the future.

From the shearing shed, Cameron walked the 700 metres along the track that led to the main road. Turning left, he circum-navigated the property, first passing the old quarry—the second place that his grandfather had forbidden him to visit—which was out of bounds because it was dangerous. A gravel ramp had been formed on the northern side, leading to the bottom of the quarry, for trucks to remove the rock. However, the rest of the walls were crumbling gravel faces, left from the removal of the stone. The edges were extremely unstable. A few landslides were testament to the fragility of the walls. Cameron once followed the distressing call of a cow to find it had fallen over the edge into the quarry, breaking two legs. Young Billy shot it, but no one attempted to remove the carcass—too dangerous.

Cameron walked along the north-eastern boundary, then down the fence line to Currawong Creek. A water treatment plant had been established on the creek just upstream from the property boundary. Binya extended over the creek to one of Cameron's favourite paddocks, called the rock paddock because it contained numerous outcrops of granite in varying sizes and shapes. Every paddock on the farm had a name. There were places you could rock-hop across the creek, but it was too steep for vehicles to access, even the tractor. To get to the rock paddock, you first had to cross the creek, then walk up the hill. The only route to the farmland across the creek required an eight-kilometre drive back through Harden, Murrumburrah and over Demondrille Hill. Cameron didn't cross the creek today but followed it along until he reached the boundary line with the neighbouring property, which was owned by Jacqueline's family.

As he strode back toward the farmhouse for lunch, Cameron's thinking moved to the issue of the sixth pallbearer. And that led him to consider Ian, particularly as he passed the rock paddock where he and Ian had spent many days playing. Ian and Cameron had grown up best of mates. They were in the same class at school and had been inseparable; "Thick and Thin," they were called. Firstly because of their close friendship and because Cameron had a chubby appearance compared to the much leaner Ian. Wherever Cameron went, Ian would follow. Where the name came from, no one knows. Some things in the country just are. That's the way it is.

The arrival of Mrs McKee into town had a significant influence on many people, none more than fifteen-year-old Cameron and his school mate, Ian. A retired music teacher, Mrs McKee had devoted her life to musicals. Some locals promoted that she came from the West End in London—a big claim for a little town such as Harden. Mrs McKee responded, pointing out that thousands of people worked in the West End, mostly earning a pittance. She said to Cameron and his classmates that very few individuals, including herself, could claim they were a product of the West End. Nevertheless, her talents excelled beyond anything Harden had seen. No one really knew why she moved to Harden, but she soon worked part-time as a music teacher at the school, as well as taking on students for private tuition.

Mrs McKee convinced the school to put on a musical—a relatively small production of *Camelot*. Students from the school made up most of the cast, supported by some townsfolk who were keen to demonstrate their hidden singing and acting skills. The quality of the production impressed everyone. It ran its two scheduled nights, which were so well-accepted that "by popular demand," as the posters said, a third show was quickly scheduled a week later.

Both Cameron and Ian had roles in the production. Cameron played the role of Lancelot, Ian the role of Maudred. They were both individually acclaimed for their performances. The review published in the Harden-Murrumburrah Express described Ian as "very good" and Cameron as "outstanding." His grandmother still had the clipping that included their individual pictures. Having your picture in the paper was a big deal.

An immediate call sounded out for a second musical. Mrs McKee recommended they work toward a production of *Les Misérables* in two years' time, the year Cameron and Ian were in year twelve at school. It would be a "bigger than ever" production involving the school and the community. Mrs McKee fostered and maintained the enthusiasm and Harden's production of *Les Misérables* premiered with stunning success. It received very positive ratings in Sydney newspapers. Mrs McKee had coerced two of her previous students from Sydney to play the roles of Jean Valjean and Cossette. Cameron played the role of Marius, the romantic hero who wooed the heart of Cossette. Ian played the role of Enjolras, the rebellious student leader.

Again, both were brilliant and the standouts of the local performers. That performance of *Les Misérables* etched its presence into Harden history. Immediately townspeople called for a third production, but Mrs McKee died the following year, and Harden never became the outback West End.

But the musicals started something for Cameron and Ian.

They began performing together; Cameron on guitar and vocals, Ian on guitar and support singer. They were popular, performing at town functions and several weddings.

Their singing really started to take off when they both went to Sydney to attend university. They started playing at one pub in the inner city and another in Darlinghurst. Through word of mouth, they were getting more bookings, so much that it interfered with their studies, but Cameron forged ahead because he could sense something bigger and brighter, eagerly anticipating opportunities that would present themselves. They were asked to audition to play at the Wentworth Hotel. The audition went well, and they were booked for their first of a regular gig two weeks later.

Three days before their first scheduled performance, Ian got word that his father had collapsed at their farm and rushed to a specialist hospital in Canberra. Ian, an only child, immediately made plans to go to his father's bedside. He wanted Cameron to come with him for support. Cameron declined, determining it was more important for him to stay and prepare for the show. He sought a commitment from Ian that he would be back for their performance.

On Friday, Ian's dad passed away. Just Ian and his mum were by his bedside. The loss of his father devastated Ian, and he struggled to support his mum. He longed for his soulmate Cameron to be there to support him. On hearing the news, Cameron didn't offer to go to support Ian, but rather contacted the Wentworth Hotel manager to tell them that he would perform solo that night. The manger asked why his mate wasn't performing, and Cameron explained that his father had just died. The manager called Cameron an arsehole for not supporting his mate and moved their date back so that they could both play.

Cameron travelled to Harden and stayed until the funeral. The day after, he returned to Sydney to resume university classes and prepare for more music gigs. Ian remained on the farm to support his mother. Two weeks later, Ian contacted Cameron to tell him he would be staying on the farm permanently to continue the family farming legacy.

Cameron pleaded for Ian to come back for the Wentworth gig—he was certain it would lead to bigger things. The gig never happened. Cameron burnt with anger and disappointment. Ian had blown what could have been something big. He felt Ian had ruined their music careers.

Ian had never confided in anyone about what had happened between him and Cameron. He had even covered for Cameron when his mother asked where he was.

Yes, they got together and said sorry to each other, agreeing to let bygones be bygones. But the Thick and Thin bond had been broken. Ian took over the running of his family sheep farm and Cameron returned to Sydney to complete his accounting studies. Cameron's music ambitions frizzled.

After graduation, Cameron got a job in a Sydney accounting firm and a few years later, an opportunity presented itself in the Dubai office for a forensic accounting position. Prior to that, Cameron received an invite to Ian's wedding. Ian asked him to be best man, but Cameron had replied that it clashed with a work commitment that he could not change. They kept in contact with telephone calls for birthdays and occasionally just the random call, but the calls had become less frequent, very less frequent.

The sixth pallbearer. He kept coming back to Ian.

But.

Back in the farmhouse, Cameron felt more at peace than he had when he first arrived. The frustration and anger had subsided. He realised that he had taken his pre-Sydney life, placed it in a box and buried it in the bottom of the cupboard. Now, he realised he had found the box, and it was time to unpack it. Although still eager to return to life and work in Dubai as soon as possible, he admitted to himself that he had enjoyed the reminiscence into his past. However, he had also uncovered the unfinished business with Ian, which left him unsettled.

Finding Jacqueline had stirred something in him, and he hoped to see more of her. His greatest comfort came from reconnecting with Grandma. If only he had done it before last Sunday. He realised he had one more thing he needed to do—and the moment to act was now.

He stood at the door of Grandma's room, his hand resting on the knob before turning it. He felt he should have knocked first, as he slowly pushed the door open. The room bore the evidence of the activity that had occurred some days previous when his grandmother had been found.

Grandma's bed had been twisted toward the open window and pushed tightly against the cupboard. She had always slept with the window open, whether in summer or winter. He guessed the bed had been moved to make room for the transfer from the bed to ambulance stretcher.

Medical waste littered the floor—evidence of the effort to provide emergency care. A roll of green oxygen tubing and a discarded oxygen mask laid abandoned nearby. The bed, stripped of its bedding, exposed a mattress reeking of human waste. The lingering smell and dark stains were vivid evidence of the state in which she had been found.

He had seen enough. *Poor Grandma.*

CHAPTER THREE

Sunday morning brought another gorgeous day bathed in blue sky, golden yellow fields and a splash of purple. Cameron slept well. Each night, the straw mattress moulded a little closer to his body. *Get in the right position and it's perfect.*

He had originally planned to spend the day buried in number-crunching, determined to solve his Pacific work case. But then, a better idea struck him—*let's go to church.*

He had breakfast on the front verandah and read Thursday's edition of the Financial Review, which he had not yet digested. He dressed into his Dubai navy slacks and a long-sleeved Lacoste shirt—a light brown design with blue and white stripes, sleeves rolled halfway up his forearms—feeling confident that he wasn't overdressed.

He arrived at the church at 9.40 am, much earlier than anticipated—still adjusting to Harden traffic. He could not recall when he had last been in a town without any traffic lights whatsoever.

Two ushers greeted him with smiles and a handshake at the door.

"Cameron, so pleased to see you. You're just the same as last time I saw you. So sorry to hear about our Amy. We loved her dearly," the first usher said, shaking his hand rather vigorously. He recognised her but could not remember her name. He replied with a warm smile and a thank you.

"Crystal, this is Cameron, Amy's grandson. He's the one doing so well in Dubai," she said, turning to Cameron, "Cameron, this is Crystal, Scott's wife. Scott is the minister—we are so lucky to have them both here."

Crystal radiated happiness with a most appealing smile, dressed in bright colours, perfect for the spring day. Cameron didn't wait for Crystal to speak, shaking her hand and saying with confidence, "So pleased to meet you. It was a pleasure to meet Scott on Friday. Harden is lucky to have you."

"All in God's placement and timing, but I must say, he has put us in a gorgeous place. You must love it as well?"

The response took Cameron by surprise, and he thought quickly for a reply, "Yes, yes. Great growing up here, but as you say, God takes you places."

"Please, come in."

Six people had already taken their seats. Two elderly ladies were on their knees praying, others fumbling through the hymn book, marking the pages as per the hymn list hanging behind the pulpit. Cameron first considered sitting in the back pew, where he and Scott had sat only a couple of days prior, but as he surveyed the chapel, he remembered that his grandmother always sat in the second row on the right. That's where he decided to go.

In the back of the pew in front of him rested a blue hymn book and a green prayer book. He wondered if they were the same ones used when he attended confirmation classes as a teenager. They looked the same. He flicked through them both.

Behind him, a few people took their seats, chatting amongst themselves about lunch.

At around five minutes before the hour, a steady flow of people entered the church; in all, around twenty-five parishioners had taken their seats. Head down, he scanned through the prayer book when his moment of solitude was interrupted by the presence of someone coming and sitting beside him—close, very close. It took a second to recognise that Jacqueline had arrived. He could smell the clean, fresh fragrance of her hair.

Over her shoulder, he could see her parents positioning themselves into their place one row back on the opposite side. Both gave a polite smile, and her mother gave a polite regal wave.

"Well, this is a surprise," she whispered.

"I always came to church back then."

"Have you been since?"

Points to Jacqueline. The shy smile on her face cemented her victory. Cameron opened his mouth to respond when Scott, the minister, broke the moment, entering from the small vestry to the side, taking his spot at the pulpit. Having met Scott casually, he wasn't expecting the black and white robe. *He really is a minister of religion,* he realised.

Everyone stood. Cameron followed. Scott welcomed the congregation. He made special reference to Cameron Blanche, in town to see his grandmother, Amy White, laid to rest. "Let our prayers be with Cameron, please. Let us all support him and his family this week."

Cameron felt Jacqueline's hand momentarily rest on his. A hot flush ran up his neck and into his cheeks. He felt disappointed when she moved her hand back to her lap.

He hadn't been to a church service since leaving Harden, but he soon got back into the swing of following the order of service in *The Book of Common Prayer.* There were the parts the minister read, then there were responses the congregation made, indicated in bold type, all laid out to follow. He may have been a little behind, but he was getting the hang of it again. *Just keep following Jacqui.*

As is customary in the Church of England, there is a time to exchange greetings with the people around you. "Peace be with you," is answered with "And also with you." Several people took the opportunity to welcome Cameron. First, Jacqui's parents, then the people behind him, and soon more followed. He found himself responding a lot with "And also with you," but never once managed to initiate a "Peace be with you."

Scott brought the focus back to the service by continuing from *The Book of Common Prayer.* Cameron whispered in

Jacqueline's ear, "Peace be with you." He could see the edge of a smile as she remained focused on the man in black and white leading the service. The first hymn was laboriously slow and seemed to not be coming to an end. Cameron sensed Scott seemed bored with it as well, when, after the second verse, he directed the congregation to go the sixth and final verse. *There is a God!* The other two hymns weren't too bad. The quality of the congregation's singing pleasantly surprised Cameron. That had certainly lifted since his previous attendance.

He enjoyed the message Scott delivered, as his opinion of him only got richer. Scott knew how to keep it short and make the relevant points. It referenced the first ten verses of Proverbs 16. One particular verse Scott read struck a chord: "In his heart a man plans his course, but the Lord determines his steps." In Scott's interpretation, he summarised: "We make our own plans, but the Lord determines how we get there."

I control my own plans and determine my own destiny, thank you very much, thought Cameron, but he wondered how opportunities like working in Dubai came about. He hadn't chased it or planned for it. It just happened. Luck, fate or God's plan, Cameron pondered. He even leant forward, got the Bible from the pew and read the chapter as Scott worked through his sermon. If it were all true, what was God's plan for him? Did anyone have a plan for him?

At the closing of the service, Scott reminded the congregation that Amy White's funeral had been rescheduled for Tuesday so that Amy's sister, Agnes, would be well enough to attend. He asked the congregation to pray for her health. Cameron's heart sunk a little when Scott invited all to stay for refreshments and to catch up with Cameron. There went any opportunity of a quick getaway.

As the congregation filed out of the church, Jacqueline and Cameron moved across to greet her parents. They chatted for a few minutes and by the time they made their way toward the door, everyone else had exited the chapel. Outside, some tables had been set up, an electric urn boiling away, along with tea, coffee, cordial and a mixture of sandwiches, slices and cake. He discovered that the Hot Bake, each Saturday, would donate leftover cakes and slices to the churches for morning tea. Rumour had it that Scott's place on the cricket and footy teams guaranteed a generous spread, and they were never short of a lovely feast.

Everyone wanted to shake hands with Cameron—he felt as if he were the honoured guest. Eventually, Cameron and Jacqueline said their goodbyes to Scott and Crystal and made their way toward their cars, where Jacqueline's parents were waiting.

"A most enjoyable morning, but back to the waiting spread-sheets—" Cameron commenced.

"Feel like a picnic?" Jacqueline asked.

"Great idea. Where will we go?"

"Cameron Blanche, I'm not amused. I recall only one place for a picnic."

Cameron thought for a second, "Of course, the rock pad-dock!" he exclaimed, loud enough to attract the attention and amusement of the few remaining people.

"Where else?"

"Mum and Dad coming?"

"No, let's make it just us. It would be good to catch up."

Cameron's morning had been good, but it just got a lot bet-ter.

Jacqueline informed her mum and dad that she and Cameron were going for lunch and she would be home sometime later. She directed Cameron to the service station at Murrumburrah, the only grocery store available on Sunday, returning shortly with a BBQ chicken, her favourite Hot Bake buns, some pre-made coleslaw and a small array of salad vegetables. They slipped by the Forbes house, where Jacqueline was living with her parents, collecting a cane picnic basket, containing all the necessities, some camp chairs and a chilled bottle of wine. A quick trip back through Murrumburrah, up Demondrille Hill and they were at the rock paddock.

It was as beautiful as ever—a breathtaking view. The paddock, so named for its numerous granite boulders and outcrops. No other paddock east or west had the same rock features. In the foreground, the hillside rolled down to the creek below. To the south, rolling farmland extended to the horizon. The Binya farmhouse stood pretty much dead centre, with the dairy to the right and the shearing shed to the left.

Further to the west, they gazed down on the Currawong homestead and farm, named after the creek. Some argued it happened the other way around—that the creek took its name from the property. Despite numerous land searches, the truth remained unclear, leaving it as a favourite topic of debate at the pub.

The Forbes, Jacqueline's parents, owned Currawong. Like Binya, it had been passed down through the generations in her family. Also, like Binya, it had been passed down through the maternal family line. Mary's parents had lived on the farm and when they died, Mary, their only surviving child, inherited it. Mary married Robert, who worked as a lawyer. Although they retained the property, they never lived on it. Robert managed the farm from town, working it himself as much he could, but like Cameron's grandmother, had farmhands doing the bulk of the work. In later years, he leased it.

The Currawong homestead stood larger and more impressive than Binya. It had been maintained and kept clean but not permanently occupied. Jacqueline and her parents would stay in it from time to time for breaks or getaways, though not often.

Cameron's family and the Forbes family maintained a close relationship. Cameron's mother, Rosemary, and Jacqueline's mother, Mary, shared a deep bond since their childhood. Cameron's father and Jacqueline's father were close friends, regularly interacting professionally.

On the first Sunday of every month, immediately after church, the two families gathered at this spot together for a picnic. Heidi, Cameron's sister, and Jacqueline, an only child, shared a close friendship. To ensure he had someone to play with, Cameron always invited his best friend, Ian, to the picnics, which was easily facilitated seeing as Ian would be at church with his family.

The boys never allowed the girls to join their games, and the boys were strictly forbidden from disturbing the girls.

Cameron and Jacqueline parked the car and made their way to the family picnic rock—a very large slab of granite flush to the ground at the very top of the hill, just before it sloped down toward the creek. Ample room to lay out a blanket, relax in camp chairs or sit on the rock. They quickly prepared the food, poured the wine, sat back to enjoy the view and chatted about anything that came to mind.

After a considerable amount of time, their idle chatter dwindled and they both sat, simply enjoying the view and moment in time, content and relaxed. Cameron had not felt this inner peace for a long time.

He broke the silence. "Ian and I would scramble over those rocks."

"Scramble over them?" she quipped. "You territorially fought over those rocks. This rock," pointing to the tallest rock, surrounded by many rocks of different sizes, "was your favourite—"

"Yep, that was my rock—" interjected Cameron.

"It was Fort Apache, you were Rusty," Jacqueline continued. "That's Indian Rock over there, Ian's rock. The aim of the game was to climb each other's rock without being caught. If either of you tagged the other, you would shout out 'Go, Rinto, go!' and you would have to return to your rock and start again. It was then the other's turn to attempt the raid. In fact, you didn't call this the rock paddock, you called it Rin-Tin-Tin Hill. Every time I saw that show on a TV re-run, I'd think of you and Ian."

Cameron's eyes remained fixed on Jacqueline in amazement, not on where she pointed. Only he and Ian played the game. "Wow, I never knew you noticed!" he said, truly in awe, almost offended that she knew their secret.

"I noticed everything about you, Cameron Blanche," she said.

Silence. A long silence.

"I, I ..." Cameron began but could not articulate the next word.

"It's okay, I shouldn't have invaded your space. I'm sorry. That was the rule, wasn't it? The boy's game and the girl's game were never to meet," she said, not raising her eyes.

"I'm sorry, Jack," he said. *Oops*, he remembered, *it's Jacqueline now*. Back then, he called her Jack—a name he never intended to use, it just slipped out one day. At first, he used it to annoy her, but it soon became a nickname that stuck, with the condition that he never say it in front of anyone else. A private name between two young kids. He recalled he sent her a Christmas card addressed "Dear Jack." Everyone laughed, ridiculing him for using a boy's name. In an act of defiance, he called her "Jack" and spelt it that way.

She said nothing. He thought he saw a tear in her eye.

With her eyes cast down, she quietly asked, "What do you remember about me, Cameron Blanche?"

He froze. He could feel sweat on his forehead and palms. Instantly in his head, he could see pimples. *No, not pimples, anything but pimples.*

"I remember calling you Jack and you didn't like it, but I kept tormenting you with it. You accepted it and you were my mate; you were Jack."

"That's about you, Cameron. What do you remember about me?"

Clear your mind, clear your mind, Cameron, clear your mind. Think. Think. He felt panic tightening his chest. He gazed across the farms, taking a moment to let his mind open the archived folders in his head. He would like to say those beautiful rich brown eyes, but he couldn't recall ever noticing them before. *How come I never noticed those eyes before?*

"I remember the day I hurt my arm at school, and I couldn't ride my bike to our home in Cunningham Street. I only had my left hand to push. You went passed, dropped your bike in your yard, ran back and pushed my bike, carrying my bag and walking me home."

She sat in silence, seemingly sharing the same memory in her mind.

"I remember being sick for about a month when I got that infection after my appendix operation," Cameron ventured. "You visited me every afternoon. You brought all my work home from school. You would stay with me while I completed my homework. I would pretend to take longer just so you would stay longer." After a pause, he added, "I never told you that."

"I knew," she replied.

"And when my dad got killed, you were at the hospital. You stayed over that night. I know you were there for Heidi, but I remember you kept checking on me. That was the last time you sat beside me in church, at Dad's funeral."

They sat in silence. A long silence.

"I love this place. I could grow old here," she said.

One side of his brain screamed to agree, but the other wanted to tell her the truth and get back to Dubai. He had not yet found where he wanted to grow old and had no immediate plans to find it.

A change of subject broke the silence.

"So," Jacqueline asked in a more casual upbeat, "Tell me, what does a forensic accountant do?"

He welcomed the change.

"Oh, you know, we search for fraud, tax evasion, hidden money from divorce settlements."

"I know about the last one, I'm dealing with you guys quite regularly on divorce cases and you are right. The amount of time people spend attempting to hide money in a divorce settlement is staggering," she said. "What I meant though, is how do you do it? How do you find hidden money?"

"Well, I first worked for a particular accountant after uni. He would say to me, 'Cam, look deep into the spreadsheets. The answer is in the numbers. The answer is in front of you.' He taught me to do Sudokus and he took me to crazy levels of difficulty. He would say, 'If you can do Sudokus, Cam, I mean really tough Sudokus, you can be a forensic accountant.' So, I did."

"But why that stream of accounting?" she asked. "I always thought you would be the next bank manager."

He gave a chuckle. "Never a bank manager, no. I don't know. I visited the shearing shed yesterday and remembered the good job I did, checking that the wool bales met all the regulations, particularly in the branding. I picked up on some that probably would have been missed. I think I always had a knack at scanning numbers and seeing patterns or anomalies.

"In my last year at uni, we had an industry placement, and I went to an accounting firm in Wollongong. They had been investigating an embezzlement by a rogue finance manager who had reportedly been doing it for years to pay gambling debts. An accountant there, nice guy but worked alone and said little, had been working on the case for ages and basically thought he had completed it. He proudly showed me how far back he had gone to a point where he assumed the fraud had run dry. I gave it a quick scan and could see a few issues and asked if I could take a deeper analysis. I expanded all the fields and asked him about some certain entries. He said they were ATO-approved tax office reimbursements. It's complicated because we were talking about historical transactions when systems were very different, but back then, companies could get reimbursed for things like tax-exempted products such as white goods," he explained.

"What, like tax returns?"

"No, they are reimbursements. This happened well before GST, very different back then. Well, I said to this guy: 'But they can't be from the ATO because they were EFTs.' Way back then, the ATO didn't do electronic transfers," Cameron explained.

"I don't get it," she said. "That's how money is transferred."

"Not back then. It had to be a manual payment. Hard to see. But if you dug, you could see it."

"Wow. How much money are we talking?"

"Into the millions."

"Are you serious? How did you see that?"

"It's in the numbers, just keep looking at the numbers."

"What happened?"

"It all went into the criminal case against him. That's where you guys take over. Another criminal in jail. Poor accountant got demoted. And I got an A for the placement. The CEO of the company wrote to the dean and said something like: 'This level of perception is a rare skill in any accountant.'"

He rarely had the opportunity to talk about his work and Jacqui's interest fuelled him to share more.

"In another case of fraud, I investigated this employee suspected of embezzlement, in my first year working for the company I work for now. It also had been going on for ages and while this fraud had been suspected, no one could put their finger on it. To cut it short, monies were being moved, legitimately, between several subsidiary companies based on a pre-determined percentage split. That's all okay. But what some people apparently didn't realise—or maybe they didn't have access to the detailed spreadsheets buried deep within the system—was that the entries were being first split down to four decimal places. Just the way the ratios had been set up. Why? I didn't really understand why. Hey! I'm just here to look at the numbers."

"Anyway, by the time it got to the published financial reports, it reported with two decimal points, right? In other words, down to one cent. Well, when I dug deep into the details, I noticed occasional transactions that only came in with two decimal points. I analysed that most of these entries came from three specific cost centres. When we drilled down further, we found they were all entered and approved by the same guy and never as part of the ratio dividend."

"How many transactions are we talking about, in total I mean?" she asked.

"I don't know," he shrugged, "but tens of thousands."

"I can't believe you could find that. That's amazing."

"Get good at Sudoku," he chuckled. "But you can apply the same skill to anything. It's simply finding what's out of place. For example," he said sweeping his hand across the view in front of him, "what do you see?"

"I see beauty, I see colour, I see—"

"No, no, what do you see? Specifics."

"Umm, I see paddocks. I see canola. I see two houses. I see ..."

He interrupted again, "Do you see the two raptors circling?"

"Where?"

"Up there," he said, pointing, "On the Jugiong Road, just left of Binya's front gate."

Her eyes pierced the horizon for a few moments. "I see, I see," she exclaimed. "But so what?"

"Well, why? Is there something dead there? Maybe not. I dunno, I'm just asking the question," he turned his focus to the right. "That freshly cultivated paddock over there."

"Yeah, I see it," she said. "But so what? What's wrong with that? It's a farm, after all."

"Well, I could ask: why? There is nothing else cultivated. Only that one patch. Unusual. And why such a small cultivation. Too small for a crop, well, a normal crop," he said.

"Are you saying—"

"I'm not saying anything. I'm just reading the numbers and asking the questions, well, figuratively speaking."

"Well, I would love it—the paddock I mean," she said. "I love the smell of freshly cultivated soil. Grandad would always say it's rotten things turning into good things. I love the smell, it's always the same. Exactly as I remember it."

"That's funny. Smell was the first thing I related to when I came back last week. On my first morning, I walked to the dairy and the smell was just as I remembered it. Yesterday—the same thing in the shearing shed. It smelt just as it had the last time I was in there."

"It's the lanoline on the wool, that's where the smell comes from," she said.

"And any good shearer will tell you it's from their sweat as well."

They both laughed.

"Well, I see Cameron and Ian scaling rocks, playing Rin-Tin-Tin. You and Ian should come out for a Rin-Tin-Tin rerun."

They both laughed.

"Have you caught up with Ian?" She hit the nerve and sensed it immediately by Cameron's reaction, "Sorry, I'm going somewhere I shouldn't."

"No, no, it's fine," he said. "Ian and I haven't been that close over the last few years."

"What? Can't be," she said. "Thick and Thin?"

He told her the story about the music gigs in Sydney. She listened without interruption. He told the story of Ian's father. She remembered that clearly. He shared what had happened with the band and how the dream fell apart with Ian gone. He told her how that had made him angry, and he had blamed Ian for the lost opportunity.

"And then I got the invite to his wedding. He rang me and asked me to be best man. I said I couldn't come. I heard it upset him," he said.

"Upset him? Sorry Cameron, you more than upset him. Not just him. There were a lot of people pissed off that you missed that. It really hurt him. And do you know who the one person not pissed off with you?"

"No."

"Ian. He never once said a negative word and even defended you when others voiced off."

For a while he said nothing, then responded, "Can I tell you something? It wasn't that I couldn't come. It was that I didn't come. And I have felt guilty ever since. I've never told anyone that. Not sure I even admitted it to myself."

Another long pause.

"I watched some of your gigs in Sydney. You remember?"

Time for honesty. "No, I don't."

"I studied at the University of New South Wales, living up at Paddington," she started. "I'd been down to see a friend in St Vincent's Hospital. I crossed the road at the traffic lights and you were crossing the road from the opposite side. I even remember the intersection, Oxford and Crown Street. We hugged in the middle of the road and we both scurried back to the other side. Do you remember?"

He closed his eyes and nodded, "Now I do, yes, I remember."

She continued, "You had just got the gig at the Courthouse Hotel on the corner and were playing that night. You invited me back and I came. A great gig. You guys were a hit, and not just with me; the crowd, albeit small, loved it. You promised me you would contact me for the next gig," she paused, "but you never did."

He said nothing.

After some moments, she continued, "Some weeks later, I saw you guys listed on a pub board in Paddington, so I went along again. You guys were even better. You promised me you would contact me—"

"And I never did," he said, completing her sentence.

Feeling battered, he hung his head in shame. "The guy at the Wentworth Hotel, when I suggested I stay in Sydney and do a solo when Ian's dad died, told me I was an arsehole. He was right. I'm so sorry, Jacqui. I don't know what to say."

They sat there for some time. "I wanted to ask Ian to be a pallbearer for Grandma, but I can't bring myself to ask him. I've got no right to ask him."

More silence.

Then, Jacqui stood up. With an affirmative tone, she said, "Well, I know where we are going."

"Where?"

"We're going right now, right this minute, out to Ian's to ask him."

"No, I can't do it now."

"It is not a suggestion. It's a direction. Time to look at the bigger picture, Cameron. Come on, arsehole, on your feet. We're going to Ian's."

Despite Cameron's immediate protests, they were already on their way to Ian's farm on the Barway Road toward Cunningar.

Jacqueline drove, based on the least amount of wine consumed. Cameron wanted to telephone ahead. Jacqueline decided they would arrive unannounced.

The property, named Whiteside, had been in the Blacka family for several generations. A large, charming white homestead, visible from the road, standing at the end of a long, straight track leading directly to the front door. With the aid of barking farm dogs, visitors rarely arrived without notice. As they pulled up adjacent to the front gate, Colleen, Ian's wife, stood at the top of the stairs.

"Don't feel good about this," Cameron muttered, as they alighted the vehicle.

"Sharpen up, arsehole, and face the music."

"Hello," Jacqueline called as she opened the gate.

"What do you two want?" Colleen quickly asked.

Jacqueline dug deep into her diplomacy skills. Dealing with difficult clients and hostile situations, combined with her charming smile and powerful demeanour, had prepared her well.

"Hi, Colleen. You've probably heard about Cameron's grandmother. He's just arrived in town and wanted to catch up with you guys."

"Been here since the middle of the week, I hear," she snapped.

Cameron tensed, suspecting that Jacqueline's strategy of an unexpected arrival may not be working as well as she'd hoped. He could see her digging deep into her legal communication skills, slowing the conversation with pauses, allowing the steam to dissipate.

Ian appeared in the doorway, carrying a baby, and his presence immediately diffused the situation. His face lit up, "Hey guys. Great to see you. Come, come in."

His welcome appeared genuine and warming. It relaxed Cameron a little, but at the same time, it heightened his feelings of guilt. Cameron and Jacqui climbed the stairs onto the verandah and followed Ian through the door, passing the rigid Colleen holding open the gauze door.

"Mind the kids' mess," Ian said, as they followed him down the hallway to the large open living room at the back of the house. Cameron knew it well. A wall of glass windows the length of the entire side wall framed a stunning panoramic view over the property, with parts of Harden visible in the distance. You could see Demondrille Hill in the background, where they had just come from. A painting awaiting an artist.

"So sorry to hear about your grandmother, Cameron. A great lady. I'm really feeling for you," Ian said.

Many people had passed their condolences over the last few days, but none of them had the effect on Cameron as it did this time. Despite his efforts to prevent it, a tear swelled in his eye.

"Thanks, Ian," he said. "The more I'm here, the more I'm appreciating the impact she had on so many people."

"She certainly thought a lot about you," Ian added.

Cameron chuckled, "I'm hearing that a lot lately. I think she has over-exaggerated a bit."

"A lot, I would think," injected Colleen, standing, arms folded, in the kitchen behind the breakfast bench that divided the kitchen from the living room.

"Come on, Colleen, not now," Ian said quietly. "Let's get a cuppa."

Colleen turned toward the stove to put on the kettle.

"Don't worry about her," Ian whispered.

"So, I see the funeral got delayed," Ian said. "I understand her sister is not well."

"Well, yes, but she will be fine," Cameron explained. "Mum stayed in Melbourne, and it was only when I got here that I found out many things were yet to be organised, and so the last few days have been pretty hectic."

"Of course, you've been too busy. There's a surprise," came the quip from the kitchen.

Ian rolled his eyes. "Ignore it, Cameron," he whispered, then in a normal volume, "No, I fully understand. I can understand just how hectic it's been. Terrible time for you."

"Now let's get a cuppa, what will it be—tea or coffee?" Ian asked to give the conversation a diversion.

Teas and coffees were sorted, accompanied by homemade boiled fruit cake. Jacqueline moved to the kitchen bench to assist with the serving. Ian moved closer to Cameron, "Don't worry about it, Cameron," he whispered, "She's been under the pump with the kids and all. It's all fine."

Cameron wasn't sure what was all fine, but he felt that Ian was genuinely pleased to see him and appeared not to be carrying any ill feelings. *Why am I?*

"Actually, Ian, there is something I would like to ask," Cameron ventured. "It would mean a lot to me if you would be a pallbearer for Grandma."

"Let me guess, two days out and one pallbearer short, so let's scrape the bottom of the barrel," came the voice from the kitchen.

"I truly would be honoured. That means a lot to me," Ian replied.

The afternoon proceeded with chatter about many things— the price of wool, availability of shearers, crops and changes that had occurred at Whiteside. Cameron mentioned seeing Gary at the country club. Ian detailed the sad demise of their property. Poor financial management and some wrong choices, he concluded.

Jacqueline managed Colleen very well. Colleen made no further commentary on the conversation between Cameron and Ian. Jacqueline skillfully engaged Colleen in chatter about anything to distract her from the discussion, even tolerating Colleen taking her through, in tedious detail, all her current crochet projects.

Cameron asked about the two children. Barry, named after Ian's father, would be celebrating his second birthday very soon. Cossette was six months old. Cameron remembered back to the *Les Misérables* performance and assumed a connection but sought no clarification. Once Ian started talking about the family, Colleen and Jacqueline joined them and both Ian and Colleen shared many antics of their young children.

As the chatter about family wound down, Cameron observed a guitar on its stand in the corner.

"You still play?" Cameron asked.

"He can sing, you know. He can do more than just back-up," Colleen snapped.

"Oh, he always could play and sing very well," Cameron replied, engaging directly with Colleen for the first time.

"He's a *very* good singer," she continued. "He does shows and lots of weddings."

"Just a bit, not that much," Ian added almost apologetically.

"He's performing a show at the country club Saturday week."

This was not the time for Cameron to announce his return to Dubai next week. He struggled to think of a response.

Jacqueline filled the vacuum. "Well, I'm sorry to say I won't be able to make it. Dad and I have a Law Society dinner in Canberra that night. What's your genre, Ian?"

"Mainly country and soft rock. There are three of us. Peta, don't know if you know her or not, is from Young. She mainly plays keyboard and manages the backing tracks. She's had experience in a number of bands. Kurt is on the drums. He is the Arnold boy, from out on the cherry farms at Young. Peta doesn't think much of him, but he's okay."

It pleased Cameron to hear Ian had kept his music interest. Not wanting to correct Colleen but playing a gig in a pub where most people aren't listening isn't what you call a show. Cameron knew Ian to be a much better guitar player than a singer, but in Harden, he's probably fine. Given the history, Cameron thought it be best not to be in town for the show. *Let's not talk about the war.*

Jacqueline changed the topic. "I'm sorry, but I need to get back to town. Mum has the Sunday roast tonight and I promised I would not miss it." She stood up and made the move toward the door. "It would be great if we could catch up again, maybe toward the end of next week? Let Cameron get over the funeral and the time with his family."

Relief for Cameron. The visit had gone well, but he now needed space. A conversation on music could lead one of two ways and he wanted to avoid opening past wounds, particularly on the back of a relatively painless reunion.

Cameron jumped to his feet. "Thanks, Colleen, for the cuppa. Great fruit cake. You guys are doing a great job with the kids. I'll call you tomorrow, Ian, with the details. Percy is organising everything with the funeral. I'll let him know you will be a pallbearer. I told him I would confirm with him after I asked you." A little lie, but he wanted to dispel any suggestion of it being an afterthought.

Ian and Colleen followed them to the door. As Cameron got to the bottom of the stairs, he turned to Ian, "It's been really good to catch up, mate."

Their eyes made contact. Cameron felt the presence of the Ian of old. "Same here," Ian said, "same here."

Thank goodness Colleen made no parting contribution.

CHAPTER FOUR

The bacon and eggs for breakfast were sizzling when the phone rang.

"Morning, Cameron. Just checking how you pulled up this morning—yesterday got a little rugged for you at times," Jacqui inquired.

"I appreciate that, Jack, all's good. Keep me away from Colleen please," Cameron responded.

"You handled it well. I could see you made Ian's day. He was so pleased to see you."

"Yeah, I could see that. It felt a bit like old times. I'll catch up with him some more. He strikes me that he is really comfortable with where he is at. Far more settled than me."

"So, what's your day?"

"Got a few things to do before Mum gets here this evening. I've also got some work things I must follow up on. Problem is I need to get onto the network and Grandma has no internet here and I can't get it in a hurry, so somehow, I must get access today."

"Come to the office. Dad has a room out the back that is often used by paralegals when he needs them. He wouldn't mind you using it."

"That would be great!" Having network access pleased him, but it excited him more that he had another opportunity to spend time with Jacqueline.

"Dad's office has moved, you know. It's no longer in Neill Street. We are in the old council chambers building in Albury Street. When will you be in?"

He had a few things to do in preparation for the funeral and would hopefully be there by mid-morning.

First, he wanted to have the farmhouse ready for his mother's arrival that evening. She always slept in her original bedroom, located on the western side of the house, known as the sun-room. His grandmother's room still had a bad odour. The soiled mattress not only stank but was an ugly reminder of Grandma's final hours. Without knowing what else to do with it, he got the farm truck and moved the mattress across to the dairy. He contacted Percy and finalised the pallbearers. *Oh shit, the eulogy.* He would have to give thought to that sometime.

By mid-morning, he arrived at the office of R.S. Forbes Solicitors in Albury Street. He had never been here before. A small but stately red brick building from the Victorian age, symmetrically square with a central front door.

Cameron entered the reception room, being immediately greeted by Mabel, the long-serving receptionist and one of his grandmother's long-time friends. Despite having exchanged pleasantries at church only the day before, the now regular exchange took place of lovely praises for his grandmother and reflecting on how dear a friend she had been.

Jacqueline appeared through an impressive solid wooden door, which Cameron later learned had been installed by Mr Forbes when he purchased the building. He greeted her with a formal, "Good morning, Jacqueline." The moment called for formality and decorum.

His eyes immediately locked onto her. She wore a stunning emerald green dress—simple yet elegant—that accentuated her figure with effortless grace. *She dresses so un-Harden-like but it's never out of place.* He loved it.

She led him through the impressive door into a hallway that bisected the building. As they walked, she pointed out Mr Forbes' office on the right and a little further down, on the left, the associate's office, currently being used by Jacqueline. Beyond that, two additional rooms—one on each side—were used by paralegals but had no permanent occupants.

At the rear of the building, a small kitchen room was tucked beside a vast filing room, filling the remaining space—its walls lined with floor-to-ceiling shelves and cabinets of various shapes and sizes, packed with meticulously kept records. Some files were securely stored in locked drawers, others on open shelving, their spines bearing the weight of a century's worth of legal history.

Jacqueline took Cameron into the paralegal office on the right. He was immediately impressed. He would expect to see such an office in Melbourne rather than Harden. He learnt that some of the décor dated back to its time as the council chambers. In the centre stood a large oak desk, in front of a black leather seat with an ornate wooden frame. Bookshelves of legal books filled both side walls. A modern computer with two large screens and a scanner sat on the table, clearly from a different era.

"This is impressive."

"Call it yours while you need it."

"That won't be long."

Jacqueline smiled and lowered her eyes, "Wait one second. I have something for you," as she darted from the room.

She returned with two coffees, "Got your favourite—a short black."

Surprise swept across his face. "Where would you get a short black coffee in Harden?"

"Now Cameron, you will have to learn to be a little less rude. Harden is not the backwater you may think it is."

He took a sip. "This is great." Another sip. "It is really great. You make a great coffee."

"I didn't. It's from Which Craft & Coffee Cottage in Murrum-burrah."

"You can get real coffee in Harden?"

"Well, you will just have to open your eyes, and maybe your mind, a little more. We drove passed it yesterday."

At that moment, Mr Forbes knocked on the open door and entered.

"Good morning, young Cameron. You do look the part behind that desk."

"Thank you so much, Mr Forbes. This is great. It really does help me out."

Mr Forbes tapped his finger on the desk. "My first desk I used as a solicitor and did so until I moved into this building. A solicitor that I had worked for when fresh out of law school left it to me in his will. It had been his father's, also a solicitor. Some history there, Cameron."

Cameron discreetly lifted his coffee off the table and again expressed his thanks.

"Jacqueline has been most helpful," he said.

"And I am sure she will be, going forward," said Mr Forbes. "Feel comfortable using the office for as long as you need. So good to see you at church yesterday. Brought back some great memories of spending time with your parents. Please let Jacqueline know if there is anything you need." He turned and left.

What do you mean, going forward? What more could there be for Jacqueline to help with? God, I hope this is straight forward. He expected it would be.

"Great coffee," he repeated.

"Your favourite," she replied.

"How would you know it's my favourite?" His love of good coffee had only developed after he left Harden.

"That day we met on the crossing near St Vincent's Hospital. We had coffee on Oxford Street, near that hotel where you had your gig. You ordered a short black."

His eyes lowered and his thoughts returned to yesterday and the failings that were revealed in his past relationships, along with what he hadn't seen or appreciated at the time. "How do you remember details like that?"

"You say you look at the numbers. Well, I'm a solicitor. For me, the answer is always in the detail," she replied. "Better let you do your work. The computer is already logged in and you're online. No porn. Dad would not appreciate that." And she turned and left, shutting the door behind her.

Cameron sat at the ornate desk, continuing to scan the room, but his mind dwelt on Jacqueline's words. He saw himself as a person who could see detail, or so he thought. How had she noticed and retained all this detail about him, yet he could recall so little about her? In their childhood, Jacqueline was his sister's friend, and they were always together doing their own thing, not interacting much with Cameron. To him, she was like a cousin. You don't get attracted to a cousin.

He had never really felt a strong romantic or sexual attraction to anyone. Yes, he had sexual encounters with a few, but not regularly or even often. He always kept himself busy with work, often going to bed scanning spreadsheets in his head. There had never been the time to let others in. Seeing Jacqueline now, as if for the first time, aroused him in a way he had never felt before. Jacqueline had always noticed him. More than just noticed him. *How could I have not seen her?*

Soon, he had two screens full of figures in front of him. He had more than a gut feeling that a gem lay buried awaiting discovery. *Focus, Cameron, it can see you.* He could see flows of money in and out of the country. The company had significant assets and a large sales turnover. Accounts balanced, but something about the payable tax bothered him. He had to find the problem. For nearly two hours, he scrolled through balance sheets and transactions. Spreadsheet after spreadsheet.

After hours of analysis and calculations, he found something. He traced transactions to an Indian-based supply company with an office in Fiji. Known fact—nothing new in that. He followed the movement of money from that company to a Nepalese company also operating in Suva. Following some deep transactional reviews and cross-checking movements of money, Cameron found a new jigsaw piece. He discovered money movements that appeared to be with institutions in the British Virgin Islands and Guam, two well-known tax havens who are also known for their iron-clad transaction security. But how did the money make its way back to the Pacific and Australia? These schemes are never direct, but rather, a rabbit warren to make them virtually untraceable.

Other arms of his company had the ability to drill deep into everything, including accounts, transactions and non-financial data transactions such as email and telephone traffic. A promising lead. He sighed with relief. After a couple of hours, he gathered the information collected so far and sent it to the office for others to sniff out the money trails. A lot more work to do, but he felt relieved that a crack in the armour had been exposed.

By afternoon, Cameron wanted to turn his attention to the detail under his nose that he had obviously neglected for some time. He knocked on Jacqueline's door and entered.

"How is your day going?"

Jacqueline smiled and immediately invited him in, directing him the to the dark red leather chairs in the corner of her office, whilst at the same time, very subtly closing the file labelled Amy White Will and Testimony that she had open on her desk. She locked her computer screen and moved to join him in the leather chairs, but not before ringing out to Mabel to bring in two coffees.

"Not a barista short black, but at least from a decent coffee machine," she quipped. "So, how has your day been?"

"Very successful," he replied. "We've been chasing down this company we believe has been evading taxes in a big way. Haven't been able to precisely identify the money trail yet, but I've found a number of transactions that someone higher up can dig deeper into. I think we might have cracked it open at last—we're in the cave, just need to navigate to the pot of gold.

"What about you?" he asked. "What exciting law brief has kept you rivetted all morning?"

"Oh nothing, just routine legal processing. Mundane stuff."

"Tell me, why are you back here in Harden?" he asked as Mabel brought in the coffees.

Jacqueline waited until Mabel left. "Dad's getting on and he's not getting through all the work. He has more than he can handle, but not enough to sustain another solicitor."

"Come on, Jack. Look at you. You're super bright. You're ..." he paused for a second, unsure how to continue.

"You're not a Harden girl? Is that what you want to say?" she asked.

"Well, you're too good for here. You could eat them in the city. I sense there must be something more."

She started with the prepared answer. "I love Harden. I love it here. I love—"

"You might love it here, but you could visit. You should be down making it big in the city."

She paused. Took a sip of her coffee. Put it back on the table and stared out the window. "Okay, you're right," she began, "I have some unfinished business I'm working on. I want to find out what happened to my mother's sisters."

He almost replied with a statement that would have destroyed everything he had built over the last few days. He wanted to ask why she would waste her time trying to solve a mystery that's half a century old. He wanted to tell her what a futile waste of her skills and abilities that would be—a cold case that had become too cold. But he sensed the moment needed sensitivity. Their disappearance half a century ago had a devastating impact on Jacqueline's mother's family and his own mother, Jacqueline's mother's best friend.

"Do you have a lead?"

In a sad, deflated voice, she continued her gaze out the window, "No. Nothing. I've come back to collect everything I can. Two people just can't disappear. There must be an answer. There just has to be! I have always wanted to know what happened, from right back when I first understood the horror of an abduction. It's one of the reasons I studied law. I thought it might lead me to the answers."

"Does your mum want you to find out what happened?"

She shook her head, "No, quite the opposite. She wants me to leave it lie—she won't talk about it."

"So?"

"I can't Cameron. I just can't."

"Didn't that guy who took the Beaumont children in South Australia have something to do with it?"

"See, that's the point, Cameron. There are so many mistruths out there. Firstly, the Beaumont children's disappearance has never been solved—but the police have always had a number one suspect. Everyone I have spoken with in South Australia shares the same gut feeling about a particular suspect. I found out that on the night the girls disappeared, he was in hospital post-surgery.

"Anyway, when you read the police report, the only supposed link to the Beaumont disappearance—which had happened six months or so prior—came down to one report that someone had seen a car with South Australian plates at the Sir George Pub in Jugiong sometime around the time of the disappearance. Jugiong is forty kilometres away on the Hume Highway. Every South Australian car travelling between South Australia and Sydney passes through Jugiong. Any day of the week, you could sit there and you'd be bound to see a South Australian number plate."

"So, the murder—"

"That's another point. Who said it was a murder?"

Cameron knew the story of the Barkley sisters very well. Everyone in Harden did. It happened at a school dance, so it's part of the school's history. Every year, on the anniversary of their disappearance, a memorial has been held at the school and flowers laid at the gate.

Cameron can remember from his first years of school, Jacqueline's mother, Mary, being the centre of attention at the ceremony. The two missing girls were Mary's sisters. Cameron's mother, Rosemary, and Mary had been very close friends from when they were little girls. Cameron recalled, particularly around memorial time, asking his mum about the mystery disappearance, but she would never talk about it. His dad had told him the story. Cameron can remember having lots of questions and his dad would always tell him what he knew.

Later, in high school, at memorial time, the social studies teacher led a project on the disappearance as part of a unit of study on community. Students gathered information and shared personal stories provided by their parents. Cameron's dad helped him gather information. His mother didn't object but wouldn't get involved. Jacqueline and Cameron were not in the same class, and she never spoke about it either. In the Forbes' house, it had always been the forbidden subject.

The Barkley's had three daughters—the youngest was Mary, Jacqueline's mother. Her two sisters, Jane and Kathleen, were older. On 17 September 1966, they went missing and no trace has ever been found. They had set out from their farm, next door to Binya, to ride to the school dance at the Murrumburrah Mechanics Institute Hall. They never arrived. Exhaustive investigations had never found a trace. In that same year, on 26 January, a similar event occurred on Glenelg Beach in South Australia. Three siblings, Jane Nartare, Arnna Kathleen and Grant Ellis Beaumont, disappeared from the beach without a trace. Many similarities between the two events were noted, such as the similarity in the names of the missing Beaumont children, Jane and Arnna Kathleen, and the sisters in Harden, Jane and Kathleen.

Mary had been too young to attend the dance and had stayed home with her mother. Mary never spoke of the event and always declared that she would not have children. Jacqueline was not planned, the consequence of very rare lovemaking with Robert, her husband. They lived in Harden and not on the Currawong farm, largely because of the events that occurred on 17 September 1966.

Cameron saw little or no value in exploring such a cold case. Nearly sixty years had passed—there had never been a location, a body, a motive, a ransom note, a weapon, a suspect or a witness identified. They may have simply met an accidental death. They were riding their bikes on a dark, stormy night. But the absence of bodies remained a mystery. Cameron could see the need to support Jacqueline and didn't want to display his scepticism. He could sense Jacqueline's deep desire to resolve the mystery.

"So, how are you going to go about this?"

"Come, I'll show you."

She led him into a room directly across from the office he had occupied for the day. Cameron immediately observed this room differed from the rest—not a legal office but more like an evidence room. A large wooden table, not a desk, stood in the centre of the room, with a single computer screen attached to a laptop. Along the side wall stood a series of trestle tables, and on them, an array of files, papers, photos and much more.

"This is it so far. I have been gathering every bit of information I can. I have every newspaper article ever written on the case—local, state and national. I have the 16mm news footage taken at the time and it has all been digitalised. I have police statements and the statements of everyone interviewed, mainly the people at the dance. I have every photo taken that I can find, not only from the media, but people around town," she said, slumping into the chair.

"And with all this—I still have nothing."

"Wow, Jack, that's an awesome start," he exclaimed, genuinely impressed. "I'd love to help you. Maybe I can have a quick read of it before I go back to Dubai on the weekend," he said. It disappointed Cameron to be leaving Jacqueline so soon, but excited to know he would be back in his accustomed surrounds.

"Maybe," she softly muttered.

"What? Maybe? What do you mean maybe?" he quizzed, bemused by her response.

"I just didn't know you had set a date," she replied. "I thought you were going to Ian's concert?"

"Yeah, I sense that he wants me to, but I just can't spare another week away from work. I'm onto something with this case now and I sense that work will ramp-up considerably."

She lowered her eyes and her voice, "I'd like you to stay around for a while."

Silence. He wanted to say, "Come back to Dubai with me," but as soon as he thought that, he asked himself what that really meant. They weren't in a relationship, yet, and he wasn't even sure if he wanted to be. He felt emotions raging inside himself that he had never felt before. He knew he would like more time with Jacqueline, but he wanted to return to his life in Dubai. His mind spun with confusion.

"Let's see, eh? Let's see what happens, but in the meantime, let me spend some time reviewing this before the end of the week." He studied her, searching for the hidden thoughts buried inside. She appeared conflicted, not sure of what the future would bring. He smiled, considered an embrace, but didn't. Soon after, he packed up his papers and set off for the farm.

The presence of a car at the farmhouse alerted him to the fact that his mother and stepfather, Paul, had arrived. He found his mum in Grandma's room, sitting on the floor, going through her mother's personal belongings. A tear running down her cheek.

"Hi, Mum, sorry I'm a bit late. Had to do some work and there is no internet here, so Mr Forbes offered me the use of a computer at his office."

"It's fine, Cameron" she sighed. "Just going through some of Mum's things. She didn't throw much out," she said with a comforting smile.

"The state of this room tells me it wasn't a peaceful end for her," his mother mourned. "To go through that alone with no one there to help—and to think she laid here for days. I feel like I wasn't a good daughter in the end."

Cameron placed his arm around her shoulder and gave her time to weep. "There is no need to feel like that, Mum. It appears worse than it was," he offered, trying to find words of comfort. "The paramedics made a bit of a mess. I got rid of the mattress to freshen the room a little."

"But to lay there all that time with no one to help. It must have been awful."

"Mum, she had the stroke, the damage had been done. She knew nothing from that point," he concluded. He didn't know this but thought it might comfort his mother.

"You tried many times to get her to come and spend time with you and Paul. You know she never left this place and never would. She said she would never leave. You can know one thing for sure: she died in the very place she wanted to," he rationalised. "It was going to happen, Mum. I think she would be pleased it happened in this room. She had outlived everyone, except Aunt Agnes."

"I know, Cameron. But I do miss her," she said wiping tears away.

"So do I," he responded, embracing her, suddenly realising he couldn't remember when he had last embraced his mother. "Love you, Mum."

They sat for a while, sifting through drawers and shoe boxes of memorabilia. Memorabilia most likely valued by no one other than his grandmother. In her bedside cabinet drawer, they found her much worn Bible, published in 1897 "in commemoration of sixty years reign of Queen Victoria," handed down to her by her mother. Cameron expected it had been held by Grandma every day of her life. Alongside it lay *The Book of Common Prayer*, printed in the 1890s.

Also in the drawer, a book titled *A Book of Golden Deeds*, written by Charlotte Mary Yonge in 1864. It seemed to be an original first edition. Cameron scanned the pages and put it aside for closer inspection. The wardrobe stored a great array of shoe boxes, each containing snippets of Grandma. Birthday cards she had received going back to her first birthday. A box containing sympathy cards following the death of his grandfather, along with the condolence book and a dried flower from the casket wreath. Cameron had wondered where all that stuff went.

There were boxes of letters she'd received. Cameron could only imagine that it was every letter she had ever received. One box was dedicated to letters from her sister, Agnes. Boxes of newspaper clippings, featuring many family members, including clippings of Cameron receiving an academic award at school and all the reviews of the musicals. A box of every set of spectacles she ever wore and a box of every certificate she had received for her prized daffodils and fruit cakes at the Murrumburrah–Harden Show, including a Championship Ribbon for the Best Daffodil!

So safely guarded for a lifetime, but what will come of it all now?

His mother prepared a traditional Binya meal of lamb chops drenched in a tomato and onion gravy, one of Grandma's favourite go-to meals. Cameron inwardly cringed when his mother suggested it but appreciated that the moment called for some nostalgia. He knew he would not find lamb chops and tomato gravy on the menu of any of his favourite restaurants in Dubai, but he admitted to himself, he thoroughly enjoyed it. They topped the meal with hot homemade custard along with a bottle of Grandma's preserved cherries. Now that, he welcomed.

Perhaps prompted by the nostalgic meal, or maybe simply because the moment in time called for it, the chatter soon turned to reminiscing about the past. "Do you remember …?" became the common prefix to every question. Rosemary recounted stories from her childhood, growing up on the farm. When Cameron complained about how long the electric jug took to boil, Rosemary reminisced about her younger years when they didn't own one. You had to wait for the wood stove to be lit and generate enough heat before you had boiling water.

Rosemary recounted the arguments that occurred when she informed her parents that Stanley had proposed. They had no problem with the proposal. Her parents very much approved of Stanley, but they had assumed he would move onto the farm and eventually take over the running of the farm. William, Rosemary's father, welcomed the prospect of an apprentice on the farm. But Stanley was enjoying his career as a banker, already living in a bank-provided house. Grandmother gave the ultimatum that unless Stanley moved onto the farm, the wedding would not be approved.

"The wise and calm council of Jacqueline's grandfather from next door convinced Rosemary's parents that the issues on the farm could be resolved and the wedding proceeded," recalled Rosemary. "A great day of celebration—we all loved it. And they loved Stanley as a son."

As the night progressed, Cameron took the opportunity to get to know his stepfather, Paul, better. Rosemary had married Paul a few weeks before Cameron finished university in Sydney.

Rosemary had met Paul, an engineer in Harden, staying in the Doncaster Hotel whilst his company completed contract work for the railway. He lived in Melbourne, where his first wife had died of breast cancer some years ago. Rosemary moved to Melbourne when they married. She hadn't found it difficult to leave Harden. She loved living in Melbourne but had found it difficult to leave her mother.

"Mum had changed a lot from the time I married your dad," she recalled. "When I told her Paul and I were getting married and moving to Melbourne, she simply said, 'My dear, follow your heart and find peace within it. My time will come if you are here or not.'"

Paul said he had never heard the family stories before and listened intently all night. He laughed a lot. At Cameron's request, Paul shared a little about his life as an engineer and how contract work had taken him to many rural and remote locations. He also shared briefly about the death of his wife. He had three children, all living in Melbourne, with grandchildren on the way.

After dinner, Cameron excused himself to do his last task before the funeral: prepare the eulogy.

The day of the funeral could not have been scripted better. Harden at its best, bathed in vibrant blue sky, contrasted with bold yellow and green fields, and that sprinkle of purple Cameron loved. It amused Cameron when he heard people congratulating his mother on her choice of casket flowers. "*A perfect match to the day,*" commented one mourner as they entered the church. Cameron smiled with contentment when his mother graciously accepted the praise for such a lovely choice. It almost made the $600 investment worthwhile.

Heidi and her husband, Bruce, had arrived on the farm well before the allocated time of the funeral. It shocked Cameron to see just how visibly pregnant she appeared and in obvious discomfort, so his resentment of her not being around to assist with preparations somewhat abated. Jacqueline greeted her at the church with the affection of a long-lost sister, lifting Heidi's spirits.

Whilst a reasonable number of people gathered to farewell his grandmother, Cameron could not help but notice the reality of living to an old age—you outlive the family and friends closest to you. As he glanced across the gathering, he could not help but think of the people who should be here but were no longer living, such as his dad and his grandfather. Much of the attention focused on ninety-eight-year-old Agnes. The greeting she received upon arrival was akin to that of the royal family, and she loved it.

Cameron felt for his mother a little, watching Aunt Agnes getting the bulk of the attention. His mother was his grandmother's only child. But his mum showed no sign of it bothering her and appreciated the moment to reflect and absorb. Mary, Jacqueline's mother, kept close company and support. He felt for his stepdad, Paul, because he knew no one, staying close to Rosemary.

Pastor Scott's leading of the service impressed Cameron, continuing to build his admiration of him. Scott spoke very personally about his contact with his grandmother and the impact she had on the congregation, describing her as a Harden treasure. He even got a chuckle when he described her as the immediate past president of Harden's Living Treasures, a segue into the legacy she would leave and what others could do to emulate her.

Aunt Agnes read the Bible reading beautifully. Cameron could see from where he sat that she had the Bible opened on her lap, not referring to it once. Using the old King James version, she orated the nine verses of Romans 8 in a manner that held the attention of the whole congregation, without exception. "For I am persuaded," she articulated with precision, "that neither death, nor life, nor angels, nor principalities, nor powers, nor things present, nor things to come, nor height, nor death, nor any other creature, shall be able to separate us from the love of God, which is in Christ Jesus our Lord." Cameron felt confident no one would dare to disagree with her.

Cameron then rose to deliver the eulogy.

"On behalf of my mother, Rosemary, my sister, Heidi, and my grandmother's sister, Agnes, I thank you all for coming today to say farewell to the Harden treasure we have just heard about. To say goodbye to our sister, mum and grandmother, and to say one final thing to her: Thank you. Thank you for the piece of you that you have permanently planted in each one of us.

I do want to start with a confession. My grandmother was a liar! Yes, I do have to set the record straight. I have been back in Harden for a few days and many of you here today have passed on your condolences to me directly, which I very much appreciate, but in doing so, something else has become apparent. I do believe my grandmother has somewhat exaggerated my status in life." Chuckles from the congregation.

"I do believe my grandmother has led you to believe I am some big financier living the high life in far-off lands. Someone asked if I had flown in on my own private jet! Sorry, Grandma. It's not true. I am a simple accountant, one of thousands doing the same thing. I work overseas simply because the company I work for has international clients and it is simply a logical place to be. At least my dad could claim to be the bank manager (more chuckles), but for me, I am a mere accountant. Please forgive my grandmother and allow her this small indulgence to be proud of her offspring. I mention this simply to put in context how much I am humbled by this extraordinary lady we say farewell to today, that she would be so proud and boastful of me to exaggerate it a little ... actually a lot." More laughter.

Cameron continued with a brief but poignant summation of his grandmother's life and her contribution to nursing, the farm and her family. He spoke of the impact she had on so many and how she had woven herself into the fabric of Harden. He spoke of her efforts in being a nurse and sheep farmer at the same time, of her managing the shearing shed, earning the respect of many a shearer. He thanked Young Billy for being his grandmother's support for many years.

"Yesterday, my mum and I were sifting through Grandma's things. We found three items in her bedside cabinet. Firstly, her Bible, printed in 1897 to commemorate the sixtieth year of reign of Queen Victoria. I can only imagine that she read from that every day.

"With it, she had *The Book of Common Prayer*, printed in the 1890s. It obviously had been a comfort to her for her entire life. And finally, this book," which he held high in his hand. "Its title is *A Book of Golden Deeds*, and it's written by Charlotte Mary Yonge in 1864. Of all the books Grandma would have read in her life, and I can assure you she loved to read, it was this book, and this book alone, she chose to keep in her bedside drawer with her Bible and prayer book.

"The book chronicles numerous 'Golden Deeds' performed by heroes and heroines in history, prior to 1864, obviously. I'll quote from the book, '*A Golden Deed must be something more than mere display of fearlessness. Grave and resolute fulfilment of duty is required to give it true weight … It is the spirit that gives itself for others—the temper that for sake of all religion, of country, of duty, of kindred, nay of even pity to a stranger, will dare all things, risk all things, endure all things, meet death in one moment, or wear life away in slow preserving tendance and suffering.*'

"There are obviously people in this book that inspired Grandma. I'm not sure why she kept it close to her, but I am pleased she did. I had to come back, spend a few days exploring the farm and find this book to remind myself that Grandma has performed her golden deed—for her family, for her church and for this community and is worthy of entry into this book."

As he drew his comments to a close, Cameron concluded that the death of his grandmother signified the end of an era for their family in Harden. He spoke of the history back to the birth of the Light Horse in Murrumburrah and the enlistment of his great-great-grandfather. He rekindled the history of Binya, the farm that had been in the family since that generation.

"And now," he said. "It is sad to say that era has come to an end. My mum, my sister and I have taken our lives to different ports, different opportunities. Not unlike our great-great-great-grandfather, who had the courage to set sail for new horizons and adventures when he boarded a ship in 1883 to take him to Australia and this district, Harden, which became our home. What will happen to the farm, I do not know, but what remains here in Harden is the legacy of the James family and my grand-mother, Amy White."

He glanced at the congregation as he stepped down from the pulpit. His mother smiled with pride for Grandma. Jacqueline made a quick sideways glance to her father, who glanced down at his order of service.

The pallbearers, including Ian, performed their duty per-fectly, carrying Amy White to the hearse, then to her grave to be buried alongside her husband in the cemetery on Demon-drille Hill.

The wake followed in the Harden Mechanics Institute Hall in Neill Street, the same hall where Amy's father Edmund had been greeted back from war and his romance with Amy's mother had begun.

Cameron's mum enjoyed her time catching up with her old friends. Paul seemed bored, occasionally striking up conversa-tion about the weather and wool prices with the odd stranger who befriended him. Coming from Melbourne, there was no one to chat about the latest AFL footy game. A lonely place for a Victorian.

Gary, who had spoken with Cameron on that first day at the country club, approached Cameron early in the proceedings. "I just want to say sorry about your grandmother," he said.

"Thanks, Gary," Cameron replied.

"Umm, I also want to say sorry for the other day and that bit about the plane," he added in a barely audible voice.

It took Cameron by surprise, taking a second to gather a response, "It's okay. Gary, I really appreciate you coming today."

Jacqueline and Heidi spent much of the afternoon together. It pleased Cameron to see them enjoying their reunion. They had been great friends as kids and seeing them together reminded Cameron of the family picnics in the rock paddock.

Cameron had the opportunity to catch up with Ian. Ian expressed again that he felt very honoured being asked to be a pallbearer. Cameron could see it had meant a great deal to him and felt it may have been more about mending their relationship than Ian's fondness of his grandmother. They spoke at length, avoiding any discussion about the past, especially the Sydney years. Ian asked if Cameron would be at his show on Saturday night. Cameron indicated that he hoped to, but plans were all still falling into place and it depended when his bosses needed him back. He didn't tell Ian that he already had booked a ticket for Thursday night back to Dubai.

Late in the proceedings, Jacqueline and Cameron found the first time to talk and were chatting about the service when Aunt Agnes arrived in her wheelchair, chauffeured by her nurse from the aged care home.

"Cameron, you haven't given me the courtesy of a hello."

"I'm sorry, Aunt Agnes, I saw you were so busy catching up with your friends," Cameron attempted in response.

"Humbug. You young ones haven't got time for older folk."

Cameron didn't have time to respond before she continued turning to Jacqueline, "So, introduce me, young man."

"Aunty Agnes, this is Jack, sorry Jacqueline, Jacqueline Forbes. You remember, Robert and Mary Forbes' daughter?"

"Of course, I remember. Watch your manners young man," she responded. "Jacqueline, my dear, I must say, you have well and truly blossomed since I saw you last." Turning to Cameron, she added, "She is stunning, isn't she?"

Cameron blushed. "Of course, Aunt Agnes. She is beautiful," his eyes momentarily caught Jacqueline's, "very beautiful," he whispered, only audible to Jacqueline.

Jacqueline dropped her head, ever so slightly—Cameron detected her smile.

Without any warning, Aunt Agnes changed the topic to something neither were expecting, not today anyway.

"Terrible thing that happened to your family, Jacqueline. I have always thought deeply for your mother and your grandparents," she stated. "Has there ever been any developments in the case?"

The question took Jacqueline by surprise, "Well, thanks so much, um, actually I do have an interest in trying to find out what happened."

"Oh, you do?" Aunt Agnes replied with surprise. "So, have you solved it?"

"No, it is still a cold case—a mystery that remains without an explanation."

"I remember it as if it happened only yesterday," Agnes said. "See Cameron, I do have a memory."

"So, you're familiar with the case then?" Jacqueline pursued with fresh interest.

"Oh, very much so," Aunt Agnes continued. "I was one of the first your grandfather spoke to when he came to collect Jane and Kathleen. He'd arrived to pick them up from the dance."

Jacqueline's eyes lit up. "Really? I haven't actually spoken directly to a witness yet. I have a copy of all the statements and come to think of it, yes, I recall yours as one of them. Sorry, I'm not thinking, my mind had not yet made the connection."

"We had lots of children at the dance, but lots were away as well because of the storm," she said. "I told your grandfather with confidence that the girls never came to the dance. We were responsible for those kids, so I took particular attention as to who attended."

"That's right, I now recall that from the statements. You were one of the chaperones at the dance," Jacqueline responded.

Cameron could sense Jacqueline found the conversation absorbing and wanting to delve deeper, but felt there would be more appropriate places for such a conversation. At that moment, Aunt Agnes's nurse came over to say that it was time to head back to the nursing home.

"Would you mind if we came and chatted with you in the home?" Jacqueline inquired.

"By all means, my dear." Turning to Cameron, she said, "You bring Jacqueline over to the home. And you better make it soon. I'm ninety-eight you know."

Cameron wanted to explain his pending return to Dubai but gave the only response appropriate, "Of course, Aunt Agnes."

"We will make it very soon, Aunt Agnes," Jacqueline replied, conscious more of her age than worrying about Cameron's schedule.

Aunt Agnes made her departure, and soon, the Forbes and Blanches (now Cunningham) were chatting as the tables were being cleared, just like old times. Everyone thought the day had gone very well, and Grandma had been laid to rest in a dignified and loving manner. She now laid in peace.

"Well, just the will to go," Rosemary said.

"Yes," Robert replied. "As you know, your mother gave very

specific instructions and insisted that it be read to all beneficiaries, which is you, Cameron and Heidi, forty-eight hours after her funeral. So, we will meet on Thursday."

Cameron heard it more of a statement of who shouldn't attend. *Bad luck, Paul and Bruce.*

"It's all quite straightforward, isn't it?" Cameron asked.

"We will meet on Thursday," stated Robert in his authoritative solicitor style. Cameron knew not to ask any further questions.

In accordance with Rosemary's wishes, a family dinner took place at Binya that night. Heidi and Bruce took over the kitchen to prepare the meal. Cameron discovered that apparently Bruce prided himself on being a very good cook: "He's always in the kitchen," according to Heidi. Rosemary prepared the dining room with all of Binya's dinner traditions, including the Royal Dalton wattle dinner set, only used on the most special of occasions. Whilst dinner preparations were underway, Cameron took Paul for a walk around the farm and along the creek.

Dinner was a pleasant gathering. Cameron felt stilted and restricted by the formality of the event. Bruce's fine dining meal of prawn bisque followed by pork chops, cabbage rolls and lentils would have impressed Master Chef judges, but Cameron would have preferred a traditional grandmother-style Binya dinner. By dinner's end, Cameron felt quite emotionally drained, and he sensed everyone else felt the same. They chattered about the service, reliving favourite anecdotes and stories. Everyone agreed that Grandma would have been well-pleased, but much of the chatter repeated what had already been said throughout the day. Cameron enjoyed much more the nostalgic story telling of the previous night. Bruce's apple sharlotka dessert typified the evening for Cameron. *Nice, but give me another serving of Grandma's preserved cherries and homemade custard and cream.*

Heidi felt quite exhausted by the time dinner finished, and she and Bruce retreated to their motel room. Rosemary, Paul and Cameron all retired soon after.

Silence pervaded the farmhouse when Cameron awoke the following morning. He felt like a pre-breakfast walk, so he quickly dressed, left the silence and headed outdoors. He had been on the farm now for a week and had not been close to a sheep, so he headed in search of some. He walked much longer than planned, to the most distant corner of the farm, before returning to the farmhouse late morning.

When he returned, he found his mum sitting on the floor of the sunroom, surrounded by boxes and suitcases she had pulled from the large cupboards at the end of the room. She sifted through an old Arnott's biscuit tin containing black and white pictures of the farm, Grandmother, Grandfather and Cameron's mother as a baby. Laying nearby was the box brownie camera, most likely used to take the photos. He picked up a handful, thumbing through them, enjoying the insights into the past.

"I'm not sure what detail your grandmother has put in the will, but I'm guessing not much," his mother said. "In a few weeks, this place will be on the market and gone for good. I want you and Heidi to give thought to what you want to take away. You and your sister have gone different paths, away from any life as a sheep farmer, which is a very wise move. You know from the last few days, there are generations of memories in this house. Days of a life on the farm are gone. Binya is over and I know that you plan to pull out of here tomorrow and not even peek in the rear-view mirror, so now is the time to find out what lives on and what goes to the grave with Grandma."

"Bit harsh, Mum!" Cameron protested.

His mother raised her hand. Cameron knew not to continue, "I'm not criticising, Cameron. I know you have moved beyond a life in Harden. But this is what I want. I want you and your sister to walk out of here tomorrow with a good bit of Binya. Not just something that you'll throw out in a few years, but something that keeps the spirit of Binya alive. Something that will outlive you."

"Like what, Mum?"

"You have a day to find that out. Your sister is coming over, and she's bringing lunch with her. Start thinking about it, Cameron," she said as she rose to her feet and left the room.

Cameron sat on the end of the bed. He hadn't given any thought to what he might keep. He sat there thinking and nothing came to mind. He quickly surveyed the room and, in his mind, he explored the house and its contents that had outlived generations. Grandma's four-poster bed sprung to mind, but he struggled to imagine it in a modern house and he had no plans of when he would return to Australia for good. Edmund James had purchased the extension dining table suite that sat up to eight people. Five generations of the family had sat around the table. *Will I be the last?* He thought of the crockery and glassware, some of it over a century old or close to it. Sad to lose it, but he struggled to see it outside of Binya. He surveyed the boxes his mother had unpacked—there were old photos, books, family records and an array of personal items from eyeglasses to smoking pipes. Grandfather's rifles stood in the corner.

He noticed several unopened boxes sitting in the back of the cupboard. He could partially see a handwritten label on one. Moving the boxes obstructing his view, it read: Cameron's Books.

He had forgotten about these books and had no idea until now where they were. He certainly had no memory of packing them into a box and bringing them to the farm. He loved reading in his early teen years and had gathered quite a collection of books. When he went off to university in Sydney, the reading required for his courses, his music pursuits and his discovery of city life left no room for recreational reading. He fingered through them, removing them one by one. A younger Cameron was coming back to him.

The first two books, his grandmother had given to him long ago. She had, at times, read pages to Cameron. They were books belonging to his great-grandfather, two books of poetry written by Major General Mackay, who had enlisted his great-grand-father into the Light Horse—written under the name Kenneth Mackay. Grandma had never let Cameron forget the story and they had relived it time and time again. According to Grandma, as Cameron recalled, Edmund had remained good friends with Mackay and visited him regularly on his property, Wallandool. He had given his grandfather two personally signed copies of his books, "To my loyal friend and comrade in arms, Edmund James," signed James AK Mackay.

Cameron held both books in his hands—*Stirrup Jingles from the Bush and The Turf and Other Rhymes* published in 1887 and *A Bush Idyl* in 1888. He flicked through the pages and could recall some of the poems. *Definitely keepers.*

He fingered through the other books that filled the box, flicking through the pages as he reminisced about when he read them. Finally, he found the last book in the box, which had been his favourite—*Kings Row* by Henry Bellamann, written in 1940. He recalled that his grandmother had introduced him to reading. She would often lend him books suited to his age. She would often tell him about *Kings Row* but told him he'd have to wait "till he grew up because it contained 'adult parts.'"

When she finally granted him permission, Cameron read it with eager anticipation, waiting anxiously to get to the "saucy" parts. He immediately identified with Parris Mitchell, a young boy growing up in his country town. Cameron could picture the town of *Kings Row* as Parris led him on a tour. As he read, he would picture places around Harden. He had seen many

American TV shows and had a real feel for the town of *Kings Row* where Parris lived. Cameron got introduced to Parris's friends, including Drake who reminded him of his friendship with Ian.

As he flicked through the pages of the book, the characters were coming back to him. He recognised the girls' names as he turned the pages—Renee, Cassandra and Randy. Cameron recalled noting the difference between him and Parris. Cameron had never had a close friendship with a girl. He and Heidi had never really been close playmates as brother and sister, though they were happy together. Jacqui and Heidi had always been close mates, but he had never been drawn in any way to Jacqui. But then again, he had not been drawn to any girl. He was a virgin when he left Harden for university.

He thumbed through the pages and came across the part that had prevented his grandmother from sharing the book. He read again as Parris and Renee played at the pond and stripped naked for a swim. They used leaves to cover their private parts, Parris using his penis to hold his leaf in place. Cameron smiled as he re-read the passage. He recalled thinking, *Grandma, this is tame.* He saw his grandmother as particularly prudish.

As kids, Cameron had skinny dipped, often with his sister, in the creek that ran through Binya and a few times with a group from school. The school outings were all very innocent, with the nakedness attracting little attention, but as puberty struck, the numbers coming to skinny dip in the creek quickly reduced. Cameron, a naive young teenager, hadn't realised the reason other kids had stopped coming. However, that was about to change. One hot, dry afternoon, a few kids went to the creek after school. Spotting Colleen, now Ian's wife, he noticed slight changes, heralding the commencement of puberty. He felt sensations within himself, he had not noticed before. Quick eye contact, a small touch, then the realisation that childhood innocence had just been broken. He never again considered skinny dipping.

A common phrase of his father had been, "when you grow up"—a strange phase he never understood until that moment. You do see things differently from that point.

But Parris and Renee returned to the pond. Cameron could recall, for the first time, getting sexually aroused as he read. He couldn't read quickly enough. He could vividly recall reading about the emotions churning within Parris. It wasn't about sex— he knew it involved something deeper. He could see that, but he had never understood love. It excited Cameron that he had found this passage—he felt that through Parris and Renee, he could understand his feelings for Jacqui. *I must be a late learner.*

Cameron knew he had to read on. Reading parts of the book that had grasped him and pulled him deep into the life of *Kings Row* were pulling him in again. He felt the emotion as he re-read the experience Parris went through when he discovered that Renee's father had found out about their encounter and then brutally thrashed her to unconsciousness, if not death. Parris himself went into a deep shock and when he recovered; they were gone, the family had left town. Renee was gone forever. Cameron remembered feeling like vomiting when he first read it. *What part of this story did Grandma not want me to read?* The moment two people felt a union that could only be expressed sexually? Or the brutal abuse of a child for exploring her own innocence? The story of Parris and Renee had never left Cameron's mind. He often thought back on it as the prospect of any relationship arose—*maybe that's the reason I've had so few?* He knew he had never felt that moment Parris and Renee had, but he knew being with Jacqui aroused feelings he had never experienced before.

Kings Row brought back other memories for him. Parris had a life-long friend, Drake, who reminded him of Ian and the bond of friendship that lasted to death, but had suffered a breakdown, not dissimilar to Ian and himself. But Parris didn't desert Drake when he needed him. Holding the book in his hand, the need to rekindle the relationship he once had with Ian became clear.

Reading *Kings Row* as a child had also changed Cameron's view of this little country town of Harden. *Kings Row* was set in a lovely little town, full of happy residents. But, as Parris discovered, underneath that veil laid a pit of dark secrets filled with death, incest, hideous revenge and many other terrible things. So much so that it led Parris to a medical career in mental health.

What lays under the veil of Harden? What secrets were being suppressed? What was at the bottom of the unsolved mystery of the Barkley sisters? Was the town harbouring a serial murderer? Were there other disappearances no one knew about?

As he read the book as a child, he would stroll through the streets of Harden, passing houses and wondering what could be happening behind the curtains. Were the people who left the town leaving for a reason? He recalled a Catholic priest who had departed unexpectedly. A popular, well-known young man involved in several of the youth activities at the school including coaching cricket, which is where Cameron had gotten to know him a little.

In the week the priest left, so did a family that lived only two houses along their street—abruptly, without warning. Cameron knew their son Rodney, a grade ahead of Cameron at school, and they played on the same cricket team together. Rodney's family had gone to the same Catholic church, but Rodney had left before Cameron could ask why the priest had left. Now, with *Kings Row* back in his hands, combined the renewed interest in the mystery of the Barkley sisters, he again pondered on the possible dark secrets Harden had hidden away.

He quickly packed the books back into the box, keeping out *Kings Row*, which he committed to reading again, along with the Mackay books. His thoughts turned to his mother's instruction to find items he would take from the farm before it sold. He definitely would keep the box of books. He hadn't given any thought to other things. He reflected upon several of the items he had rediscovered over the last few days—his great-grandmother's four-poster bed he loved to sleep in. *But where would I put it?* He couldn't take it to Dubai. He would love to keep the dining table in the family—he hoped Heidi or Mum would claim it.

He picked up Grandmother's commemorative centenary crystal bowl, celebrating Australia's first one hundred years. *That would be nice to pass on.* Maybe Heidi could keep it to pass onto her expected child in anticipation of the third centenary celebrations? The swan lake painting in the bedroom would make a good keepsake. The Alfred Meakin dinner set—a quick Google search dated it between 1900 to 1920. It struck Cameron that he sat in a museum, not only of his family but of the pioneering history of Australia. It saddened him that it would soon be a faded memory, lost to those beyond his generation.

He thought smaller. He liked the old day-to-day cutlery that had been set on the table every meal for generations, including Dixon Kangaroo spoons, well over a century old, along with bone-handled knives of the same vintage. He grabbed a few settings of cutlery. He wanted to find something unique to the farm. *I know it!* He went to the bathroom and took the cake of soap. In some ways, he could argue this cake of soap is well over a hundred years old, at least its origins were. Grandma stipulated a cake of soap had to be fully used. Waste not. When it got too small to effectively hold, but most importantly before it broke into two, the new cake of soap would be opened, used once or twice to soften it, then the soft remnants of the old cake would be moulded against the new cake. After a few uses, they would meld into one, the remnants of the old cake wearing down until it disappeared to nothing, ensuring every final lather bathed a soul. Cameron took the cake of soap to continue the tradition. For the first time in over one hundred years, a new virgin cake of soap sat in the bath soap-holder.

In a similar fashion, his grandmother ensured the very last squirt of the toothpaste left the tube and was used to brush a tooth. His grandfather had developed a clamp that he would screw onto the bottom of the tube. At the time, toothpaste tubes were aluminum. You would turn the clamp to expel the toothpaste, rolling the tube, like the old sardine can lids. As you required more, you would screw the clamp until it finally came to rest hard against the top of the tube without a drop of toothpaste remaining inside. Cameron thought back to being chastised for grabbing the tube of toothpaste and simply squeezing. "Waste, waste, waste," his grandmother would say. She continued the clamp on the new plastic tubes but found it not as effective. She solved the problem with a modification of a bulldog clamp to keep the tube rolled up. Cameron unscrewed the clip from the tube and took it. He put the clamp, cake of soap and cutlery in his bag, ready to leave tomorrow after the will reading. He checked his booking on his phone and smiled at the confirmation for a late Thursday night flight.

It shocked Cameron when he realised a good deal of the day had slipped by. He needed to attend to some work matters that would be best done connected to his online files, still only possible at the R.S. Forbes Solicitors office. It would also give an excuse to make contact with Jacqui, which pleased him. But after giving thought to the will reading tomorrow, he concluded that the moment called for a separation of the legal process and personal friendships. Probably best not to go to the office. He could get by with what he could do with the offline files on the laptop.

CHAPTER FIVE

Thursday at last. Time dragged ever so slowly toward the sched-uled 10 am will reading. The formality, or what Cameron thought, pageantry, associated with the will irritated him immensely and he grew increasingly impatient. He packed his belongings and would leave for Sydney directly from the office of R. S. Forbes Solicitors. Rosemary said she would come back, clean up and leave for Melbourne. Heidi would be meeting them at the office.

Rosemary and Cameron arrived in separate cars to find Heidi waiting in reception. Mabel, a long-time friend of Rosemary's, greeted them with the formality of a special occasion. Mabel directed them to take a seat in the reception. Cameron's frus-tration grew as they sat silently in wait. *Can we just get this over and done with?*

Precisely at 10 am, while the grandfather clock in the recep-tion hammered out its chimes, Jacqueline Forbes entered through the doorway leading to the offices. Cameron could not help noticing that she was wearing yet another stunning dress—a bright blue that lightened the otherwise sombre setting. She smiled, greeting everyone with a very formal demeanour.

"Good morning," she welcomed, stepping across the small reception room to another door. "Please, come in," motioning everyone into the large boardroom.

"Do I bow?" he whispered as he passed Jacqueline, receiving in return the briefest hint of a smile, but nothing more.

Cameron had not been in this room before and quickly scanned the surrounds. A large picture hanging on the western wall depicted the last council meeting held around this very table, before the chambers were relocated. The large ornate table occupied most of the room, surrounded by matching wooden chairs with leather seat inserts. Robert Forbes sat on the first chair with his back to the door. Cameron observed a second door at the end of the room, which he assumed accessed the offices. Mr Forbes rose and formally shook everyone's hand.

Jacqueline stood at the head of the table. "Please take a seat," she directed.

Three manilla folders were positioned in front of three vacant chairs where they were ushered to sit. Rosemary sat next to Robert. Heidi sat opposite Robert, and Cameron opposite his mother. Jacqueline sat at the head of the table. Robert wore a black suit, white shirt and dark blue tie, complementing Jacqueline's bright blue business dress, both in stark contrast to the casual dress of Rosemary, Heidi and Cameron, leaving Cameron feeling somewhat underdressed.

Robert Forbes spoke first. "On behalf of your mother and grandmother, I thank you all for attending today, each a beneficiary named in the will and testament of the late Mrs Amy White. These proceedings are being delivered in a manner prescribed by the late Amy White and with respect to her, we will deliver those requests without explanation or justification.

Really and truly! This is an old lady in Harden who owned a modest farm. *Formality overkill.*

Robert Forbes proceeded, "I am most honoured to be named in the will of Mrs Amy White as executor of her said will and testament. I can advise that I have been appointed by the probate court to wind up her affairs. Today, I have appointed legal assistant Ms Jacqueline Forbes to chair this meeting and commence with the reading of the said will of Mrs Amy White. Any questions before we start?"

He broke the silence after a few seconds and continued: "Ms Forbes, I hand it to you to lead the proceedings."

Ms Forbes opened the leather folder in front of her.

"In the folder in front of you is a copy of the will. I will proceed to read it in full. Please feel free to follow. The will and testament is made by Amy Mavis White, of Binya, Jugiong Road, Harden, New South Wales, Australia 2587. I make this will and testament in five parts: Part A: Appointments; Part B: Distribution of Estate; Part C: General Provisions; Part D: Definitions and Interpretations; Part E: Execution."

Cameron flipped through the pages in front of him, following the headings laid out through the document. Jacqueline continued to read the will verbatim. "Robert Forbes is appointed trustee to execute the will. Scott Bennett is appointed executor if Robert Forbes is unable to perform that role." After a brief pause, she moved to the distribution of the estate.

"I distribute my estate in two parts. I firstly distribute my personal financial wealth and possessions. This includes monies held in the balance of investment accounts in my name at the time of distribution, the balance of bank accounts in my name and any cash in my possession at the time of my death.

"It does not include monies held in the Binya operating account, to which I am a signatory.

"It does include provision for the payment of my unsecured debts, funeral expenses and the costs associated with my estate.

"It does not include any outstanding debts owed by the operational account for the property, Binya.

"The balance of my estate is to be divided equally between Rosemary Mavis Cunningham, Cameron Stanley Blanche and Heidi Elizabeth Peterson (nee Blanche). If any beneficiary was not to survive me, the balance of my estate is to be paid to the remaining beneficiaries. If all beneficiaries do not survive me, the estate is to be held in trust for future direct descendant grandchildren. Any income received from that trust is to be divided amongst the living grandchildren at the time."

That made sense to Cameron except for the exclusion of the farm. He gestured to interrupt but Jacqueline immediately raised her right index finger and gave Cameron a direct stare, surprising him. He immediately obeyed. Robert Forbes nodded to Jacqueline to continue.

"In relation to the farm known as Binya. Binya has been owned by the family since its purchase by Edmund James following the First World War. It is my wish that it stays in the family. I, therefore, leave the farm to my grandson, Cameron Stanley Blanche, to manage and run the affairs thereof. Binya is not to be sold. Cameron shall also receive the balance of the Binya operational account, which is to be used for the running of the farm and shall receive an income to be agreed by the beneficiaries from the Binya operational account. Any surplus profit is to be distributed equally to all surviving beneficiaries on an ongoing basis. He has the freedom to make appropriate business decisions in relation to the property. I have confidence that decisions will be made in the spirit of my wishes.

"It is my wish that the farm, Binya, be passed on through generations to come. At any time, the beneficiary who holds ownership of the farm may choose to transfer the ownership to another beneficiary or direct descendant of a beneficiary, with agreement of the surviving beneficiaries or their direct descendants.

"In the event that no beneficiary is identified to continue the operation of Binya, the property is to be bequeathed to St Paul's Anglican Church, Harden, for them to do as they wish."

Jacqueline continued with all the legalities in the will, but Cameron heard none of it. His mind was frozen. When she finished, and for what seemed like a very long time, there was silence. Cameron stared at the copy of the will in front of him. All eyes in the room were on him, except Robert Forbes, whose eyes were fixed on the gold pen he rolled back and forth through his fingers.

Cameron spoke. "So, what does that mean?"

"Means you are a farmer. Swap your leather shoes for a pair of boots, Farmer Cam," Heidi said, with a grin.

"But I can't be made to live on a farm in the middle of nowhere."

"It's what your grandmother wishes, Cameron," Rosemary said.

"Grandmother, yes; parole officer, no," he quickly responded.

Robert Forbes took control with the authority of a solicitor who had conducted these proceedings many times. "I will speak as the executor of this will. I have the highest respect for your grandmother—she has always been, and remains, a dear and precious friend. You know of the bond that ties our families together."

Well, actually, your wife's family, if we are being so damn precise.

"My duty to your grandmother is to execute this will to her satisfaction. My reasoning in involving Jacqueline is that there are avenues you have, which may conflict with my role as executor to discuss. Wills can be contested. There is a lot of water that can pass under this bridge. Jacqueline assures me you are a brilliant problem solver, Cameron. You are an intelligent man. My professional and personal advice to you is to work this through. But I appeal to you to honour your grandmother. I can tell you, in all my legal career, I have never seen anything like this in a will and I will be frank with you, I am still trying to work out the legal details that sits behind her decision. But let me tell you what your grandmother said when I told her that. She gave me that familiar little grin and said, 'You can do it.'"

More silence, the clock in the foyer could be heard ticking. Cameron felt giddy. Did he really own a farm now? He could see Jacqueline felt his anxiety and sensed she wanted to comfort him. He felt she understood the conflict going on in his mind. *I can't be forced to own a farm.* Jacqueline lowered her eyes and kept her composure.

Heidi sat relaxed and even a little excited. *Of course she is relaxed. She hasn't got to come back here and live and still gets an income for the rest of her life.*

He glanced across at his mum, searching for a lifeline.

"Cameron, I didn't know Grandmother's plan," Rosemary stated. "But when you think of it, she would never give up Binya. We must consider what she wants."

Robert Forbes took control. "Let's wrap up here for now. Cameron, Jacqueline is going to have a talk with you. Settlement of a will does not happen overnight. The period to contest a will is up to twelve months, but we can wrap it up a lot earlier if we get it sorted out. Choosing to contest the will is a prerogative you all have. Mind you, I have never dealt with a will being contested over what you got, it's normally what you didn't get.

"Before we go, I do have one other bit of information for you all. Regarding the first half of the will, it is far too early to start talking dollar amounts but, let me give you some idea. Your grandmother was a wise businessperson, always frugal. She was the wise farmer who stored the grain. That didn't stop when it came to money. We can go through details later, but your grandmother had basically three sources of income and financial assets that were not the property of Binya. As you know, she worked for a long time as a nurse and put away a lot of money that has been invested for many years. In her accounts, I can't find much evidence at all of her spending any of her money. Your grandfather had a life insurance policy that your grandmother received and invested without touching it. She received an income from the farm, for her entire life, over and above the farm working account, which was how your great-grandfather Edmund James had set it up. The gross cash value of your grandmother's holdings, aside from Binya, before we consider deductions, is in the vicinity of $2.8 million. And can I add that on top of all that, the Binya operating account is in a very healthy position."

Rosemary, Heidi and Cameron sat in stunned silence. *She lived on the farm as if she had no money, spending nothing, everything being recycled, nothing being thrown out, yet she had near three million dollars!*

Rosemary spoke first, "I had no idea."

Cameron reacted, "What the hell? Why did she keep so much money?"

"To give to us, Cameron," Heidi said. "Maybe we give her what she wants."

"I have one more formality for the meeting," Jacqueline added. "There are processes of probate that must be undertaken before a will is settled. A person may choose to contest a will for a period of twelve months from the date of death. However, after the grant of probate is made by the court, the executor can start to distribute the estate. The estate will not be distributed until at least six months after the date of death."

"Well, I'm leaving for Dubai right now," Cameron said.

Robert Forbes responded. "And no one can stop you, Cameron. However, I urge you to think of not only yourself. My recommendation to you, not as a solicitor, but as a family friend, is to stick around for a few days at least and a way forward may become clear. Today is not the day to explore that."

As they left the office, Cameron walked past Jacqueline. "Are you okay?" she asked.

"No," he replied. "Why didn't you warn me—give me a hint?"

"Because you are a professional—I knew you would understand why I couldn't."

He kissed her on the cheek, "I'm sorry. Meet you at Fort Apache at two, eh?" The slight smile accepted his invite. He had planned to be on the road by then, but he still had time to get to his flight if he left later. He would decide then.

Rather than head for Sydney as planned, Cameron returned to Binya, as did Heidi and his mum. The sudden, unexpected fortune had Rosemary and Heidi in good spirits. They knew it was best to leave Cameron alone. He sat silently in deep thought. He had just inherited close to a million dollars. But he also now had a farm to run. He could not process what this meant for his future. He had his career in Dubai. He had a job—a good job. He didn't see himself becoming a sheep farmer. Well, he didn't think so. And he had a plane to catch later that night.

He escaped to the verandah for some private space. Young Billy came to the farmhouse, wanting to chat with him. *Why him? Why not go see Mum?* Everyone knew him as Young Billy, but he had not long ago celebrated his seventy-third birthday. He had been working on Binya from before Grandfather William died. Young Billy had found Grandfather William the day he died. William had been attending to the sheep in the quarry paddock and dropped dead with a heart attack. Young Billy had been driving into town and saw the truck parked near the quarry with the dogs still having the sheep rounded-up in a mob, but he could not see William, so he stopped, and that's when he found him.

Young Billy's father, also called Billy, but known as Old Bill, had been great friends with Cameron's grandfather. Old Bill died well before Grandfather William died, but the name, Young Billy, had stuck. After William died, Young Billy basically worked the farm by himself and would never let Amy increase his wages.

"You got a minute, Mr Blanche?" Young Billy asked.

Cameron so much wanted to say no, but he didn't, "Sure, come, take a seat on the verandah."

"Well, you see Mr Blanche—" Young Billy started, but Cameron interrupted.

"Come on Billy, you've called me Cameron all my life, cut out this Mr thing."

"But you're a big international businessman—"

"Cut it out Billy or I'll dump you in the dipping trough," snapped Cameron with a laugh.

"Well, Cameron, as you know, I have been doing this job

from before you were born. Started helping your granddad when I was a young'un. Truth is, there is nothing young left in this old bugger. I've stuck it out to help your grandmother. She was always against getting anyone else in, but Cameron, I just can't keep going and, more the point, I can't keep up. Every day, I'm stuffed before smoko. Things are going backward real quick. Sheep need attention and there is a busy time coming up with lambing, drenching and shearing, of course. Fencing is in a bad way. You'll find me like I found your grandfather if I keep going," he said, with tears in his eyes.

Cameron didn't know what to feel. *What a day.* It's not even his farm and he loses his only employee. *And why come to me? Who says I'm running the farm?* He wanted to tell Young Billy to go and see his mother, but he knew that would achieve nothing.

Cameron knew he had to solve this for Billy. Billy had been his grandmother's number one supporter. *Fix it, Cam.* He put his arm around Billy's shoulders. "Leave it to me, Billy. My grandmother would not have survived here as long as she had if it wasn't for your heroics. We love you, Billy. Here's the deal. Keep pottering around the place as long as you like, or for as little as you like. I'll get someone in to help. We'll work it out. Go and rest up, Billy."

"It's a good farm. In fact, it can easily be one of the best in the region. It's good soil. Grows good grass for the sheep. Pests and weeds are low, we've kept them under control, but a fair bit of work is needed now or they will get away. Water supply is great. You're still on a gold mine here, Cameron. Don't sell it. Your grandmother would always say: 'Cameron will do a mighty job here one day.'"

"Thanks, Billy, now you get home before lunch and give that ticker a rest," Cameron replied.

Young Billy's words shook Cameron. He could feel the responsibility resting upon him and he owed it to Grandma to do something about it. His immediate plans had never included owning Binya. He surveyed the farm from where he stood. He scanned over the shearing shed and beyond, scanning to the left, down over the creek, the rock paddock, further around to the dairy, the night paddock beyond that and finally the farmhouse. Work needed to be done, yes, but his grandmother had always said Great-Grandfather Edmund could not have picked a more perfect location for a farm to grow wool. He had no idea of the state of the books, but his grandmother's fortune seemed to indicate things were stable, financially, and Mr Forbes had described the finances as "healthy." *But what did any of that have to do with a respected forensic accountant working internationally?*

He had to talk to Annand in Dubai. This morning, everything appeared so clear and straightforward, but now he felt hopelessly confused.

Sitting alone on top of Fort Apache, he watched Jacqui arrive. He had taken the time to walk up from the farmhouse. With style, she navigated through the barbed wire fence and wandered down to the rock. His rock.

"Not surprised you would be sitting there, Farmer Cam," she said as she approached.

"Come on, don't make it worse."

"I bought some soother," she said, lifting a cooler basket with a chilled bottle of Sauvignon Blanc and some glasses, cheese and biscuits.

"You know, one half of my brain wants me to be angry and hop in my car and drive to the airport. But the other side says, what the hell is going on? You can't walk out now."

"So why aren't you on the Hume Highway heading for Sydney?" she asked.

"I rang my boss. He is quite happy with me working here for a little longer," he explained.

"That's a big turnaround from the urgency when I first came over. Apparently, the work I sent through the other day uncovered a lot more than I even expected. Not only is there no more required from my end at the moment, but he told me to watch the news over the next few weeks. May have earned another bonus. They are happy for me to stay here for now, for a week or so anyway."

"I'll ask again, why are you not on the Hume Highway to Sydney?"

He hates it when people see through him. He sat silent for some time, searching for what to say. He could say, because you're here. There was truth in that. He could say, because of his love for his grandmother and his mum. There was truth in that. He could say lots of things: Ian, Young Billy, the farm, the smell. But on the other side, he could think of many reasons why he should be at the airport.

"Young Billy came by to see me this morning; he's retiring," Cameron huffed. "Already lost my entire workforce."

After a moment, he continued. "Billy said something that my grandfather once said. I can't remember much about my grandfather, but the few memories I have are very clear. One thing I remember is that he would say, 'This is a gold mine, Cameron.' I remember thinking, at the time, that he meant a real gold mine. Anyway, that's what Young Billy said today. He admits it's rundown, but he said it's on a gold mine, just as Granddad had said. And I remember Grandma telling the stories of Edmund James, the war hero, establishing this place after the war. There is something in me that wants to keep that."

He paused, "I wanted to stay ..." He moved his fingers ever so slightly so that they rested on hers, "Because ..." Another pause, "Because ..." Then barely a whisper, "Because of you."

Their eyes locked. He recalled the beauty of the moment between Parris and Renee. *Was this love?* She slowly leant forward, and they locked in a kiss: the softest, most sensual kiss he had ever experienced. He wanted to slow it down and experience it frame by frame.

"Have I finally caught my Rusty, my Rin-Tin-Tin boy?" she

whispered. "I never thought those dreams on this very rock, way back then, would ever come true."

"Thank you for waiting," he softly replied.

She opened the wine. They sat in silence, taking in the spectacular view of Binya in its full blaze of colour.

"But Jack, I'm not a farmer. I am not a small-town boy. I love the city. I love my job. I'm good at my job. I don't want to give that up. Let's not kid ourselves: working the land is not all roses. There were many years where I watched my grandmother get bugger-all for the wool. She once sold sheep for fifty cents a pen—that's fifteen sheep! She sold another mob for zero cents a kilo directly off the farm and told me she got the best price going."

"Yes, I've dealt with many a sheep farmer's bankruptcy where zero cents a kilo was the going price. I've even had cases where we have settled for negative prices. It's just another way of charging the owner for the cost of killing the stock and disposing of them. Of course, there are those bad times. Farming is a cycle. The industry has become much better at planning for those ups and downs.

"Overall, your grandmother did pretty good, as you can see from the figures today. And without breaching professional confidentialities, you haven't seen the farm account yet. Anyway, your mum can access that. She is the signatory on that account, but I don't think she has ever used it because your grandmother took care of everything. Your mum is the business back-up signature. You better get your mum to visit the bank."

"But I feel I don't want to do it. I can't do it. I want to do something else. If I come back to this purely on emotion, I'll soon regret what I missed out on—what I could have been doing somewhere else in the world."

"Cameron Blanche, the smart, switched-on forensic accountant who can't see past his own nose. You haven't begun to think how you could make this work. The will doesn't say you have to live on the farm, well not permanently; I even emphasised it when I read it: '*I therefore leave the farm to my grandson, Cameron Stanley Blanche, to manage and run the affairs thereof.*' Manage and run. Think outside of the box, Cameron. You can make this work."

"You mean a George Street farmer? It's not big enough to produce that income."

"Come on Cameron, let's put two things together: your focus on the numbers and my focus on the detail. Your job as a forensic accountant pays well, you've just inherited a fortune, the farm is debt free and has its own financial reserve—a significant reserve. It supported your grandmother, and she didn't physically work the farm."

"Yeah, but Grandmother kept every bit of string, didn't drink wine, didn't go clubbing, didn't go on holidays—"

"Cameron," she yelled. "I think I am falling in love with you because you're irritating me so much. The big picture, Cameron!"

She had a point. He felt that love comes with that wisdom that gives you insights into the other's mind, and he felt she had some idea of the turmoil in his. He was falling in love because he saw someone who wanted to invest her love in him. She could make him a better person.

Thoughtful silence.

"Okay," he said. "Let us give it a thought but don't make me commit. I don't want to give away what I'm good at. I do want to get back to Dubai."

"Us give it a thought?" she quizzed. "Cheers," she said as she held up her glass.

"Cheers."

They embraced for another enduring kiss.

"So, if you're not leaving town, you'll be going to Ian's concert Saturday night?"

He threw back his head—something else he'd been hoping to dodge.

"You do have to face it, Cameron."

He knew he had to, he just had to build up the courage. He had been thinking of Ian since rediscovering Drake. He wanted to share some of that with Jacqui, but not at this moment.

"You're right, I will go. Just scared though."

"Scared of what?"

"Scared of facing the truth that I was wrong."

"Cameron, the water that has passed under the bridge is now out to sea, let's focus on the water yet to come."

"You'll come?" he asked.

"I told you. Dad and I are going to a legal dinner in Canberra," she replied. "But anyways, you need to do this yourself."

"Your plans for the week?"

"Well, on Tuesday, I am going to do the re-enactment of the ride Jane and Kathleen took to go to the dance, from the house down there," pointing to their family homestead.

"I remember. I'd like to come."

She swung around to face him, "Would you? I've been hoping you would."

"Well, you know—numbers and detail combined seems like a good combination."

They stood up, held hands and walked back to her car. He placed his arm around her waist, and she did the same. It felt natural. Though mentally exhausted, he drew strength from Jacqui. Uncharted territory for him to navigate, but it felt good and right.

CHAPTER SIX

Cameron expected to feel better the next morning but didn't. Sleep had not come easy as his mind wrestled with the conflicts within. He knew it had little to do with the farm but more to do with Cameron Blanche. All night, he had tossed and turned, thinking not only about his future, but where he had come from. Who is Cameron? Who is Ronnie? He had not told Jacqui about Ronnie.

In Dubai, no one knew him as Cameron—or even Cam. Back in Sydney, his friends gave him the name Cam, but in Dubai, they called him Ronnie. A one-liner, tossed out at a party, that had stuck. When he arrived in Dubai, his work mates—a mix of Australians, Americans, two Brits and one German—took him out for introductory drinks. The conversation ebbed and flowed, weaving through various overlapping topics. At some point, amidst the many congruent conversations, one of his new workmates asked for his name. "Cameron," he replied. One of the English guys sounded out his name in an elongated, slow drone: "C-a-m-e-r-o-n."

"That's not a name that flows nicely off the tongue," someone responded.

"Well, my mates in Oz call me Cam," he replied.

"That's even more dicky," another responded. "Sounds like part of a car engine." They all laughed and shrugged their shoulders. "Why Cam?"

"Well, it's just short for Cameron—us Aussies do that a bit, shorten names. So, take the Cam out of Cameron."

"That's just dumb."

"Well," proclaimed one of the Englishmen, "if we can only use half your name, let's use the back half, not the front half: I proclaim you Ron from Australia."

From there, it morphed into Ronnie and it stuck.

So, for the past few years, it has been Ronnie when in Dubai and Cameron, or Cam, in Australia, depending on if he was in Sydney or not. Amongst family, it was always Cameron. He observed that Jacqueline's name had morphed from Jacqueline to Jacqui to Jack and back to Jacqueline. Furthermore, he noticed that her name varied to fit the moment and the audience at the time. If you got it right, fine, but if you got it wrong, her reaction let you know it.

He struggled to identify himself—*Cameron or Cam or Ronnie?* Maybe Cameron belonged in the past, someone he wanted to leave in the past. He liked the new person, Ronnie. Ronnie sat well with his work and life in Dubai. Ronnie would have been far more suited to the Sydney singing gigs, and he often wished he had discovered him earlier. He thought he knew Ronnie well.

But over the past week, he had once again found Cameron, or maybe Cameron had found him. Given the unplanned nature of his trip, a trip he didn't want, he had not given Cameron a thought until he was back in Harden and people were calling him Cameron. The problem is that Ronnie didn't know Cameron. *How do I explain that to Jacqui? And now Cameron owned a farm—what did Ronnie think of that?*

He found his mother in the kitchen having breakfast. It quickly became clear to Cameron that her mind had been preoccupied overnight thinking about the way forward with the will. As he prepared his morning coffee, she bombarded him with her thoughts: "What are you going to do? It's what your grandmother wanted. It is your responsibility to your family. You're not going to contest the will, are you? You're going to have to stay until this is sorted out, you know."

"Stop!" Cameron yelled. "I have six months to decide what I am doing. There is no rush."

"Well, what happens in the meantime?"

"I'm not going back to Dubai straight away. Not sure when. I'll work something out, but it will be soon."

He hadn't told his mother of the conversation with Young Billy. He would manage that. If he is responsible for running the farm, he didn't want his mum or Heidi interfering. As far as he understood the conditions of the will, the running of the farm would be his call. That part he liked.

"But we must know what you're going to do, Cameron. The farm is not going to run itself. You've got to make some decisions."

"Mum, I've got it, okay? Mr Forbes said it himself—we have time."

"Well, things are not going to happen if you're back in Dubai. Someone must take control."

"Okay, Mum. You want me to take control? Be careful what you wish for. Firstly, that means that until the will is executed, nothing changes. Nothing leaves the farm—so that boot-load of stuff both you and Heidi loaded up must come back."

"Now you're being stupid. Don't be a dickhead."

"No, everything stays until I say so and the will has been executed."

Paul had arrived for breakfast, now standing in the doorway, reluctant to enter. Rosemary turned to him for support. "Paul, he's being stupid. He says we can't take our share of things."

Having heard the exchange, Paul pondered for a moment. The pause gave a few seconds for the tension to dissipate. "Actually, he is right. Until the will is executed, nothing should change."

"That's just being childish," Rosemary protested.

"You did say it's what Grandma wanted," Cameron added with delight. So, his mother unloaded their car and grudgingly put everything back in its rightful place and left to return to Melbourne.

"You will have to get it all back from Heidi," his mother directed as she left.

"Of course, Mum," he replied, having no intention to take any further action.

To clear his mind, Cameron went into the offices of R.S. Forbes Solicitors and buried himself in his work. Before doing so, he rang Ian to confirm he would be at the concert tomorrow night "as planned." Ian sounded very excited and instructed Cameron to give the ushers at the door his name and they would direct him to his seat. Cameron didn't understand the need for that at a pub gig, ignoring it as unnecessary information.

After a few hours, Jacqueline interrupted, letting him know her dad closed the office precisely at 5 pm. Now that circumstances had changed a little, he realised he needed to make arrangements for NBN access for Binya. Satisfied with his day's work, he soon closed the computer and went to Jacqueline's office to let her know he was finished. He glanced at the time and realised there was a small window of time available, so he offered to spend a few minutes reviewing the Barkley files. Entering the room he had nicknamed the evidence room, he began familiarising himself with the material Jacqueline had compiled. After a short while, Jacqueline joined him, enthused by his interest.

Cameron began scanning through the police statements, immediately noticing a striking similarity—they were all very short and lacked detail. They shared a common theme: no one had seen the girls at the dance. Only two statements specifically referenced seeing the girls—those from their mother and their surviving sister, Jacqueline's mum, Mary, who had been a very young child at the time. Jacqueline's grandfather, Cecil Barkley, the father of the missing girls, provided a statement indicating his plan to return to the farm to take the girls to the dance. He had spent the day assisting on a friend's property. He had been delayed because the threat of an approaching thunderstorm necessitated the need to move a large quantity of grain to a storage shed, and that task had been complicated by the breakdown of one of the trucks. Cecil seemed to be the only person who could fix it. By the time he had arrived home, the girls had already left. He didn't know they were not at the dance until he went to pick them up.

After reading through the statements a couple of times, he asked Jacqueline, "Were there any statements taken to verify your grandfather's whereabouts?"

"Umm, I don't know. I can't recall seeing anything. I am sure I got all statements from the police, and they all seemed to be together in recorded file boxes."

"Are you sure you got all the file boxes?"

"Well, yes," and giving more thought to it, she added, "yes, there were only two evidence boxes marked 1 of 2 and 2 of 2."

"That doesn't seem like much."

"Well, that's the very point. There is so little evidence. Sorry, no evidence," she stated. "No bodies, no pieces of torn clothing, no missing bikes, no nothing. There's nothing."

Her hands were raised, her palms open, her face twisted in frustration. He felt the pain that the lack of any evidence had caused over all these years.

He sat down on the corner of the table and took her hands and held them together in his, "I understand, but I would have thought there would have been some collaboration of your grandfather's movements, his relationship with the girls, his—"

She pulled her hands away with a fright. Her twisted face suddenly turning to one of shock, eyes wide open, eyebrows raised. "What? Are you jumping to the conclusion that my grandfather is a suspect?"

He hesitated for a moment, unsure if he should wear the hat of a supporting close friend, or the hat of a forensic investigator. He chose the latter. "Jack, listen to me," a break from the office naming conventions. "Let me be frank. Maybe it's that I've watched more TV murder mysteries than you, but here's the drill. The people I deal with at work are very sophisticated. They hide behind assumptions of logic and a veil of numbers. If you are going to make progress on this, you need to have a cold, callous methodology. Question everything, rule out nothing."

She was a solicitor. She had passed Law 101. She put her arms around his neck and laid her head on his chest. A pause.

She stood back, restored her solicitor disposition. "Sorry. You're right. I feel embarrassed I hadn't noticed that before. I can only assume they had verified things like that."

"Do you know if any questions were ever raised about your grandfather?"

"No, none at all. In fact, quite the opposite. Mum won't talk about it, but Dad says it broke his heart. I was young when he died and my memories of him are faint. He spoke little. I can't recall him laughing and only an occasional smile, but he would pat me on the head and say, 'Stay close to your mum and dad.' He was a kind, loving father that adored his three girls, and from that day, he became a broken man. I would have loved to have known my real grandfather."

He opened his arms, and she rested her head back on his shoulder. A warm tear ran down his neck.

"And I am sure the police would have verified his whereabouts. It would be good to find something that closes that off. I'm sure the police at the time had no reason to question it. But if we are going to find anything here, we need to turn over every stone. So, what have you got planned?"

"Well, I am re-enacting the bike ride, remember?"

"Great idea, so when?"

"If you happened to notice the dates, next Tuesday is the anniversary of when they went missing, so I'm thinking Tuesday morning."

"Good, but why Tuesday morning? They rode the bikes in the evening?"

"Because I thought it would be cooler then," she muttered, appearing very embarrassed.

"This is what we should do," Cameron flicked through some of the witness statements, searching for the time. "Your mum says they would have left between 5.30 and 6 pm. We leave then and we will ride in the same light they did."

"Okay," she said. "The other thing I want to do is talk to your Aunt Agnes. She's the only person I have spoken to who attended the dance. I'd like to get to her before ..." she paused, thinking of the correct way to complete the sentence.

"Before she croaks," he said. They both laughed. "You're right. Let's do that later in the week."

"Sounds great," said Jacqui. He liked Jacqui more than Jacqueline. She appeared more comfortable with Jacqui. Jacqueline personified her solicitor mode. *Don't cross Jacqueline.*

Mr Forbes appeared in the doorway, heralding the time of 5 pm. Time to leave.

"Would you mind if I took some of this and analysed them at home?"

"Not at all. Home, is it?" she added with an inquiring grin.

"Back off, not that quick."

They exchanged good nights in the presence of her father, and all left the office.

Cameron spent that evening and most of Saturday meticulously reviewing the statements and police reports, trying to gain as much information of the incident, searching for any possible thread worth pursuing. By late Saturday, he had assembled a timeline.

Jane and Kathleen had ridden home from school and arrived around 4 pm, their normal routine. They were full of anticipation for the school dance that evening. From the time they arrived at home, they were bubbling with excitement, eager to get dressed in their new dresses. For the girls and their school mates, nothing beat the school dance. Their father had planned to drive them to the dance after he arrived home from a neighbouring property, where he had worked for the day, however their mother had received a telephone call shortly before the girls arrived at home saying that there had been a delay due to a truck breakdown and their father may be late. Finding that pleased Cameron because it collaborated Cecil's delay before the girls even went missing. In that phone call, the caller cautioned about an approaching storm. Their mother, Louise, had devised that the back-up plan would be for the girls to ride into town on their bikes, as long as the approaching storm didn't strike. Cecil would pick them up at the end of the dance.

The statements of Louise and Mary had described the girls as excited and happy about attending the dance and that riding their bikes had not phased them. They regularly rode their bikes to school and town, a trip of about twenty minutes. Their mother stated her reluctance to let them ride and tried to persuade them to wait because of the storm. Cameron speculated that the girls were so anxious to get to the dance, fearing that their mother would delay them, that they may have snuck away on their bikes somewhere between 5 and 6 pm. When their mother went to check on them, Mary, the youngest daughter, told her that they had already left.

The storm struck between 6 and 6.30 pm, and both their mother and father had concluded that the girls would have got there safely before it struck. Cameron could find nothing to validate the time or specifically at what location the storm struck. Cameron knew from his own experience it could be raining at one spot and dry only a short distance away. A consensus across numerous statements seemed to confirm that the storm had struck before the dance started. It was also apparent that it had continued to rain heavily well into the evening. A few statements spoke of the reduced number of children attending the dance because of the storm. Dance organisers had reported that they were not concerned about children not being there because of the storm.

No one could recall seeing Jane and Kathleen. From the wording of the statements, it was clear to Cameron that everyone had been asked that question. Their bikes were not found at the Murrumburrah Mechanics Institute Hall, the location of the dance, or anywhere along the road where they would have travelled. Cameron tried to piece together the details, mindful that the events occurred in a very different era, having no mobile phones, no social media and no internet.

According to his statement, Cecil Barkley arrived at the hall at about 8.45 pm for the scheduled 9 pm finish. He parked on the opposite side of the road in front of the flour mill and watched the door of the Murrumburrah Mechanics Institute Hall, waiting for his daughters to appear. At 9 pm, children started to come out the front door. Departures soon dwindled to the odd child exiting, and after a few minutes, he got out of his truck and went into the hall. Inside, he found the adults who had supervised the dance cleaning up. He asked a number of them where Jane and Kathleen were, and none could recall seeing them. A number of statements listed Agnes, Cameron's aunty, as one of the adult supervisors he had spoken with.

Cameron concluded from the evidence that, at first, no one showed any concern. A lot of children were unexpectedly absent. Each person Cecil spoke to individually could not recall seeing the girls. Cecil became a little more anxious when the supervisors came together and unanimously agreed that they had not seen them.

One of the schoolteachers volunteered to drive to the Harden Police Station and soon arrived back with a police officer. Cecil rushed home to check if the girls had already arrived home.

After confirming that they had not, he returned to the hall. Word went out that the Barkley children were missing.

According to the newspaper report, "a hundred" gathered to search, but Cameron could not find that officially confirmed anywhere in the notes. A reporter from the Harden-Murrumburrah Express arrived on-site. The story said the reporter had turned out as a volunteer to search. Cameron's sceptical mind suspected that the reporter was more likely in pursuit of a good story rather than driven by some altruistic passion to assist in the search. *He just happened to have his camera with him.* The reporter took several photos, mainly of all the people who turned out to the search, the cars and trucks gathered in front of the hall that night, as well as many more photos over the coming days.

The Murrumburrah Mechanics Institute Hall quickly transformed from a school dance hall into search headquarters. Given the recent disappearance of other children in Glenelg, South Australia, national media vans soon arrived in town.

Over the coming days, a wide and exhaustive search took place, which was well-documented in police reports and newspaper clippings. A party of forty volunteers walked the road from their farm to the hall, searching for any sign of the girls, but found nothing. The storm had potentially washed away evidence. Police reports concluded that the girls had ample time to arrive before the storm but added that it may have started to rain. Cameron had no doubt there had been a storm, but he could not confirm precisely when and where the storm had struck.

Cameron agreed with Jacqui's assessment that the story ends there. No sign of the girls, no ransom notes, no clothing, no bikes. Nothing. Even the theories seemed to be light in substance. Statements satisfied Cameron that nothing suggested any involvement from Cecil. Cameron saw no reason to query that any further. He wished he had checked for that before confronting Jacqui. *Poor research. Sorry Jack.* No reports of anyone "acting strangely" around the hall or the school were found.

He read the articles suggesting a connection with the disappearance of the Beaumont children in South Australia, agreeing with Jacqui's assessment that the "evidence" relied totally on a sighting of a South Australian number plate at Jugiong, twenty-six miles away, on the main highway linking Sydney and South Australia. And that sighting had been three days after the event. Police recorded that they had dismissed that theory. *Good work, Jack for following it up anyway.* Some conspiracy theorists had pointed out that Jane had the same name as one of the Beaumont children, and Kathleen was the middle name of the second Beaumont child, which supposedly proved to be a point of connection. Cameron just shook his head.

The investigation remained open, but nothing more had been added to it. The town moved its focus to an annual memorial that Cameron himself had participated in as a school student. Fifty years on, nothing had changed.

Cameron had no idea what to do next. His opinion had not changed from his first reaction when Jacqui had told him about it a few days ago. *This is a waste of time.* He sat at the Binya dining room table, sipping a white wine and randomly picking up reports, statements or photos and pondering on them. He saw his Aunt Agnes in at least two photos depicting the shattered staff who had been caring for the children. Generally, the photos were of poor quality. Photos were black and white, taken at night in dim light.

Cameron smiled when he noticed what he thought to be his grandfather's International truck pulled up near the hall. He had responded to the call to search. Many years later, Cameron would enjoy riding in the old truck. Though age had wearied it since the photo was taken, he remained confident it was his grandfather's. He could see that there were many very similar trucks on the poor black and white photos. He felt pride that his grandfather had answered the call to help and turned up so rapidly on the night. He and Cecil had always been close mates.

But where to go from here, he had no idea.

Being so engrossed in the research, he ran late for Ian's show. In reality, he'd allowed it to delay him. He longed for a legitimate reason not to go. He lamented Jacqui's absence, wishing she could be there. He needed the support. Sitting by himself in a half-empty club trying to stay enthused didn't appeal to him.

He had been told that the show would start at 7 pm. The car clock showed 19:10 as he drove up East Street and approached the Harden Town & Country Club. To his surprise, the street overflowed with cars, making it difficult to find a parking spot. When he secured one, he had a distance to walk back to the club, arriving about twenty minutes late. He made his way inside, swinging into the bar, expecting to hear Ian singing as he entered. Instead, silence filled the bar, with only a few people in sight. For a moment, he thought he must have the wrong venue.

The barman observed his obvious disorientation. "You lookin' for someone, matey?"

"Ah yeah, I thought Ian Blacka was here tonight," Cameron responded in a rather confused voice.

"He's already started mate, you're late," the barman replied.

"Late, um?" Cameron scanned the room: no noise, no people.

"Out the back, mate, in the auditorium," the barman added. "You can go straight ahead at the foyer or cut through here behind the pokies."

During his visit the previous week, the club appeared largely unchanged. He had not noticed the significant addition at the back of the club—an auditorium with a 400-seat capacity.

As he approached the usher standing at the door, she asked, "Are you Cameron?"

Rather surprised, Cameron replied "Sorry I'm late."

"That's okay," the usher replied. "Colleen told us you would be late and asked that I take you down to your seat."

Thank you, Colleen—not.

She opened the door and motioned for Cameron to follow. The moment he stepped inside, a blast of music and song hit him, making him gasp. Ian's rich and commanding voice filled the room. Cameron expected to be sitting in a bar watching Ian standing in the corner singing mostly to himself, as they had done in Sydney. Instead, he found himself in the middle of a full-scale professional concert with Ian performing on a proper stage with an auditorium that appeared very full.

He gazed down on the stage, sunken, into the corner of the large theatre, with tiered seating angled at forty-five degrees to both sides. He counted roughly ten or so rows of seats and, along the front, a series of tables with additional seating caught his eye. The usher led him to a table where Colleen sat—the only vacant seat he could see.

Collen gave him a cursory glance. "Could have guessed you didn't have a watch," she grunted.

"Sorry," Cameron muttered, trying to think of an excuse, but rather simply left it at that. The usher leant down, quietly asking if he wanted a drink. Cameron ordered a glass of Sauvignon Blanc wine. She returned shortly after with what appeared to be a glass of Coke.

"Ah, I asked for a Sauvignon Blanc," Cameron stated.

"Ian said you would ask for that. He said to bring you this."

Cameron didn't know what to say or do. He quickly glanced across at Colleen. Her eyes were focused on Ian performing and didn't appear to notice, but Cameron detected the slightest hint of a grin on an otherwise straight face. He took a deep breath. *What the hell?* He sipped his drink—Bacardi and Coke. Of course, his teenage go-to drink. Ian had remembered.

Ian sang "The Green, Green Grass of Home." Country was

not Cameron's genre, particularly old country. *This is going to be a long, long night.* Cameron sat just off to Ian's left. Ian didn't seem to acknowledge him, but Cameron assumed he must have noticed him. Ian sat on a stool, strumming his acoustic guitar and commanding the microphone. Two electric guitars rested on stands behind him. Over Ian's right shoulder, Kurt sat surrounded by his drum kit. To Ian's left, more directly in front of Cameron, Peta played keyboard and managed additional backing music and mixing through the control desk beside her.

Cameron took a moment to absorb everything. The venue impressed him, and the quality of the singing and music had the large audience fully engaged. He recalled Jacqui's words, "Cameron you need to open your eyes—and your mind." He realised how much he hadn't seen. Returning to Harden, he had expected to find everything just as he left it. But things had progressed—he simply hadn't noticed. He could see, if he chose to, a barista, a church minister with fresh ideas engaging well with young people and a quality music venue. Now, he was witnessing a quality musician he felt he should have known already existed.

Ian transitioned smoothly into his next number, "Clancy of the Overflow." Despite not being a country fan, this song had always transported Cameron to the romanticism of the Australian sunburnt plains. Ian and Cameron had often sung it in their gigs. Ian sang with genuine passion, bringing Clancy vividly into the auditorium. Cameron could sense the burning sunset—the smell of the shearing shed, the smell of the dairy. *And I somehow rather fancy that I'd like to change with Clancy.*

"Way Out West" ignited the audience—their feet stamping and hands clapping. *"Living and working on the land"*—Ian made it sound very attractive. Surrounded by people who felt an affinity with rural living, Cameron could sense the values and fulfillment that everyone else in the room thrived on. Maybe he had missed something when he packed his bags and left.

The next two songs tore at Cameron's emotions. Ian slowed the pace, shifting the mood in the room as he strummed John Mellencamp's "Smalltown." *"I was born in a smalltown."* As Ian sang, Cameron felt himself being drawn back to a place he had once rejected. His eyes, initially focused on Ian, became transfixed by the vibrations of the base drum immediately behind Ian. He gripped his glass of Bacardi and Coke tighter and tighter as Ian's words drilled deeper and deeper into his mind.

The spell held strong as Ian moved into Bruce Springsteen's "My Hometown"—another song that Cameron had occasionally performed in the Sydney gigs. Ian repeated the introductory chords several times before singing the opening words. Cameron's eyes remained fixed on the beating of the base drum, his mind singing the words, even before Ian sang. Vivid images of the town he had been rediscovering over the past week flashed through his thoughts: *"Son, take a good look around; this is your hometown."* Cameron accepted it: *This is my hometown.* More than that, he could see and feel the Cameron he had left behind.

Another realisation pierced his emotions. The brilliance of this performance stemmed from Ian's amazing singing voice. As Ian sang, Cameron glanced around the audience. They were captivated, hanging on every word he sang. They weren't just listening to him—they were absorbing him. Ian had become an extraordinary singer. His voice had matured, developing a rich huskiness, the perfect tone for the power ballads.

Then, a chilling irony froze Cameron. He had left Harden to chase fame and fortune, singing in Sydney—but it never came. Meanwhile, Ian had returned to Harden and found his music career, achieving everything Cameron had longed for. The resentment Cameron had harboured—believing Ian had destroyed their music dreams—suddenly felt baseless. He now felt guilty: *Had I, in fact, held Ian back? Maybe Ian has always been great and like everything else, I didn't see it.*

The interval broke Cameron's trance and the grasp on his

glass. Ian came directly off stage to Cameron and gave him an embrace.

"Thanks for coming. Great to see you here," Ian greeted.

"Sorry for being a little late. Mate, that was bloody amazing," Cameron wanted to say more but struggled to find words that could express his emotions.

"Heaps more to come."

They were soon interrupted by a seemingly endless line of people wanting to congratulate Ian on the show so far. Ian excused himself, on the pretence that he, Kurt and Peta had to map out the second half of the show. Colleen chatted with well-wishers from the audience. Her pride of Ian shone brightly. Cameron ordered another Bacardi and Coke and sat in silence, happy to give his emotions a break.

The second half commenced with a rendition of "Hallelujah"—a song Cameron had sung in Sydney. Ian sang it better. "Summer of 69" followed. It had often been their opening number in Sydney, and again, Ian produced a much superior performance. Cameron's ego was getting a battering. Another Bacardi and Coke was his response.

As the concert built toward the end, Ian started to introduce the last bracket. The audience erupted into applause immediately as Ian began. Cameron scanned the audience, and he sensed they knew something he didn't.

"If you are new to Harden," Ian introduced. "I need to tell you that several years ago, this town banded together to produce a magnificent performance of *Les Misérables*, now etched into Harden history. I'd like to share a couple of numbers from that production."

A silence fell over the auditorium as Ian delivered a deeply moving rendition of "Bring Him Home," supported by an orchestral backing track, managed by Peta. Cameron could feel the emotion in the room. Every person hung on every note, and

Ian delivered with perfection. The final syllables of "Bring Him Home" hung in the air and were followed by a deafening silence until the room erupted into a standing ovation.

Without introduction, Ian continued with "Empty Chairs and Empty Tables," another song from *Les Misérables*. Cameron had played the role of Marius in the production of *Les Misérables*, performing this song for which he had received critical acclaim. Another rousing response from the audience. Cameron's eyes swelled with tears—Ian had performed a flawless rendition.

On that standing ovation, Cameron assumed the concert was over but could sense the audience knew there was much more to come.

"Do you want one more?" asked Ian.

Loud applause.

"MORE!" cried the audience in unison.

"Do you mean more, or do you mean 'The More'?"

An even louder cry of "The More" followed by very loud cheering.

Cameron spun around. *What's going on?*

"For those who have not been here before," Ian continued as the crescendo subsided. "It is tradition that we close out the concert with a performance of 'One Day More.' We call it The More. But when I say we, I mean we. I mean all of us. We are the Harden-Murrumburrah Choir!"

More thunderous applause as Kurt and Peta came forward and set up three additional microphones, placed on either side of Ian.

"But tonight, we have something even more special. Tonight, Marius himself returns to us, Cameron Blanche. As many of you would know, Cameron's grandmother, Amy White, passed away recently."

Spontaneous applause broke out in tribute to Cameron's grandmother.

"Yes, we do honour a Harden legend in Amy, and may she rest in peace with God. But tonight, we have with us Cameron, aka Marius, who will be joining us for tonight's performance."

Another round of rousing applause followed.

Cameron sat in stunned silence. *No, no, no!* He didn't want to be on stage. But the enthusiasm of the applause told him the decision had already been made. Ian ushered him to stand between him and Kurt, who stood a microphone and music stand in front of Cameron. On the stand, Cameron saw a sheet with words, highlighted and colour-coded.

Kurt, whispered in his ear, "You only need to sing the green bits. We all sing the black bits! Others sing the other bits."

Some relief for Cameron—he didn't have to remember all the words. But he had not sung any of this for years and now stood in front of hundreds of people, now next to someone who could really sing, and much better than him. He feared he would be humiliated and wanted to return to his seat.

Cameron soon discovered that Kurt, Peta and Ian would sing most of the key solo lines, supported by some audience members. A chorus singer from the production, who had been Eponine's understudy, sang Eponine's lines, while another person from the production sang Javert's lines from where he stood. Cameron recognised many of them as they sang. Kurt and Peta filled in the rest. They were ready and Peta pressed play on the orchestral backing track.

Following Ian, Kurt and Peta's lead, the audience stood and began to sing. Only a few bars in, Cameron felt the vibe. Everyone sang as if they had rehearsed for weeks. Goose bumps quickly covered his neck and arms. It was inspirational. The audience participation was exhilarating. Overwhelmed by the emotion of the moment, Cameron quickly slipped back into *Les Misérables*, barely needing to follow the words.

Without introduction, Ian, Kurt and Peta led the audience into a rousing performance of "Did You Hear the People Sing." Ian, Kurt, Peta and Cameron sang solo a line of each verse, with Kurt pointing to Cameron every line he had to sing. Cameron required little direction and sang his lines with passion as if he had rehearsed repeatedly. A stunning performance by all—tears streamed down Cameron's face. The standing ovation lasted for a long time. It had been the best *Les Misérables* bracket of all their concerts. Many tears filled the room, not just Cameron's. Cameron caught Ian's eye and they embraced. Nothing needed to be said.

On the cue of the applause, the usher opened the doors, but no one had moved. It seemed no one wanted to move. Ian didn't do his standard audience bow, but rather turned, picked up his electric guitar and took his seat on his stool. He made no eye contact with anyone. Cameron glanced at Kurt and Peta. They exchanged glances, shrugged and returned to their positions as Cameron made his way back to his seat. Ian, eyes focused on nothing but his strings, began strumming some chords, appearing oblivious to anyone or anything in the auditorium. People found their seats again and a silence descended again.

Don't spoil the moment. A good performer knows the moment to end a show, haven't we just had that? Cameron was nervous for Ian.

A hush enveloped the room, the only sound being the softly strummed chords. Cameron could see the doors were open and more people were crowding at the door. Ian continued to strum the chords. Kurt quickly resumed his seat behind the drums, brushing the symbols, adding rhythm and depth to the unfolding music. Peta followed, tentatively latching onto Ian's chord progession. Cameron could see the nervousness in her eyes, darting from Ian to Kurt and back as if unsure of what to do. She followed Ian's lead, anticipating his every chord.

Ian began singing, "*Stood there boldly, sweating in the sun, felt like a million, felt like number one, the height of summer I'd never felt that strong. Like a rock."*

The "k" in rock resonated through the theatre, hanging in the air and in Cameron's mind. A shiver traced through his body. His eyes welled with tears.

Kurt appeared to be in his element. Cameron watched him touch the drums and cymbals with the gentleness of a skilled drummer. Peta appeared nervous—her eyes continuing to dart from Ian to Kurt, following Ian's chords on her keyboard.

The second stanza started. Ian sang every syllable with emotion and clarity—with calmlness and gentleness. The audience sat in complete silence. Cameron remained frozen with emotion. At the end of the third stanza, the scale lifted. Kurt and Peta followed, the music rising again for the chorus, then escalating further for the next verse. As Ian sang, the swelling of emotion and beat reverberated through the auditorium, leading into a perfect guitar solo masterclass by Ian. Cameron did not move. He could sense the audience was equally engaged.

Ian built the guitar bridge a level higher every time he played through the chords with perfection and clarity. He repeated and repeated, higher and higher, cutting through the air with every note. The emotion in the room became palpable. Ian held the high note for an extended moment, fading it out once again to almost silence. Kurt and Peta followed, fading out, leaving just the softest of sounds from Ian's guitar.

"Twenty years now, twenty years, I don't know
I sit, and I wonder sometimes where they've gone.
And sometimes late at night
Oh, when I'm bathed in the firelight,
The moon comes callin', a ghostly white and I recall I recall ..."
Every word spoke to Cameron, haunting him. Where had his twenty years gone? The words, the beat, the guitar lingered in the room like a ghostly presence. Cameron wondered if anyone

dared to breathe. Kurt momentarily took the spotlight, pounding the drums with all his might as Ian ascended his scale, "... *Like a rock, like a rock*," then a bridge that built and built and built, ascending each time to a new height. Kurt controlled the beat with perfection, allowing Ian's words to crystalise the moment. Then, they combined to build to a climactic end. The emotion built to an explosive level. Ian brought it down for a final time, and with the quietly played solo, softly sang the chorus, "*Like a rock, I was strong as I could be. Like a rock, nothing ever got to me. Like a rock, I was something to see. Like a rock.*"

Silence—as if no one in the audience knew what to do, until an eruption of noise and applause filled the auditorium as everyone rose to their feet. And it just didn't stop. It became a moment that would be talked about in the Harden Town & Country Club for many years to come. Cameron hadn't moved. His body felt numb—he sat drenched in emotion. Even Colleen could sense that he needed a moment alone. The "k" in rock echoed in his mind. He didn't know where the last years had gone or what he had missed. *Cameron or Ronnie? Less clear— where to from here?*

The audience slowly made their way out. Cameron headed to the bar to wait for Ian.

"A nightcap, mate?" asked the barman. "You look like you need one."

"A Bacardi and Coke please."

"Some show eh!"

"Awesome. That ending, I don't know what to say ..."

"We call those moments around here a 'Blacka moment'. He pulls them out of the hat quite often. I've seen it before—when the doors open, but no one comes out. Word races around out here, so you'll see people rush around saying 'there's a Blacka moment' and everyone crowds the door."

"He's pretty good", Cameron lamely responded.

"Pretty good? Mate, I've worked in many pubs and clubs, backpacking all over the world and he's the best I've ever seen. He should be in the big time."

Cameron could do nothing but agree.

After a short while, Peta also made her way to the bar. Recognising Cameron, she introduced herself.

"So, you're Ian's friend from school? Living in Dubai I hear?"

"Yes, that's me. Peta, is it? Ian speaks highly of you. Been around the music field a bit, I hear?"

"Yeah, done a bit—played the country music scene for a long time. Had some good gigs, toured with Tom Jones once, but developed a bit of a throat problem. Told to give it away or lose my voice. Doing the odd bit with Ian seems pretty much the right balance."

"Won't be if you keep having nights like tonight."

"Yeah, tonight has been something special. For me, it's probably been the biggest night since a Tom Jones finale!"

"That's a big call!"

"Ian's big. He is better than he thinks he is. I've done a lot of the big gigs, like the Tamworth Country Music Festival. I can get him a gig. A good gig. But he won't be in it."

"If every show is like tonight, I can see why."

"There was something different about tonight. I've never seen him so tense about a show. So much longer than we have ever done before. More rehearsals than normal and much more new material than we have ever attempted on one night. Don't know why."

Cameron knew—it was for him. "I still have goose bumps from that last number. I'm ringing wet."

"I think everyone does. I didn't want to do it—I've never played it before. We did rehearse it a couple of times, but it wasn't on the playlist. It surprised Kurt and I when he started playing it. Kurt has drummed it for another guy he plays for over at Cootamundra. Ian probably only went ahead with it because Kurt was so keen."

Cameron recalled the dynamics he observed, particularly between Kurt and Peta and it now made sense. "I think he did an awesome job on the drums," he said.

"Don't get me wrong, he did. To be honest, Kurt and I have never got along much, but tonight, he redeemed himself. Take my hat off to Ian. He stuck by Kurt and never gave up on him. Suppose there is something to learn in that."

Cameron felt the dagger—it pierced deep. Ian had stuck up for Kurt in a way he had never stuck up for Ian. He felt gutted.

"So, what are you up to? Going back to the high life in Dubai?" Peta asked.

"Don't know about the high life. Not sure what's next for me," Cameron replied. What a different statement he would have made a few days ago, when Ronnie knew exactly what he wanted to do.

"But you've packed your bags and made the choice to pursue an international career. Not many from Harden have done that," she said.

"Well, that's just it," he replied, "none of it has been planned, as such. My dad was a bank manager, so probably no surprise I have always been good with numbers."

"Did you want to be a banker too?"

"No, no," he replied. "That's the point, there has never been a big plan."

"Well, you must have known what you were going to do when you finished uni?"

"Not really. Be an accountant in Sydney and do music gigs at night, I guess" he replied. "Got a job with a firm that has overseas offices, got interested in a specific field of accounting. They asked me to do some work in their Dubai office. Same work, same firm."

To Cameron's relief, Ian joined, having finished the pack up and chatting with the well-wishers. "How is everyone?"

"Recovering. One hell of a show, mate," Cameron stood up and reached out his arms and embraced Ian. "The Best. Awesome. I don't know how else to describe it."

"Must have grown up with a good mentor," Ian responded.

Cameron dropped his head, knowing that he had never been the mentor he should have been.

"Hey," Ian added. "You did great up there with the *Les Mis* set. Pity you're not hanging around; you could join us more."

Now Ian is offering him a job as a sidekick, backing singer. For the first time, that didn't offend Cameron.

"Pity," he replied.

"Well, time we all went home," Ian glanced at the door. "Got a big day tomorrow: lamb marking. Colleen will drive your car home, Cameron. I'll follow in the truck and pick her up. Let's go."

Cameron thought briefly about debating a trip with Colleen but realised that the Bacardi and Coke total for the night didn't leave too many options. Cameron saw the irony in the entertainer, who had just completed one of the best shows Harden had seen, a show many an entertainer would dream of pulling off, and he's already focused on working sheep in the morning.

"Why do sheep on a Sunday?" Cameron asked.

"You do it when you can get the people to do it," Ian replied. "Number one secret in farming. You got to let it drive you."

Colleen drove Cameron's car to Binya. Neither spoke. Cameron had no problem with that, he was well beyond having any conversation. Ian followed in his truck.

Arriving at the Binya gate, Colleen directed, "You can make your way home from here. Don't crash."

"Goodnight," he said, as he got out, opened the gate and got in the driver's seat.

CHAPTER SEVEN

Cameron awoke much earlier than expected the next morning, feeling slightly seedy and in search of Panadol. He had planned to attend church, but he knew what he had to do. After a quick bath, followed by an even quicker breakfast, he jumped into his car and drove to Ian's property.

As he approached Whiteside, he could see the cars gathered at the sheep yards. He expected to be early, but he could see the action was already well underway. A large yard of sheep waited to the left of the pens where the procedures were taking place ready to be processed. At the far end of the yards, more sheep that had already been attended to were yarded, waiting to return to their pastures.

Farm activities like this were a bit like shearing—everyone would come together to get the job done. As a kid, just like the shearing time, Cameron would join the team to attend to the lambs. This included earmarking, drenching, tail docking and castration. It's a big job to bring all the sheep and lambs into the yards, so it made good sense to do as much as possible while the mob was gathered.

At about three months of age, lambs were earmarked. Castration and tail docking were done when lambs were much younger, but some were always missed. Earmarking provides the opportunity to ensure that the whole mob had been attended to. Finally, it presents a good time to drench the sheep with vaccines to prevent worms and other infections.

Cameron could see about eight or so people hard at work on a typical lamb production line. No one stopped to acknowledge his arrival. A good day's work depended upon an efficient, smooth workflow. One person herded the sheep into the first large holding yard with the aid of sheepdogs. Well-trained dogs did the bulk of the work with minimal input from their master.

Mobs of sheep would be moved into smaller yards and then broken into even smaller groups within sheepfolds. Although there were several sheepfolds, Cameron noticed they were operating only one today. In the first yard, sheep would be visually checked for tails or those needing castration. Those requiring attention were caught and held while their tails or testicles, or both, were removed.

The lambs were then guided into a race—a long chute designed to manage the lambs in a single file. Here, they were drenched by placing a dosing gun in their mouth and administered a dose of vaccine. Following drenching, they were moved into the final race where two farmhands earmarked the lambs. Using a pair of pliers embedded with the farm's registered trademark, the farmhand would take the left ear of a female lamb, or the right ear of a male lamb, place it in the pliers and squeeze. Blades would slice the trademark into the ear before the lamb was released into the final holding yard. From there, the lambs would be grouped into mobs and herded back to their respective paddocks on the farm—a task that would have been impossible without highly skilled sheepdogs.

Cameron could see that the production line had been put in place and was running efficiently. He spotted Ian at the first pen, attending to the castration and tail docking, dressed appropriately for the part—obligatory long sleeves, a large white apron dripping with blood and other remains and a face shield. Cameron immediately realised he had dressed like a city tourist in a short-sleeved shirt and baseball cap. *Didn't remember the dress code for working in the sun all day with sheep full of burrs— long sleeves are a must.* Feeling very out of place, Cameron grew even more determined to work long and hard—and be one of the last workers standing.

"Well, well, didn't expect to see you here," Ian greeted him with a cheerful grin. "You pulled up a lot better than I expected."

Cameron didn't let on how seedy he felt on the inside—the Panadol barely keeping his throbbing head at bay. "As you said, get the work done when people are available," Cameron responded, giving Ian a friendly slap on the shoulder. "Can't go back to Dubai without sheep dung under my nails. Now, what can I do?"

"Well, we've already done the bulk of the lambing work. Today is about earmarking and wrapping up—finding any that we missed castrating or tail docking. There appears to be quite a few that still need attention. After that, we are drenching them," Ian said, pointing down the race.

"Why don't you jump in the yard here and help Natalie—she's from the neighbouring property. Check if the lambs need castrating or docking. If they do, bring 'em over to me."

Cameron introduced himself to Natalie, who he hadn't met before. She appeared to be in her late teens, with a welcoming smile, wearing dark glasses. Her outfit was both stylish and practical—a blue checkered long-sleeved shirt buttoned to the top and secured with a brown scarf, all topped with a light fawn felt fedora. Not only very dressy, but it offered excellent protection—an extremely practical protection from burrs, sun and dust. It amazed Cameron how clean she still appeared to be.

It had been a long time since Cameron had handled sheep. While he'd done yard-work in the past, he usually chose tasks that involved less manual handling of the sheep, like drenching. He paused to observe Natalie for a moment. She clearly knew her craft well. With sharp eyes, she quickly identified lambs needing attention. Within seconds, she had one held under its front legs, its back resting against her chest. Securing the lamb on the top rail, she secured its rear legs in place, exposing the testicles for Ian to whip his knife into action and remove what he had to in seconds.

Cameron watched in awe. *Okay, a high standard to emulate.*

He thought about complimenting her but realised she was already focused on catching her next lamb. Feeling very self-conscious, Cameron knew all eyes would likely be on him. His first unsuccessful attempt to catch a lamb resembled the greasy pig chase at the Harden Show. (He never did catch that pig.) As the lamb darted, kicked and made its escape, Cameron could feel his face burning red, and it wasn't from sunburn—at least not yet.

Eventually, he managed to catch his first lamb. With its legs kicking wildly, he wrestled it to the railing. Ian assisted, using his elbow to hold the lamb steady while completing the castration. Cameron braced himself for laughter and jibes, but surprisingly, he heard none. Meanwhile, Natalie had already finished three lambs and in pursuit of a fourth as Cameron struggled with his second.

Moments later, he nearly lost his balance while lunging for the next lamb's leg. If not for Natalie, he would have faceplanted into the dirt. Still in the process of securing her own lamb, she instinctively used her left leg to pin the one Cameron was chasing against the fence railing, giving him just enough time to grab hold of it. The entire manoeuvre happened behind her, and he had no idea how she even knew he needed help.

At first, the work didn't get easier, and the lambs were winning in terms of points. But Cameron kept a close eye on Natalie, watching her technique. He admired how she led by example rather than giving him a condescending this-is-how-you-do-it lesson.

He kept telling himself, *I've picked up hundreds of lambs.* Gradually, the muscle memory returned to his arms and legs. *Pick up the lamb from behind, tuck the left arm high under the front legs, lift with the right arm from behind the back legs, rest its bum on the rail so that the groin is exposed, and tail is clear of the rail. Move your right arm to stop the back legs kicking.*

Hold still while the castration is completed, and the tail is docked. Simple—once you got the technique right.

Once he found his rhythm, Cameron got the technique flowing—even with the hangover. While Natalie continued to significantly outpace him, after a couple of hours, he started holding his own. His pace increased to a point that another person joined in to assist with the castration and docking. However, the lambs were carrying many burrs, and as the day wore on, the constant scratching of the burrs against his arms became increasingly painful. They were inflamed and scratched, resembling the inside of a sliced cherry.

By lunchtime, any image as a city kid beginner had vanished. He had slotted in well to the production line and was fully accepted by the group. Trestle tables and chairs had been set up under the shade of nearby gum trees for all the workers to break for lunch. Colleen and a team of ladies delivered a broad selection of sandwiches and an impressive array of slices and cakes. At the end of the table sat two coolers—one filled with cold water and the other with homemade lemonade.

Cameron relished the lunch, but he was hurting. His arms were raw with pain, and his back ached from the repetitive strain of lifting. Despite this, he gave nothing away. No one would have guessed the raging discomfort he felt as he suffered in silence, determined to hold his place amongst the team.

After lunch, they continued with the last of the castration and docking. He picked up the first lamb with ease, but he had not anticipated the excruciating pain. It felt like sandpaper being scraped on red raw, sunburnt skin. His eyes watered, but he refused to let go of the lamb. Determined not to be defeated, he braced himself for the next. With each lamb, the pain intensified, the burr-covered wool digging into his already shredded arms. With each lamb, he forced himself to mentally prepare for each wave of agony. There would be no surrender.

Ian noticed Cameron's arms had begun to bleed, yet he could see the determination etched into Cameron's face. Evaluating the production line, Ian identified that the bulk of the castration and docking work was nearly done, while other tasks required more help. He redirected Cameron to the drenching.

Drenching involved far less handling of the lambs. They were already in a race, so the operator had the rather simple task of holding the lamb's head, placing the nozzle of the drenching gun deep into its mouth and squeezing the gun to give the lamb the required dose of vaccine—vital for the management of worms and parasites. Cameron strapped on the drenching pack—a container of the vaccine about the size of a large backpack—and took up his new task. He spent the rest of the afternoon holding lambs steady, squirting the mixture down their throats and pushing them through the gate.

Finally, all tasks were complete, and the sheep were ready to move back into the paddocks. They were herded into their respective mobs and, with the aid of motorbikes and sheepdogs, guided back to their paddocks. By late afternoon, everyone congregated back at the yards and assisted in cleaning up all the waste and putting away the equipment. Those who had come from neighbouring properties made their way home.

Ian turned to Cameron. "Why don't you clean up in the guest house and join us for dinner on the porch? Some of the others are going home to freshen up and will be back."

Cameron readily accepted.

"Great. I'll let Colleen know you're coming."

Ian gave Cameron a big smile and a hearty slap on the back. Cameron winced in pain but felt the bond they had shared for so many years—the bond that had connected them as kids. But Cameron could see the transformation in Ian. He had developed into a leader. He could see it last night on the stage, and he could see it today on the farm.

Ian had been the follower—Cameron had been the one in control. It had been Cameron who set the rules for the games in the rock paddock, Cameron who talked Ian into going to Sydney for university, and Cameron who organised the music gigs. Cameron couldn't recall a time when he had ever stopped to ask Ian what *he* wanted.

Now, things were different. Ian stood tall, confident, and self-assured, leading with a natural authority that Cameron had witnessed firsthand throughout the day and last night. Ian had guided the team with encouragement and support, ensuring a quality job got done efficiently. Last night, Cameron had seen Ian subtly orchestrating every detail.

Cameron saw a quiet strength in Ian's demeanor. There was an unmistakable inner peace about Ian—an inner peace that Cameron didn't have. For all his accomplishments, for all the praise his grandmother showered on him, Cameron couldn't help feeling envious. Ian had something intangible, something priceless: contentment. It was a calmness, a self-assurance, that Cameron couldn't quite grasp but deeply longed for.

The guest house had been a favourite place for Ian and Cameron to hang out in their youth. Cameron made his way to his car, trying to disguise how much it hurt to walk or stand upright, or how much his arms raged with pain, and drove the short distance back to the homestead.

He gingerly made his way from the car, around the back of the homestead and past the porch to the guest house. He found the door open, a fresh towel waiting on the end of the bed—all so very familiar to him. It made him feel good. He realised he had left his phone in the car all day and checked it for the first time. There were several missed calls and texts from Jacqui wanting to know his whereabouts and if he was okay. One message mentioned that she had driven to Binya to check on him.

He had thought about Jacqui throughout the day. He wanted

to tell her about the concert, or more accurately, to debrief the concert. He opted to text her:

Sorry Jack, been helping Ian with sheep all day. Left my phone in the car.

Her reply was instant.

Good to hear you're okay. I was thinking you may have gone back to Dubai.

No, all good.

How was the show?

Bloody good. Awesome.

I know. He puts on a good show.

Why didn't you tell me it was a show?

Because you had to find out yourself. It's your journey.

Sorry I didn't contact you. Left my phone in the car. It's been a full-on day but really enjoyed it. Don't tell anyone, but I can hardly move.

Lol. Did you want to drop by?

Ian has asked me to stay for dinner, I'm sure he wouldn't mind you joining.

You need some time with Ian. I'll catch up tomorrow. xxx

He focused on the xxx. He had never imagined that xxx on a text would make him feel so good. *I think I'm becoming a romantic.*

He stripped off his clothes and made his way to the bathroom. The hot shower relieved his aching muscles. He muffled the scream of the initial excruciating pain as the hot water met his raw, sunburnt, burr-scratched arms—but his perseverance through gritted teeth was soon rewarded as the hot water began soothing his aching muscles. When he finally finished, he stepped out of the shower, dried himself and buried his head in the towel to dry his hair as he walked back out into the guest room.

"Brought you over some fresh clothes of Ian's. I'll think they'll fit."

Pulling down the towel from his head, he saw Colleen standing at the door with neatly folded clothes. He quickly lowered the towel into a more modest position, covering his nakedness.

"Oh, thanks. Never thought of that."

An awkward moment of silence.

"We will be on the porch shortly for a drink with the others," she said before turning to leave.

"Ah, Colleen ..." he called out. She turned and faced him. Another moment of awkward silence. "You seem angry with me."

"Not angry. Just giving you what you're worth."

"What?" he fastened the towel around his waist. "What are you talking about? I've never done you any harm."

"No harm? No, because Mr International-Too-Good has got what he wants and treats everyone else like pawns."

"What the hell are you talking about? I've done nothing but take the opportunities that came my way. Sure, it's taken me to some great places—"

"I don't give a shit where it's taken you. You've never looked over your shoulder to see who you've trodden over, have you?"

"That's bullshit."

"Bullshit, is it? So, where was Ian, then?"

Cameron struggled to get his thoughts together. Yes, he felt guilty over the coldness that had developed in their relationship and regretted it. "I didn't tread over him. Our interests changed. We just drifted different directions."

"Drifted different directions? Bullshit. You didn't get the band gig you wanted, blamed Ian for it and dumped him."

"Okay, it was a disappointment, but I didn't blame Ian for that," he muttered, knowing only the first part of that statement was true. He wanted to retract it. He stared at the ground. "I didn't abandon him. We just went our own ways."

"Christ almighty, Cameron," Colleen's face flushed a deep red and she took a step toward him, finger outstretched waving in his face. He could feel her anger. "He was hurting, Cameron. Hurting real bad. His father died. His mother had no idea how she would survive, let alone run a farm. He needed support. You were his best mate. Who else did he have?" Tears swelled in her eyes.

Cameron hung his head. "I called him," he mumbled, eyes fixed on the ground.

"Called him! Wow! Glad to see you busted yourself."

Cameron felt yet another dagger pierce him.

"And where were you at our wedding? He wanted you to be best man," she continued.

"That was different," Cameron struggled to find his words. "There was a thing happening—"

"Whatever," she stepped toward the door. "Always something else. No Ian in any of it. You are just full of bullshit, Cameron Blanche."

Silence.

"And you can put that thing away too. I see it's gotten no bigger than last time I saw it."

For a moment, Cameron didn't understand, until he realised that he been so blinded by the conversation that the towel had long dropped. He stood completely naked. He quickly reached down and grabbed the towel at his feet to cover himself.

"Colleen. Ian is my best mate. I haven't had a friend like him since Sydney," Cameron said, eyes swollen with tears.

"We'll be out for drinks shortly. Dress in more than that," she said before turning and leaving.

Cameron stood frozen for some time. He cast his eyes down. *It isn't that small, is it?* For a moment he couldn't think of when Colleen had seen him naked but then remembered the last skinny-dipping adventure at Currawong Creek.

Cameron laid on the bed for some time, replaying Colleen's words in his mind. Deep in his heart, he knew they were true.

He should have supported Ian more when his father died. Sure, the wedding had clashed with some work commitments, but he could have done more to make it work. It wasn't that he couldn't—it was that he didn't want to. Too gutless to confront the situation, he'd found an excuse to hide behind.

He had always believed Ian had made the wrong choices—should have come back to Sydney, should have continued his studies, should have continued playing music with him. But now, he could see he centred his own life on himself to further his own interests. He had only seen Ian as a means to achieving what he wanted. He hadn't seen Jacqui. He hadn't had a romantic relationship with anyone because he made no room for anybody else. Cameron now understood why he hadn't wanted to come back to Harden: because he knew he would find the old Cameron there, and Ronnie didn't want that. His mind floundered somewhere between Cameron and Ronnie.

A yell from the porch brought him back to the present. "Hey, Cameron, you haven't gone to sleep in there, have ya?" Laughter followed. Time to join them.

Cameron stepped onto the porch, where Ian, Colleen and about half the group who had worked the sheep earlier were now gathered, drinks in hand, clean and refreshed. To Cameron's irritation, none of them seemed to be in any pain. Most of them were Ian's extended family, including an uncle and some cousins. Two boys from the neighbouring property, one of whom was Natalie's brother, made up the group. Natalie had gone home. Cameron recognised a couple of Ian's cousins from school days but hadn't known them well.

Ian introduced Cameron to the group, describing his background, including his career in Dubai. Cameron winced. *Skip that bit for now.* Cameron immediately downplayed any importance of his job, as he had throughout the week.

Despite his desires to shift the focus, the group had a genuine interest in knowing more about Dubai. How hot did it get? Where does the water come from? Is it all sand? Had he been in the tallest building? Has he seen the seven-star hotel? He chose not to tell them that he and some work mates had stayed there a night, costing them a few thousand dollars each. A lesson in not accepting a dare when you are drunk at a pub.

On several occasions, Cameron tried to steer the conversation back to farming and the sheep industry. He asked if Merino was still the best wool, knowing it would spark a lively debate. Everyone relaxed and engaged in the conversation, and Cameron found himself fitting in well. They listened intently when he spoke, laughed at his jokes and asked many questions. When he deflected a topic, they simply said, "Tell us about it next time," as if they assumed there would be a next time.

At one point, Ian's uncle said, "When you got out of your car this morning, I chuckled to myself and said to the boys 'Give him half an hour and he'll be on his way back to the city.'" Everyone laughed. "But matey, you stuck it out. You did a bloody fine job. Hats off to ya. But one piece of advice—next time, wear a bloody long-sleeved shirt. You're going to make a bloody fine sheep farmer."

The group erupted into laughter, raising their glasses—or beer cans—in a collective toast of "Here! Here!" One by one, they clinked drinks with Cameron. Colleen headed to the kitchen to collect food, and Ian fired up the BBQ. Two of the cousins sat with Cameron to ask more questions about Dubai. Cameron enjoyed the chatter, but the uncle's words lingered in his mind "You're going to make a bloody fine sheep farmer."

People left early after a hard day's work but not before expressing how much they had enjoyed the night—good food, lively chatter and very enjoyable company. Cameron had enjoyed their interaction as much as they seemed to enjoy his. After the last cousins had left, Colleen moved into the kitchen and the kids had long since gone to bed, leaving Cameron and Ian alone. Ian began cleaning the BBQ.

"Got to say," Ian remarked, scraping the grill, "you really helped get through that mob today. Would've taken a lot longer without you."

"Thanks, mate. Had to come."

"Had to? How come?"

A long pause followed.

"I owe you."

"Owe me?" Ian continued scaping the BBQ. "Owe me for what?"

Another pause, "I don't know," Cameron admitted. "I don't know if it's an apology, an explanation or just an admission that I let you down."

Ian gave the BBQ a few more scrapes, put down the spatula and moved off the porch into the darkness, signalling Cameron to follow. They walked away in silence.

After a few minutes Ian spoke, "It took me a while to realise our lives had reached a point where we had different roads to follow."

"I was an arsehole," Cameron stopped walking and turned to his friend. "I treated you badly. And I don't know why."

"Oh, the why is the easy part," Ian said, staring into the darkness. "It's because, up until then, we were doing things that we both wanted to do. You were—you are—my hero. I always looked up to you as the big brother I never had. But when Dad died, everything changed. I realised I needed to be here. More than that—I *wanted* to be here on the farm. It was the easiest decision I have ever made. I could so clearly see that it was the right thing to do."

He paused, then added, "But here's the big thing: I realised I went to uni in Sydney to be with *you.* I played in a band so I could be with *you.* Mum even said I was Cameron's shadow."

"You're not exactly making me feel any better here," Cameron said, scanning the same darkness in search of solace.

Ian shrugged. "It was my issue to deal with. I just didn't understand it back then."

For a time, neither spoke.

"Colleen said you were really hurt that I wasn't around when your father died—or for the wedding. I can explai—"

"Stop," Ian interrupted, his tone calm but firm. "We're not going to do that. Yes, it hurt, but I never once criticised or complained. Yes, some people read me like a book, sure, but I knew we had to grow up. Losing Dad hurt bad, and yeah, I felt like I'd lost my big brother too. But we had to grow up and I knew that."

"But I let my little brother down," Cameron said. "I should have been there for you. I am truly sorry. I was being a dick. I've never saw beyond myself—it was all about me. But from what I see here, you're one damn good sheep farmer. I've heard the talk. This town respects you—a lot. And last night! Man, oh man; just brilliance. I couldn't match any of that. I want to live in *your* shadow."

They both stared into the darkness. After a pause, Ian continued, "The saddest song I often sing is 'Puff the Magic Dragon.' I remember crying when I heard it as a kid, and it saddens me even more now."

"Why do you sing it?" Cameron asked.

"Because it reminds me of you, or more the point, us," Ian replied. "Every time I sing it, I think of you and me. See, it's Jacky Paper that's gone, Cameron. Puff's still up there, on those rocks where we used to chase Rin Tin Tin. But it's us who's gone. We just grew up and travelled different paths."

"Why didn't you sing it last night?"

"I had it on the playlist," Ian admitted. "But when I got to it, I choked. I wouldn't have gotten through it with you sitting there."

They stood in the darkness for a long time.

Finally, Cameron broke the silence, not lifting his eyes.

"There's something I need to tell you," Cameron confessed, turning toward Ian. "I had my ticket booked to fly back to Dubai straight after Grandma's will was read. I was going to hide behind another lie and say I got called back urgently. But things changed.

"Grandma has left the farm to me. There are conditions. I can't sell it, and if I do, all proceeds go to the church. She has this thing about keeping it in the family for generations to come."

Ian laughed, shaking his head. "So, Cameron Blanche is a sheep farmer. I'll be damned. My uncle must have known!"

"No one knows yet," Cameron said. "You're the first. Well, other than Jacqui."

"So, what are you going to do?" Ian asked.

"I have no idea!" Cameron cried, throwing his hands into the air, staring into the black abyss of the night sky. "It's doing my head in. I don't know what to do. I don't know if I'm Cameron, Cam or Ronnie."

"What? Who the hell is Ronnie?"

"I'll fill you in on that another time, another beer or two," Cameron said with a helpless smile. "But in Dubai, they call me Ronnie. I'm beginning to realise Cameron is a different guy. I haven't seen Cameron for a long time—I've just met him again."

"Well, fellow farmer—" started Ian.

"Come on mate, cut it out," Cameron interrupted. "I don't know if I am, that's the point."

"Sorry, mate, not making light of it," Ian responded. "Okay, big brother, I'm here to help. I have no idea how to work through all this, but we will. But now I know why you came today: for your first lesson!"

"Cut that out," Cameron responded, shoving Ian's shoulder, knocking him off balance. "I came today because I needed my little brother."

They both laughed and gave each other an embrace.

"Colleen hates me," Cameron said.

"No, she doesn't."

"Yes, she does."

"Well, you know what my father would have said?"

"What?"

"Love her more."

CHAPTER EIGHT

Cameron woke up sore and stiff. But his discomfort reminded him of his day, making him feel good. Standing at the kitchen sink, waiting for the jug to boil for his morning coffee, he could see Young Billy's truck coming down the track. He quickly went out to greet Young Billy as he passed by the farmhouse.

Young Billy waved. "Going to check the sheep this side of the creek."

Despite his stiffness, Cameron jumped in the truck, much to Young Billy's delight. This time, Cameron sent a quick text to Jacqui to let her know. They spent a couple of hours checking the mobs. Cameron listened intently to Young Billy's observations about the condition of the sheep as he inspected them. He didn't tell him about the farm or the will.

Back at the farmhouse, Cameron particularly appreciated the bath more than usual. He filled it far higher than Grandma would have allowed. The water was so hot he could barely tolerate it as he slowly immersed himself, soaking his aching muscles until they were tender, and he could move without excruciating pain. He soaked until the water was barely tepid. Later, Cameron drove into town, stopping at the Which Craft & Coffee Cottage before arriving unannounced at R.S. Forbes Solicitors with coffee for everyone, including Mabel on the front counter. He gave the excuse that he was there to work, but he really wanted to see Jacqui.

He felt even better when Jacqui appeared equally excited to see him. Coffees were distributed and once alone, Jacqui cradled his cheek in the palm of her hand and, with the softest of touches, kissed his other cheek. She didn't rush it. He felt a hot flush rush through his body and could feel his heart racing. "Thank you for the coffee," she whispered.

She stood back and they moved to the chairs in her office.

"So, tell me about the weekend."

He slumped back in the chair, unsure where to begin. The will reading felt so long ago.

"I missed you, Jacqui. I needed you."

"No, Cameron. I feel this is a journey you had to take."

"I honestly don't know where to start. Mum and I exchanged a few words on Friday. The concert was unbelievable, and yesterday Ian and I had a real heart-to-heart."

"Let's start at the end. Where are you now?"

"Actually, I'm not in a bad place. If you asked me if I've burnt my ticket back to Dubai—no, I haven't. Part of me is definitely still there. I do love my job, but I also know I've been a dick. I think back on the way I've treated Ian and I'm ashamed. And for reasons I don't understand, I've deleted so much of my life growing up here in Harden. I'm hearing about things I never noticed but have been right in front of me. Even since being back here, I haven't noticed what's around me. I couldn't even see Harden had decent coffee! I know I need to find myself again. I was pissed off with Ian and blamed him for us not achieving what we could in Sydney. But I came back to find he is an incredible singer and entertainer. He is in a great spot with the farm and his family, and he's so in touch with his inner self. I went out in search of that. He found it here in Harden."

Mr Forbes knocked on the door and entered without waiting for an invitation.

"Sorry Jacqueline, but I do need some urgent work on the file for the sale of the McDougall property. Issues have come up with the financing, and we need to act fast to avoid the sale collapsing. I need you to follow it up with urgency. Sorry, Cameron."

"Not at all. Sorry, Mr Forbes, I didn't mean to hold Jacqueline up—I'm just enjoying the coffee. I have work to do myself, which is why I came in. If it's okay, I'll use the back room again?"

"Of course, Cameron. You know you are most welcome."

Jacqueline took the file from her father, "No problem, I will get onto it straight away."

Mr Forbes excused himself and left, leaving the door open—a subtle reminder for Cameron to leave.

"It sounds like you've come a long way, Cameron. Let's talk more about it later," giving him a parting kiss.

Cameron made his way into the spare office and immersed himself into a couple of hours of work. For the first time since being away, his supervisor emailed asking when he might be returning to Dubai, stating that there were some files needing Cameron's attention, but he didn't elaborate. The email puzzled Cameron because the advice he received only a few days before implied that there wasn't anything requiring his immediate return. But Cameron didn't seek any clarification and simply advised that his return date may become clearer by next week.

Cameron and Jacqui snuck away for a quick lunch at the Which Craft & Coffee Cottage and made plans for tomorrow's re-enactment.

Tuesday dawned with the repeating brilliant blue sky, but a bank of ominous clouds were emerging on the horizon. Another unusual email arrived from work, requesting an urgent review of some Lebedev files. The Lebedev family owned a Russian company with an office in Dubai, primarily engaged in engineering and mining, along with some property development.

Although Cameron had never dealt with the Lebedev files, as they had never required any forensic review, he had developed a friendship with two Lebedev brothers. The Lebedev company was managed by Adrik Lebedev and his two sons, Aleksander (Alex to Cameron) and Matvei. During a night out in Dubai, Aleksander unexpectedly greeted him at a popular bar, recognising Cameron from the office. That chance meeting developed into a friendship, and so Cameron (Ronnie),

Aleksander (Alex) and Matvei (who Cameron would call Matey) regularly socialised.

Nonetheless, Cameron went to the R.S. Forbes Solicitors office to review the files and prepare the reports. The people at the Dubai office were aware that he socialised with the brothers and, as a rule, reviewing their file could have been perceived as a conflict of interest. In fact, he had fostered the friendship with the Lebedev brothers on the basis that he didn't handle any of their files. It also troubled him that he didn't normally deal with property clients. Nevertheless, he undertook the review.

At first glance, everything in the files appeared normal. Having limited experience with property files, he methodically scrolled through the spreadsheets unsure at first as to which specifics to analyse other than core accounting reviews. He observed an unusual number of transactions for the same amount of money, but that alone wouldn't raise alarms. Property and deposit returns, as they were identified, were regular transactions for property management and it wasn't unusual for deposits to be the same amount, assuming the apartments had the same contract value. However, the similarity seemed a little odd since apartments values varied based on things like floor level, corner apartments and the view. With no reference point to assess whether the amounts were excessive or not, he noted the transactions. He also noted that it might indicate they may not be the best quality properties. Poor properties had a higher turnover of tenants, resulting in more deposit returns.

A quick review of the ledger of debtors appeared to support this assessment because there were many repair and maintenance invoices. He noticed the absence of some ledger accounts he would expect on a property account, such as municipality bills or government charges, but then again, they simply may be on a different billing cycle. He noticed that several transactions came from external entities where the invoices were not individually identified, but then again, it was not an abnormal form of batching. The bottom line—the ledger balanced. Nothing struck him as alarming and he failed to see the urgency of the review, or why he had been asked to review the file, given that property accounts had never been his specialty.

Before he closed, he cast one last eye over the screen, through the lens of money laundering. He felt more in his comfort zone—the bread and butter of forensic accounting. He scanned the spreadsheets in search of patterns. He found nothing unusual at first, but as he scanned deeper, some anomalies began to become evident.

He scanned for amounts paid that, when added together, equalled a payment received. He found an entry of $78,600 received and three payments of $26,053 paid out on the same day. Two payments drilled down to $26,053.33, whilst the third was $26,053.34. *If this is money laundering, they are amateurs*, he thought. He found a rather large payment of $650,000 and went searching for payments that matched that amount. A day after the receipting of the money, seven separate payments of different amounts went out to seven different accounts, which added up to exactly $650,000. *Coincidence?* Maybe. He found a few other similar matches. At the end of the day, they may or may not mean anything.

He completed his assessment, noting the observations he had made, and emailed his report back to the office. Cameron still couldn't understand why the files had been sent to him.

By mid-afternoon, Jacqui and Cameron were able to get away to undertake the re-enactment. Jacqui borrowed two bikes, and Cameron arranged for Ian to take them and the bikes in his truck to the old Barkley—now Forbes—property, where they would begin the ride. Jacqui had assumed they would ride out directly, but Cameron insisted on re-enacting the bike ride as closely as possible to how the girls would have done it.

"If they started at the house, so do we."

Driving down the track to the Currawong homestead felt surreal. Cameron guessed the three of them had different emotions and expectations, but no one spoke. Ian dropped them at the front of the house and left, seemingly pleased to be leaving.

Cameron and Jacqui stood silently looking at the two-story house. Cameron felt like he had stepped onto the set of a thriller movie, inspecting a house full of evil spirits. He scanned the second-floor windows expecting to see a figure or a shadow.

"You been here before?" Jacqui asked.

"Yeah, a couple of times as a kid, as I remember. It's familiar, but not familiar, if that makes sense," he shielded his eyes from the midday sun, surveying the house and surrounds. "So, no one lives here now?"

"No, not for a long time," Jacqui replied. "After Grandfather died, Grandmother lived here until she died. I remember Mum and Dad would bring me out here for weekends and we'd stay over, but I think Mum always felt uncomfortable. Anyway, that seemed to fizzle out."

"But it seems well-maintained," Cameron observed.

"It is. The farm is leased to the Moffatts who run sheep on it. As part of that deal, they're responsible for maintaining the house. It's cleaned and dusted regularly, and the yards are always in top condition."

"That's bizarre."

"Not wrong there."

Scanning the surrounds, Cameron asked, "Has anything here changed? Is it the same? The driveway, the trees: is anything different?"

Jacqueline turned her body a full circle, "It's so much the same, it's eerie."

A visible shiver passed through her body.

They stared at the house in silence for a few more moments. "Let's go in," Cameron suggested.

When Jacqui turned the key to open the large, solid wooden door, Cameron noticed her beautiful brown eyes glistening with tears. His eyes scanned the interior, searching for anything that might tell him something. He could recall being here, but a long time ago.

"Nothing has changed much on the inside either," she said. "Some things have been taken into the house in town, but not much."

Cameron shifted into forensic mode, his mind instinctively scanning, as it had been trained to do so—but this time he replaced his spreadsheet with a real whodunit mystery. His eyes scanned for anything that may be a clue. Jacqueline led the tour, pushing open the door to reveal a hallway leading to the back of the house. To the left, the space opened into a lounge. Cameron opened the closed door on the right, exposing a formal study with a distinctive legal décor. A staircase led to the upper floor, while the hallway extended to additional rooms, including a dining room, a vacant games room and a utility room. Toward the back, a door led into a very spacious kitchen facing the back of the house, with a big wooden table in the centre, both wood and electric stoves and a rather large walk-in butler's pantry.

Cameron had never seen such a large pantry. "Wow, that's big. Did the pantry get used much?"

"Oh, yes," Jacqui replied. "Grandma's favourite room. She always said, 'This is my space—everyone else out.' I was never allowed to play in there."

"I assume the bedrooms are upstairs?" Cameron asked.

"Yes, up here," she said, leading the way. Cameron couldn't recall ever being upstairs on his childhood visits.

At the top of the stairs to the left, the main bedroom occupied the entire space, from the front to the back of the house, including large robe areas and an ensuite. On the right, three smaller bedrooms lined a short hallway. Jane and Kathleen each had a room facing the front of the house, while Mary, Jacqueline's mother, had the room in the back corner. Both Cameron and Jacqui felt extremely uncomfortable in Jane's and Kathleen's rooms. Jacqui's eyes swelled with tears, noting that everything had been left untouched since the girls had gone missing. The beds were still made with the sheets they had last slept in the night before they disappeared—the same sheets their parents had expected them to come home to. Jacqui explained that her mother wanted it kept that way. Cameron picked up a hair-brush—its bristles still holding strands of hair. He noted it might be useful for DNA analysis down the track, but assumed the police had already collected their samples.

"We'll need to come back in here," he said.

"Why?" Jacqui asked.

"To look at everything. Everything can possibly tell us something," he replied. "The reality is that we don't know what we don't know. We need to search for love letters from any boys, notes, diaries—anything."

He pulled open a drawer in the desk.

"Don't!" Jacqui cried.

"Don't what?" he asked, startled.

"We can't go prying. I feel like I'm violating them," she said, her voice trembling.

"Jacqueline," he said firmly. "You're a lawyer. Do your job."

She gave him a startled stare, then began to cry. Cameron stepped over and took her in his outstretched arms. She laid her head on his shoulder, her warm tears soaking through his shirt. After a few minutes, she softly said, "You're right. We have got to do this. I've never done anything like this before. You seem to know what you're doing."

"I am trained to snoop. That's what I do—and it's what we need to do here."

Cameron sensed that Jacqueline's personal proximity made

it difficult for her to approach the task with the detached objectivity needed for a thorough forensic investigation.

"I need you, Cameron. I need your help to do what needs to be done."

She stepped away and opened the drawers in the study desk, followed by the clothes drawers. In Kathleen's room, she discovered two diaries and a drawing pad. The sketches in the pad displayed impressive artistry but gave no reason for suspicion. Inside the cupboards, they found the girls' school bags. Cameron could only assume the police had reviewed these pieces of potential evidence, though it surprised him that they hadn't been held in evidence as part of the investigation. It is still an open case.

"We'll come back and collect these," he said. "You have a look first, and I'll have a scan after that."

"To find everything I miss," she replied. He leant over and kissed her on the cheek.

"You just have to approach this as a forensic investigator—not as a teary niece."

They spent a few more moments rummaging through drawers and cupboards, knowing they would come back for closer inspection. Finished there for now, they headed downstairs to begin the bike ride.

"I don't believe this," she said as they stepped outside, "I think a storm is coming."

Dark grey clouds gathered in the south-west.

"You could not have scripted this better, Jack. Let's get going. It's almost 5.30, about the time they would've left. We need to ride as we imagine they might have. But we also need to put our detective eyes on and watch for anything suspicious."

"What exactly are we looking for?"

"The same as upstairs. We are scanning for what we don't know that we don't know," he said, mounting his bike and starting to pedal.

"Oh, I had no idea it would be that easy," she said, following him along the dirt track.

"And, by the way, we are doing it three times," he added.

"What?"

"First, we'll ride it as they probably did—fast, to get to the dance as soon as they could. I've measured it on Google—it's 4.7 kilometres. Google says that's fifteen minutes. Then, we'll ride back taking the time to examine anything we think we need to. Finally, we'll ride it a third time for a final check, but in reality, to get home."

Jacqui laughed. "Or get wet. You seemed to have this all worked out."

Cameron realised he may have overstepped the mark and taken control of Jacqui's project. *I'm doing it again aren't I, doing what I want to do.*

"Sorry, Jack. I'm getting that lesson a lot lately. I know—it's not about me," he said, twisting his clenched hands on the handlebars. "This stuff is second nature to me—sifting through the pan in search of a speck of gold. It's what I do."

"It's okay, Cameron. I think we've already proven I really don't know what I'm doing. I hadn't even considered the detail you're thinking about. I appreciate it and I know I need your expertise. Let's do it together, eh?"

He turned his bike around, pulled up beside Jacqui, leant over and kissed her on the cheek. "Let's get started."

They began riding. Cameron knew the girls were experienced bike riders. They regularly cycled into town, including to and from school. The dirt track leading from the homestead to the road stretched only a few hundred metres and presented no challenges. It was in good condition, well-maintained, and Jacqui could not remember it otherwise.

As they rode, Cameron shared his thoughts and observations with Jacqui. They were soon on the Jugiong Road, which gently rose and fell in elevation, but Cameron could not describe any stretch as steep. The final incline required the most pedal power of the whole trip, though both agreed it fell well within the capacity of the girls.

For experienced riders aged fourteen and eleven who knew the route well, the ride presented no significant challenge. In fact, Cameron considered the ride home slightly steeper than the ride into town. Cameron noted the sweeping ninety-degree bend at Weirview Road as the only significant directional change.

They reached the Murrumburrah Mechanics Hall in eighteen minutes and sat on the steps of the hall, drinking from their water bottles.

"Well, what did you see?" Cameron asked.

Jacqui thought for a minute, sipping from her water bottle. "Nothing, really. A nice, pleasant ride through beautiful countryside. Not very helpful."

"Actually, very helpful."

"Nothing isn't helpful," Jacqui replied, turning her head and giving him a puzzled look.

"Not true. The fact that there is nothing tells us exactly that: there is nothing. It tells us that there is nothing on the trip re-enactment that stands out as a contributing factor. If that is the case, we can discount it and move on. Even with the cloud cover, the light levels were fine, the ride was enjoyable, not physically demanding. I can see why their parents weren't phased by a bike ride."

"But we already knew that."

Cameron shrugged his shoulders, "Assume nothing. Validate everything. I counted four cars going in the opposite direction. Three overtook us, including that one truck. Did the side wind of that truck bother you?"

"No. I felt it, but it didn't knock me off the bike."

"I have no idea of the road conditions back then—whether

traffic volumes were higher or lower or if the shoulders were narrower or wider. But I see nothing today that suggests passing vehicles were an issue."

"Wow, Mr Sherlock. You really counted the cars?" Jacqui laughed lightly. He gave her a silent momentary stare.

"Sorry," she said, wincing.

On the return trip back, they rode slowly, scanning for anything unusual. They paused at several gates and entrances for closer inspections. Jacqui shared her observation with Cameron that the open terrain meant a vehicle couldn't enter the road unnoticed, nor could the riders have missed seeing an approaching vehicle. The two intersections—one at East Street and the other at Weirview Road—were T intersections entering from the opposite side, making it unlikely that a vehicle could've entered at high speed without being seen.

They guessed the bitumen strip of road may have been narrower in the past. Cameron searched for areas where a car could have parked to intercept or lure the girls. Nothing stood out. They stopped at the Currawong gate. Cameron ruled out the possibility of anything occurring along the track from the homestead to the gate. Open paddocks flanked the track, leaving nowhere to conceal bikes. Their father had travelled the same route shortly after the girls, and he hadn't noticed anything unusual.

Cameron also concluded that any incident in town would have drawn more attention and likely would have been witnessed. If something had occurred during the ride to the dance, it would most likely have happened within the three-kilometre stretch between the front gate of the property and the edge of town, a section that took no more than nine minutes to travel.

As daylight faded and the storm threatened, they headed back into town. This time, Cameron stopped occasionally to examine a few ditches and culverts. Police reports noted that two days after the girls disappeared, four constables and forty volunteers had conducted a foot search along the entire road. They were searching for signs of an accident including blood, clothing and belongings. The report also noted the storm that struck that night, bringing heavy rain, continued through the night and into the next day. It concluded that nothing had been found to suggest an accident or foul play.

As they neared the edge of town, it began to rain. They headed for the Forbes house, but the storm broke, drenching them in torrential rain. Reaching the house, they dropped their bikes on the lawn and rushed to the back door. They walked through the kitchen and into the hallway where Jacqui asked Cameron to wait until she fetched towels before they entered the carpeted rooms of the house. She disappeared through her room on the right, heading to the bathroom ensuite.

Within moments, Jacqui returned, towels in hand, standing in front of Cameron. His eyes suddenly widened as they locked onto her sleek white cotton top, now completely saturated and clinging like transparent wrapping to her beautifully shaped figure. He froze, unable to move, as a stimulating sensation rushed through his body. He felt his body responding involuntarily. Jacqui slowly lowered her hands to her sides and let the towels drop to the floor. Moving slowy but deliberately closer to Cameron, she embraced him gently, moving her lips to unite with his in a warm lingering kiss. Their rain-chilled bodies contrasted with the heat of the kiss, which seemed to last forever. Every second of it etched itself into Cameron's memory—it was unlike anything he had ever experienced.

Eventually, Jacqui stepped back slightly. Without breaking eye contact, she ever so slowly peeled off her soaked top and unclipped her bra, letting it slip to the floor. Cameron felt he might lose control at any moment. Reaching out, he cradled her soft breasts in his hands.

The slamming of the back door suddenly broke the moment.

"Hello, I'm home," Mr Forbes called. Cameron detected that as code for: "I'm here, make yourself decent."

Jacqui giggled and darted into her room, leaving Cameron standing awkwardly in the hallway. On the floor directly in front of him lay Jacqui's white top and bra. At the precise moment Mr Forbes turned the corner into the hallway, Cameron flicked the towel with his toe, hoping it would cover the evidence laying on the floor before him. Fully aware that his dripping wet trousers clearly highlighted the physical evidence of his raging emotions, he sought his own cover. In one quick swoop, he bent down picking up the towel, hoping to keep Jacqui's belongings concealed, positioning it appropriately, he hoped.

"So sorry, Mr Forbes. We got caught in the storm. You must have literally followed us in. Jacqui—sorry, Jacqueline—went for a shower and told me to wait here," Cameron stammered.

"Well, she's not much of a host is she, Cameron?" Mr Forbes replied. "We have another bathroom off the laundry. Why didn't she direct you to there?"

"It's okay, I'm happy to wait."

"Come this way," Mr Forbes said, turning and leading him to the laundry bathroom.

Cameron followed, clutching the towel bunched in front of him, hoping Jacqui's top and bra were out of sight. The shower provided a welcome reprieve and a chance to calm down, though his sunburnt arms still stung. Drying off, he noticed the clothes were gone. Jacqui must have silently retrieved them. Cameron assumed they were in the clothes dryer in the laundry that was tumbling away. A clean T-shirt, ironically white, had been left on the chair. He slipped it on and wrapped the towel around his waist.

In the kitchen, Mrs Forbes had arrived home and was now unpacking groceries. Cameron greeted her warmly as he passed, then headed to the lounge where Mr Forbes sat with two cans of beer on the table beside him.

Mr Forbes invited Cameron to join him. They chatted about the weather, the lambing season and cricket. Cameron felt uncomfortable dressed only in the towel and Jacqui's borrowed T-shirt.

"So, have you had a chance to consider the will yet?" Mr Forbes eventually asked.

Cameron suspected this moment had been crafted for a private, man-to-man discussion.

"It certainly wasn't what I expected," Cameron admitted.

"Yes, a confounded thing to put together. Your grandmother could be quite demanding and specific, particularly when it came to the will."

"I will be honest with you, Mr Forbes, I really enjoy what I do. I think I'm good at it, and I know that other people think I am good at it—" Cameron started.

"They must," Mr Forbes interrupted, "to send you to Dubai."

"Well, I didn't come here to give that up, and I'm a bit dirty on my grandmother for assuming that I would without ever talking to me about it."

"I wouldn't put it like that, Cameron."

"Well, she wants me to be a sheep farmer."

"Not exactly, Cameron. I knew your grandmother well. She deeply valued her heritage. Lived by it. Guarded it. She was so proud of her father and his legacy. He established the farm for his children and their children. Do you know your family history, Cameron?"

"A bit, yes. I know all about the 1st Light Horse, the Mackay connection and all that. Grandma would tell us often."

"Well, I suggest you find out everything you can, otherwise it fades away from this point and could be soon lost forever. Agnes is nearing a hundred now. She is your source," Mr Forbes said. "Get to her while you can. At least do that for your grand-mother, before you make any decisions. Do you know why your great-grandfather called it Binya?"

"It means 'resting place.' I remember that."

Ignoring Cameron's response, Mr Forbes continued, "I'm not sure where he got that word from. I looked into it once; in indigenous languages, it is more used as a term for 'mountain.' There's a winery—in South Australia I think—that produces some lovely wine under the name 'Binya Station' who claimed that Binya meant a place of rest. I recall their claim: 'This wine is a tribute to the resilient vines that stand amidst the rocks, providing a comforting and bold respite amidst the rugged beauty of the Australian landscape.'

"I used that quote in a speech about your grandmother at her retirement," he said, chuckling at the memory. "But Cameron, the point is not where he got the word from, but what it meant to him, your great-grandfather. That is what he believed. Your great-grandfather's dream, Cameron, was that the family, for generations, would find rest there.

"But wars are a terrible thing. Both sons were killed. Agnes got married and left. Your grandmother had her career in nursing. It appeared that your great-grandfather's dream may well be over in one generation. But they underestimated your grandmother. This town has never seen a matriarch like her. In a world that is based on paternal power—which father begat which father—your grandmother stood up as a matriarch. But she only had the one child: your mum. Now the hope of a future lies with you."

"And Heidi, she has a responsibility; she could be the next matriarch."

"It rests with you, Cameron Blanche. It rests with you," Mr Forbes took a large mouthful of his beer and shuffled back into his chair.

"Jacqueline tells me you are meeting with Agnes later in the week. Talk to her. Get the history when you can. You need to see this from a different perspective, Cameron.

"This isn't about sheep. It's not about being a sheep farmer—it's about your heritage. Your Grandmother, a nurse, made it work. So can you, Cameron."

At that moment, Jacqueline joined them, fresh and radiant, wearing a skirt, a pale pink shirt and obviously no bra. Cameron immediately felt his body react under the towel he was still wearing. He could feel his pulse racing.

"Hello, how's your day been, dear?" Mr Forbes asked.

"A great day," she replied, beaming. "Just a little wet," turning to Cameron, she added, with a sly wink, "and steamy."

Cameron blushed.

"We did the re-enactment today—" Cameron blurted, hoping for a quick change of topic.

Jacqueline interrupted softly, "Cameron, we don't talk about that around Mum."

Mr Forbes added, "I'd like to hear more, but not here at home."

Mrs Forbes entered, wiping her hands on her apron, "I'm assuming you're staying for tea, Cameron?"

Before Cameron could even think of a reply, Jacqueline spoke, "No, Mum. Cameron and I have some unfinished business from today. We are going back out to Binya as soon as we can give Cameron his dry trousers back. Actually, Cameron has bought a bottle of wine so, to be safe, I might stay over—there's plenty of spare rooms out there."

Cameron's heart pounded. He had heard of spontaneous orgasms—*Dear God, not now, please!* Noticing the slightest twitch of the corner of Mr Forbes' lips, Cameron knew that he understood the nature of the "unfinished business," causing him to blush even more.

They were soon naked in Great-Grandmother's bed. Cameron had had sex, but never a lesson in lovemaking like this. He had never known the difference. The emotions inside him were something he had not experienced. They kissed and caressed for what seemed like forever. Jacqueline rolled Cameron onto his back and positioned over him. She softly, most gently kissed him, her tongue tracing a delicate path down his body—across his chest, along his abdomen—and then he gasped. He had never experienced exhilaration like this. She continued. Cameron's mind sang: *I'm in love.*

Cameron awoke the next morning, with Jacqui contentedly sleeping beside him. He gently ran his hand over her naked body. She stirred and they laid there, united in each other's comfort.

"We've got to go to work," he whispered.

"I know the boss."

"That's why we have to go to work."

They both giggled, embraced and made love again.

Cameron dropped Jacqueline at home so she could collect her car and change into her work attire, while he headed to the Which Craft to get the coffees. Arriving separately would be diplomatically the correct thing to do. Jacqueline immersed herself in her work, whilst Cameron went to his temporary office and opened his computer. More emails relating to the Lebedev files greeted him, deepening his curiousity. Why such interest? And why him? He emailed Annand, his supervisor, asking these very questions, but got no response. It appeared they were trying to track some cash flows, but to do that effectively, he needed to be provided with more information.

Curiosity got the better of him. Allowing for the time difference, he waited until Annand would be at work and then rang him. Annand, sounded evasive and noncommittal, repeatedly diverting the conversation. Later, he got a call from a Dubai number he didn't recognise—it was Annand. The message was simple: ask no questions, be careful what you say on the phone, keep emails brief and on topic, only do financial reports that you have been requested to do so and above all, remain silent. Say nothing. Nothing. The concern he could hear in Annand's voice worried him. It sounded big and it sounded bad.

Cameron confirmed the arrangements with the residential aged care facility for their visit the next day with his great aunt. The staff reported her to be in lively spirits, eagerly anticipating the visit.

Cameron got about his business—across the hall, Jacqueline did the same. Mr Forbes walked down the hall with a contented smile. All was good.

Jacqui stayed over again that night, under the pretense that they were heading off early for the visit to Aunt Agnes in Bowral, a two-and-a-half-hour drive. For the second consecutive morning, Cameron woke with Jacqui beside him. Life was good.

When they arrived at the aged care home, the staff said that Aunt Agnes had been full of anticipation for their visit, having spoken of little else for the entire week other than her pending visit of an "international visitor" and a "high-level lawyer." Aunt Agnes had insisted that she be given one of the private reception rooms, normally reserved for grieving families. Cameron and Jacqui were amused. Aunt Agnes greeted them with high spirits. If nothing else, their arrival had made her week.

First, they exchanged idle chatter about how the family was doing, how beautiful Amy's service had been and what a great eulogy Cameron had given. Aunt Agnes then turned to Jacqui.

"Now, dear Jacqui, what a beautiful young woman you have become. So, tell me what you have found out about your aunties."

Aunt Agnes's personalisation surprised Jacqui. Jacqui had never referred to them as "her aunties."

"I don't believe we have anything more to tell you other than what you already know. I am sure you know more than what we do," Jacqui replied.

"Tell me, dear," Aunt Agnes leant closer, "what are you trying to achieve?"

"I want to know what happened to the two girls, my mum's sisters, who just vanished without a trace."

"And how does knowing what happened change anything?" asked Aunt Agnes, her face showing no emotion.

Jacqui momentarily turned to Cameron, her face twisted with confusion, before focusing back on Aunt Agnes.

"I'm sorry, Aunt Agnes, I don't know what you're asking. Two young girls are dead. I know that can't change. But it's left a hole in a lot of people's lives not knowing what happened. It has destroyed many people. My grandfather, my mother. I want closure. I want to know what happened. Is that unreasonable?"

"No, dear, it's not unreasonable. And I ask myself the same question. There are so many mysteries in life. But after all this time, it is most likely going to remain a mystery. I have nothing I can tell you that will give you answers," Aunt Agnes leant back clasping her hands in her lap, one palm resting in the other.

"Thanks, Aunt Agnes," Jacqui responded. "I understand. You are the first person I've spoken to who witnessed the events that night. That's a perspective I've never had."

"Let me tell you what I remember," as Aunt Agnes began her story. "The school dance was always a big affair. All the high school children could come and most did. Children loved it and the town would always build up to it. Girls and their mothers would spend endless hours selecting material and making dresses. The boys who could gather the nerve would ask one of the girls to be his partner.

"As you probably know, a big storm struck that night, causing so much confusion. But there were no phones like there are today, so we had no way of knowing who was coming and who wasn't.

"I will be honest in saying that until your grandfather walked in, I had not noticed if Jane and Kathleen were in the hall or not.

"Probably the thing I remember most from that night was your grandfather coming. Most children had left the hall. Some were still waiting. Your grandfather came in and chatted for a few minutes with some of the other dance chaperones before he even asked about the girls. I can still hear his words: 'Anyway, where are the girls? We'll head home.' Only then did we look at each other and piece together that no one had seen them.

"But even then, there wasn't a great deal of panic. We would find them somewhere. No one had ever gone missing in Harden. Your grandfather said he would go home and check. He came back about twenty minutes later and that is when people really got concerned."

"Could you be sure they were never at the dance?" Jacqui asked.

"That's a good question. There was someone running around saying she thought she had seen them. I think it was Mabel Baxter. But everyone else was sure they had not seen them. We checked the bike racks once we heard they had ridden their bikes there, but there was nothing. Yes, I can say they were never there.

"Do you know if any other children came in from out Jugiong way?" Cameron asked.

"I can't remember that, but the police took the details of everyone that attended. I know they checked on every child listed to attend but hadn't come. Everyone was accounted for, except the two girls. As for who was coming from out Jugiong way, I can't remember," she replied. Cameron could recall seeing the attendance list and noted that he would follow up on that.

"Aunt Agnes," Cameron asked, "could you please put the girls aside for the moment and just tell us about the night."

"As I said, everyone eagerly anticipated the dance. Those who had arrived enjoyed themselves. It lacked its normal hive of activity due to the reduced numbers," she covered her mouth with her hand and spoke softly. "One thing we had to always police were the couples that would go down in the grass behind the toilets. With the reduced numbers and all the supervisors, the children could not sneak away so easily, so there was no naughty business that night." Everyone grinned.

"Were there any strangers around on the night?" Jacqui asked.

"No, no. We knew all the parents. There were half a dozen or more chaperones, plus those helping in the canteen. We would have been alerted to a stranger. The band was from out of town. Cootamundra, I think. But even some of them were known to the locals. And they were setting up from well before and played all night."

Jacqui asked, "One more thing. Police reports said that Kathleen had planned on meeting a boyfriend at the dance. Were you aware of that?"

"Yes, Lyall Billings," Aunt Agnes said with a sweet smile on her face. "I knew nothing about it before the dance, but it was one of those stories that did the rounds after all this happened. The story goes that he waited for Kathleen, and they were going to kiss for the first time that night." They all gave a giggle. "When I first heard the story, I recalled that Lyall had spent the beginning of the dance standing by the front door reaching his neck out obviously looking for someone or something. I said to him 'What are you doing, Lyall?' He blushed and said, 'Just looking, ma'am,' or something like that. Poor soul. He never got a kiss. Lyall is still alive you know; you could talk to him."

Cameron saw no need. Just another casualty to carry the pain of the night. Police had investigated it and he accepted what he had read in the report.

Jacqui pulled several photos out of her briefcase. "Aunt Agnes, I want you to flick through these photos and look at them one by one, and just speak to each, describe them, highlight anything," placing a stack of photos in Aunt Agnes's lap.

Aunt Agnes methodically worked through all the photos. Most of them she had seen before. She remembered a remarkable degree of detail. She identified many people in the photos, even pointing out Cameron's grandfather.

"I recall your grandfather answering the call," she said. "He turned up on the evening of the dance and again the next day. He helped on all the searches. He even walked along the road all the way from their property to town with the other searchers."

"How would Granddad have known?" Cameron asked.

"You forget about Harden, Cameron," she smiled. "Everyone knows when they need to. Sometimes they know too much of other people's business."

Cameron and Jacqui glanced at each other and smiled.

As she scanned through the photos, she noted, "There's your grandfather's truck."

Cameron and Jacqui were impressed with Aunt Agnes's clear memory. Cameron had identified the same photo of his grandfather's truck lined up outside the Mechanics Institute.

They continued sifting through the photos with Aunt Agnes giving her rundown of people, places and who owned what truck. Examining another picture taken the next day, she pointed to another truck, "There's your grandfather's International again."

Cameron had a closer examination. Noticing it captured a different angle, more a side-rear view, "I don't think so, Aunt Agnes; I don't think that's Granddad's."

She looked again, "Young man, that's your grandfather's. Are you questioning me?"

"But—"

"Cameron. I know your grandfather's truck."

Cameron took the photo and laid it on the table and searched back for the previous photo, putting them side by side. "See," he said, "That truck has a box on the back, this one doesn't."

"I'm telling you, it is your grandfather's truck," Aunt Agnes insisted.

"Well, what's that?" asked Cameron, pointing to the box on the back of the truck in the first photo.

"That's just a toolbox your grandfather had. If he had the sheep cage on the back, he always had to take the box off. Sometimes on, sometimes off."

Cameron put his forensic eyes on and checked for other points of comparison, such as marks, wires, mirror position, etc. She was right—the same truck. He turned the photos over to check the date. One was taken the night of the dance with the box, while the other, taken the next day at the search base headquarters, set-up in the Mechanics Hall, with no box.

"I've never seen this box on his truck in all my life," Cameron said.

"You weren't born then, Cameron," rebuked Aunt Agnes. "He used it all the time. I can even tell you where he got it— the old piano box. I believe the old piano is still in the Binya lounge. Your great-grandfather had the piano shipped out from England. Your grandfather said the box was a perfect width to put on the back of his truck. He said it would be great for tools and stuff. It was a bit of a family joke that your grandmother got the piano and your grandfather got the box."

Cameron remained adamant he had never seen it on the farm. Given its age, it had most likely decayed and finally got to a point of being kindle for the fire.

Jacqui, frustrated they were getting off topic, felt they should wrap up. They had been talking for well over an hour and Aunt Agnes appeared weary, so Jacqui started to bring the discussion to an end.

"Aunt Agnes, you have been most helpful, and we don't want to exhaust you," Jacqueline said. "It has been a delight to chat."

"For your satisfaction, Jacqueline," Aunt Agnes said, "it would be nice to have answers. But there are many mysteries in this world. The sad thing about this ordeal is that your two aunts were not the only victims. It changed your mum, even at her young age. She became a shy young girl, never participating much in town life. Your grandfather died of a broken heart. I admired him greatly. He continued to see the good in the world. He thanked God every day for what he had. But he never stopped grieving his two children.

"And Cameron, your father was also a victim. In later years, he became a heavy drinker. He never had been before. To his credit, he stuck by Cecil. He supported him every day. When Cecil had his heart attack, he would drive to Sydney and sit with him. When Cecil went into a coma, which he never came out of, William came by our home here in Bowral. Upset they wouldn't let him see Cecil, your father came back here and gave me a letter for Cecil and asked me to see it got to him.

"That was the last time I saw your grandfather. He dropped dead of a heart attack out attending his sheep. Both died within two weeks of each other. From memory, Cecil never regained consciousness to know William had died. See, Jacqui, you may or may not find out what happened, but nothing is going to change for those affected."

"What came of the letter?" Cameron asked.

"What?"

"The letter," Cameron replied. "You said he gave you a letter."

"Oh, I don't know, Cameron. I would have sent it, I suppose."

"But you said Cecil died just after that."

"Oh, Cameron, I don't know, I can't remember," Aunt Agnes replied, getting frustrated by Cameron's questioning.

"More than enough," intervened Jacqui. "Aunt Agnes, you have been very helpful."

"You will come back and visit I hope?"

"Most definitely," Cameron said. "I would like to know more about my great-grandfather Edmund and the family."

He chose not to tell her about the will.

"Please do," she said as she pulled at the shawl over her legs. "I do have a black chest full of our family memorabilia. It belonged to your great-grandmother—her glory box. It's with one of my nieces from my husband's side of the family. Why I left it with her, I don't know. Anyway, I'm going to write to her and have her send it to you. It has everything I have about your family and Binya."

As the nurse wheeled Aunt Agnes's chair from the room, Aunt Agnes turned to Jacqui, "Young Jacqueline, do be careful what you wish for. Well, I do hope you come back soon."

At ninety-eight, they hoped so too.

Cameron and Jacqui dissected the information as they drove home. The subdued mood reflected a day that had revealed little. They debriefed what Aunt Agnes shared and concluded it added nothing to what they already had. Jacqui was disturbed by Aunt Agnes's parting words.

"What did she mean by that?" she asked.

Cameron shrugged his shoulders. The comment didn't bother him. He agreed with the likely conclusion that they may never find out what happened. He saw Jacqui's pursuit as more and more futile. But he could sense the importance for Jacqui that she had tried to find the answer. Jacqui decided not to stay the night. It had been a long day following some rather sleepless, but unforgettable, nights.

CHAPTER NINE

Friday morning began with fresh emails from Dubai. Cameron had enough data downloaded on his laptop that he could work on them at the farm. He texted Jacqui to let her know he may be in later. He wanted space to forensically dissect the information they had received yesterday, not that he had any reason to feel excited. His only recurring thoughts were of his grandfather's truck. The difference bothered him. He also wanted to catch up with Scott Bennett, the minister, for a chat.

After breakfast, he strolled over to the machinery shed that lined the western wall of the shearing shed. His grandfather's old faded blue International truck stood in the end bay at the northern end of the shed. It obviously hadn't been used for many years. The tyres were flat and perished. He opened the driver's door to be immediately confronted by a wall of cobwebs. Grabbing a nearby broom, he cleared the thick veil of cobwebs to view the cabin and gain access. He sat behind the wheel and slid his fingers along the top of the visor, finding the key still sat where his grandfather and Young Billy always placed it. He inserted it into the ignition, turned it to the on position and pushed the start button. Nothing but a repetitive click. He never expected it to start, but he smiled as his mind flooded with old memories of sitting on his grandfather's lap to start the truck.

He got out and swung up onto the tray. The rear tray had wooden side rails about half a metre high that could be lowered or removed altogether. Standing at the back of the tray, facing the cabin, he could see the metal frame with horizontal wooden rails holding an array of chains, dog leashes and ropes, just as he remembered it. In his mind, he visualised a piano sitting there. He imagined a box of the same size would be a perfect fit, ideal for storing tools. But he had never seen such a box in his lifetime. Scanning the machinery shed, he found nothing resembling it. An old wooden crate, left out in the weather, that had once delivered a piano back in the 1800s, was unlikely to still exist. His theory that it had long become firewood, was most plausible. But he couldn't understand why the box appeared in one photo and not the other, taken only twenty-four hours apart.

He made his way back to the homestead. Passing the mirror on the duchess, his reflection shocked him. His shirt and trousers were a mess following his excursion into the truck, covered in cobwebs and dust. His hair was much the same. He had no option other than another quick bath and putting on some fresh clothes.

Refreshed and in clean clothes, he journeyed into town—his first stop: the church. Pulling up beside St Paul's, he found the church locked, as he expected, so he walked toward the manse. Scott spotted him and greeted him warmly, making Cameron feel welcome and in the company of an old friend.

"Well, Cameron. How are you? I've been thinking of you, wondering if you were still in town."

"Yeah, still here. That's a bit why I was hoping for a chat."

"By all means. The kids are inside, a bit noisy. Are you comfortable chatting in the church?"

"Not a problem at all."

"Great. It is for some, you know," Scott laughed. "I think they worry some type of spiritual power will invade their soul."

"An exorcism or something," Cameron joked.

"Nah, we don't specialise in those. You'd have to go to the Catholics for that."

Cameron spun and stared at Scott.

"Only joking, Cameron," they both laughed as Scott unlocked and slid open the heavy bolt guarding the front door of the church.

Cameron felt comfortable in Scott's company and on safe ground to share his emotions. Together, they made their way inside. "I have an office—come whatever room—up the front there, but it's probably more comfortable here," Scott said, pointing to the back pews.

"This is fine," Cameron replied, and they sat and chatted for nearly two hours. Cameron told him about the will and the decisions that he had to make. It had been becoming increasingly clearer to Cameron that there were ways to make it work. He knew he could own and run the farm from Dubai. That no longer concerned him. He knew the real torment. He told Scott who Cameron was. He introduced Cam. Then, he introduced him to Ronnie. Cameron once lived in Harden, Cam grew up in Sydney and Ronnie now lived in Dubai. He told Scott about his history with Ian and rediscovering Jacqui—who, in herself, seemed like three people: solicitor Jacqueline, friend Jacqui and soulmate Jack. He described the transformation of the young girl he once knew as his sister's friend into the beautiful woman who stirred feelings in him he had never felt before.

Scott listened intently, his gaze never leaving Cameron. Cameron could sense his interest and compassion. He could see it in his eyes. Finally, he reached a point where he had no more to tell.

"Wow," Scott responded. He paused for a moment or two, reaching out his arm, patting Cameron on the shoulder. "You've just introduced me to three wonderful people—Cameron, Cam and Ronnie. But here's what I hear: those three people have one thing in common. They are you. They aren't three separate people. You've adapted yourself for the different environments you find yourself in. That's not a bad thing."

"Yeah, well, there is a problem. I don't know if I like all of them," Cameron admitted, hanging his head, almost in tears.

"But you own the choice. Don't live only to please others. First, be who you want to be," Scott said, opening his hands as if baring his soul. "I used to drink and go clubbing and thought I loved it. I don't anymore. I used to enjoy living in the inner city. I don't anymore. None of it's bad. You might think I simply don't do those things anymore because I'm a minister. But it's not that at all. I don't do them because I don't want to. I've chosen not to. I have found who I am and who I want to be."

"It would be simple if I knew who I wanted to be," Cameron interjected.

"Sounds like you and Ian are in a good space now. Continue to build it. You have a confidante—two actually, Ian and Jacqueline. You can't erase the past. Sometimes, it hurts when you look back, so just focus on the future. Let things evolve at their own pace. It sounds like you and Jacqueline are really coming close. But here's the obvious thing to me: both of them, Ian and Jacqui, only know Cameron and maybe Cam.

"As for Cameron or Ronnie, well, you must decide—or maybe not decide, but discover. You need to determine who and where you want to be. You may be seeing it too black and white, one or the other. Maybe it's somewhere in the middle. It will come to you. You've been on a great journey, Cameron. None of it's bad. Just let it evolve to where you want to be."

They sat back in the pews and relaxed, chatting for some time. Cameron felt much better. He still hadn't resolved if he wanted to continue living in Dubai or Harden, but he walked away feeling the question didn't demand an immediate answer. He agreed with Scott. He just had to let things evolve. He felt grateful for finding a new friend, someone he could confide in. It had been so long since he'd had that. *Cameron Blanche, best mates with a minister!* He decided he would go to church on Sunday.

Jacqui rang, asking him to pick up the files they had taken yesterday to Aunt Agnes's from her home. She had been reviewing them before breakfast at the table in the formal dining room but forgot to put them back into her briefcase. Knowing her mum didn't like anything about her missing sisters in the house, Jacqui had chosen the formal dining room, knowing her mum didn't use it much, particularly this early in the day. She hoped her mum hadn't stumbled upon the files.

When Cameron arrived at the Forbes house, he found Mrs Forbes pottering in the kitchen. Her good spirits reassured him that she hadn't been into the dining room and, therefore, had not yet discovered the files Jacqui had left behind. She offered Cameron a cup of tea and he knew that question had no decline option, so he politely accepted. As she prepared the tea and cut slices of her recently baked boiled fruit cake, Cameron made his way to the dining room and found Jacqui's material on the table in neat piles, with one file of statements opened. As he began gathering it together, his phone rang—a call from Annand in Dubai. For privacy, he stepped back out into the driveway to take the call.

Annand's questions related to the Lebedevs, particularly about Cameron's connections with Aleksander and Matvei. Cameron had never made his friendship a secret, but he hadn't talked about it at work, so it surprised him to get the direct question. He confirmed that Alex, Matvei and he would often socialise. Annand would not elaborate any further but said he would be in further contact. Cameron was quite disturbed that Annand had advised him to avoid using the Lebedev names in any emails and not to electronically exchange any information with them or make any phone contact. Furthermore, he advised him to be careful of what information he shared on his Dubai phone. Fortunately, he had not used it the entire trip because he opted to use his Australian work phone that he still had active.

Back inside, he found the kitchen vacant, so he proceeded through to the formal dining room. As he approached, he could see Mrs Forbes at the table glancing over the open file. She held a photograph in her hand. He paused, standing quietly in the doorway not wanting to invade the moment or startle her. After a short while he quietly stepped into the room. Although she didn't acknowledge his presence, he sensed she knew he was there.

After a few minutes she spoke, "I don't know why she won't just let this go."

"I'm so sorry, Mrs Forbes. She forgot it this morning when she went to work and asked me to come and collect it."

She continued to stare. "Just let it go."

"I understand," he replied, "Jacqui—uh, sorry, Jacqueline—is trying to bring closure for everybody, simply by knowing what happened."

"But we do know, Cameron. We know they went missing and they are not coming back," she said, her eyes gazing out the window and her fists clenched. "If we dig deeper, we might uncover something even more painful. I can accept they went missing. Don't ever ask me to accept that they were raped and brutally murdered."

Turning to face Cameron, she added, "Promise me you will never find that out. Promise me."

Tears streamed down her face.

Cameron stepped forward and wrapped his arms around her. She laid her head on his shoulder and cried.

After a few minutes, she stepped back, "I always liked it when you called her Jacqui. I even liked it when you called her Jack. Robert hated it. You can call her what you want," she said, then whispered, "but Jacqueline when Mr Forbes is around."

"Guaranteed."

"Promise me you will look after her well."

He had no idea what Jacqui had told her about their relationship. Maybe she just had a mother's intuition. "I will, Mrs Forbes," he assured her.

They stood in silence for a few minutes before he asked, "Mrs Forbes, may I ask you something really difficult?"

"I may not answer."

"Can you tell me what you saw that night?"

Silently, she stood gazing out the window for what seemed a very long time.

"It was a long time ago," she commenced. "I was very young. It's like remembering scenes from a movie—you only remember bits and pieces. We got home from school. Jane and Kathleen were so excited about the dance. I was far too young to be going. I remember Mum coming upstairs, telling them Dad might be late. Kathleen said they could ride. I can't remember Mum saying they couldn't—they rode that road every day. Mum said to wait to see when Dad came home. Time passed and I know the girls were getting anxious. They were so worried they would be late. They were in Kathleen's room. They shut the door, and I could hear them whispering. And from then, it all went very quiet. I think they had worked out their plan. They never knew, but I had listened at the door, and I found out Kathleen was going to meet a boy at the dance. I've never told anyone that."

Cameron pulled a chair out from the table and motioned Mrs Forbes to sit. He pulled a second chair and sat beside her.

"After some time, they came out. I was sitting on my bed in my room. They stopped in my doorway and told me that they were going to ride their bikes to the dance and not to tell Mum. I saw them tip toe down the hall and disappear down the stairs. I shut my door because I didn't want Mum asking me where they were. I looked out my window. I saw them wheel their bikes along the back of the house and disappear around the back of the shed. That was the last time I saw them.

"After a while, Mum came upstairs. I heard her go to their rooms. Then, she came into my room. I told her they rode their bikes. Mum wasn't all that upset. If Dad had not come home,

I am sure she would have let them ride anyway. But she was annoyed that they had sneaked off without telling her."

"You said that you were in your room?" Cameron softly asked.

"Yes."

"Your room was the one at the end of the hall facing the back of the house?"

"That's right."

"So why did the girls wheel their bikes past your room and then down around the back of the shed?"

She thought for a moment. "You're right—they should have gone the other way. But wait, that would have taken them past the kitchen window. Mum was in the kitchen. They didn't want her to see them."

"You said that they went around the shed. Are you sure they didn't go along the side of the house, back around to the front?"

"I close my eyes and the most vivid memory I have of the whole event is that last moment I saw them pass around the corner of the shed—that image has never left me."

"But that doesn't make sense, the track is at the front of the house."

Mrs Forbes sat silently for a moment, before speaking. Thinking. "There was the waterworks track."

"The what track?" Cameron asked.

Mrs Forbes told Cameron about a track built by the waterworks company that ran along the side of Currawong Creek, passing through several properties—Currawong, Binya and beyond. It connected to the Jugiong Road only a kilometre from town, about 300 metres, just beyond the edge of Binya's boundary line below the quarry paddock. The first part of the track still accessed the waterworks, off the Jugiong Road.

Cameron stood, his heart racing. He had a development—the only development he knew of. He needed to tell Jacqui.

"Mrs Forbes, I know that has been painful, but I thank you so much. Let me clean all this up—out of sight and out of mind for you."

"Never out of mind, Cameron. Never."

He could feel the depth of pain and grief that had scarred this family since that day. He understood Mrs Forbes desire to leave things be and her fear of what the investigation might uncover. But the forensic side of his brain had sprung into overdrive.

He gathered the files and drove straight to the offices of R.S. Forbes Solicitors. Jacqueline was typing on her computer as he invited himself in.

"Cameron, I'm busy at the moment—"

"I've got a breakthrough!"

"What are you talking about?"

"I was talking to your mother—"

"You did what? Talked to my mother? About this?" She pointed to the folders in Cameron's arm. She stood upright, walked around her desk and snatched the files from Cameron. "You shouldn't have talked to Mum without me. You should not have talked to Mum about this, period."

"Sorry, but you sent me. When I got to your mum's place, I found her in the dining room thumbing through the files," a slight variation to the truth but he considered it an acceptable condensing. "Look, Jacqui, I asked your mum one question. That's it. Anyway, she told me something very interesting."

"You interrogated her?"

"No, no, nothing like that. I asked one question, and I even asked her if I could ask it."

"What did you ask her?" she asked, her voice the tone of an interrogator.

"I asked her what she saw that night."

"That's it?" as if expecting something more profound. "And?"

"They never rode their bikes along the road."

"What? There is no other way."

He recounted the conversation almost word for word. He could see her mind working through the details.

"I do remember that track," she recalled and she searched her mind for a memory, any memory. "It ran through several properties. The first part from Jugiong Road to the waterworks is still used as far as I know, but it runs through the Moffatt's property. It used to follow the creek, but I don't think it's been used for years. In fact, I think Granddad removed the gate that used to go into Binya. Cattle had got through or something like that."

"But we are talking about fifty years ago," he said. "I think we should go and find it now."

"Cameron, I can't. I've got to get these affidavits completed by first thing Monday."

"That means you've got the weekend."

She pondered and, in an impulsive moment, she locked her computer, picked up her bag and headed for the door. Cameron took a step back as she strode past and out the door.

"You don't talk to Mum without talking to me first," she commanded, as she passed by him. Cameron said nothing, following her to the car.

They drove in silence.

Arriving at Currawong homestead, Cameron indicated he first wanted to go to Mary's bedroom and verify her mother's account. Standing at the window, they could see precisely what Mary had described, and the direction she saw Jane and Kathleen go. Cameron and Jacqui walked past the kitchen window, confirming the assumption that they could have been seen if they had gone that way.

Cameron could still feel Jacqui's anger, but it quickly gave way to the euphoria of the first case development in fifty years. No bikes today—they would simply walk the track from the house to the road. At the creek's edge, they turned east, following the bank where, in places, remnants of a track remained visible. The gates were just as Jacqui had described. Some were in place, particularly where they formed part of an internal property fence, but at boundary fences, the gate had been replaced with a solid fence, or an old, padlocked gate still stood and showed no sign of having been opened for many years.

They followed the track, speaking little along the way, not stopping until they reached the Jugiong Road. Using his phone, Cameron measured the distance—approximately two kilometres. The track joined the road about a kilometre from town. He recalled stopping at this spot during their bike ride a few days earlier. Just a typical farm entrance that had not been used with any frequency for a long time. A gate sat well back from the fence line to allow for a steep thirty-metre decline leading to the road. On Tuesday, they had assessed it unlikely that a vehicle exiting the track would have not seen two bikes on the road and would have been moving slowly. But new scenarios were now feasible—two bikes coming down a steep muddy hill in the rain, unable to stop in the wet muddy conditions, being hit by a passing vehicle.

"What do you think?" Jacqui asked as she surveyed the area.

"Very plausible," Cameron responded, continuing to scan the surrounds, processing everything he could take in. "You wouldn't ride a bike along there now, but fifty years ago, most likely. If we accept what your mum says, there is no reason not to believe they came this way. What do you think?"

"This makes much more sense to me," she replied. "I can close my eyes and see two bikes racing down that bank and into the path of a car. But the problem remains—no car, no proof of an accident and no bodies."

Cameron wandered over to the road's edge, noticing a relatively deep stormwater pipe under the entrance to the gate. *Had it been there fifty years ago?*

"It does change the narrative," Cameron said. "We can say they came this route. Now, we need to consider all the possible scenarios. Being hit by a car is just one."

As they walked back, they discussed some of those possibilities.

"So, let's work through them," Cameron suggested.

"It makes abduction less likely," Jacqui reasoned. "Who would be hanging around this track waiting for two young girls to pass. No one would have been expecting them," deduced Jacqui.

"I agree with you," concluded Cameron. "It does bring the creek into play. A storm, heavy rain, flooded creek. We can't rule out drowning, slipping into a swollen creek."

"Quite feasible but the bikes or even bodies should have washed up somewhere."

"Bodies could go a long way in a flooded creek and as far as I know, there were no searches done of the creek."

"Highly unlikely that two bikes would lay around for fifty years and not be found."

"You would think so," Cameron agreed. "And no reports of washed-up bodies either."

They were soon back at the homestead, and Cameron drove Jacqui back to the office. She chose not to come to the farm that night, wanting to finish her work and she had promised to take her mum to the Cootamundra markets the next morning. She invited Cameron to join, but he saw the value in some mother-daughter time. He told her that he intended to go to church on Sunday. They agreed to meet after church for a BBQ lunch at Fort Apache and Indian Rock. Cameron indicated he would invite Ian and the family.

As they parted, Cameron leant over, embraced Jacqui, and they held each other tightly.

"Sorry for talking to your mum," he whispered.

"You shouldn't be," she replied. "I can see how the moment

in time simply unfolded, and you were wise to take it. I suppose it just frustrated me that I've done so much and got nowhere, and in five minutes you get the biggest breakthrough."

"Sorry. I'll slow down."

"No, you won't. You are the forensic accountant. You have the skills to search and find the speck of gold in the pan. I need your help. I need you."

"Let's do it together," he responded, drawing her close for a long hug. "What I do find interesting is that such an obvious piece of information had not been detected before. I'm not sure how thorough the police investigation has been. Surely there must be more to find."

"Let's find it," Jacqui replied, giving him a departing kiss. "But keep me informed."

On Sunday, Cameron enjoyed the church service. He sat in Grandma's pew, with Jacqui joining him when her family arrived. He glanced over to Mrs Forbes, who offered him a very warm smile. Cameron appreciated sitting in the congregation simply as himself—neither as the grandson of Amy White nor as the boy from Dubai. As the congregation shuffled out the church door, Scott greeted Cameron with, "And who would this be today?"—causing them both to laugh loudly. Jacqui appeared confused, having no idea what Scott meant.

Straight after church, Cameron and Jacqueline headed to the picnic site. A few minutes later Ian and Colleen arrived.

"I haven't been back here for years," Ian remarked, scanning the view. "You been here before?" he asked Colleen as she joined him carrying Cossette.

"No, never, but you've told me a lot about it," Colleen responded.

"You remember our rocks?" Cameron asked.

"Most definitely," he said, giving Colleen the Rin-Tin-Tin run down of Fort Apache and Indian Rock.

"Have you been here before, Jacqueline?" Colleen asked.

"Yes. Jacqui's fine, by the way," Jacqui replied. "Heidi, Cameron's sister, and I were good friends. So, while they went off and played Cowboys and Indians, Heidi and I played with our dolls on these rocks." Everyone laughed.

Everyone enjoyed the afternoon. Ian took two-year-old Barry for a walk across the rocks. Too young for defending castles just yet. As they returned, Cameron quietly asked Ian, "Find any dragons, mate?"

"Just dragon poo," Ian said with a smile. He gazed over the landscape, holding Barry's small hand. "He is here if you want to find him."

"Maybe we just need to know he's not far away," Cameron replied.

"And we move onto other toys," Ian responded.

Cameron scanned the scene around him—Binya, the farmhouse, the crops, the mobs of sheep, Currawong Creek, the rock paddock, Jacqui, Ian, Colleen and the kids. He felt a profound peace he hadn't felt for a long time.

CHAPTER TEN

The sun shone brightly through the window, telling Cameron it had long since risen. He had slept solidly, the best he had slept since arriving back. A strange thought woke him—he wanted an umbrella stand. Since being caught in the rain, he wanted to put an umbrella in the car. Particularly at the farm, where the car parked outside the yard fence, some twenty metres or more from the shelter of the porch. Clearly, he needed something to put an umbrella on the porch, ready for use on exit. He thought of an old milk can—no better place than the dairy to find one. Once he had located a milk can, he planned to go in pursuit of an umbrella. He had noticed big colourful ones at the Which Craft Cottage in Murrumburrah.

So, even before morning coffee, Cameron headed for the dairy, greeted by its distinctive smell, exactly as he remembered, making him feel at home. No fog this morning. He stepped through the dilapidated fence into the territory his grandfather had forbidden him to enter. Since returning, he hadn't seen a snake on the farm, so he considered it safe.

He walked into the back room of the dairy, the dumping ground for everything. To his surprise, he couldn't see a milk can in sight. He ventured deeper, moving and lifting a whole range of relics and junk in his search. The shed, being only about four metres wide, didn't take long to search. He moved toward the back past the old milking machinery, chicken nests and egg boxes, crawling over several old lawnmowers, including a few ancient push mowers. He maneuvered around an old wringer washing machine and black and white TV, passing by not one, but two kitchen sinks. He poked through the wooden box standing along the back wall containing bike parts, a car muffler, garden tools and numerous fox and rabbit traps, but no milk can. The dairy seemed to have everything except a milk can; at least he found no snakes.

Disappointed, he returned to the homestead for breakfast, savouring each spoonful of his Sustain cereal. Then, suddenly, he froze. His spoon slipped from his hand and clattered into the bowl, splashing milk and cereal across the table. His gaze locked. He didn't blink. A revelation had just struck him. His heartbeat thundered in his ears. He sat motionless for several minutes, his thoughts racing, his mind churning through the data.

He abruptly pushed back his chair, stood upright, strode to the verandah, pulled on his boots and marched back to the dairy. He moved with purpose—through the fence and into the shed, throwing obstacles aside like a snow plough carving through a snow drift.

There he stood—dumbfounded. It had stood in the same spot all his life. He could not remember it ever not being there. He'd seen it on his last two trips into the dairy. He'd seen it every time he had been in the dairy. He stood in front of the old piano case. It wasn't on his grandfather's truck, it was here. It had been in front of Cameron the whole time.

Cameron began ravaging through the box and the items surrounding it. Thoughts of a snake never entered his head. He knew his mum's bike was hanging next to the box. The smaller bikes were also hers from younger ages. Tyres, tubes, wheels and bike chains hung on the wall. After removing the car muffler, garden tools and many other bits and pieces, he uncovered an array of bike parts, chains, seats and cables—a complete bike shop. Behind the box, wedged between it and the wall, he could see more bike parts.

A closer inspection sent a wave of anxiety rushing through him. Two small frames—very old, twisted and damaged—lay before him. Nearby, bent and broken bicycle wheels rested in a heap.

Anxious to dig deeper, he switched on the torch in his phone, the beam slicing through a darkness that had not been disturbed for many years. As he directed the light into the box, his breath caught in his throat. The beam of light illuminated something distinct—a large dark stain spreading across the floorboards of the box.

There are times a forensic mind goes into a crazy "what if" mode. He stood deep in that zone now. *Take control, Cameron, take control.*

Grabbing a nearby crowbar, he wedged it under one of the wooden box's floorboards, breaking away a piece roughly 10 cm x 25 cm. Cameron turned and walked out of the dairy, tightly clutching the piece of timber. He shuddered at the thought of what he may be holding in his hand.

Back at the homestead, he sat on the edge of the verandah, studying the wooden floorboard, like he would a spreadsheet. In the daylight, the stain appeared a lot lighter than it had in the darkness of the dairy. *Don't overthink this,* he cried to himself. But his gut churned and his heart pounded so hard he could feel it in his temples.

When Cameron did his forensic accountancy, he knew exactly when he had found that one piece of evidence that exposed an otherwise hidden crime. He had that feeling now. But he could see lots of variables. He could hear his lawyers at work declaring it circumstantial: *So, you found a piano box. So, your grandfather used it on his truck. So, sometimes he took it off his truck. So, you found bike frames on a farm where there were heaps of bike frames.* All circumstantial. But he held a piece of timber that might bear a blood stain. That constituted evidence—if it was blood.

Questions swirled in his mind. He struggled to make any sense of his discovery. Why hadn't his grandfather disposed of this stuff? *It's a wooden box for crying out loud. He could have just burnt it. Anyway, what about bodies? We have no bodies.*

Cameron went inside and sifted through Jacqui's research

material that he had been reviewing. He found the two photographs of his grandfather's International truck—one with the piano box on, one without. The first photo had been taken late at night shortly after the girls were found to be missing, and the second, taken the next day. The box was on the truck in the first photo, but had been removed by the time the second photo was taken the next day. Why would it have been necessary to remove the box in that time?

Cameron recalled seeing a magnifying glass in the drawer of the telephone table. He fetched it and examined the two photos closely. Despite being very blurry, the magnification identified that the truck appeared muddier in the second photo compared to the first. The search had begun in the rain, so mud could be expected. But the greater build-up of mud along the side of the truck did seem odd.

A horrible thought entered his mind. He picked up the photo taken on the first night. Could he be looking at the bodies of the girls in this photo? Could they be lying in the box parked just out front of the Mechanics Hall—right where the dance they were to attend had taken place? The thought sickened him. His imagination ran wild. *Is it a blood stain in the bottom of the box?*

Cameron thought back to last week when Jacqui had been upset for not keeping her informed. He should tell Jacqui straight away. He pulled his phone from his pocket and hesitated. This was her mission, her project. But this was his grandfather. If he withheld the information, Jacqui may never forgive him. On the other hand, sharing the information prematurely may cause unnecessary anguish. He only had one fact—he had found a wooden box his grandfather had once used on his truck. Jacqui already knew that a box had been removed from his truck the day after the disappearance. *So, what really do I have to tell Jacqui?* He stared at the piece of wood taken from the box, rotating it in his fingers as he considered what he should do.

There is no proof it is blood. He turned it some more. Telling Jacqui facts, yes. Sharing wild conjecture could just confuse and mislead her, no, he concluded. He would find out more before he shared the find. He knew one thing—he was desperate to prove his suspicion wrong.

He wanted to quickly shower—*still no damn shower.* He made his way to the kitchen and filled the jug. His phone rang. He recognised the +971 code from Dubai, but he didn't recognise the number—he calculated 4 am in Dubai. Best to answer it.

"Hello?"

"Ronnie, its Annand. Just listen to me. Listen closely. Don't call again on this number. A ticket has been booked for you on tonight's flight out of Sydney. When you get to Dubai, go straight to your apartment. We'll contact you there."

"What the hell is going on Annand?" he asked. "Something has come up here, I can't leave today."

"That's not an option, Ronnie. I can't tell you anymore at this moment. Don't answer any other calls from Dubai other than this number. And don't ring back on this number."

"Am I safe?"

After a pause, Annand relied, "You have done nothing wrong. Quite the opposite. Just do what I tell you and you will be safe. We will be in contact tomorrow. Don't tell anyone you're coming."

He immediately disconnected, before Cameron could respond. *What the hell?* After feeling so much peace this morning, this last hour overwhelmed him. He felt scared and confused.

From memory, Cameron knew the flight flew at 11 pm. He would have to check in no later than 9 pm. Sydney is a four-hour trip. He checked his phone—just before 11 am. He had no more than about six hours to get everything organised. Communication from Dubai back to Australia sounded as though it might be problematic. He rang Jacqui.

"Good morning," she greeted, with a bright and cheerful tone. He pictured her smile and imagined her kiss. "Pleasant surprise. Am I getting a coffee this morning?"

He winced. "Something's come up," he stammered nervously. "Umm, don't ask any questions just now, but please, just trust me. Can you buy a mobile phone in Harden and have it activated immediately?"

"Yes, dear, at the electrical store in the main street," she replied. "But you're scaring me, what's going on?"

He noted Jacqui had called him "dear." If only he had time to enjoy the moment.

"I'll explain when I get there later. Please just do this for me. Get a phone that is in your name but on a completely separate account to any account you currently have, and make sure it has international roaming."

"Am I about to go overseas?" she asked. He could hear the anticipation in her voice.

"Sorry, I'll explain later. Just do it straight away."

Her reserved reply carried a hint of fear. "Okay."

The farm first. Ian could watch over it, but he couldn't work it. Nor could Young Billy hang on. Cameron had another idea. He jumped in his car and drove to the Country Club. His hunch proved right—he found Gary sitting at the bar. Same seat as on his first visit. It wasn't that long since opening time, so Cameron hoped for a coherent conversation.

Cameron walked directly to Gary, no time to order a drink. "Hey Gary, you got a minute?"

Gary was surprised and more importantly, sober. "Hi, Cameron. How are you going? You still in town?"

"Yeah, Gary, I am going to be around for a while longer, but I have to go south for a bit, I've got a favour to ask."

"Gee, yeah, I guess so," Gary said hesitantly. No one had asked him to do anything for a long time, let alone give him the time of day. "You want me to do something for you?" he clarified.

"Yeah. I need you to work the farm for me for a few weeks."

"What the hell? You haven't read my credentials, have ya?" Gary replied, his ruddy face reddened even more. "I'm not chasing charity."

"Listen, Gary, I'm not dumb. I've heard the story. I'm guessing you're pissed off because you probably had little input into any of those business decisions that went south. And frankly, if you are not bright enough to learn something from it, you are probably the wrong person so say no. And I'm not giving out any charity. I want someone who will work their arse off. I'll pay you shit to do it, if that makes you feel better. I need someone who can take care of the daily things that need to be done to run a sheep farm."

"I can work a sheep farm, Cameron. It's just that no one believes it anymore."

"Well, I'm giving you a chance. Young Billy has been doing it for ages but one day soon he's not going to wake up. And I've been called away suddenly. Come on, Gary, what is it?"

Gary stood up. Grabbed his broad brim hat off the bar, put it on his head. His eyes swelled with tears, "No one's given me the time of day since all this happened," he said. "I'm in. When do I start?"

"You just did," Cameron replied, shaking his large, calloused, trembling hand. "Give me your number, I or Ian will ring you."

Cameron returned to Binya to find Young Billy. Fortunately, he could see his truck over in the night paddock, so drove directly across to the gate. Billy saw him coming and drove to meet him. Cameron explained that Gary would be coming on board as an interim measure as he would be going down south for a bit.

"Catching up with Mum?" he asked.

"I hope so."

"Gary's a good kid, he'll do fine," Young Billy appeared relieved, but Cameron sensed Young Billy saw this as the end for him.

Cameron added, "Remember what I said the other day. You can stay on for as long or as little as you like. Ian is going to be overseeing things. Gary and Ian will watch out for you. You're family, Billy."

They embraced.

"Thank you, Mr Blanche."

"Billy!"

"Thanks, Boss," Billy walked away, the first time Cameron had seen him smile since he had returned. Cameron walked back to his car. Now to see Ian—*Please, please, Ian, agree.*

He drove to Ian's place, hoping to find him at the homestead having lunch. Fortunately, he hadn't yet ventured back into the paddocks for the afternoon's work. Breaking the rules, Cameron told Ian he had been called back to Dubai urgently and he didn't know for how long—hopefully not long. He stressed to Ian that, without exception, he could not tell anyone, not even Colleen, that he would be back in Dubai.

"I'm telling everyone else that I'm going down south."

"Are you safe?" Ian asked, his face etched with genuine concern.

Cameron gave the best answer he could. "I think so. They do play by different rules over there."

They briefly discussed the priorities for Binya. Cameron kept it simple: maintain the status quo, produce a good mob and get a healthy wool cheque. He would talk with Jacqueline about access to finances. He told Ian that Gary would be taking over from Young Billy, filling him in on the conversation he had with Billy.

As he jumped in the car to leave, Colleen came running down the front stairs.

"You won't be away long, will you?"

"No, just some things I need to do, you know."

"Thank you, Cameron. Ian has found you again. That's good. But you're still a dick," she said as she ran back to the house.

Cameron smiled. For the record, he thought his penis had gotten bigger.

He told Jacqui much more than the others. She had a genuine concern for his safety. He downplayed the risk. *When all this is over, I promise to tell the truth.* He told her there were critical files that required complex analysis. He made no mention of the Lebedevs.

They quickly negotiated what had to be done to finance Ian. Robert Forbes had the financial control. Ian would simply need to come and see him. Jacqui would inform Ian.

Jacqui mentioned something he hadn't thought of—wills and power of attorney. He had a will—everything to Mum and Heidi. He nominated Ian to be his power of attorney. Jacqui produced a few documents for Cameron to sign and would get Ian to finish it off. Not quite the normal process.

Jacqui had bought the phone he had requested—the only phone he would call her on. He promised to try and keep in touch but warned her there may be times when he couldn't call, assuring her that it wouldn't necessarily mean something was wrong. She would have to be patient. No texting. No social media.

With all the business finished they stood. Jacqueline embraced him and they kissed passionately.

"Do one more thing for me before you leave," she said softly in his ear, "Make love to me."

She locked the door. His heart raced, and his body trembled. He thought lovemaking on office desks only happened in the movies. He wondered if Mr Forbes or Mabel had any idea as to the business transaction currently unfolding.

Cameron didn't tell her about the piano case. He knew it would most likely be a problem down the track and it very much tempted him to break his previous resolve, but he reminded himself of the work needed to validate the findings. He truly feared what the truth may reveal and that would have a major impact on their relationship.

Back on the farm, he called his mum to let her know he had decided to go away for a little while, ensuring her that Ian and Jacqui had everything under control. He packed quickly, knowing that he had all his belongings in Dubai. He included the never-ending cake of soap and toothpaste winder, determined to keep those Binya traditions alive. He made sure he had his computer and all the Lebedev material saved on disc and burned all the paper working copies and notes in the kitchen stove. By 4 pm, he had left Harden, on the road to Sydney, with the broken plank of piano case in his bag.

Cameron struggled to concentrate on driving. On numerous occasions, he ran off the edge of the bitumen, requiring immediate steering correction. His mind functioned like a very full hard drive—slow and sluggish. He hadn't given a thought as to when he may return. He was more anxious as to what awaited him in Dubai. He put faith in Annand's assessment that he would be safe. He felt increasingly uneasy about the broken piece of wood in his luggage. He could be holding the piece of evidence that would condemn his grandfather as a murderer. It sickened him even more as he thought what that might mean. Had he molested and raped them? Was Mary's greatest dread about to be realised? He felt increasingly nauseous and at times felt he would vomit.

Numerous times he considered discarding the broken piece of piano case into some unsuspecting bush. He saw an exit sign for a rest area, prompting an immediate decision to stop. Having parked the car, he walked to the rear and opened the boot. Only then, he noticed the sign directly in front of the car, pointing toward Belanglo State Forest. His mind almost imploded. He instantly remembered Ivan Milat, the notorious psychopath serial killer who murdered seven backpackers in the early 1990s and buried them in the Belanglo State Forest. The realisation that he had almost disposed of the last clue of Jane and Kathleen into the killing fields of Milat paralysed him. He fell on all fours and vomited.

After a few minutes, he stood, resting his head on the open boot-lid of the car. He wanted to tell Jacqui. *No, Jacqui could not know this.* He stood motionless.

A car pulled alongside him. "Are you alright, mate?" a young man asked. A similar aged woman sat in the passenger seat—a surfboard strapped to their roof racks.

Cameron pulled himself together. "Thanks, mate. Yep. I'm fine, just stretching the legs."

"You've been standing there for ten minutes," the man said. "You haven't moved. Thought I'd seen my first dead man stand-ing!"

Cameron forced a laugh. "No, all's good. Been driving a long time, just feeling a bit of motion sicknesss."

"Can we get you anything?"

"No thanks, mate. I'll get some fresh air and I'll be fine," Cameron replied, glancing at the pair, seeing a genuine concern on their faces. "You guys are champions. I wish the world had more people like you."

"There are heaps of us. Just keep your eyes open. You look after yourself," the man replied, and they drove off. Cameron felt he needed to be reminded that there were good people in the world.

Cameron closed the boot, removing nothing. He then noticed a small monument nearby and moved closer to inspect it. He had stopped at a resting area called the James Gordon VC Rest

Area. The monument held a plaque that told the story of James
Gordon:

> *On the night of 10th July 1941 during an attack on "Green-
> hill" North of Djezzine, Private Gordon's Company came
> under intense machine-gun fire and its advance was held
> up. Movement even by single individuals became impossi-
> ble, one officer and two men being killed, and two men being
> wounded in the effort to advance. The enemy machine-gun
> position which had bought the two forward platoons to a
> halt was fortified and completely covered the area by our
> forces. Private Gordon, on his own initiative, crept forward
> over an area swept by machine-gun and grenade fire and
> succeeded in approaching close to the post; he then charged
> it from the front and killed the four machine-gunners with
> bayonet. His action completely demoralised the enemy in
> this sector and the Company advanced and took the posi-
> tion. During the remainder of the action that night and
> the following day, Private Gordon, who has throughout
> operations shown a high degree of courage, fought with
> equal gallantry"*
> *[London Gazette: 28 October 1941.]*
> *James Heather Gordon was born at Rockingham, Western
> Australia on 7 March 1909. He died on 19 July 1986 and
> was buried in the Karrakatta Cemetery, Perth, Western
> Australia.*

The story resonated with Cameron. He felt the isolation
James Gordon must have felt as he moved forward alone to
overcome the enemy. It echoed the isolation he now felt. Only
he held the potential to solve a mystery that had torn at the
hearts of many for a long time. But doing so could expose the
crimes of his grandfather.

His thoughts drifted to the stories of his great-grandfather, Edmund, who had been one of the first to enlist in the 1st Light Horse Regiment. It was his great-grandfather's moment of pride and glory to be the first to ride with the Light Horse and defend righteousness.

Confronted with the service of James Gordon and his grandfather, a deep feeling of responsibility weighed heavily on Cameron. Likewise, he must act to defend the truth. Cameron walked back to the car and resumed his journey.

He pulled into the Sydney Airport domestic terminal before realising he had completed his journey. For a moment, he could not think what to do next. A sign for AVIS Rent a Car reminded him that first he had to return the car he had originally rented on his arrival. He had extended the rental on several occasions using the Avis app but was now returning it well before the checked return date.

"Is the car fully refuelled?"

Refuelled? At no point on his journey, or before he commenced, had he checked the fuel gauge.

"How much fuel is in the car?"

"No idea," Cameron responded. This car return would not score him any bonus points but rather, additional charges on his final bill.

Departing the rental car depot, he suddenly realised he had returned to the domestic terminal, not the international terminal on the other side of the airport. An inquiry at the service desk in the airport directed him to the transfer bus.

Finally, at 8.30 pm, he made it to the international terminal. He had no ticket but assumed he had been booked on the Emirates flight. Not sure exactly what to do, he approached the Emirates customer service desk. Following the debacle at the rental return, he knew he had to focus and approached the desk with more composure and determination.

"Good evening. I understand you have a ticket for me," he said confidently.

"Thank you, Sir. I am sure we can help. Your name please."

He stated his name and extracted his passport from his pocket. She quickly entered his details into the computer, tapping the enter key a couple of times. Cameron noticed the subtle shift in her expression, the fleeting change in her demeanour and the quick flick of the eyes.

Without a word, she approached the nearby supervisor. Cameron observed a quick verbal exchange, followed by a millisecond glance in his direction. The supervisor spoke into the mic on his shoulder, then moved directly toward Cameron, with purpose.

Cameron's breathing quickened. His foot began tapping the floor.

"Good evening, Mr Blanche. My colleague here will take your bags. Please come with me and I will escort you to your lounge."

Cameron wanted to ask a lot of questions: *Where am I going? Do you need to see my passport? Do you want to know if I've got batteries in my luggage?*

But he asked nothing and followed the supervisor.

Escorted down a corridor, Cameron came to a security post. At this point, he went through standard screening, but there were no other passengers in sight. An immigrations officer cleared his passport, and he received his boarding pass. Glancing down, his eyes suddenly widened when he saw he held a first-class ticket. His reaction made those around him laugh. His company had only ever flown him economy. A few business class trips thanks to points upgrades, but never first class. The supervisor escorted him to a very elite VIP lounge. Cameron didn't know there were VIP lounges. He definitely didn't know he was a VIP.

Cameron soon found himself in the luxury of a very exclusive lounge. There were very few other guests, or if there were any, he couldn't see them. The décor exuded luxury and sophistication, crafted to evoke calmness and tranquility. He saw no liquor bar or self-serve food bar. He felt like royalty, being ushered into a private room, introduced to a personal waiter and advised that he would see to anything Cameron desired. The waiter asked Cameron for a drink order and seemed deflated when Cameron requested a Bacardi and Coke. A rare wine or sophisticated cocktail may have been more the order of the day.

Following an extremely stressful day, for the first time, he felt a little more relaxed. But why first class? He could only assume that he got the last remaining seat on an otherwise full flight. His supervisor, Annand, would be pissed, particularly if it was coming from his budget. The thought calmed Cameron a little and he smiled.

Soon the waiter returned, "Another Bacardi and Coke."

Cameron, at first, didn't realise it was a statement, not a question, as the waiter handed him a second drink and gave him a menu to select food. Given the last twelve hours, Cameron gratefully accepted being a sponge and absorbed every aspect of the service. He enjoyed a meal of sumptuous Australian seafood, paired with premier Australian white wine. Following his meal, he accepted the offer of a massage and spa shower. Never had he travelled in such luxurious indulgence. He shut out the darkness and anxiety in his mind and relaxed.

The same supervisor returned to escort him onto the plane. No boarding call. In fact, still no other passengers in sight. The supervisor escorted him to the door of the plane and bid him a pleasant journey, personally handing Cameron over to the flight attendant. No request to see the boarding pass, the flight attendant, dressed in her formal first-class suit, welcomed him, "Come with me, Mr Blanche; we have your suite waiting for you," escorting him to suite 1B, front row, centre of the plane. Not a seat, a suite, the flight attendant called it. Cameron was more than impressed—the biggest airplane seat he had seen, which at night, transformed into one of the most comfortable beds he had ever slept in. He tried to act cool, as if a seasoned frequent flyer. Inside, he felt like a kid locked in a confectionery shop.

Josephine, the flight attendant, gave him a detailed description of the suite, including his private mini bar, "Just press your button and we can restock that at your request," the Byredo skin care collection, the Bowers and Wilkins headphones and detailed instructions on how to operate the full-size computer/ TV screen.

"Mr Blanche. May I familiarise you with the shower?" Josephine escorted him into the eloquently appointed bathroom and demonstrated all the features, inviting him to come back and enjoy a shower whenever he wanted to during the flight, even though he just had an amazingly relaxing shower in the lounge. He was given a set of night clothes that he could change into when he showered. He was advised to leave his clothes in the shower, and they would be pressed for him and stored until they were required.

Josephine offered a tour of the private bar at the back of the plane. He impressed himself, explaining that he regularly used the bar when travelling business class and there would be no need. He settled back into his suite and smiled. Annand would be pissed. He still didn't understand why he had to come back and why all the secrecy. But for the first time, he didn't care.

Ronnie would later find that the first-class ticket was not courtesy of Annand's generosity, rather it was part of a well-rehearsed high security witness protection program. He had company. Two Dubai Police secret service officers were escorting him. One in seat 2A, directly to his left and one row back, and one in 1C, to his right, behind the dividing screen. His movements had been monitored from the time he arrived at the airport. Every movement on the flight would be monitored. When he went for a shower, which he did twice—after dinner and before landing, a secret service officer stood at the base of the stairs. When he spent time in the bar at the back of the plane, so did a secret service officer. When he slept, neither secret service officer slept. Whenever the door to Ronnie's suite was closed, theirs were always open.

The fourteen-hour uneventful flight passed by all too quickly in a haze of indulgence and comfort. He could do this for a lot longer. He got some sleep, interrupted more by time at the bar than the worry on his mind. Upon arrival into Dubai, another chaperone guided him to a private buggy that took him directly to a first-class arrival gate, reminding him that his first-class flight included a chauffeur-driven limousine to his accommodation.

"Where do I collect my bag?" he asked.

"It will be waiting in your limousine."

How silly. How could I forget that.

Cameron convinced himself he could do this again. In what seemed like minutes from when he left the plane, he sat in a limousine, feeling like a person of importance. He sat back to enjoy his journey down Sheikh Zayed Road, heading to his Dubai apartment, unaware that a Dubai Police secret service officer was driving him. The cars in front and behind were undercover police vehicles. Exiting the limousine at his apartment block, the early morning oven-like humidity welcomed him home. Within minutes, he stood in the comfort and privacy of his twelfth floor apartment. Comfort, yes. Privacy, no. His apartment was heavily bugged including microphones, cameras and highly sophisticated WIFI and social media scanners, but he didn't know that yet.

CHAPTER ELEVEN

He had caught that flight from Sydney to Dubai several times, but never had he been home this early—7.08 am according to his wall clock. He would like to say, *good to be home*, but that didn't describe how he felt. He found the apartment just as he had left it, but it felt foreign. His cleaners had obviously maintained their routine and it glistened in its sterile showroom-like presentation.

Typically, he would come home from a fourteen-hour flight feeling unslept, seedy, grimy and sweaty. He would first have a shower followed by a big breakfast. However, in the last twenty hours, he had soaked in so many showers and had not stopped eating, including a five-star three course breakfast just before landing. He wanted to ring Jacqui, but remembered the instruction of *no phone calls*, even though he had the "secret phone" purchased by Jacqui. Instead, he opened the computer and scanned his emails. Nothing new—nothing that shed light on his summonsed return.

For a while, he simply sat, expecting to hear from Annand at any moment. He would have been bored, but his level of anxiety prevented that. Waiting but not knowing what for and why made him more anxious. His thumb rubbed the palm of his hand so persistently that it appeared bruised. Unpacking his bag took a few minutes—he left all his newly purchased attire at the farm. It was pointless bringing additional attire home to an already full wardrobe. After changing into fresh clothes, he resumed sitting and waiting.

A glance at the time: 9.15 am. *How long would I have to wait?* He considered visiting his favourite coffee shop, but he recalled Annand telling him not to leave his apartment. *Does Annand know I am here?* He remained unaware of the detailed tracking that had followed him from the time he arrived at Sydney

Airport—or that authorities knew exactly what room he currently stood in and the last email he had just read.

Cameron picked up the book he had been reading before leaving—John Grisham's latest novel, *Gray Mountain*. He had left it on the bedside cabinet with the intent of packing it in his hand luggage to read on the plane but had forgotten to pick it up as he walked out. He tried to pick where he'd left off. The story of a lawyer working for a major law firm in New York who lost her job after the crash of the Lehman Brothers, starting anew in some small town somewhere in Virginia. Flicking through the pages, he struggled to focus. He closed the book and put it back on the table. "Try being a sheep farmer," he mumbled out loud to himself. He sat back down on the white leather lounge chair and waited.

Not long after 10 am, a knock at the apartment door broke the silence.

When Cameron opened it, Annand stood there, accompanied by five imposing men, two in suits, two Arabs in traditional Arabic kanduras and one in police uniform.

"Good morning, Ronnie. Welcome back," greeted Annand. Cameron had to immediately make a mental adjustment—back in the world of Ronnie.

I need to introduce you to a number of people—"

Before Annand could continue, one of the men dressed in a kandura, stepped forward. "Mr Ronnie, allow me to introduce myself. My name is Mr Abdullah, Lieutenant Colonel in charge of the International Fraud Investigation Unit of the Dubai Police. Mr Mustafa here is from the UAE Embassy, Mr Simons is from the World Bank, Mr Donald is from Interpol Criminal Investigations and Major Juma is from my office, reporting direct to me."

Ronnie didn't speak. *Whatever this is, its big shit—definitely not about a parking ticket.* His mouth went dry, thinking he faced imminent arrest. His mind reeled, struggling to adjust to being called Ronnie and the Arabic convention of the constant use of the title Mr combined with first names.

"I know you have no idea why we are here. Come, let us sit and we will explain," Mr Abdullah said, holding his arm out to guide Ronnie forward.

They sat in the lounge. Mr Abdullah determined where each person sat. He directed Ronnie to the single lounge chair in front of the corner window. Ronnie braced himself to be interrogated about something he had done in the office. His mind rapidly scanned all his current accounts and whilst financial fraud may well be amongst that, he failed to understand why it would capture this audience. But instead of interrogating him, Mr Abdullah launched into a detailed explanation of the events leading to their meeting.

Mr Abdullah began with an overview of money laundering—how big the crime had become on the world stage and how the Dubai Government worked with Interpol and the World Bank to stamp it out. He spoke with the authority of a commander, raising his index finger high, commanding that Dubai would not be a haven for money laundering. Ronnie listened intently, wondering what the hell this had to do with him—a relatively low-level accountant. Had he missed something very significant in his accounts?

Then, Mr Abdullah sharpened his focus. "Our attention has narrowed to one company, and Mr Ronnie, in some ways, you have led us to that company."

Ronnie sat forward abruptly. "All that Pacific stuff I did for the Sydney office? I've given all my findings to them," he said, pointing to Annand, "but I told them a lot more work needed to be done."

"Wait, wait, Mr Ronnie," Mr Abdullah interrupted. "Do you think I would have an interest in the Pacific? No, no. This is much closer to home. So close, in fact, you can see it, Mr Ronnie. I know you know the Lebedev family, correct?"

"Yes, I do. I don't do their books. But Mr Annand, here, asked me to review some files only in the last week or so. I sent them back to him."

"Mr Ronnie, I directed those files be sent to you. Mr Annand acted on my orders."

"But I've never worked on their accounts. I don't even have access to them, other than the files I was sent."

"Perhaps we need to clarify something for you. If you were a suspect in this case, this discussion would not be happening here and would be a very different discussion with specialised interrogation teams.

"Mr Ronnie, we have conducted a very thorough investigation of your activities. We know you do not provide any accounting services to the Lebedev company. We know you have never accessed any of their files other than those sent to you recently. Those files were sent to you for two reasons. Firstly, I am told by Mr Annand that you are developing quite a strong reputation as a forensic accountant—you find things other people do not. Secondly, we closely observed your responses to those files. If you had any involvement in fraud, we suspect your responses would have been very different. More importantly, we are following up on some of the, can I say, 'discrepancies' you identified, which even our teams had not identified."

"It's not rocket science."

"I have had that discussion with my team," Mr Abdullah replied. "I might send some people to you for tuition at a later date. Allow me to continue.

"Our interest in you stems from your relationship and social interactions with members of the Lebedev family. We will talk about that shortly. We believe that you are ignorant of the illegal activities being undertaken by the Lebedev family—just as your company seems to be."

Ronnie could not miss the glance toward Annand as he made this observation.

"That brings me to the second reason we are having this conversation and why it is happening in this room. It was you who first alerted us to this case of money laundering."

Ronnie's eyes widened with shock. "What, me? How?"

"Over your shoulder, Mr Ronnie," Mr Abdullah said, motioning with his eyes.

Ronnie turned and saw nothing out of the ordinary. A mass of high-rise apartment buildings standing outside his twelfth-floor windows, all of which were there when he left.

"What I believe happened, Mr Ronnie," Mr Abdullah continued, "is that you often shared coffee breaks with some of our police officers who frequent your office from time to time—Mr Majid in particular."

Ronnie nodded cautiously.

"One day, you mentioned the apartment block beside your residence and the patterns you observed with the apartment lights at night, along with some other comings and goings. Do you recall?"

"I do," Ronnie said, recalling the curious patterns of lights turning on and off. "But it was nothing more than a casual observation. Everyone laughed at me and said I've been looking at too many spreadsheets. Majid said I needed to get a life—or maybe a girlfriend."

They all chuckled.

"Well, Mr Ronnie, Mr Majid followed it up. Have you ever noticed the name of the building?"

Ronnie twisted his head—Babki Towers. He hadn't paid any notice to the name. It had never meant anything to him.

"'Babki' means money in Russian," Mr Abdullah explained. "In itself, insignificant. But Mr Majid is an astute officer and investigated further. And Mr Ronnie, you may well have cracked one of the biggest money laundering schemes in the world. Cash rents from fictitious tenants are processed from company to company, enough to lose the detail of any non-existent tenants. Those fake tenants 'live' in apartment blocks like Babki Towers, hidden by apparent light activity in the apartments to give the illusion that they are occupied."

Ronnie stared at the building. He pictured in his mind the curious light patterns he had observed. He never imagined he had a front row seat to money laundering fraud.

Mr Abdullah broke the silence. "Now, don't get me wrong, Mr Ronnie, it has been a long journey from strange light patterns to a major case of money laundering. That brings us to the next part of this investigation. Now, please tell us about your relationship with the Lebedevs."

"I really wouldn't call it a relationship," Ronnie replied, a little more relaxed. He sat back in the chair a hand on each knee. "I remember being out for drinks one night, at The Observatory bar down at the Marriott. Alex, he is the older brother, walked past me, recognised me from work—his family did a lot of business with other accountants in the office—well anyway, he saw me and came over and said hello and we had some drinks at the bar. That's when I met his brother, Matey—at least, that's what I call him. His name is something like that. After that, we caught up often for drinks."

"Where have you met them?" asked Major Juma, the guy in police uniform.

"A few different places—we liked checking out new venues as well. Our regular spots were The Observatory, the Buddha Bar, or if we were up the other end of town, we often went to The Address Hotel—top floor."

"Have you ever been to their private residence?" Major Juma asked.

"No, only to bars and restaurants. We've attended events together, like the Rugby 7s and the World Cup horse race. Their company hired a room at the World Cup," Ronnie searched his memory. "That's about it. It's probably been no more than a couple of times a month. And to be honest, they've been good social company."

"Have you ever met their father?"

"No, never," Ronnie leant back in his chair. "He was supposed to be at the World Cup but for some reason, he wasn't there. No idea why."

"Okay, Mr Ronnie," Mr Abdullah said, taking control of the meeting again. "That brings us to the reason we are here today."

Ronnie interrupted, "What, there's more?"

Mr Abdullah gave a slight grin but ignored the question. "Whilst we believe we have our case, some crucial links are still missing—particularly the connection between Babki Towers and the Lebedev company. We suspect the link runs through a company called Rendezvous, which funnels cash through one or more shell companies, all originating from the Lebedev villa.

He paused for a moment. "You may be the connection that can make that link."

"I don't know what you mean," Ronnie responded.

"The Lebedevs are a very private family. You seem to be quite privileged—you were the only non-family member at the World Cup event and your social meetings other than some of the lady friends present."

"I don't know about that, there were sometimes a lot of people there," Ronnie interrupted.

"We have a considerable amount of photographic evidence from sources such as CCTV and sources I cannot disclose. You are in a number of those pictures. We have undertaken extensive checks on the other people, and you appear to be the only non-family person present."

That surprised Ronnie, but when he thought about it, it didn't. His hands were sweaty. Hearing of this surveillance that had been happening and how he had been identified in photographs at the events made him feel quite violated.

"So, what's so important about that? I wasn't part of their fraud schemes, and they never talked about any stuff like that," Ronnie said, now sitting upright and eyes engaging with Mr Abdullah. "I'm glad I've fulfilled my role as a good standing citizen and told your officer about the lights, but I can't see what more this has to do with me."

"We are satisfied with what you have told us," Mr Abdullah said, pausing, locking his eyes directly on Ronnie. "But Mr Ronnie, you can now help us close this case. We want you to get invited into the Lebedev villa."

Ronnie suddenly felt sick—very sick. It was now bigger than anything he had ever imagined. Instantly, he saw the immense danger in being asked to cross the path of Russian criminals. *Take me back to Binya. Jacqui, I need you.*

Ronnie didn't respond. His elbows rested on his knees; his forehead cupped in his palms. He had had enough.

"We will leave it at that for today," Mr Abdullah said. "Here are your instructions for now. Firstly, you need to know that your apartment here is being fully monitored. Cameras, microphones, your computer, even all your WIFI traffic. That is not about monitoring you, but on the chance the Lebedevs may contact you or even visit. It is also to protect you. We are dealing with Russian criminals who have few boundaries. Please live normally. We will respect your privacy, and anything not related to this investigation will not be retained. Legal documents have been prepared that ensure nothing can be used in any other legal proceedings against you."

Mr Abdullah paused for a moment and allowed his officious style to drop a little and with a grin, "But please, Mr Ronnie, don't purchase any online porn."

"But I haven't got any!" Ronnie blurted.

"We know," Major Juma said, with a grin.

Laughter rippled around the room. *Why does everyone think I have porn?*

Mr Abdullah continued, "We want you to lead a normal life. Spend time with the Lebedevs and try to enter their personal space and, we hope, their villa."

"And what am I supposed to do when I'm there?"

"One of your skills is your ability to observe—you see things others don't. Scan for any leads whatsoever: any mention of companies, names, properties—anything like that. You impress me, Mr Ronnie, and I have a lot of experts on my team. Mr Annand is the only other person outside of the authorities who is aware of what is happening."

Annand interjected, "We have a normal schedule of work for you to keep you occupied."

Ronnie nodded silently, frustrated that his forensic eye could spot unusual lights on a building but failed to see Jacqui, or Ian. He wished he could stop noticing things like a stain on a piece of timber. *Why can't I just look at things normally?*

Mr Abdullah resumed his authority, speaking in his commanding tone. "You cannot share this with anyone. That includes your solicitor friend, Jacqueline Forbes. Yes, you are being monitored. By the way, leave Cameron in Australia. You are Ronnie. To change that now would raise suspicions. You are also being protected. Secret service police have been by your side since your arrival at Sydney Airport. I trust you enjoyed our first-class service—it's the most secure place for you on the plane. One day, I will ask you which seats our two secret service police officers occupied. They accompanied you all the way. I will see how observant you are," he added with another rare smile. Ronnie's mind flashed through the cabin of the plane. *Let me think about that.*

"There will be no secret service in your apartment, but they are not far away. If you think you know who they are, please do not acknowledgment them or make contact with them. I stress, the secret service is not here to monitor you, but to protect you and, through you, gather information about the Lebedevs. Your point of contact with us will be Major Juma. He will provide you with a phone number that will be safe from any detection.

"Thank you for your time, Mr Ronnie," Mr Abdullah concluded, and they left.

Ronnie felt so drained; he didn't move. Annand hung back slightly to be last to leave. He turned to Ronnie, "See you in the office tomorrow."

Alone, Ronnie turned his head glancing at Babki Towers. Only a few weeks ago, he enjoyed being a simple accountant, doing his job and reveling in Dubai's social life. Two weeks later, he owned a farm, had fallen in true love for the first time and uncovered the possibility that his grandfather had killed two young sisters. Now, he found himself in the middle of one of Dubai's biggest money laundering schemes—facing so much danger from Russian criminals that he required secret service police protection. If that wasn't enough, he now had to infiltrate the world of Russian criminals and expose them. He had rediscovered Cameron but now thrusted back into the world of Ronnie. *I could have been checking sheep for flies.* Leaning forward, he buried his face in his hands and cried.

He woke a couple of hours later. The irony struck him of being on a fourteen-hour flight in the luxury of a first-class bed, only to come home to sleep in a chair. It must be a withdrawal symptom from economy class. He felt a little better, however, he was emotionally drained. One minute his thoughts were on how he would meet his Russian friend Alex, the next thinking of a piece of wood in his luggage that could condemn his grandfather. Then, his thoughts returned to Jacqui. He so much wanted to ring and talk to her. He picked up the phone a few times but put it back down.

Mr Abdullah had told him he could lead a normal life. He interpreted that as he could ring Jacqui. *Anyway, they are going to know who I ring.* But he knew the issue was not about if he could ring, but rather a question of what he would say—would he tell her about his discovery in the dairy? He didn't want to believe it himself. He wanted to prove it wasn't true. To tell her would break his own rules of investigation and deduction: you don't jump ahead of the facts. What fact proved the presence of a blood stain? Were the damaged bikes Jane's and Kathleen's? Why would he lead Jacqui up this path if it may not be true? Any respite from his short sleep quickly evaporated. He put the phone down knowing it would only be a matter of time before he picked it up again.

He texted instead.

Hi Jacqui. Good flight. Scored a first-class upgrade. Oversubscribed flight apparently. All is good here, but I can't discuss it. Got a lot to do. Will call in a few days. Missing you. He pressed send. Only the last sentence was really true. He typed again: *I love you.*

A reply came a few minutes later: *Miss you too. Hope we can talk soon,* followed by a love heart and hug emoji. He smiled and felt less alone.

Surveying the unit, he found its stark white sterility cold and unwelcoming. His cleaners, Muhammad and Mia—a Filipino couple—had maintained the spotless presentation of the apartment in his absence. They were very reliable, cleaning every Thursday since he had moved in, and even taking care of his washing and ironing.

He found the refrigerator empty. Muhammad and Mia must have cleaned it and disposed of the stale and expired items, so he decided to go to the shop for food supplies. He caught a taxi to the nearby Carrefour supermarket and stocked up. He found little difference between shopping in Carrefours and shopping in Australia. Australian produce dominated both the meat and the fruit and vegetable sections; even Australian pork was available—though in a separate section for non-Muslims.

Ronnie soon reminded himself why he enjoyed grocery shopping in Dubai more than Australia. In Dubai, with no local food production, all fresh food was imported. Everything was always available, sourced from wherever it was in season from around the globe. What he enjoyed most were the constant supplies of cherries—his favourite. He never found them out of stock; only the country of origin varied.

The cherries always reminded him of Harden, just a short distance from the heart of Australian's mainland cherry-growing heartland. He had grown up believing Australian cherries were the best, but now, he embraced and enjoyed all international varieties.

Back at his unit, as the evening approached, Ronnie contemplated plans for dinner. He rarely ate at home, so he considered dining out options. He definitely didn't want to see the Lebedevs tonight, so he decided to head to the Irish Village at Al Garhoud. He had taken Alex and his brother Matvei there once to watch Russian Igor Kunistyn compete against Indian Sondev Devvarman in the Dubai International Tennis Championship. They were not impressed that Kunistyn lost in the first round in straight sets, 6–1, 6–4. Even though they returned to watch Djokovic win the final, Ronnie could not persuade them to join him at the Irish Village, located under the tennis stadium. One of Ronnie's favourite bars, but not the scene for two partying Russians seeking someone to share their bed with that evening. However, Ronnie felt very much at home there, as did many of the Aussies, Brits and Irish expats working in Dubai.

Ronnie hadn't adjusted to a life of constant surveillance. It felt strange knowing that someone observed and listened to everything he said and did. He felt like Truman Burbank in the movie *The Truman Show*. *I'm a real-life Jim Carrey.* Living by himself, he never shut the bathroom door to shower or use the toilet. Conscious of being observed, he instinctively shut the door, then laughed at the futility of it—of course, they would be interested in knowing what went on behind a closed door.

Accepting they were ever-present, he called out, "Okay guys, I'm heading to the Irish Village. I'll be under the James Joyce portrait. If you want a ride in the cab, I'll wait a few minutes for you."

He smiled, remembering he could not identify or communicate with the secret service police.

"I'll shout you a drink. I'm assuming you're Muslim," he added, "So it'll be a Coke."

Once outside, he hailed a taxi—always an easy thing to do in Dubai. He hopped in, leaving the door open for a few seconds.

"Are you waiting for someone?" the driver asked.

"Maybe," he replied. After a brief pause, he shut the door, and the taxi pulled away.

At the Irish Village, Ronnie was pleased to find his favourite table—beneath a painting of James Joyce—unoccupied. He ordered a pint of Amstel Lager and a glass of Coke. As the drinks were delivered, he went to the bathroom, located nearby. When he returned moments later, the Coke was gone. Smiling, he enjoyed the first sip of his ice-cold Amstel Lager.

He didn't seek out the secret service officers. Not because Mr Abdullah told him not to, but because he intended to enjoy the game. Knowing they were there gave him a genuine sense of safety. He had always regarded Dubai as the safest place he had ever lived. The irony of having personal protection here when he felt more at risk on the night-time streets of Sydney or Melbourne had not escaped him. But then again, he had never upset a Russian criminal before.

Having enjoyed his beer, he ordered another one, along with a T-bone steak, salad and chips. A reasonable gathering of people occupied tables in the courtyard outside, but most were inside due to the heat. Like every visit to the Irish Village, he thoroughly enjoyed his meal, washing it down with the last mouthful of beer. He called the waiter, settled the account and went to the bathroom in preparation to leave.

On exiting the bathroom, he noticed a full glass of beer and an empty glass at his table. Ronnie smiled, sat down and took a sip. Yes, Amstel Lager. He picked up the glass, yes, an empty Coke glass. He smiled. *This is going to be fun.*

The night felt too young to go home, so Ronnie headed to the Eclipse Bar at the InterContinental Dubai Festival City—another of his favourite bars. He'd taken Alex and Matvei there, but they found it too dark, too small and few people—which were all the reasons Ronnie liked it. He called it his secret bar, hidden away on the twenty-sixth floor. It had no signage and the entry door was tucked away out of sight; you could only find it if you already knew about it.

He settled at a window table, taking in the stunning view of the Dubai city skyline. He could only see three other people—a couple at the far end and a woman at the bar that he assumed was a prostitute. Her glancing attempts to make eye contact soon confirmed that.

The waiter arrived and he ordered a Bacardi and Coke, which was promptly delivered with the customary mixed nuts. He kept a glancing eye on the door. After some time, two women entered, bubbly and chatty. Not prostitutes or secret service, concluded Ronnie. Another couple arrived and headed for the more secluded end of the room, and after a while, the couple who were there when he arrived left. No customers for the prostitute. There never appeared to be. He thought that if he went out the door, he would find an Arabic-looking guy in a dark suit leaning against the wall smoking, waiting for his exit. But he didn't peek.

Nearing the end of his drink, the waiter arrived with another Bacardi and Coke. Ronnie raised his arm to indicate to decline.

"They said it's your favourite. Enjoy," the waiter said with a smile, putting it on the table and returning to the bar.

"Did they include a cheese platter?" Ronnie muttered to himself.

The waiter soon arrived back with a cheese platter. Ronnie smiled. This is going to be a good relationship. His mysterious secret service man needed a name. As he sipped, several names went through his head. He tried to recall characters in his favourite books, but nothing came to mind. Chuck Nolan had Wilson on his island in *Cast Away*. He thought of Truman in his movie. Truman had Christof, the director. Ronnie needed someone. He pondered, sipping his Bacardi and Coke.

"Sidney!" he suddenly called out. Everyone suddenly turned their eyes upon him, expecting more. He ignored their sudden attention. "That's it!" he exclaimed, then in a little quieter voice, "Sidney it will be. Thanks, Sidney."

Ronnie finished his Bacardi and Coke, nibbled a bit on the cheeses and left. He exited the sliding door—no one on the other side. He navigated the left and right bends to the elevators. Still no one. He went to the foyer on the ground floor, finding it rather empty. No one obviously looking out for him. *You're good, Sidney.* The doorman hailed him a cab and Ronnie headed home. He didn't turn around, but knew Sidney wouldn't be far behind.

CHAPTER TWELVE

He didn't rush into work the next morning. On his arrival, a warm and welcoming reception greeted him. There were many condolences. Despite the comments, he felt no one had truly missed him except Annand. Ronnie found his office unchanged. His desktop was clear.

Company policy dictated that no papers whatsoever were to be left on a desktop after work for security reasons. The policy existed to prevent situations where sensitive information could be inadvertently seen by the wrong eyes. A cleaner once used a Post-it note left on an accountant's desk to obtain the mobile telephone number of an internationally well-known football player and contacted them directly. Since then, anything left on a desk resulted in a reprimand.

Ronnie fired up his computer. He was hoping to use his work as a distraction from the many thoughts churning in his mind. Emails and files were up to date. He opened the latest email from Annand titled *Immediate Work Task*. Attached was a file, *101 Extreme Sudokus*.

Ronnie walked to Annand's office.

"I've seen your email with my tasks. That's a mountain of work to get through," he said flatly.

"Mr Abdullah doesn't want you overloaded," Annand replied.

"But he also said, 'life as normal,'" Ronnie responded. "I also have to keep myself busy or I'll go crazy."

"Understood," Annand said. "You still have the monthly reviews of all your customers. I know there are some outstanding inquiries amongst them, nothing out of the ordinary, but they need closing. The monthly financials will need to be out by the end of next week. As for specific forensic projects, you've wrapped everything up until we hear more on the Pacific investigation from the Sydney office. At the moment, I don't have another major forensic project to throw your way."

"I need to do something that is totally not related to any of this shit. My mind needs to be distracted."

Annand paused briefly, before adding, "Abdullah doesn't want you doing anything with the Lebedev file. He thinks that could compromise your position with them."

"They aren't the only company on our books. Come on, Annand, there must be something else. I need a distraction."

"Understood. Let me go through a few things and see what I can find."

"Thanks. I just wanted to make sure you don't expect me to sit around playing Sudoku all day. I may well want to flex some hours on this other thing, so don't come chasing me if I'm not here."

Annand nodded.

"Don't worry, I am sure Sidney will let you know if there is a problem," Ronnie said with a wry grin.

"Who's Sidney?"

Ronnie had already left.

Moments after Ronnie arrived home that afternoon, a knock on his door followed him. Opening it, he found Major Juma from Dubai Police standing there.

"Major Juma," Ronnie opened the door wider. "Lucky—I just got home."

"We know when you are home, Mr Ronnie."

"Of course," Ronnie replied, still getting use to the new norm.

"How are you doing?"

"You are watching everything I do, but you don't know? I'm just fine," Ronnie responded with a touch of sarcasm.

Major Juma raised his eyebrows slightly. Ronnie could sense a sympathetic understanding to his circumstances.

"I'm sorry, Major."

"I understand, Mr Ronnie. We are only here to help and protect you."

"I know. The last couple of weeks have been an emotional roller coaster ride for me."

"We know, Mr Ronnie."

Ronnie wanted to ask them to drop the 'Mr,' but he knew how entrenched it was in Arabic protocol and custom—it would not change.

Major Juma proceeded to provide Ronnie with an undetected telephone number he could use to contact him directly. Ronnie was becoming increasingly fascinated with the intricacies of surveillance. The more the Major explained, the safer and more secure Ronnie felt. The telephone number he provided belonged to a legitimate medical home care supplier. When called, it provided standard menu options: press one for administration, two to place an order, three to follow up on an order, and so on. However, one option, 717, wasn't listed. Major Juma explained that pressing 717 connected directly to his phone. Ronnie tried it. *How cool was that*! He could ring Major Juma without leaving any trace whatsoever.

Major Juma also installed an app on Ronnie's phone. On the surface, it advertised events at the Dubai Mall—something every mobile phone in Dubai should have. However, the app featured a hidden function. Ronnie could take photos using the app, but they would not be stored on his phone. If he was caught or suspected of taking photos, his phone could be searched and no trace of the photos would be found. The photos taken through this app would be instantly uploaded to the secret service police and disappear from Ronnie's phone.

Major Juma also asked a number of questions that Ronnie found unnecessary given his constant surveillance: Had he contacted the Lebedevs? Had he discovered any link to Babki Towers?

As Major Juma stood to leave he asked, "Is there anything else I can do for you before I leave?"

Ronnie sat silent for a moment, then stood to face Major Juma. "Yes, Major Juma, there is one thing I want to talk to you about. You've been monitoring me and my ..." he hesitated, almost saying girlfriend, but quickly corrected himself. "Ah, my friend. You would be aware of the matter we are researching, I assume?"

"Yes, we have been monitoring your computer traffic and your telephone conversations with her. But we haven't monitored your every movement or any face-to-face conversations with her. I presume you are referring to Jacqueline Forbes. We know she is a solicitor. As we have said, you are not a suspect; therefore, we have had no reason to monitor your conversations that closely in Australia, knowing they did not include the Lebedevs.

"Okay. Well, there is something I have been assisting Jacqui with, of a personal nature," Ronnie said, proceeding to give a summarised version of the case of the missing Barkley sisters and their efforts to investigate the case so far. He detailed the discovery of the piano box, its unexplained removal from the back of his grandfather's truck and his subsequent discovery on the morning he left Harden to come back to Dubai.

Major Juma listened intently, appearing genuinely interested. He acknowledged he had some awareness of their investigation, but it had been ruled out-of-scope of matters relevant to any Dubai Police investigation.

Ronnie excused himself and went to his bedroom, returning with a small parcel wrapped in a pillowcase.

"And so, Major Juma, this is a piece of board from the bottom of that piano case. I found it just before Annand rang me to come back. I need to know if that stain on the board is blood. I need to know if my grandfather is a killer."

"I assume you are asking me to have this tested?"

"In summary, yes."

Major Juma remained silent for some time before speaking.

"I have two things to say. Firstly, when all this is over, I want you to work for me. Your analytical and forensic skills are unique gifts. Secondly, what you're asking for is, shall I say, very difficult. Particularly here in Dubai, where there are very strict controls governing the management of evidence. You can't simply walk into a police lab and have something tested. Evidence must be part of a case, with a case number, appropriately recorded in the evidence inventory. The log needs to link it to a specific location, specific time of identification as evidence, including details of who logged it at the time. My official answer is that you must surrender this evidence to the Australian Police and have them investigate and test it."

Ronnie made no comment.

Major Juma paused for some time, before adding, "Leave it with me. One more observation about what you just told me: Don't rush ahead with wild assumptions. You have the forensic skills. Blood on a piece of timber alone, even if it is blood, doesn't make your grandfather a killer."

He stood, bid his farewells, and promptly left with the piece of timber tucked discreetly in his folder. Ronnie had the impression that the last fifteen minutes of surveillance tape might quietly disappear.

Thursday felt like a normal workday for Ronnie. With a steady flow of routine work, the day passed quickly. When work colleagues asked him to join them for weekend drinks, he suddenly remembered Thursday heralded the end of the working week. His mind was still operating on the Australian weekend—Saturday and Sunday. In Dubai, the weekend consists of Friday, the Muslim Holy Day, and Saturday, with Sunday being the first day of the working week.

The invitation excited him—exactly the diversion he needed. However, he knew his priority was to make contact the Lebedevs.

He particularly wanted to avoid meeting them at work. Now more than ever, work and pleasure needed to be separated.

Although Ronnie had Alex's number, he wanted their meeting to feel like a chance meeting, just like his first encounter. He reluctantly declined the invite to join his work colleagues and, after a fresh shower and change of clothes, headed to The Observatory bar where he had first met the Lebedevs. Unfortunately, no success. He walked the entire length of JBR hoping to see them, but without success. Eventually, he went home disappointed.

Friday is a quiet day in Dubai, being the Holy Day, but comes alive as a party town at night. Time to hunt again. He tried several places, with the last stop being the Buddha Bar. Initially, he sat at the bar by himself and had a couple of drinks, observing the guests as they passed by. Later, he walked through the lounge, discreetly examining every alcove as he passed by.

Suddenly, out of the darkness, a shout, "Ronnie!"

He stopped and turned, seeing nothing but a sea of faces in a darkened sunken lounge before Alex emerged from the darkness. He and his brother, along with several other people, were in the lounge, obviously enjoying their evening.

"Aussie, how are you? Have not seen you for so long!"

Ronnie quickly explained that he had been to Australia for his grandmother's funeral.

"Sorry to hear that man. I was in the office a couple of times but didn't see you."

Although Alex appeared genuinely pleased to see him, Ronnie could see by his body language that he was keen to return to his group. He sensed there would be no invite to join with them tonight. That suited Ronnie. From what he could see, it appeared a little too intimate and steamy. But the brief contact had opened a bridge, and he hoped they would follow up with him over the coming days. After sharing pleasantries and a hug, Alex rejoined his group.

"Give me a call and we'll catch up soon," Ronnie said as Alex turned.

"Will do," Alex replied before disappearing back into the dimly lit alcove.

Matvei, who had his arm around a girl whose dress hung dangerously low, gave Ronnie a wave.

Ronnie found his seat still vacant. A waiter caught his eye and glanced to the side of the bar, pointing to a pint of beer and an empty glass, indicating they were for him. A sip confirmed an Amstel Lager, along with the empty glass that had contained Coke. The coaster under the beer had a smilie face drawn on it, followed by an exclamation mark.

"Thanks, Sidney," he said to himself with a smile. He didn't look around—*let's play by the rules.*

Ronnie woke on Saturday feeling slightly more relaxed and secure. His bedroom overlooked the desert away from the high-rises. A combination of desert dust and heat haze most often meant poor visibility, but he still found it a very relaxing scene. He did a little calculation, concluding it was early Saturday afternoon in Harden.

He sent Jacqui a text:

If your free ring me from the rock paddock.

Give me twenty minutes. Three red hearts attached.

"At last, I get to hear your voice again," Jacquie greeted him. "Are you okay?"

Ronnie could hear relief in her voice.

"I'm good. Hearing your voice makes me feel even better," Ronnie replied, feeling more relaxed than he had been since returning. "It has been really hectic since coming back, but I'm slowly getting it all back under control."

"Are you safe?"

He had to be careful knowing ears were listening, "I'm fine, I am working on a very sensitive case, and I have crazy deadlines to meet. That's why I had to come back. A day can be a lot of money in the finance world. I can't discuss it, anyway. Not even with the others at work. Just getting my head around it all is why I haven't phoned you."

He didn't want to lie but genuinely wanted to put her at ease about his safety. No talk of Russians for now.

"You're telling me it's a big firm, surely they've got someone else who can do it?" he could hear a longing hope in her voice.

"It's stuff I've worked on before and know it inside-out. They all want Ronnie."

"Who?"

Shit. He had let his guard down. His palms suddenly felt sweaty, but he thought for a second, took a stabilizing breath, and concluded it was time for honesty.

"They call me Ronnie over here," he said as blandly as he could.

"You didn't tell me that," she responded.

No more lies, he committed to himself.

"I'm sorry. I thought of it a few times, but it never seemed the right time or even relevant. Everyone calling me Cameron sounded good. It seemed more suited to the timing and events. Grandma only knew me as Cameron. I didn't even revert to Cam—that only started at university and in my Sydney time."

"So, what do you prefer?"

"That's something I'd love to talk with you about, but that needs a good wine at the top of the rock paddock."

"Well, that's where I'm sitting now. And I brought my wine," she said softly.

"It would be so much better if I was there with you," he responded. He felt a self-satisfaction that he had told the truth, "Ronnie started as a joke and stuck as a nickname. No one knew me as Cameron, so Ronnie it was."

He paused as he carefully chose his words. He wanted to be honest.

"But what I have realised is that Ronnie is a different person. Being back in Harden, I realised I'd forgotten Cameron."

He paused and could hear her breathing on the phone.

"But you helped me find him again."

After a further pause, she replied, in an almost whisper, "And who do you want to be?"

Honesty. Honesty. You must be honest. "I want to be me. Maybe that is a little bit of both. I may not be the Cameron Grandma boasted so much about and I don't want to be the Cameron that was an arsehole to his best mate. But I don't want to be the Ronnie that has abandoned everything from the past. I want to be the person that does remember everything about the people who are important to me. I want to be the person who loves you."

He heard a faint sniffle and imagined a tear rolling down her cheek. "I love you, Cameron Blanche."

They continued with idle chatter. She hadn't heard from Ian, so they assumed things were well on the farm.

"Actually," she said, "I can see a truck down there on Binya now. It appears to be parked along the fence line near the creek."

"Is it a white Toyota?"

"Give me a break, Cam, it's a long way away. I can see it's not white—more of a blue colour."

"I think Gary's truck is light blue, I saw him drive off from Grandma's wake. That's a good sign—Gary is working on a Saturday."

"I love what you did for Gary."

"He did it for himself. He'll be fine."

"I love you, Cameron."

"Any developments on the investigation?" he asked, nervously.

"No, without you, it seems to go nowhere. In fact, I am feeling I know less now than when we did the re-enactment. I'm thinking more about the theory that they drowned in the creek with some flash flooding. But where are their bikes, and where are their bodies?"

The piano case. His palms were sweaty again—beads of sweat formed on his head and back of his neck. *Honesty. Be honest.* He went to tell her but stopped himself. She knows about the piano case. As for the rest, too much conjecture and no proof. Major Juma's words rang through his mind: there was no evidence to convict your grandfather. No, he would wait.

"You there?" she asked.

He jolted back into focus, "Sorry, just distracted. I don't know how long it might be before I'm back. If you come across anything let me know."

"I thought about chatting with Aunt Agnes again. She really is the only person with any link back to them."

"I don't see the value, myself. I can't see anything else she may be able to share."

"Yeah, you're probably right. I'll think about it."

"But Aunt Agnes would enjoy a visit anyway."

Her voice went soft and low, "Where do you want to meet when you come back? My desk or Great-Grandma's room?"

Sidney is going to love this part.

"I'll take both."

"And what do you want?" she asked.

"All of last time and double," he replied. "Oh, Jacqui, why had I not seen you before?"

"Because this Ronnie guy you speak about was in the way and you had to grow up, I suspect." Then she added, "I love you. Got to go."

He felt a sense of relief and a longing to be back with Jacqui.

Soon after, he got a text from an unlisted number. As he recalled, you couldn't have an unlisted number in Dubai.

Taxi booked. 11 am. Irish Village.

Good on you, Sidney. His beer sat waiting for him when he got face-to-face with James Joyce. He could only guess that Mr Abdullah and Major Juma were not aware of the understanding Sidney and he were forming.

When he arrived home that night, Ronnie felt a sense of calm. Stepping onto his verandah, something he rarely did when the temperature was 42°C, according to his phone. He cast his eyes over at Babki Towers, reflecting on how the simple observation of light patterns could have led him into the situation he now found himself. Lights in the unit directly across from him would go off precisely at 9.28 pm, except Saturdays. On that night, they went off at midnight, and on Tuesdays, they remained on all night.

Surveying the facade, he had noted a repeating sequence: two floors with lights on, followed by two floors where there were no lights at all, then another two floors with all lights on. The same pattern repeated every night until 10 pm, after which the lights turned off one by one, three minutes apart. In the middle apartments, lights were on every Friday night. Patterns would change periodically. Some apartments would be in permanent state of darkness for a week or more at a time. *Vacant*, he assumed. Now he knew nobody lived behind any of the lights, *or so they say.*

The ground floor had shops, a convenience store on one side and a dry cleaner on the other, both of which he visited regularly. More shops operated inside the glass doors, but he had never been inside to explore. A steady flow of people appeared to and fro through the front doors every day. He could only accept the police's claim that the apartments were vacant.

CHAPTER THIRTEEN

No more contact with the Lebedevs for over a week. That disappointed Ronnie given his quick encounter with Alex. However, he accepted that it wasn't unusual, as they sometimes went weeks without contact. Ronnie realised he needed to make things happen quicker.

He updated Annand on the lack of contact and shared his concern that just waiting for a chance meeting could take a long time. Most of his interactions had been spontaneous. Invitations to events, were often verbal invites offered at one of those spontaneous meetings. He had never instigated the contact. To do so now may make them suspicious.

Ronnie devised a new plan. He asked Annand to organise a work meeting for the Lebedevs to attend. The meeting would not involve Ronnie. Surely that would not be suspicious because they were frequently there for meetings. Ronnie advised Annand to simply leave the rest to him.

Annand did his job well and scheduled a meeting that didn't appear to anyone to be out of the ordinary. Even the finance team doing the meeting weren't aware it had been staged. A few minutes before they were due to finish, Ronnie, rather clumsily, entered the room with an arm full of folders, balancing a cup of coffee, as if expecting the room to be vacant. Acting surprised, he apologized for an apparent scheduling conflict in the room bookings. Ronnie placed the folders on a bench at the head of the room, excused himself and indicated he would wait outside for the meeting to finish. No hurry.

Once the meeting concluded, the door opened and Ronnie re-entered, greeting Alex and Matvei, whilst the other finance officers departed. Ronnie steered the conversation into social chatter, suggesting it would be great to catch up sooner than later. Matvei stated that they had a meeting in the Burj Khalifa on Thursday and suggested they meet for drinks immediately following, at the At.Mosphere, the highest restaurant and lounge in the world on the 122nd floor of the Burj Khalifa. Ronnie's plan had succeeded, impressing himself with his skills of manipulation. Alex and Matvei excused themselves, leaving Ronnie to start his online meeting. He sat in the meeting room, alone, enjoying his coffee.

On Thursday evening, they met as planned at the At.Mosphere bar. It was a very enjoyable night; Alex and Matvei were chatty, participating in conversation across a wide range of subjects including football and tennis. Ronnie promised to take them to an upcoming cricket match at the stadium, featuring Australia. They were enjoying themselves so much they stayed for dinner at the At.Mosphere restaurant. Ronnie didn't resist sharing in a dinner well beyond the $1,000 AUD.

During the dinner, Ronnie suggested they go for a desert safari on the weekend. Alex and Matvei declined, declaring they were celebrating their father's birthday on Saturday with a cruise in their private yacht around the World Islands. Ronnie drooled, expressing his disappointment that he had never seen the World Islands.

"Would you like to join us?" Alex asked, sparking an immediate reaction from Matvei.

Alex and Matvei spoke between themselves in Russian, before Alex turned to Ronnie.

"Dad doesn't like visitors much. He doesn't speak much English. He likes to keep very much to himself."

"But, hey, the yacht's big," Matvei interjected with a grin. "Plenty of space and if things get uncomfortable, we can always lock you in the cooler or toss you overboard."

Both boys laughed. Ronnie broke into a sweat knowing that is exactly what they would do with him if they knew his reason to be there.

"Don't worry," Alex said. "There will be some others on board. We're tired of just partying with Pappa. We need some life. And I think he'll like you."

On the way home, Ronnie updated Sidney. When he arrived home very late that night, he found Mr Abdullah waiting in his apartment. Mr Abdullah complimented Ronnie on his efforts— first in arranging the meeting, then securing the invitation to the yacht. Mr Abdullah explained that their intelligence indicated that no business appeared to be conducted on the yacht. It rarely moved from the wharf, despite being maintained by a full-time staff. Getting into the villa remained the goal; however, becoming acquainted with the father, Adrik Lebedev, increased the likelihood of that significantly.

The surveillance capacity of the Dubai Police continued to impress Ronnie. He hoped their protection skills were equally as impressive. Ronnie went to the kitchen and made two coffees in his Barista Plus. Returning, he found Mr Abdullah standing at the window.

Gazing over at Babki Towers, Ronnie observed, "I'm impressed you could deduce money laundering out of a pattern of lights. I've been observing the building ever since our first meeting. Other than the lights, it seems to be a pretty normal high-rise. Cars going in and out, people going in and out. I can't believe no one is living there."

Mr Abdullah stared at the building for a while before responding, "Using apartment buildings to cleanse money is not new. What changes is how the trail is disguised. Sometimes, it's just a vacant building. But not all vacant buildings are being used for that purpose. Buying a vacant building, owning it for a while, and later selling it to make a capital investment, is a legitimate transaction." Mr Abdullah shrugged his shoulders.

"Sometimes, a building that is being used for money laundering is the neighbourhoods' worst-kept secret. But most times, they will go to great lengths to disguise it. First, bonds from fictitious tenants are collected in cash payments."

"But what about ID?" Ronnie asked.

Mr Abdullah brushed the question away with a dismissive wave. "There are ways around that. In terms of money laundering, it's about separation. Making sure the left hand is not connected to the right hand—immigration on one side, accounts on the other. And the key is ensuring that money flows through multiple companies; so, by the time it reaches the person receiving it, any connection to fake tenants is untraceable.

"Now, we are shutting down the amateurs very quickly. A Band-Aid doesn't cover everything. But when you get to more sophisticated operations, it becomes more difficult.

"Things like these lights are simple covers these criminals use to try and hide what's going on. Varying the lights simply gives the illusion of occupancy.

"Then, you make the place appear busy. Shops on the ground floor. Always people coming in and out. Babki Towers has tenants on the first few floors. Those tenants may be suspicious about the rest of the building if they realise its empty, but there is often something that pressures them not to see it—cheap rent, employment with the company, that sort of thing. Babki Towers underground car park is rented out to surrounding places and businesses that don't have car parks, so cars are always coming and going. People can only exit the car park through the ground floor foyer, so there is the appearance of heavy pedestrian traffic.

"Dubai is a place where people don't want to get involved. They choose not to see what they don't want to see. You won't find anyone who would have a suspicion about Babki Towers, except maybe the handful of tenants and the shop owners, who, if you check, would be getting a very good deal. What do you Aussies say, a good wicket?" Mr Abdullah asked with a grin.

"Of course," he continued, "this is only the start of the process to clean money. Fake tenants pay in cash—illegal money of course—that is then properly receipted and banked. To lessen the potential of tracking, that money may pass through a few companies. Some of them are legitimate, registered companies but are used for this processing. This removes direct links between the fake tenant and final recipient of the money. Recipients receive money in a legitimate cheque or transaction. There are common ways to move money, like repayment of deposits that were received in cash from fictitious tenants. Then, there are false invoices for what appears to be legitimate work, such as repairs and maintenance.

"Actually, we don't see many like Babki Towers anymore, where it is basically the whole building being used. Many of the criminals these days will use vacant rooms in a building, say 25 percent, which can be much more easily disguised, except for the interfering tenant who wants to know why they never see their neighbours," Mr Abdullah concluded.

Ronnie found the explanation fascinating. It surprised him how complex, yet simple, the process could be. Ronnie appreciated the explanation—it may well help him understand variances in the spreadsheets he may be analyzing.

When Mr Abdullah left, Ronnie said out loud, "Apologies up front, Sidney, but you might have to close your eyes. I've always slept naked. If you're going to move in, you'll have to get used to it. I'm tired of wearing pyjamas just for you."

Ronnie received instructions from Alex to arrive at the Dubai International Marine Club by 9.45 am on Saturday morning. Arriving well before, he nervously waited by the marina's edge until Matvei picked him up in his Porsche.

"Hey, Matey," Ronnie greeted, as he dropped into the low bucket seat.

"Gidday, Aussie," Matvei replied in his broad Russian accent.

As soon as all were on board, the yacht began pulling away from the jetty. Adrik and Alex were the last to arrive. The overwhelming size of the yacht left Ronnie in awe. He struggled not to appear like a kid entering a theme park for the first time. He had driven past the marina many times and admired the yachts; however, being on board, he found this one bigger and whiter than he had ever imagined. Everything gleamed white, including the white leather lounges. Ronnie counted about fifteen people on board, not counting staff, though it was difficult to count because they were scattered across three above-deck levels, and he had no idea if people were below deck.

Aside from Adrik, Aleksander and Matvei, there were six other Russians—four men and two women on board. Noting a definite resemblance, he assumed they were extended family. Ronnie recognised two from the Dubai World Cup event. Two Russian gentlemen, about Adrik's age, leant against the ship's rail drinking Ryumka, a high-class Estonian vodka. Ronnie recalled being introduced to Ryumka by Alex and Matvei at one of his early encounters, resulting in a hangover that lasted a week. The two men stayed close to Adrik throughout the cruise. Everyone Ronnie could see appeared Russian, making him feeling very isolated.

As the yacht made its way out of port, the formalities began on the aft deck. Alex introduced Ronnie to his father. Amongst the Russian dialogue, Ronnie could make out the words, "Aussie," "accountant" and "football." At what seemed the right moment, Ronnie extended his hand to shake Adrik's hand. Adrik took it and gave him a very firm handshake.

"Aussie," Adrik said with a big grin, "you know Tim Cahill?"

Ronnie didn't follow football, or soccer as he knew it, but knew of Tim Cahill. His stepfather had once met him at a business fundraiser.

"My dad has met him. A great player. Great head ball," Ronnie surprised himself with that response off the top of his head.

Adrik's eyes lit up. "Da da da!" he exclaimed, turning to Alex and speaking in Russian.

"He says you're a friend of Tim Cahill's," Alex said, laughing, loudly.

Ronnie went pale. "No, no, tell him no. My stepfather only met him once, tell him," Ronnie pleaded.

Alex laughed harder. "Don't worry. That's close enough."

Ronnie already wanted to jump overboard.

"You play, you play?" Adrik asked, pointing at Ronnie.

"Only at school. Long time ago," Ronnie replied.

"He teach at school," Adrik said to Alex, who had tears of laughter rolling down his cheeks. Turning back to Ronnie, Adrik added, "Teach my boys."

Alex laughed even more. Ronnie turned pale as the colour drained from his face but laughed as well because it seemed like the right thing to do.

Adrik grabbed Ronnie's hand again and shook it vigorously. "Wine, wine," he said, turning to the waiter and pointing at Ronnie.

Alex politely led Ronnie away and the introductions moved on to the next guest.

"Aussie man. You're a hit. He has never reacted like that to a guest before. Better brush up on your football history," Alex teased.

Ronnie appeared pale and sweaty. He had never been to a football match. Ronnie, Alex and Matvei moved upstairs to the next deck. Adrik stayed on the main deck. Later, they returned to the main deck for lunch. The furniture had been rearranged and Adrik now sat at the head of a big square table large enough for all guests. The two other older Russians were sat on either side of Adrik with Alex and Matvei next to them. As they entered, Adrik waved to Ronnie, pointing to the chair next to Alex, on Adrik's right.

"Aussie mate, you are getting VIP treatment," Alex exclaimed.

The rest of the cruise went smoothly and quietly for Ronnie. Fortunately, Adrik spent his afternoon reminiscing in Russian with his old friends, drinking premium Estonian vodka. Ronnie had joined Alex and Matvei on the upper deck. Returning to the main deck to use the bathroom, Ronnie noticed the absence of Adrik. He had gone to the master bedroom for a sleep and would not be seen again for the entire cruise.

By late afternoon, the yacht had moored at the wharf and Ronnie bid his farewell, thanking Alex and Matvei for a very enjoyable day. They expressed their pleasure in having Ronnie join them and passed on that their father had expressed a desire to meet with him again. Apparently, a highly unusual request. Ronnie, who could not recognise Tim Cahill in a line-up, had been a smash hit.

Ronnie would not have to wait long for a follow-up visit. Due to his lack of interest in football, Ronnie didn't know that UAE and Qatar were playing a friendly match in Dubai the following weekend. Adrik had instructed Alex and Matvei to "Bring that Australian man." When Alex called to invite Ronnie, he laughed, advising Ronnie "Brush up on your football lingo."

During the week, Ronnie contacted Ian, who gave him a good report on the farm. Gary had settled in very well and was doing a great job, showing a lot of enthusiasm. Young Billy had the highest praise for him; "He's at work at sunrise and goes home with the setting sun," he reported. Sheep inspections were up to date, and fence lines were inspected and repaired. Gary had even sought Ian's permission to break up some of the mobs, based on their condition, to ensure they were getting the greatest nourishment. Young Billy reported he simply had nothing to do, having to convince Gary to let him milk the few cows.

Realising he had not organised a pay for Gary, Ronnie instructed Ian to find out the going rate, add 20 percent and speak with Jacqui about how to get that from the farm's account.

Ronnie also spoke with his mum, who shared the family updates. She and Paul were in a good space and Heidi's pregnancy had progressed well as she approached eight months. His mum asked Ronnie what his future plans were. He told her that he hadn't made up his mind yet but didn't intend to stay in Dubai forever though he hadn't set any time frames, yet.

Despite no immediate plans to return, after every phone call with Jacqui, he longed to be back. He thought of Jacqui every day. In her last phone call, she recounted their first moment after being caught in the storm, standing in the hallway in her wet T-shirt, followed by a night of the most sensual lovemaking. Ronnie felt hot and excited and longed for Jacqui to be beside him.

Ronnie had always kept his body clean shaven. No passionate reason other than it made him feel cleaner. Given the hectic nature of the last few weeks, he had neglected his standard routine of personal hygiene. Standing in front of the mirror, he concluded that he didn't like the current appearance of his body. On impulse, he armed himself with shaving cream, a shaver and mug of hot water and went about removing the unwanted body hair, particularly from his pubic area. It immediately felt clean and soft. He inspected his effort in the mirror, and he was well-satisfied. Only after he finished, he remembered the cameras. "Sorry, Sidney," he said out loud, blushing with embarrassment.

Ronnie approached the upcoming football match with conflicting emotions. He felt excited about going to the match with Alex and Matvei but dreaded the expectations Adrik may have about his football knowledge. Realising this could be a major step to getting into the Lebedev sanctum, he set about improving his football knowledge. To prepare, he found a couple of past UAE games to watch online. He read about the healthy but strong rivalry between UAE and Qatar. Adrik supported the UAE. Ronnie found out they were the team in white and red—*that would be helpful.* Everything he read rated Ali Mabkhout Al-Hajeri UAE's top goal scorer and had played the most matches for the UAE. Khalid Eissa, the goalkeeper, seemed the easiest name to remember. He also found out that in the last three encounters between Australia and the UAE, they had drawn twice, but Australia had won their most recent encounter, 2–0. *Ouch—best avoid that.* He purchased an Australian jersey and was now good to go.

Alex informed Ronnie that a limousine van had been arranged to take the party to the game at The Sevens Stadium. A total of nine were going, some of whom he met on the yacht cruise, Ronnie assumed. Ronnie would be collected on the way. However, mid-afternoon, Ronnie received a call from Alex indicating a change of plans. His father wanted to go direct—no pick-ups on the way. He was a no-fuss man. He gave instructions for Ronnie to meet them at their villa.

"Not a problem," Ronnie responded, almost unable to contain his excitement. Alex texted him the address.

"Yes!" he screamed. "Did you get that, Sidney? I'm going to the villa. Stay close."

The Lebedev villa sat on the Dubai Palm, the world's largest man-made island, consisting of sixteen fronds in the shape of a palm tree, housing many millionaires' residential villas and apartments. Ronnie had booked a limousine rather than the standard taxi. He wanted to rise to the class of the moment. He found the fronds to be individually guarded, with a security gate positioned at the entrance of each frond. His limousine stopped at the security gate and a security officer approached seeking the villa number they were visiting. Ronnie provided his name and his National ID, when asked. The security guard returned to his office, made a phone call, and within a few seconds, the gate opened and the limousine moved forward.

He located the villa about halfway down on the right side. It was big, as expected, but others in the street were bigger. It appeared to be U-shaped with a central courtyard. A circular drive led to the entrance. As the limousine slowed to a stop, a concierge appeared, opening the door and ushering him up the few stairs to the main entrance.

If the villa had not impressed him from the outside, once inside, he was overwhelmed with the sheer opulence. The large hexagonal-shaped entrance foyer gleamed with white tiles and a towering LED light glass dome. The two stories above his head dazzled in a vibrant mix of colours. He guessed each floor to be five metres high. The skylight towered high above him. Grand double doors were on either side of the entrance, while twin curved staircases led to the second floor.

A second usher guided Ronnie through the foyer into a large open area. Beyond that, the rear of the residence offered a sweeping view of the palm canal. A stunning pool dominated the patio, where a small group of people had gathered. An usher motioned him forward to join his hosts.

Alex greeted him warmly and immediately led him to his father. Adrik's face lit up as Ronnie approached.

"Mr Aussie!" he greeted. "Come, sit, sit."

Ronnie sat in the seat offered to him, next to Adrik. Adrik spoke in Russian to the man sitting on the opposite side to Ronnie. He understood the words "Tim Cahill," but nothing else. Adrik seemed genuinely pleased to see him, pulling at his Australian jersey.

"Da da da," he said with a big grin.

Another waiter rushed to Ronnie's side with a glass of Estonian vodka, which he disliked but pretended otherwise. Adrik resumed his Russian conversation with the older man beside him and, for some time, Ronnie sat silently, taking in the villa.

From what he could see, the whole downstairs, except for

the doors in the entry foyer, appeared to be open space for entertainment. He could see the kitchen to the right. Numerous staff with food and drinks were entering and leaving from two swing doors—like a commercial restaurant kitchen—a door for entry and a door for exit. At the opposite end of the house, left of the entry hall, he could see part of what appeared to be a very large dining table. He could see a large deer head hung on the far wall with extraordinarily large antlers. *Must be a Russian thing*, he thought. An elevator connected to the top level, supplementing the stairs he saw near the entrance.

Soon, Alex began asking the group to make their way to the limousine van waiting to take them to the Dubai Sevens Stadium complex for the match.

The Lebedev's private box overflowed with alcohol and food. Ronnie felt free to be the Aussie wild boy, fitting of his reputation. Adrik, translated through Alex, asked Ronnie to name his favourite UAE player. "Ali Mabkhout Al-Hajeriu, of course," he swiftly replied.

With every goal the UAE saved, Ronnie gave an Aussie cheer, sparking a hearty response from Adrik. Unfortunately, the UAE went down by one goal in the ninety-third minute. The fact that you could lose a game in the ninety-third minute of a ninety-minute game baffled Ronnie. "Just stop the clock," he cried. "That's how it is done in rugby league." Those around him laughed.

Ronnie had a great night. Despite the loss, everyone enjoyed it and most importantly, Adrik had a smile on his face for most of the night, that is, until the whistle condemned the UAE to defeat. He had particularly enjoyed the antics of "the Aussie kid." Alex told Ronnie that he hadn't seen his father laugh so much in years.

They returned to the Lebedev villa close to midnight. Ronnie intended to head straight home, feeling he had done enough to open the door for a future visit. He ordered his limousine and asked to use the bathroom. Others were waiting to use the downstairs bathroom, so Alex directed him to another bathroom.

"Go up the stairs, turn left. Go down the hall and the toilet is on your left," Alex instructed.

Ronnie ventured up the stairs and turned left as instructed. He found the door to the first room on the left open and light on. He could see an ensuite behind a partially open door in the back corner of the room and genuinely assumed that to be the toilet he had been directed to by Alex. He entered, but within seconds, he realised he'd made a mistake. He stood in the middle of a very formal, officious office. *It could be Adrik's*, he thought, and most certainly knew he shouldn't be there.

He took a couple of steps forward. He could hear his breathing so loudly that he feared others may hear it also. A very large wooden desk dominated the room, the desktop was untidy and scattered with papers. He quickly scanned the room, his eyes darted wildly as he shuffled a few pages. He could feel the blood pounding through his ears. And then he saw it—an invoice with the "Babki" written boldly on the top. He gave an audible gasp. His hands were trembling.

He fumbled for his phone and quickly searched for the app that Major Juma had installed. His hands were trembling so much that he found it difficult to open the app and press the button to activate his camera. Panicking, he shuffled through some papers, clicking the button and trying with all his might to stop his hand from trembling. He had no time to read any of the papers—he just picked and clicked. A file surfaced under the invoices labelled "White Birch." Inside were more invoices titled "Babki." He kept taking photos as he flicked through papers at an increasingly frantic rate.

His heart stopped—he heard voices coming up the stairs. No time to get out. Indescribable panic. He dived into the toilet and locked the door. Sheer fear gripped him. *I'm going to shit myself.*

He quickly plunged for the toilet seconds before his bowel exploded. The voices were now in the room—he recognized the voices of Alex and Matvei.

He sat frozen in sheer terror. He heaved as if about to vomit. A thought struck him: the best defense would be offence. He flushed the toilet, making as much noise as he could, washed his hands and opened the door, ensuring to leave it open, walking out, eyes down, fastening his zipper.

"What the hell are you doing in here?" Alex demanded.

Ronnie jumped with fright, seemingly unaware of their presence. "Going to the toilet," Ronnie casually replied. Well, he hoped it sounded casual, "This is where you told me to go."

"No, I said go down the hall and the toilet was on the left."

"The door on the left was open, and I could see the toilet," Ronnie explained, gesturing emphatically, pointing from the door to the toilet. "So, I assumed this is where you meant. I could see the toilet." *If I don't sit soon, I'm going to faint.*

"The door was open?" Matvei interjected.

"Yeah, and all the lights were on. Sorry guys—I really needed to shit."

"The toilet is down the hall." Alex stated in a matter-of-fact tone.

"How the hell am I supposed to know that when you lit up this one?"

Alex and Matvei exchanged eye contact. Matvei walked past him, into the toilet, "Holy shit, Ronnie! What have you been eating? If you lit a match right now, we'd explode!"

Following a slight pause, both Alex and Matvei laughed. Ronnie laughed, but out of relief.

Ronnie saw his chance to build on his alibi.

"Sorry, guys. If I had to hold on another second, I would have shit in my pants," Ronnie said still feeling he could easily do that again at this very moment, if they needed proof.

"Miscommunication," Alex muttered. "This room is out of bounds."

"You should lock it then," Ronnie retorted.

"It always is," Matvei declared, glaring at Alex.

"Someone may have been in here while were away," Alex said, directed at Matvei.

"Or the old man forgot to shut it again," Matvei replied.

Seizing the opportunity, Ronnie glanced around the room as if for the very first time, feigning a newfound interest. "Hey, guys, this is a really neat office. Very grand and stately."

The dark, formal décor contrasted the downstairs styles. The furniture was ornate, beautiful timber. A large stag head hung on one wall, while a large portrait painting of a senior man hung on the opposite wall.

"Who is this guy?" Ronnie asked, pointing to the painting.

"He is our grandfather," Matvei replied, gazing at the painting. "Grigory Lebedev. He started this whole business with a lumber yard in Russia—then salt in Siberia."

Ronnie took the opportunity to take his phone from his pocket and quickly click a photo of the stag.

"Hey, hey, no photos, no photos," Matvei cried.

"Sorry, guys. I've never seen a stag that big," Ronnie said, immediately handing the phone to Matvei without hesitation.

Somewhat surprised by Ronnie's quick reaction, Matvei, took the phone and opened the picture gallery. Ronnie held his breath, knowing his life depended on this very moment and Major Juma's technology. Matvei opened the gallery revealing a blurry photo of the stag, testament to Ronnie's shaking hands. Matvei deleted it and the gallery immediately scrolled to the next picture. Ronnie exhaled when he saw a picture of the football match. Matvei continued scrolling.

"Hey, these are great," Matvei laughed. "Look at the old man! I've never seen him so happy."

"Show me," Alex said, and for the next few minutes, Matvei focused on reviewing the pictures with Alex.

Ronnie quietly exhaled, then inhaled. He could breathe again. Tension in the room dissipated with each photo. By the time they got to photos of the yacht cruise, all three were reminiscing two fun trips.

Alex brought the focus back to the room, "Come on, guys, we got to get out of here. The old man would kill us all if he found us here."

As they walked down the stairs, Ronnie overheard Alex whisper to Matvei that they must make sure Pappa shuts the door every time he leaves. "This is the third time this week we found it open."

Ronnie's nerves continued to calm. He impressed himself with his escape skills.

Downstairs, they found Adrik still in a good mood. Matvei took Ronnie's phone and showed his father some of the photos of the football match. Adrik's eyes were bright with enjoyment and face alight with a smile. Ronnie's eyes never left the phone as it circulated the room. He wouldn't feel safe until he cleared the villa. His clothes were wet through with sweat. He watched as his phone continued to be shared for all to see the photos. Only he knew they were holding the very thing that would condemn them all to prison.

He wanted to leave—now. He made eye contact with the doorman, who gave the slight nod indicating his car had arrived. The doorman opened the door, and after what felt like an eternity, Ronnie cocooned himself in the limousine and headed home.

I'm breathing again, or still. Thank God.

"Sidney. I need to see them now."

It was after 1 am when he opened the door of his apartment, finding Mr Abdullah, Major Juma and Mr Donald from Interpol waiting. Ronnie's eyes were widely dilated, and he felt sweaty and anxious. Major Juma met him at the door and put a comforting arm around his shoulder.

"Come, Mr Ronnie, you can settle now. You're safe," Mr Abdullah said. "Tell me, are you hurt in anyway?"

Ronnie shook his head.

"Are they following you or suspecting anything?"

"No, it's all cool," Ronnie replied, focusing on Major Juma. "You would be pleased with me. I think I passed my first spy test."

"We've seen your photos, and we have the team already analyzing them. From what we see, they are potentially significant pieces of evidence. We need you to take us through all the events from your first arrival at the villa. Don't leave anything out," Mr Abdullah said as he pulled the drapes closed. "It's our turn to study the numbers. But first, make this machine of yours make four coffees."

Ronnie took them slowly through all the events, in detail, trying not to leave anything out. He described how he innocently ended up in the room, was discovered and how he defused their initial suspicions, convincing them he had inadvertently stumbled into the room. They were all confident that Ronnie had maintained his cover.

Major Juma gave him a slap on his back. "You are most definitely going to work for me after this," he said with a big welcoming smile.

Mr Abdullah maintained a more formal demeanour. "It is a remarkable story, Mr Ronnie. You demonstrated an exceptional ability to cover your presence and divert their suspicions. It is somewhat unfortunate for you that the story you have just shared will never be retold. It never happened. If those of us present were ever to hear this story, we would deny that we ever heard it. But, before it is erased from our memory, I commend you for a remarkable effort.

"What you have uncovered, unfortunately, is not evidence, or not in the true meaning of the word. It is proof to us that the evidence exists and where we can find it. Before that, we need to determine if it is worth discovering. Whilst it seems critical, we must be sure that our official discovery of it does not jeopardise us losing something more critical.

"Our investigators are telling me there are many invoices detailing names and apartments in Babki Towers. There is a list of names with passport numbers and National ID numbers. We are still determining if they are real or fake. We suspect the latter. There are certainly receipts for payments of rents and deposits in cash.

"We see invoices and receipts to a company called 'White Birch.' What else did you see about White Birch?" Mr Abdullah asked.

"I can tell you I didn't read anything. I just flicked and clicked," Ronnie explained. "But I do recall that one folder I opened had 'White Birch' written on the front. I don't know if the photos showed it but there were lots of folders on the desk and I think there were boxes, like file boxes, on the floor."

"Perfect," Mr Abdullah said. "Did you see anything about Rendezvous?"

"Not that I recall," Ronnie admitted. "But I literally only had seconds. I didn't go through everything on the desk."

"What you have given us is invaluable. You have done exceptionally well. Did you see any security in the room like cameras?" Major Juma asked.

Ronnie sat upright, suddenly alarmed. "I didn't look, I don't know."

"Don't be alarmed," Major Juma reassured him. "I would suspect not. I am sure there is a lot that happens in that room that they wouldn't want recorded. But, we do implore you to be extra vigilant over the next few days and be alert to any changes in behaviour from any of the Lebedevs. We have achieved the purpose of the mission. We have confirmed a link between the Lebedevs, Babki Towers and a third party, White Birch, which we had not heard of before."

Mr Donald from Interpol had been listening all night and taking copious notes, "If I remember correctly, the white birch tree is sacred in Russia—it's a national symbol, as I recall."

"Then it's definitely a piece of this jigsaw. Let's go and do our homework," concluded Mr Abdullah. "Mr Ronnie, maintain normal contact with the Lebedevs and let us know anything you hear. I also want to find out who these two older men are with Adrik. We've got your photos from the yacht and the football match. We also have our own. Stay in touch."

Ronnie glanced at the clock—3.20 am. He had survived the scariest day of his life. A story he would never be able to tell a soul, not even Jacqui.

CHAPTER FOURTEEN

For the next three weeks, things returned to normal for Ronnie, or as normal as his life could be. He heard nothing from Mr Abdullah or his colleagues. He became so accustomed to the surveillance and protection that he rarely gave it a second thought. He had certainly lost any concern for what Sidney saw or heard. There had been no reason to alert Sidney to anything. His beer and Coke ritual at the Irish Village continued, along with the occasional wine at the Eclipse. Every time he entered his apartment, he announced his arrival with, "Sidney, I'm home."

He socialised with the Lebedev brothers on a couple of occasions. Ronnie thought it was important that he keep that as normal as possible. Alex or Matvei gave no indication they were suspicious of Ronnie's activities in Adrik's office. On the contrary, Ronnie felt that they were growing closer. They were telling Ronnie every time they met that their father always asked about "the Aussie" and telling them to bring him over again. Ronnie always responded with "love to," even though he never wanted to set foot in the villa again.

Ronnie felt guilty for enjoying their friendship while actively assisting in their likely arrests. He didn't like being dishonest. He hadn't been honest about many things. He thought of his grandfather and the secrets he kept. He thought of what he had not told Jacqui.

He knew the importance of maintaining his contact with Alex and Matvei. Mr Abdullah and Major Juma wanted that. It not only maintained his cover, but he could continue to observe any change in behaviour from the Lebedev family that could indicate they were becoming aware of the police investigation or lead to the discovery of fresh evidence.

Work returned to a new norm—some new accounts, not all of them forensic analysis. He and a small team were assigned to support a start-up company developing Middle East alternate energy options, including wind and solar. They had an exciting proposal, still in its infancy, to turn the Palm Jebel Ali, an undeveloped Palm that dwarfed Palm Jumeirah, into a huge wind and solar farm.

Ronnie found the financial modelling exciting. There were long-term employment opportunities to be based in Dubai to support of the project, and that interested Ronnie.

But his social life didn't fuel a desire to stay. He had attended a few functions with his friends from work, the same group who had given him the nickname Ronnie. He enjoyed their company but not with the same enthusiasm as before. The bright, loud, alcoholic-fuelled nightlife of the club scene lacked the appeal it had a few months ago. A night at the Town & Country Club in Harden had a very different appeal.

His thoughts were increasingly drawn back to Jacqui and Ian. He felt a depth in those relationships that he didn't feel with his loud drunken Dubai friends. The stag head he never saw in Adrik's office, which he had never been in, kept reappearing in his mind, a reminder of where he didn't want to be. Conversely, every time he got an update on the farm, he felt more excited. He had taken up reading about the wool industry. Ian told him that Gary was keen to talk more about stock breeding and artificial insemination.

"Gary has a great head for sheep. He's a real asset. I would never have guessed it from my memory of him at school," Ian reported. Gary wanted to talk about other breeds. Like many Australian sheep farms, Binya had been a generational Merino farm. Gary had a keen desire to branch into other breeds such as Corriedale and Polwarth and wanted to undertake further research of the French Merino, the Rambouillet. Cameron, not Ronnie, would follow up Ian's calls with surfing the internet to explore Gary's ideas, always leaving him with a desire to explore further and deeper. There was a science and complexity to the wool industry that he had never known about.

Ian had another concert coming up, this time in Cootamundra. Apparently, the word had spread about his last concert, and he was in demand. He had two shows locked in at the Harden Town & Country Club, and the first was already sold out. Ian informed Cameron that the Harden Show Society wanted Ian, Peta and Kurt to play an outdoor concert on show night at the next annual town show, early in the new year. Ian had suggested that they could make room on the stage for Cameron to join them. Cameron didn't say no.

Every few days, Ronnie spoke with Jacqui. She had been doing a lot more legal work because her father had been unwell, suffering several severe headaches a week. On one occasion, the ambulance transported him to Canberra. Jacqui had a return visit to Aunt Agnes and shared with Ronnie everything Aunt Agnes had told her. She repeated much of the information she shared on the first visit. Aunt Agnes had shed further insights into the profound impact of the disappearance on Jacqui's grandfather and grandmother and how the loss of two daughters had shattered and permanently changed their lives. Both had personally held themselves responsible. Cecil regularly went to church, seeking forgiveness for failing as a father. Jacqui's grandmother had rarely left the farm after the disappearance and would always set the dinner table for five. Jacqui said her mother had never told her that.

Aunt Agnes had also spoken about the impact on Cameron's grandfather, William, and the friendship between him and Cecil, Jacqui's grandfather. Two best mates and neither recovered. She lamented once again about the death of both being so close together. Aunt Agnes told how Cameron's grandfather would often visit Jacqui's grandfather and just sit. When Cecil was in a Sydney hospital with a failing heart, just prior to his death, Cameron's grandfather drove all the way from Harden to Sydney to see him.

Jacqui passed on that Scott, the minister, had been asking after him and sent his regards. He missed Scott, hoping to build their relationship in the future.

Ronnie welcomed the long conversations with Jacqui; however, after each new conversation, the guilt grew about the information he had not yet shared. He was tempted many times to share his discovery of the piano box, but every time he withdrew, convincing himself that what he had found had not proven his grandfather's involvement in their disappearance.

Jacqui had never inquired anymore about Ronnie. Cameron liked that.

Mum and Paul were doing fine. Heidi had a healthy baby girl—another unlikely sheep farmer.

So, whilst he felt comfortable with life in Dubai, his thoughts of being with Jacqui were foremost in his mind. He didn't know when he would be allowed to leave Dubai, let alone when he would actually do it. He wasn't even sure if it would be a return-trip or a one-way trip.

On a Thursday afternoon, everything changed. Ronnie arrived home from work to find a welcoming committee waiting for him: Mr Abdullah, Major Juma, Mr Donald from Interpol and Ronnie's supervisor, Annand. Only then did he realise that he hadn't seen Annand in the office that day.

Mr Abdullah began with a lengthy description of the development, once again praising Ronnie's skills. *I'm getting tired of that message.* By now, Ronnie knew it was an Arabic tendency to summarise every time. Mr Abdullah confirmed that the photographs Ronnie had taken of the Babki invoices linked the money laundering operations to the Lebedevs. But more significantly, the identification of the company known as White Birch had expanded this into a far greater case and had cracked open something far larger than the Lebedev's affairs—a significant link exposing a far greater network. White Birch was not a Lebedev company, but rather, a separate company owned by Sergei Volkov. Mr Abdullah identified Volkov as one of the older men that Ronnie had met on the yacht and at the football match.

Major Juma, sitting beside Ronnie, put his arm over his shoulder and vigorously shook his hand.

"You have done what everyone else has not been able to do!" exclaimed Major Juma.

Mr Abdullah's sharp glance at Major Juma suggested he didn't appreciate the interruption and resumed control of the meeting.

"Which brings us to why we are here now," Mr Abdullah continued. "Dubai Police and Interpol have determined that we need to act now and with haste. There are other aspects of an international nature that, whilst connected, we are not at liberty to go into with you. But we do need to move to our next step and quickly. Our intelligence has found that some key players are about to leave Dubai."

"So, what's the next step?" Ronnie asked, hoping that the Lebedevs may soon be off UAE shores.

"Arrests," Mr Abdullah replied quietly.

"Great," Ronnie responded with relief. "I just want to get on with normal life. I'm happy to not see them ever again."

The four men exchanged glances and focused back on Mr Abdullah.

Mr Abdullah turned and locked eyes with Ronnie. "It's not going to be as simple as that."

"Yes, it is," Ronnie insisted. "Just go and nab them and I'll get on with my life and never look at lights again. I promise to tell nobody."

"Mr Ronnie," Mr Abdullah said solemnly, ignoring Ronnie's response. "There is an opinion, not only shared by us, but by many in the organisations we represent, that an arrest will put you in considerable danger. Arrests will upset some very influential Russians."

"They don't suspect me, do they?"

A long pause followed, that Ronnie heard as a thundering silence.

"That may change after the arrests have been made," Mr Abdullah admitted.

"But why? They don't know about any of my involvement, right?"

Mr Donald spoke for the first time, "Because they are Russians. You must think like a Russian. They have been running a very successful money laundering business for some time. Suddenly, they are all sitting in a prison with plenty of time to think. Who lives next to Babki Towers? Who works in the accounting company they use? Who has been inside the very secret Lebedev villa? And who was found in the office of that villa? Who is the one outside person to socialise with Mr Adrik and Mr Sergei? And, perhaps most importantly, who amongst all those people is not Russian?"

Ronnie fell back in his chair, holding his head in his hands, pulling at his hair. A rage of anger could be heard in Ronnie's voice, "You guys lied to me! You said I would be safe and now you're telling me I'm a dead duck. Well, thank you very much."

He threw his head back on the chair, staring at the ceiling, arms laying by his side, palms open—a posture of capitulation.

A tense silence filled the room for what felt like minutes before Mr Abdullah quietly continued, "Mr Ronnie, you are safe. Our plan will keep you safe. You will never give evidence as a witness. None of the photos you took will ever be used. There is simply no need. We intend to retrieve the documents as part of the raid, ah, the arrest."

"It doesn't sound safe to me. Again, am I safe or not?"

Ronnie asked, pointing to Mr Donald. "Go on, answer his question. Doesn't sound safe to me."

All eyes focused on Mr Abdullah.

"We have a plan to protect your innocence," Mr Abdullah said. "But it will involve your participation. If we follow that plan, you will be safe."

"Participation?" Ronnie responded. "You've had my participation. Who else has stuck their neck out throughout all this?"

Another moment's silence. Beads of sweat ran down his neck. His eyes were red, and his pupils were dilated. His temples were throbbing, he could count his heartbeats.

"Listen carefully to all of what I am about to say. I need you to concentrate," Mr Abdullah continued. "Our intelligence tells us there is a dinner on Saturday night at the Lebedev villa to which you have been invited—"

"I haven't told them I'm definitely coming yet," Ronnie interjected. "I'm a bit over the Lebedevs and I hate soccer."

He hadn't replied to the Lebedev's text invite yet but had reluctantly accepted that he would.

"Let me finish," Mr Abdullah insisted. "On Saturday, you will be at the function at the Lebedev villa. Mr Sergei will also be in attendance, according to our intelligence. The villa will be raided by Dubai Police. All those present will be arrested, including you. You will be taken to prison and interrogated. You will be held in a different part of the prison and appropriately cared for. You will be questioned as a suspect. The Lebedevs and all his Russian family and friends will be asked to detail your involvement.

"This is all being done for a reason. The Russians will see you arrested as a suspect. They will be interrogated about your involvement. It will be the Russians who declare your innocence. That declaration will come from them, ensuring your safety."

"How do you know that for sure?" asked Ronnie. "They'll throw me under the bus."

Mr Simon interjected, "We are driving the bus, Mr Ronnie. Russians don't fabricate stories—they deny or hide their actions. Or they arrogantly demand they have the right to do what they have done. They have no shame. There is nothing in the evidence that can be used to link you to their elaborate schemes. They gain nothing by accusing you. You have never worked for Mr Sergei. You don't even know what Mr Sergei does. You have never done the Lebedev's accounting. The very nature of the raid is that it is so unexpected that there is no time to plant any fabricated evidence. But most importantly, there is no advantage for them in trying to implicate you.

"The one thing we do need to do is to make it obvious to the Russians that you were not involved in any way with uncovering this criminal network. You will never be suspected."

"Are you confident this will work?" Ronnie asked, staring Mr Abdullah directly in the eyes.

"Mr Ronnie, I have every confidence in you. More to the point, I will go to any length to protect you and yes, this will permanently sever you from them, I am most sure. But, it will also sever you from us, which is important for your safety, and that saddens me deeply."

Ronnie's eyes locked with Mr Abdullah's. He glanced at Major Juma. He had confidence and faith in both of them.

"So, what happens after all that?" Ronnie asked, turning back to Mr Donald.

"You will be held for a few days. There will be interrogations, ahh, interviews. The Russians will see that you are being dealt with as a prisoner under investigation. It will be determined that you are innocent and released to the Australian Embassy, who will see to your safe return to Australia."

"So, I'm being kicked out of Dubai?"

"Not kicked out, Mr Ronnie; you're going home, where it is safe," Mr Abdullah responded.

They sat in silence as Ronnie contemplated what he would have to go through.

"So, when does this happen?" asked Ronnie.

"Saturday night, as I said before, at the function you are invited to," Mr Abdullah replied.

"Yes, Mr Ronnie, tomorrow will be your last full free day in Dubai. And that comes with one very big warning. No good-byes. Sunday and beyond are just normal days in your diary waiting to happen," advised Mr Abdullah.

After a pause, Ronnie said, "I don't know if I can do this."

"I don't know anyone I would have more confidence in doing this than you," Mr Abdullah said. "Skilled secret service officers would struggle to pull off your escape from the Lebedev office. Furthermore, these arrests will change money launder-ing around the world for a long time. You are changing history. This case will be talked about and used as a case study in law schools and law enforcement agencies. With one sad fact—you will not be acknowledged in any of it."

The words didn't sit lightly with Ronnie. He had seen the numbers. He had done his job, even unwittingly, in part. But his mind struggled to comprehend what it all meant. *I'm going to spend time in a jail cell.*

"Will I be safe in prison? I hear it's a pretty rough place. I don't want to lose my anal virginity. There is only so far I am prepared to go for this charade."

Major Juma gave a reassuring smile, "Where you are going is a prison by name, but you will be comfortable and protected. I doubt you will see anyone else at all."

"So, for the rest of my life, I'll be flagged as a criminal?"

"Absolutely not," Mr Donald interjected. "There are many international standards and codes that protect you. None of this will appear on any record and you will be well-compensated, the details of which will be provided in due course."

Mr Abdullah stressed, "No communication whatsoever. Complete silence. Please, no Australian phone calls. But do text the Lebedevs and confirm you are coming."

The four men left. Ronnie felt numb. He scanned what had been his home for a couple of years. He had loved his time here, but it no longer felt like home.

"Sidney, you know where. Time for my last drink with James Joyce."

The Irish Village buzzed with a larger-than-normal crowd, but his favourite table sat vacant awaiting his arrival—he was very relieved to find a beer waiting for him. *Good on you, Sidney.* For the first time, Ronnie pondered how this surveillance worked. How and by whom were the drinks being purchased? He paid for most of them, but on some occasions, the drinks simply appeared. Did the bartenders know the secret service agents? He concluded that he didn't know, and he had no desire to find out. He knew that he intended to enjoy every last bit of it.

A waiter passed by, and Ronnie ordered another drink. It arrived shortly after.

"Thanks, mate, much appreciated," Ronnie said.

"Are your mates coming back?" asked the waiter.

"Sorry, um, what do you mean my mates?"

"The guys that got us to clear the table. Somehow, they coerced that couple out there to move," he said, pointing to a table outside. "They had sat here to avoid the 40°C outside sauna. I don't know how they coerced them to move. I think they are paying for all their drinks."

Sidney, you work in mysterious ways.

After a couple of beers, he decided he wanted somewhere quieter, and so he decided to leave, but not before going to the table the waiter had pointed to, explaining to the couple that his friends had not joined him and they could have the table back.

He bid a final farewell to James Joyce.

Ronnie found the Eclipse Bar busier than normal, but fortunately, there was one free table between two occupied tables against the window.

Ronnie gathered that the three women at the table behind him were Australian teachers from the Australian International School in Sharjah. He gathered this from their accents and their rather loud chatter. Australians often gathered in this bar, and he had chatted with some staff from the Australian school before. At the table on the other side, sat a couple, the woman facing away from him, sitting across from her partner. He guessed that they were Middle Eastern, but they were not in traditional dress, so maybe Jordanian. Unusual to see Middle Eastern couples in a bar, but not the first time. The woman radiated exceptional beauty. Her partner seemed younger—jet black hair, neat cut above the collar and a well-trimmed mutton-chop beard—*newlyweds*, he guessed.

Ronnie sat alone, not only physically but mentally. He closed out the chatter of the nearby Australian girls. Whilst more guests than normal patronised the lounge tonight, he liked the quietness and darkness; well, except for the Australian girls. Surveying the city skyline, he recalled it had always ranked as his favourite view in Dubai. Close but far enough away that you could not see or hear the hustle and bustle. No prostitutes tonight. Too busy. Always scared away by crowds, particularly mixed crowds. As he slowly sipped his drink, he became increasingly melancholic. Over the next couple of hours, Ronnie ordered more drinks than he normally would. Numbers in the bar dwindled, the Australian teachers had left. Thank God. The couple across from him were still enjoying their night and another couple had entered and sat at the far end of the bar. He had often enjoyed the bar to himself, but that's okay. The ambience and the distant view calmed his thoughts. There was no rush tonight.

Eventually, he called the waiter over to settle his bill. "But the tab has been paid, Sir. Three Amstel Lagers, two glasses of Sauvignon Blanc and four Cokes."

Ronnie smiled knowingly. "Thanks, Sidney," he said out loud and left.

Downstairs, he signaled to the very tall doorman for a taxi, who immediately motioned Ronnie toward a white limousine waiting at the curb. The driver alighted the limousine and opened the rear door.

"No, no, a normal taxi will do."

The doorman shook his head. "No, my dear Sir, we are informed that this limousine has been pre-paid and is for you."

Ronnie hesitated. *Booked by the Russians to lure me to my death? Or is it Sidney taking care of me?* What the hell, if it were the Russians, at least Sidney wouldn't be far behind.

Sleep did not come easy, maybe fuelled by a little too much alcohol, but most from the distinct fear of prison. Leaving Dubai so abruptly disappointed him. No goodbyes. But these thoughts were replaced with the anticipation of returning to work in the Sydney office, the farm and, of course, Jacqui. He tossed and turned as the minutes painstakingly ticked by.

When morning light appeared, he lacked any enthusiasm to move. Being Friday, the Holy Day, he suddenly realised he had already worked his last day in Dubai. He would not see his work colleagues again. That made him feel sad.

His phone rang—Jacqui. *No phone calls. No phone calls. You can't answer it.* He replied with a text: *Can't talk today. Will ring in a couple of days. All is good. No worries.*

He opened Spotify, selected the album titled "Old Stuff," and hit the shuffle button. He immediately recognised the intro bars being strung on the guitar. "Shit," he muttered, throwing his head back on the pillow and closed his eyes.

"LA's fine, the sun shines most of the time, and the feeling is

'lay back.' Palm trees grow and rents are low, but you know I keep thinking about making my way back."

The melody transported him back to a time Ian and he performed it together. The song had struck his emotions when Ian sang it at his concert.

"'I am' I said, to no one there. I am lost and can't say why. Leaving me lonely … still."

That single word, 'still,' hung in the air forever. It resonated in his brain. Ronnie felt the tears swell in his eyes. He felt very much alone.

Over the last few weeks, he had been torn between his own New York and LA. But this morning, as the song crescendoed, he no longer felt lost. He had been on an emotional journey not knowing who he was or who he wanted to be. Things were becoming clearer—much clearer.

The song reached its peak: *"'I am' I cried … 'I am' said I."* He sat up and cried out with conviction: "'I am' said I."

Cameron is in charge. Survive the Russians and prison, then, Cameron will be home.

Finally, around 9 am, Ronnie rose from bed and fired up the barista. His phone rang. Mr Abdullah. Of course, Ronnie realised that Mr Abdullah would not call until Sidney had alerted him that he had risen.

"Good morning, Mr Ronnie. I am ringing to see how you are feeling. Is there anything we could do for you?"

Ronnie sensed a real feeling of compassion and concern in his tone.

"Thank you, Mr Abdullah, I do appreciate you calling," Ronnie replied with genuine appreciation. "I will be honest; I will be pleased to go home. I'm not saying I don't like Dubai. In fact, I have come to like it very much. But my recent trip back home has made me realise much of me still lives back there."

"We will ensure you will safely return home to Australia.

We don't want you to go home with any bad memories. I am sorry this has happened all so quickly. If we can't let you say goodbye, we can make your last day memorable. I have arranged for a chauffeur-driven limousine to be at your disposal all day. Feel safe; one of my staff will drive you. I have instructed him to take you wherever you want.

"In addition, because this is your last free night, I offer you a room in any location in Dubai you may want. Anywhere, Mr Ronnie; the choice is yours."

"Very generous, Mr Abdullah, thank you. I'll take the penthouse at the seven-star Burj Al Arab," he replied, tongue in cheek.

"It can be arranged," Mr Abdullah replied.

Ronnie immediately regretted being so insincere. *He is a nice guy. This isn't his fault. He does care,* "Sorry, a joke. I haven't given it any thought. I just might like it here. Babki Towers puts on a good light show."

Mr Abdullah gave a chuckle. "Let Sidney know what you want and we will oblige. And, by the way, wherever you go and eat, drink or buy, your tab will be taken care of," and he hung up.

Ronnie appreciated the genuine sincerity of the call. But it surprised him that Mr Abdullah had acknowledged Sidney by name for the first time. Did he know about the drinks, he wondered? Or the more private moments in his apartment? Out loud, he said, "Sidney, you're the best. You can be my wingman any day. I will miss you."

Ronnie had no idea how he wanted to spend his last day as a free man in Dubai. He knew what he didn't want to do—go anywhere where he might bump into the Lebedevs. He wanted to get out of the JBR. He headed back to where he had first lived, Deira, courtesy of Mr Abdullah's limousine. He strolled through the Deira City Centre, thinking of all his shopping expeditions—grocery shopping trips to Carrefours, the endless clothing stores with 80 percent off sales and the seemingly unlimited number of restaurants and fast food franchises.

He got a bowl of New York Fries for morning tea and ate lunch at PF Chang's for old time's sake. Over lunch, he thought through how he would spend the afternoon and evening. He had not discounted spending his last night in his apartment. But the more he thought, the more tempting a final night of celebration appealed to him. He considered taking his last abra ride on Dubai Creek or a swim at Atlantis, but those are too close to the Lebedevs. A final viewing of the Dubai fountain—maybe.

Then, suddenly, he knew what he would do: he would spend his last night of freedom in the Dubai desert at the Bab Al Shams Resort eating at the outdoor restaurant and staying overnight. He conveyed his desire to Sidney and went back to his waiting limousine and simply hopped in, advising the driver, "Via Al Lisaili, thank you."

He loved the camel farms at Al Lisaili, and he had a desire to see them one last time. He had always been fascinated with the Bedouin nomads—never settling in the city, choosing to stay in the desert living in their primitive desert homes. They were known for their hospitality and strong sense of community. Many didn't own vehicles and if they did, they were farm vehicles. To Ronnie, they were a mysterious Arabic group that kept to themselves and regarded their camels as precious possessions. He regarded the nomads as the true, genuine Arabs. Camel herders were regarded as the most prestigious of the Bedouins, followed by the sheep and goat herders. Cattle herders ranked lowest. Bedouins living in Al Lisaili were camel herders, breeding camels for sale. An average camel sold for around $90,000 AUD. Prices had reached upwards of $2.5 million AUD. And they remained in their primitive desert nomadic dwellings.

What can I learn from the Bedouins?

Of all the memories he would take from Dubai, the Bedouin were one of the most endearing.

Arriving at Bab Al Shams, an entourage of staff greeted him. *Mr Abdullah, you have made phone calls.* His room—in fact, rooms—were a lavish suite, aptly named The Royal Suite. He purchased a pair of designer brand swimmers, charging them to his room and spent a couple of hours lounging in the pool, enjoying the poolside bar. And poolside meant poolside—underwater seats, the bar literally forming the edge of the pool deck, lapping the water's edge. The waiter stood in his sunken bar on the other side. At sunset, he strolled across the sand dunes—dunes that stretched to the horizon, where the sun was bidding its farewell. The dunes appeared untouched, except for the waved sculptured ripples formed by the wind, waving lines that ran in perfect symmetry across the dunes, vividly enhanced by the setting burnt-orange sun. The only disruption was his own footprints as he made his way across the nearby dunes. The gentle breeze had started its process of returning the patterns determined only by the dunes and the wind. By morning, any trace of his presence would be gone forever. The image left a lasting impression of the end of his Middle Eastern sojourn.

Later that night, he enjoyed a dinner at the outdoor Al Hadheerah desert restaurant before heading back to his suite designed for many but occupied by one.

CHAPTER FIFTEEN

By midday Saturday, Ronnie had returned to his apartment. Mr Abdullah and Major Juma were waiting for him. Ronnie tried to conceal his nervousness, although his fingers were in constant motion and his legs felt weak. They made coffees and sat around the living room. Major Juma had mastered his Barista Plus.

"There are no changes to our plans. Our intelligence says the dinner this evening is going ahead as planned. We believe that besides you, Mr Sergei Volkov and two to three of the Lebedev cousins, who you have previously met, will be there. We now know they all work for Mr Sergei. Very little separates the Lebedev and Volkov operations," Mr Abdullah reported.

Ronnie listened but didn't concentrate. He felt rather detached. He had the vision of the burning orange sun setting behind the sand dunes last night and his fading footprints. He thought of the Bedouins, their footprints blown away every day, to be renewed again and again.

He tried to focus on Mr Abdullah.

"We are not going to tell you anything about the operation. Your protection is strengthened by the element of surprise, not expectation. Neither Major Juma nor I will be there. You will not recognise any of our officers. But they all know you, Mr Ronnie. They are thoroughly briefed and will treat you no differently than the others. You will be arrested and taken to our facilities. You will be interviewed like any other suspect. Do you have any questions?"

"No," Ronnie replied, rubbing his wet palms on his right leg that rapidly tapped the floor repeatedly.

"You must relax. If Lebedev saw you now, he would suspect a rat."

Major Juma reached into his pocket and removed a small bottle, "Please take one of these just before you go. It will calm you."

Ronnie took the bottle and placed it on the coffee table. "What is it?"

"Just something our doctor gave us that will calm your nerves."

Ronnie didn't question any deeper. He trusted Major Juma.

"When will I be back here?"

"We haven't determined how your actual discharge will occur. We will be guided by Interpol and the Australian Embassy, but it is possible you will not be back in this apartment," Mr Abdullah replied.

"So, do I pack up now?"

Mr Abdullah responded quickly. "No, it is crucial you leave this apartment on the premise that you will be back here tonight. Go downstairs, buy fresh bread and fresh milk. Make sure you chat with the shop owner."

"So, how do I pack up my stuff?"

"Don't worry about that," Mr Abdullah replied. "We will take care of it."

"Get Sidney to pack it up for me. He'll do a good job."

"Inshallah," smiled Mr Abdullah.

Mr Abdullah and Major Juma stood. Ronnie followed.

"You will go to the villa in a standard rented white limousine. It will pick you up at 4.30 pm. The limousine is standard, but the driver will be one of our secret service men. Don't acknowledge that please. Just a normal limo ride, all prepaid on a credit card," Major Juma explained.

As they left, Major Juma turned, "As you Aussies would say, see you on the other side," and he closed the door.

Ronnie followed Mr Abdullah's suggestion. He visited the shop on the ground floor of Babki Towers, where he regularly shopped for his daily needs. He knew the owners, Akshat and his son Aarush. Both were always keen to discuss cricket with Ronnie. He bought milk and bread. Aarush wanted to show him some news on Australian cricketers in an Indian magazine.

"Next time, Aarush. I will catch it next time," Ronnie said and returned to his apartment.

Long before the scheduled departure time, Ronnie put on the Australian football jersey he had worn to the game. Maybe a little underdressed, but soon that wouldn't matter. A loud Aussie thing to do, something Ronnie would do. But he also thought that would clearly differentiate him in the sight of a fully automatic rifle.

"Just kidding," he said aloud, trying to convince himself.

At 4.30 pm, he took one of Major Juma's pills and opened the door to leave. He turned, scanning the apartment for the last time. "Thanks for everything, Sidney. If we don't meet again, all the best."

Downstairs, he found the limo waiting. The sleekness of the police operations made him feel safe. He trusted Mr Abdullah and Major Juma. He felt they had invested in him and would protect him.

Upon arrival at the Lebedev villa, the doorman escorted Ronnie to the back patio. On this occasion, the door to the room on the right was open, revealing a large pool table. Outside, near the swimming pool, he found the Lebedev family enjoying drinks.

Alex greeted him, "Hey Pa, see who we have here," escorting Ronnie across the terrace. Adrik's face beamed and he extended both arms. Ronnie leant down and gave him an embrace. "Tim Cahill, Tim Cahill!" Adrik said in his Russian-English. Ronnie wasn't going to miss this at all. But the football jersey worked perfectly as a good ice breaker.

The Lebedev cousins arrived and drinks around the pool were broken by Matvei searching for an opponent in a game of pool. When no one accepted, he asked again, turning to Ronnie, "Hey Aussie mate, you guys play this in the pubs all the time. Come on, want a go?"

Ronnie hadn't played pool for some time but had been pretty good at it in Sydney. He had won the meat tray on the pool table in many a pub pool night. He thought that if he could funnel his concentration into the game, it would take his mind off the imminent raid.

Matvei, Alex, Ronnie and two of the cousins gathered in the pool room, drinks in hand. Adrik, Sergei Volkov and one additional person, who Ronnie thought could be Sergei's son, remained beside the pool. A full-size pool table stood in the middle of the room. Very little else occupied the room other than stools and standing tables. No stag head to un-remember, noted Ronnie. Matvei invited Ronnie to break, being the guest. Balls scattered and the game commenced. Matvei immediately pocketed two solids. A disappointing first shot from Ronnie, his ball fading well to the left of the pocket. A shot he should have got. *Concentrate. Relax. Breathe slow.* Ronnie could see that Matvei had immediately assessed him as an amateur and oozed arrogance, confident that he had already won the game. Matvei had no clear ball to easily pocket, electing to play a ricochet that nudged two of his solids toward the top left corner. Ronnie played a nice soft shot, positioning the 10 ball for a future pocket into the top right corner.

On his next shot, Matvei sunk his 1 ball into the bottom right corner. He could have sunk one of his balls in the top left corner but opted to dribble a third ball into the cluster to give him three balls surrounding the pocket, in an arc, waiting to be pocketed. *So, the cat thinks he is going to play with the mouse for some entertainment before he pounces.* Matvei's only other ball sat down the other end of the table quite close to the edge, just past the middle pocket. He proudly surveyed his shot and smirked with pride. It didn't concern Ronnie that Matvei played very well. But his arrogant attitude pissed him off. Without Ronnie realising, the impending raid momentarily no longer had complete control of his mind.

Ronnie knew his position seemed hopeless. He still had all seven balls on the table, none of them in good positions. On this shot, the best he could do would be to get the 12 ball near the centre left pocket, setting up for the 10 ball. But that would open the game for Matvei to sink the three balls around the top left pocket and that would only leave one to wrap up the game. Ronnie concentrated. He had a high-risk plan. He could hit the 12 ball basically into no man's land but in so doing ricochet it into the black, moving it so gently toward the top pocket to stop a millimetre from the hole, thus blocking Matvei's three balls from dropping. A millimetre too far and the black would drop, handing the win to Matvei. *Go for it.* As he lined up, no one got excited because they could see that the shot would not send his 12 ball anywhere close to a pocket. Ronnie concentrated. He went for the shot. Into the 12 ball, it rolled forward with sufficient pace to clip the 8 ball, which, in turn rolled ever so slowly to the left, heading straight for the pocket. Matvei could see the black ball heading for the top pocket and moved to start preparing for the next game. But the black ball continued to slow, slower, slower, then stopped right on the lip of the pocket. Ronnie had held his position from the moment he struck the white. Matvei's eyes dilated in horror and anger.

The cousin standing behind whispered in Ronnie's ear, "I don't believe it. You played for that shot. That is the best shot I've ever seen."

Ronnie moved away from the table. Matvei, visibly shaken, badly missed the next shot. Matvei's face turned red with anger. All eyes gazed upon the Russian. The quiet room just went quieter. Ronnie took control, sinking three balls with crispness and precision, positioning the white near the cushion, leaving Matvei no clear shot. The game had become a tense dual. No one spoke. It came to the point where Matvei now only had the three balls to play, the black standing between all three and the pocket. He had no option but to play a shot that would ricochet one of his balls into the side of the black, which may cause it to bounce off the cushions and out. He attempted but the black sunk and the game went to Ronnie on a foul.

Before the black had sunk, Matvei cried for "best of three." His Russian accent clearly conveying that was not a question.

Matvei broke and the game started far more intensely. Ronnie's pool skills were coming back to him. He now had a feel for the cue. He had a feel for the pace of the table. He had adjusted to the room and the light. He knew he could match Matvei. It moved from a game of potting balls to a strategic combat to outplay each other. Ronnie potted the first ball of the second game—a shot from the bottom left corner to sink a ball in the top right corner—not an easy shot. He would need to pass one of Matvei's balls by the width of a hair. Everyone held their breath as Ronnie played the shot and gave an audible expiration when he got it.

"Cues on the table, hands on your heads," yelled a loud stern, steady, unknown voice.

Everyone simultaneously turned to see four riot police in full riot armour gear, with automatic rifles aimed at them. Not even Ronnie had seen them enter the room.

"Hands on heads!" shouted the commander.

Ronnie laid the cue on the table and obliged.

"What the hell?" cried Matvei.

"No talking. Put down the cue!" yelled the commander. Matvei complied.

And with that, the raid was over. No gun shots, no one wrestled to the ground, no body contact, no noise. Nonetheless, Ronnie could feel his trousers were wet and his heart racing. It surprised Ronnie how unemotional everyone appeared to be, apart from Matvei, whose arms were waving, his eyes dilated, his face red with anger, as he yelled in Russian.

They were marched onto the back patio where Adrik and Sergei were still seated—two riot police behind them, automatic rifles across their chests. One cousin, who stayed outside, stood near the back wall of the house, handcuffed. All five from the pool room were stood beside him. Riot police stood in a line in front of them with automatic weapons at the ready. Two other police officers handcuffed each individual and completed body searches. Meanwhile, a team came down the stairs, reporting no one found upstairs. Ronnie noticed that more police were gathering the staff together in the kitchen area.

Standing beside Alex, Ronnie whispered, "What the hell is going on?"

Before Alex could respond, the same officer who had done all the talking upstairs yelled "No talking!" A nearby policeman butted Ronnie in the midriff with the butt of his rifle. It hurt and partially winded Ronnie. Two officers moved forward, grabbing Ronnie by each arm, and marched him to the other side of the line, placing a wider separation between him and the cousin he now stood beside. No one moved. No one spoke. Even Matvei stopped yelling.

It surprised Ronnie how quickly and quietly the whole raid had been completed—over in seconds and in relative silence. No weapons were found on any of the suspects and Ronnie observed none being brought forward by the other police from inside the villa.

After a few minutes, three Dubai Police appeared, wearing normal police uniform. Only one spoke. He said very few words, all spoken in English, announcing they were under arrest and would be taken into custody for questioning. They were to remain silent and instructed not to talk to each other. Another police officer arrived with a folder. He flicked through the papers in the folder as he stood in front of each individual one by one. Ronnie surmised they were matching faces to photographs.

Eventually, the senior police officer, who appeared to be in charge, pointed to Ronnie. "You," he said with a commanding voice. "Your name?"

"Ronnie Blanche."

They again thumbed through the papers. Ronnie gathered that they had no picture for him.

"You live here?"

Adrik spoke, "No, he Aust—"

"Shut up," yelled the police officer. "Did I ask you?" Adrik attempted to speak in Russian, but the police officer closest to him smacked him in the shoulder with the butt of his gun.

The officer turned back to Ronnie. "No, I am just visiting," Ronnie responded, his voice trembling despite his efforts to stay composed.

"You work for them?"

"No."

"You live in Dubai?"

"Yes, I work for a finance company here."

"Russian company?" he asked.

"No."

"Nationality?"

"Australian."

"Why are you here?"

"They invited me. I am friends with Alex and Matvei."

The police commander fingered through the papers, this time eyeing both Alex and Matvei. Ronnie's legs quivered. He could feel his wet groin, hoping it could not be seen. *Are these guys really good at what they do, or do they really think I'm involved?* Ronnie reminded himself of his faith and trust in Mr Abdullah and his team.

The three uniformed police moved back to the pool's edge to confer, speaking in Arabic, but not loud enough for anyone to hear. They returned, addressing the senior riot officer.

"Arrest them all, including the Australian visitor. Take them to the central jail," the senior police officer commanded.

After some further Arabic discussion, the three uniformed

police departed. The prisoners were led one by one out to the street into a much more dramatic and chaotic scene. Dozens of police vehicles of all shapes and sizes—several riot vehicles, prison trucks and other police vehicles—crowded the driveway and street. As the prisoners were marched to the transport vehicles, Ronnie observed boxes of equipment and trollies being taken into the villa for what would be a very thorough forensic investigation of the house.

Adrik and Sergei were put into the back of separate police cars and taken away, each escorted by police motorbikes. The remaining six individuals, including Ronnie, were placed into the back of a police van, three on either side. Two police positioned themselves at the front of the truck, which also departed with a police motorbike escort.

As the truck prepared to depart, the police officers were momentarily distracted by their radios.

"What the hell is going on?" Ronnie whispered to Alex, sitting beside him.

"Nothing. We'll sort it out. Don't you worry."

Russian optimism or arrogance—Ronnie couldn't tell.

Ronnie found the long trip extremely uncomfortable. The hard bench provided no cushioning from the relentless bouncing, each jolt tearing at his shoulders cuffed behind his back. The cuffs dug deeply into his wrists. There were no windows. It stunk of stale sweat and urine. Ronnie found the heat unbearable. They were tightly packed, shoulder to shoulder. Even the two police officers' uniforms were drenched with sweat.

Opposite Ronnie sat Matvei and two cousins who were silent. At one stage, Matvei and Alex were trying to communicate through eye contact. Both wore a face of defeat. Matvei mostly had his eyes shut and head bent back. The police officers kept their fingers on the triggers of their guns, their gaze fixed directly ahead.

Eventually, the truck slowed, turned sharply, and bounced over a series of speed bumps, each one causing a tearing pain in Ronnie's shoulders. They came to a stop. The police officers didn't move.

After a few minutes, the truck moved off again. Ronnie assumed they had passed through a security gate. They drove another short distance, stopping again, then moving slowly before finally stopping. The dim light from the small slit above their heads darkened—they must be entering a building. The police officers still didn't move—their faces said they had done this routine a thousand times before.

When the back door of the truck finally opened, Ronnie observed they appeared to be in a large garage. About ten metres from the back of the truck stood a row of armed guards. Ronnie guessed they were prison guards. They were in a different uniform, equipped with different rifles—smaller weapons than the police. Smaller budget, Ronnie surmised. Two unarmed guards stood ready at the back door of the police van wearing epaulettes on their shoulders indicating they were of higher rank.

One pointed to the cousin sitting on the bench directly opposite Ronnie, "You! Out!"

Two more guards appeared from beside the van. The cousin stumbled out, being offered no assistance and disappearing out of sight. Several minutes later, the same command was shouted at Ronnie. Once he had stepped down, he could see they were parked parallel to a large building with double steel doors adjacent to the truck. After a short pause, the doors opened automatically. A firm hand in the middle of Ronnie's back pushed him into a large brightly lit foyer. He expected to see the cousin who had preceded him, but Ronnie stood alone with the guards in a large reception room.

In front of him, two guards sat behind a curtain of iron bars. The two armed guards remained behind him. When asked, he provided his name, date of birth and nationality. The guards removed the handcuffs. Ronnie appreciated the immediate relief.

"Everything in your pockets on the bench," the guard at the counter commanded. Ronnie complied.

"Your clothes," the guard commanded. Ronnie removed his Australian football jersey and his jeans and placed them on the bench. He stood on the cold concrete floor in nothing but his underpants.

"All your clothes," the guard commanded. Ronnie hesitated briefly before removing his underpants, placing them with his other clothes. He noticed the guard's eye inspect his clean-shaven pubic area, raising his eyebrows slightly, before exchanging glances with his colleague. Ronnie fixed his eyes on the wall behind the officer's head and made no response; however, he found the procedure humiliating and he felt violated.

"Watch," the guard commanded. Ronnie removed his watch and placed it with his other possessions.

Still naked, a gentle shove in the back pushed him through a door on the right. He walked down a corridor and then he was directed into a large open shower room containing six shower-heads. One wet patch on the floor suggested the cousin who proceeded him had just finished.

A guard pushed Ronnie to a shower, then both guards stood, watching his every move. Only one tap—the tepid water soothed his hot body. The water automatically cut off after two minutes. From the shower room, a baton prodded him toward another room where there were prison clothes waiting for him. He expected bright orange, but they were a dull matt grey. No underwear. A pair of buttoned trousers, which were slightly too big and a buttoned top, almost a good fit, and a pair of scuff shoes.

The guards led him down yet another corridor to a locked door. One guard pressed a button and after a few seconds, the door opened into a brightly lit corridor that had more of an office appearance, but Ronnie had no doubt he was in a prison. A row of solid doors lined the hall on either side. A guard stood outside one door. Ronnie was pushed past that guard to another room further down and then stopped.

The guards ushered Ronnie into a plain square room with a table in the middle. One chair on one side and two chairs on the opposite side. No windows. Everything painted matte grey. *So, this is an interrogation room.* It felt isolating and barren, much more than he imagined it would. Ronnie's eyes glanced for the two-way mirror like he'd seen on TV, but was disappointed to see only the four plain grey walls, and cameras in the ceiling at every corner. One guard ushered him to the single chair and moved back to stand near the door, the other guard stayed standing outside the door. Ronnie assumed the guard he saw in the hall stood guard outside the room the cousin had been taken into.

Ronnie sat in silence for some time. "Water?" he asked. The guard didn't respond.

A man and a woman in police uniform entered and sat opposite Ronnie.

"Name?" the man asked.

"Cameron Blanche," Ronnie replied.

"Is that the name you go by?"

"No, in Dubai they call me Ronnie."

"Why is that?"

"It's a nickname given to me by friends."

"What is on your passport?"

"Cameron Blanche"

"What does the Lebedev family call you?"

"Ronnie."

"Do they know your real name?"

"That's a good question," Ronnie replied. "I have no idea. But I think not. No one in Dubai calls me anything but Ronnie."

The questioning shifted to broader topics—when did he come to the UAE, his work in Australia, where he had lived just prior to coming to the UAE, where he worked now, what he did at work, etc. They asked about his recent travels, reasons for travelling and if he had ever been to Russia. Eventually, the policewoman, flipping through papers, steered the interrogation into specifics.

"How do you know the Lebedevs?"

Ronnie recounted his initial contact with Alex and subsequent social events, meeting Matvei along the way. He spoke about the outings to the Rugby Sevens, the Dubai World Cup and the recent trips on the yacht and to the villa.

"How many times have you been to the villa?"

"Only twice. Once when Alex invited me to join the family at the UAE football match with Qatar. We met at the villa and went to the game. After the game, I called a limo and went home. The second time was today."

"Where have you been in the villa?"

Ronnie tensed. "From the front door to the entertainment area and the patio. And today, we played pool in the pool room. I hadn't seen it before."

"Have you been upstairs?"

Ronnie's heart rate suddenly increased. "Only to go to the toilet."

Questions continued about his work and the Lebedev files. They asked about his involvement with Sergei Volkov. He replied that he had only seen him at the social functions and other than welcomes and goodbyes, he had not spoken with him.

The interview went longer than Ronnie had expected. No questions about Babki Towers. No questions about White Birch. Ronnie had not expected this level of questioning. He could only assume it to be important for his freedom—his potential involvement had to be investigated, discounted and documented. Ronnie noted that for every question asked, he could give a truthful and honest answer.

The interviewers left the room. After a few minutes, the second guard entered, and they escorted Ronnie from the room, down the long corridor and through a door at the opposite end from which he entered. Each room he passed had a guard standing outside the door. Ronnie assumed that each of those who had been arrested were in a room being interviewed.

The guards led Ronnie to a car and drove a short distance to another set of buildings still within the prison walls. Ronnie was directed into a single-story concrete building, which had a different feel and appearance but the same matt grey colour. They walked him into a room about the size of a two-star roadside motel room containing an unmade bed with a folded blanket in the corner, a square metal table and two metal chairs, a small bench secured to the wall and a small bookshelf above it. In the back corner stood a shower room with no door, containing a standard prison toilet, a showerhead on the wall, a small basin and the luxury of a high-mounted barred window too high to see out of. The solid metal cell door locked behind him with a clang. He sat on the bed and waited.

The prison cell felt cold and lifeless. Ronnie was convinced that time moved slower in this environment. He expected to be sitting behind bars—facing other prisoners staring back at him but instead found himself alone in a concrete block. Although larger than he imagined, a concrete block is a concrete block. What wasn't concrete was steel, including the toilet. No luxury of a toilet seat. The bed, a single steel structure bolted to the floor, covered by a thin non-absorbent mattress. Ronnie quickly concluded that he would not survive in a prison.

Later in the evening, after eating his first prison meal of curried sausages and rice, followed by melted ice cream and terrible tasting jelly, Ronnie's door unlocked and Mr Abdullah, Major Juma and a third man introduced simply as the superintendent of the jail entered. Ronnie had dosed off on the bed but immediately sat upright at the loud clanging of the metal door.

"I'm reasonably impressed with the holiday home," Ronnie remarked.

"You are being held in the Diplomatic Detention Centre, which is contained within the jail," Mr Abdullah explained.

"Are the others here?" Ronnie asked.

"No," Mr Abdullah replied. "May I say, they are having a more United Nations experience."

"Won't they think it odd that I'm not there with them?"

"None of the prisoners will have contact with each other for some time. That is part of normal investigatory procedure—no opportunity for them to collude their stories.

Mr Abdullah continued, "We have now completed all preliminary interviews. As you can see, it has taken well into the evening. We can inform you that no evidence has been given that suggests you were aware of or played any part in any illegal activity connected to the Lebedevs or Mr Volkov."

Mr Abdullah opened a plain manilla folder, perusing the pages it contained. Ronnie could see handwritten Arabic notes. "I must say, all prisoners speak well of you. Generally, the prisoners said very little and made no admissions of guilt, but when asked about you, they were a little more responsive."

Mr Abdullah thumbed through his handwritten notes as he spoke, "Alex described you as a mate. He said you met socially and he spoke of the outings, such as the World Cup and football. He made no mention of you in the villa other than you had been there on one previous occasion, only briefly."

Turning the page, he continued, "Matvei, much the same, except he added 'He can play pool, the bastard.'"

Ronnie smiled. *Yes, beat the smart arse!*

"Matvei mentioned his father wanted you to visit because his father said you knew Tim Cahill. When asked if you knew Tim Cahill, he replied, 'Stuffed if I know.'"

Mr Abdullah raised his eyes at Ronnie.

Ronnie shrugged his shoulders and smiled.

"Adrick Lebedev said nothing the whole interview, except when asked about you, he replied 'Tim Cahill, Tim Cahill.'" Mr Abdullah again raised his eyes toward Ronnie.

Ronnie chuckled. "He had this idea I knew Tim Cahill. When I got introduced to him on the yacht, the only word I understood when he greeted me was football. I know nothing about football, but I remembered that my stepdad had once gone to a business lunch and had been introduced to Tim Cahill, the guest speaker. From that time on, Adrik went crazy about Tim Cahill every time he saw me. If Tim Cahill walked in here now, I wouldn't recognise him."

Mr Abdullah flipped through a couple more pages, "And there is really nothing more. Sergei Volkov struggled to remember who you were. He said he had only been introduced to you once and the cousins offered nothing, one couldn't remember your name."

Mr Abdullah closed the folder and summarised what Ronnie could expect. "From here, we will continue our investigation and finalise matters when we are sufficiently satisfied your involvement is not suspected in anyway, and you will be duly released."

"Thank God! I can go home," Ronnie rejoiced.

"Unfortunately, it is not quite that simple," Mr Abdullah clarified. "Yes, we are satisfied of your innocence. For your own legal protection, the formal investigatory process must prove that and be fully documented. I think you call it due diligence.

"Furthermore, and most critically, we must also afford you proper witness protection. We will involve the Australian Embassy in that process. We have already briefed the Australian

Ambassador, and he informs me that they have briefed the Minister for Foreign Affairs in Australia. That will take a little while."

"Holy shit," Ronnie responded. "Does this nightmare ever stop getting bigger and bigger?"

"On the contrary, this is making it smaller and smaller, ensuring your safety and freedom," Mr Abdullah defended.

"So, I could be here for ages?"

"Not at all. Once we finalise the documentation proving you are no longer a suspect, and your witness protection is in place, things will move quickly. Sometimes, the witness is out of the country in hours."

"Can I ring Jacqui?"

"I'm sorry, not yet," The superintendent shook his head. "Your only contact will be with your legal representation. But at this stage, that is not required. The Australian Ambassador is representing your interests."

Ronnie stared at Mr Abdullah his eyes pleading for some leniency.

Mr Abdullah stood to leave, "I will have someone contact Jacqui and give her reassurance."

"Sidney?"

Mr Abdullah paused, "Leave it with me."

On the third day, Ronnie heard the key in the lock. Two guards entered, ordering him into a vehicle and drove him to the interview rooms. In a well-executed move, they led Ronnie into the corridor at the precise moment Alex entered from the opposite end of the corridor, escorted by guards. A chance meeting timed with military precision. Their eyes met for a few seconds as they were directed into neighbouring interview rooms. Ronnie could see the resignation in Alex's sunken eyes.

The same two interviewers asked Ronnie similar questions, with some added specific questions about his knowledge of White Birch but no specific reference to the documents he had photographed. All questions he could answer truthfully. They left and Ronnie sat in silence, accompanied by a lone guard standing near the door.

After a considerable amount of time, the door opened, another guard whispered in the ear of the guard in the room and they both left. Ronnie had grown numb to long periods of nothing.

Eventually, the superintendent entered the room. "Mr Blanche, what is about to happen is a breach of protocol, but I am allowing it. Alex Lebedev has requested to meet with you. There will be no one else in the room, but you won't be alone," he glanced up at the cameras. "Do you agree?"

Ronnie nodded. Ronnie suspected this wasn't such a breach, but rather another scene in their scripted charade. The superintendent continued, "My advice to you is say very little," his eyes again glancing at the cameras.

After a few seconds, a guard opened the door and Alex walked in. Ronnie stood to face him. Before him stood a broken soul—no fight left in this Russian. Ronnie had an instantaneous and unexcepted swelling of emotion and tears, embracing Alex. They held the embrace for some time before moving apart.

"Umm," Alex began, his voice breaking as tears streamed down his face. "I'm so sorry you have been dragged into this. We have told them you didn't know anything. The big guy told me you are being released and are not a suspect," he paused for a second and then continued. "I guess Pa had good reason for never bringing people to the villa, especially good, decent people."

"We're mates," Ronnie replied. "If the police are good at their job, they would have questioned me anyway, even if I never went to the villa."

Ronnie felt sickened by the betrayal he was concealing. He had very much enjoyed Alex's friendship and knew he would do Ronnie no wrong. But he also understood the gravity of their crime and he must pay.

"You're a good guy, Ronnie. Very few people make my pa happy, but you did."

"I hate football."

Alex attempted the faintest of a smile, "That's what makes you a special person, Ronnie. You could teach us Russians a lot."

"How is your father going through all this?"

"You're the first person I've seen," Alex replied. "But they tell me he is fine. They won't be getting much from him. He is old-school Russian style. He would still think all this is a legitimate way to make money."

They embraced again. "So, what happens next?" Ronnie asked.

"Not your concern, Ronnie," Alex dried his face with his shirt. "The lawyers will push for some type of plea bargain. I won't be able to meet you at the Buddha Bar for a long time. My lawyer said they may try and negotiate an extradition or prisoner swap with Russia, but I can't see that happening. If it did, it could be years. Do the crime, do the time, they say."

He turned and knocked on the door, which promptly opened, and Alex left.

Ronnie felt conflicted. He was wanting to feel relieved—it is finished, but a guilt gnawed within for not being honest with Alex. They broke the law and must be punished. He had no problem with that. But he felt he should have been honest with Alex. *It was me, Alex. I led the police to you. You did wrong and you needed to be punished for that.* But he knew that even if Alex accepted that, there would be many other angry Russians that wouldn't, and they would come in pursuit of him.

CHAPTER SIXTEEN

The guards returned Ronnie to his cell in the Diplomatic Detention Centre, where he laid on his bed, feeling a deep sadness and a longing for the rest awaiting him at Binya. Its familiar smells were calling him home.

A couple of hours later, two guards woke Ronnie, prodding him with their batons, gesturing him to move to the car. He was driven the short distance to the front reception building, stopping at a different door on the opposite end of the building to the interview rooms. Guards escorted him down a long corridor to another door. Expecting another interview room, it surprised him to enter a large boardroom. A very long board table ran the length of the room, with many people seated around it—several people he recognised, others he did not.

The jail superintendent introduced everyone just the same: "I believe you've met Mr Abdullah, Major Juma, Mr Annand, Mr Simons from the World Bank and Mr Donald from Interpol. And this is Monsieur Fredeaux, a very senior agent from Interpol who has flown in from headquarters in Lyon, France. Finally, you may be familiar with the Australian Ambassador, Mr Kemp."

Ronnie would never have recognised the Ambassador, having never met him or known his name. He found out later he had driven from Abu Dhabi accompanied by a small contingent of staff, who were sitting behind him wanting to appear important, or so it seemed.

Mr Abdullah opened proceedings. "Thank you for joining us, Mr Ronnie. I told you that when things happened, they would happen quickly. After this meeting, you will walk from this prison a free man, released with no charges and no suspicion of a crime. You will be on a plane to Australia tonight. As we have previously indicated, you will be afforded all the protection appropriate for your ongoing safety. You will leave here protected by a witness protection program overseen by the Australian Government.

"Before we outline that plan, we believe you need to understand the significance of this case and the need for such protection. As Major Juma has previously indicated to you, this case will be referred to in criminology programs around the world for years to come. For better or worse, you will be the silent hero who exposed one of the most significant cases of money laundering in recent times. However, that will remain known only to those in this room. Monsieur Fredeaux will explain further."

"It is an honour to meet you, Mr Blanche," Monsieur Fredeaux began. "I must say your story is an extraordinary one. You may think that your discovery of a high-rise building next to you being used to launder money is what made this case extraordinary, but that is not the case. The true importance lies in your discovery of White Birch, which has international ramifications. I understand you took great personal risks to uncover this. Your findings exposed a complex, multi-country operation. Money laundering is just one piece of this criminal empire you have unearthed. The invoices you discovered led us to specific accounts in the Philippines. It is not your Russian friends that are the big players, they are small pawns. White Birch is a web that brings this together, and Mr Volkov is the big fish.

"Since you were arrested, there have been arrests in the Philippines, India, Kenya, Sudan, Singapore, Indonesia and one in Tonga, and the arrests are still ongoing as we speak.

"You may find some comfort in that the evidence in this case will start with those accounts in the Philippines, not with a villa in Dubai. In fact, Mr Volkov may be extradited to the Philippines to be charged and trialed there. No one else will come to know that it was you who cracked this open, Mr Blanche, but we will be grateful to you for years to come," Monsieur Fredeaux bowed gracefully, prompting applause from those around the table.

And all I said was that it amused me to how lights turned on and off. Nonetheless, he appreciated, from his forensic accounting background, just how big this had become and the impact on international finances. The people he dealt with are on the periphery, the end players. He could see now that the Lebedevs had inadvertently led authorities to the core of the operation. Professionally, he was well-pleased. Personally, he just wanted to go home.

Monsieur Fredeaux continued, "Which brings us to the terms of your witness protection. You will be going home this evening. From the time you get off the plane you will have a new identity."

"What?" Ronnie exclaimed. "A new name? That's stupid. You just said you've caught the ringleader. Anyway, what's the point in changing my name when everyone in the Sydney office knows who I am. That's just absurd. Let's all go back to just being normal."

"You will not be returning to your job in Sydney. The risk is too great. Somewhere, someone could make a connection. The last thing you need is to be known as the boy that brought down White Birch."

"What, I lose my name and now my job?"

"There are some important details we need to work through," Monsieur Fredeaux took his seat and gestured to his left. "Let's start with your compensation. Mr Annand, can you proceed?"

"Yes," Annand said opening the folder before him. "Ronnie, the company is very impressed with your work, not only because you have uncovered the fraud, but you also safeguarded our significant financial interests. You will be compensated for loss of future income, given that it would be unsafe to return to your employment."

"I've accrued a lot of leave," Ronnie interjected. "I hope you include all that and what about my superannuation?"

"Ronnie, please. Allow me to finish. You will be compensated to the sum of 1.85 million AUD dollars."

Ronnie suddenly inhaled, causing him to cough. The room fell silent. After a minute he raised his eyes at Annand, still in a state of shock. "1.85 million, eh? Like not 1.9 or a round $2 million?"

A chuckle rippled around the room. "I didn't do the calculation," Annand replied sheepishly.

Monsieur Fredeaux resumed. "Mr Simons?"

Mr Simons spoke calmly. "The World Bank and Interpol have been working together for some time to wipe out money laundering. As part of that campaign, confidential rewards are offered for significant information. Whilst the existence of such rewards is known, the details are confidential. Those rewards are in five tiers. The highest tiered reward that has ever been paid out is tier three and that has been done four times. In partnership, Interpol and the World Bank have agreed to pay, for the first time ever, the tier five reward. One of the reasons for that agreement is in recognition of your brave efforts in gathering information and your involvement in the actual arrest."

"And what is that worth?" Ronnie asked.

"5 million dollars, USD," Mr Simons coolly replied.

Stunned silence filled the room for a considerable time. Ronnie couldn't speak. His accountant brain told him that's more than $7 million AUD. He closed his eyes to see that in numbers. When he opened them, all eyes in the room were fixated on him.

"May I move to the question of your identity. We have some suggestions," Monsieur Fredeaux continued.

"My name. I don't need to change my name. I won't change my name."

"Not for nearly $9 million AUD and the comfort to go to sleep without fear every night?" Monsieur Fredeaux asked.

Ronnie glared at him and said nothing. *Well, I didn't say never.*

"My name is not Ronnie anyway."

"We all know your real name is Cameron."

"No one knows me here as Cameron."

Mr Annand interjected, "He's right. He has only ever been known as Ronnie."

Major Juma added, "In all of this investigation he has only ever been referred to as Ronnie by all those arrested."

"But what about in Australia?" asked Monsieur Fredeaux.

"I've never been called Ronnie in Australia," Ronnie replied. "I'm going to have some say in my future. I will go back to Australia as Cameron James. James is the surname of my great-grandfather who rode in the 1st Australian Light Horse Regiment. He bought a farm in Harden and called it Binya. I'm returning to Australia to assume ownership of that farm and I'll own it as Cameron James."

He folded his arms and stared at the table.

Monsieur Fredeaux turned to the Australian Ambassador, "Well, Mr Kemp? Your government will be responsible for managing the witness protection program, so the decision must be yours."

The Australian Ambassador, Monsieur Fredeaux and Mr Abdullah huddled at the far end of the room. After some lengthy discussion, they returned to their seats. The Australian Ambassador spoke, "I will have a temporary passport drawn up for tonight's flight, made out in the name of Mr Cameron James. It will be delivered to the airport before boarding. Mr James, your new passport will be handed to you in Sydney." Turning to the jail superintendent he added, "If you can assist with appropriate photographs, that would be greatly appreciated."

The Ambassador added, "Ah, may I add Mr James, the rewards previously detailed have already been deposited into your existing UAE accounts as Cameron Blanche. That is significant. You received them as a UAE resident, with no intention of returning to Australia. That ensures the Australian Taxation Office has no claim to any income tax on those amounts."

"Are you certain about that?" asked Cameron.

"A line in the sand is a line in the sand. That line for you was drawn earlier today. Call it your new birthday," the Ambassador replied.

"In final summary, Mr Blan ... Ah, Mr James," Monsieur Fredeaux stated, "there are some agreements and conditions you will have to sign with the Ambassador present. These agreements include conditions relating to non-disclosure, witness protection, the change of name, restrictions on returning to the work sector without the clearance of the Australian Government and your obligations to keep in contact with the appropriate authorities as required."

"Thank you, Monsieur Fredeaux. Excuse me now—I have sheep to grow."

Thirty minutes later, the final formalities of release were completed. Dressed in civilian clothes provided to him, Cameron James emerged from the prison.

Mr Abdullah, alone, stood by his car, waiting for him. "I'll be your chauffeur today. I'll take you to your apartment where you can collect what you want to take with you on tonight's flight. The Australian Embassy will ensure the rest of your belongings make their way to you."

"Can I call Jacqui?" asked Cameron.

"From the airport," Mr Abdullah said. Cameron shook his head in frustration, "As you heard Mr Cameron, there are major players in this game—far bigger than the Lebedevs. Let's leave no cracks. In fact, give me your phone."

Cameron rummaged through the bag of personal items that had been returned to him by the jail clerk. The mobile was out of battery.

"I'll keep that," Mr Abdullah said.

"But I need to get my contacts."

"No, you don't," Mr Abdullah said. "Ronnie doesn't exist anymore."

"I do have another phone from Australia," admitted Cameron.

"We know, Mr Cameron, but that phone is in the name of Jacqui Forbes. There is no link to Ronnie Blanche."

"What's my baggage limit?"

Mr Abdullah chuckled as he deciphered Cameron's cryptic question. "Yes, it is first class. The Ambassador's expense account this time—not mine."

Mr Abdullah dropped Cameron at his apartment building and advised he'd return at 10 pm for the 2 am flight. There was no Ronnie. Scanning the apartment, he decided he would take very little: no clothes and no furnishings. His Dubai years belonged to another life. He packed the Binya cake of soap and toothpaste winder. When the time came to leave, he took one last look at the Dubai skyline and closed the curtains.

Cameron was sitting on his lounge when Mr Abdullah returned. His one small carry-on bag packed and waiting beside the door.

"Travelling light, Mr Cameron?"

"Ronnie stays here. I won't be seeking anything else to be returned to Australia."

Mr Abdullah simply nodded.

"Please do me one favour, Mr Abdullah."

"Of course. Tell me."

"After I am gone, please have Major Juma come back and collect my Barista Plus. He knows how to work it now."

"No, no Mr Cameron, we can't—"

"Mr Abdullah, please. I have asked for little. This small token would mean a lot to me."

Mr Abdullah was about to protest but could see the compassion on Cameron's face.

"Please," Cameron pleaded.

"For you, Mr Cameron, I promise. And by now, you will know I will be faithful to my promise."

Mr Abdullah drove to a special entry point near first-class arrivals. They were met by a team of airport police who escorted them into the airport. Cameron was processed through a normal security check, albeit at a private gate. Papers were exchanged at passport control and they proceeded.

Expecting to head to the first-class lounge, Cameron discovered that within Dubai Airport, similar to Sydney, there were exclusive lounges beyond the first-class lounge. He knew of an exclusive VIP lounge. However, he soon discovered the very exclusive VVIP lounge that only the precious few ever entered. Primarily used for sensitive diplomatic movements and the superstars of superstars, this catered for the very high-level security risks. There were no signs, no grand entry, the door camouflaged into the bland sand-coloured wall.

The VVIP lounge provided a stark contrast to Cameron's diplomatic quarters of the last week. It could only be described as opulence on steroids. Designed around a very Arabic theme, it offered a series of large *majlis*—some arranged with couches, others set for traditional floor seating. Dedicated staff stood ready to fulfill any need, with access to any food or drink he wanted.

Major Juma was waiting for them when Cameron and Mr Abdullah arrived. Soon, the staff from the Embassy delivered Cameron's temporary passport. Opening it for the first time, he saw his new name in writing—Cameron James. His eyes reddened with emotion. It was new, but it was old. Cameron studied it again. *I know who I am.* He had found himself. Not in Dubai, not in the pubs of Sydney, but in the history of his great-grandfather in Harden. Home on Binya awaited him—his true home.

The Embassy staff briefed Cameron on his upcoming meeting with the Foreign Affairs staff in Sydney. He would meet at the airport, accommodated in the city overnight, and in the morning, he would meet Foreign Affairs staff and Federal Police. Cameron listened to the details with frustration because he simply wanted to go home. For just under $9 million, however, he could spare the time for the pitstop.

Mr Abdullah and Major Juma waited nearby as Cameron sat largely by himself. Mr Abdullah had his phone to his ear most of the time. Cameron had no interest in finding out why. Major Juma was regularly checking if Cameron wanted anything.

A little later, Cameron noticed a strikingly beautiful woman enter the lounge, dressed in a traditional abaya and hijab. Far from concealing her beauty, the silky black abaya and deep blue hijab enhanced it. He initially assumed her to be another traveller.

However, Mr Abdullah greeted her at the door and immediately escorted her to Cameron.

"I would like to introduce you to someone whose name I can't disclose, as you will understand," Mr Abdullah said, his voice carrying a hint of amusement. Cameron's gaze remained fixed on the woman as Mr Abdullah added, "Mr Cameron, please meet the person you know as Sidney."

Cameron's expression shifted so dramatically that the woman identified as Sidney burst into laughter. Mr Abdullah and Major Juma joined in the laughter. Sidney extended her hand for a handshake, a gesture Cameron hesitated to accept, unsure of cultural protocol. Her hand remained extended, so Cameron accepted it, shaking her hand. The firmness of her handshake made his face flush with embarrassment.

Struggling to form words, Cameron managed to softly stammer, "I'm sorry."

"Sorry for what?" she asked with a warm smile.

He didn't know what for either.

"I offered my hand," Sidney replied. "Refusing it would have offended me. And I regard Ronnie as a dear friend who has earned my respect."

Mr Abdullah and Major Juma excused themselves, leaving Cameron and Sidney to converse in one of the *majlis*. Cameron opened, "So, you're the Sidney who handled all my drinks?"

Sidney smiled, "It was a twenty-four-hour operation over several weeks, so it physically couldn't be always me. But yes, many times it was. Lucky for you, I only drink Coke. I received an alert every time you went out, which wasn't all that often, so I managed to keep an eye on you. I personally oversaw you much of the time."

"Someone really watched me every time—at the Irish Village and the Eclipse?" Cameron asked.

"Most definitely," she confirmed. "At the Irish Village, you had your James Joyce seat, we had our preferred spot, too."

"But the Eclipse Bar never had anyone in there."

"The hotel security room monitors every camera in the building. An officer would always sit in there when you were in the bar and there was an officer always outside."

"But I never saw anyone when I left."

"We knew you were coming from the cameras. It's not that difficult."

Cameron frowned. "I never saw you or anyone watching me."

"Twice, I sat in direct line of sight of you at the Irish Village. I was wearing western clothing of course. And on your last visit to the Eclipse, when it was very crowded with those noisy Australians, I sat directly in front of you at the next table. My back was facing you."

Cameron's eyes widened, "Really? I always thought I'd recognise secret service officers, if I saw them. I imagined you would be behind a tree or something."

Sidney laughed, "Sometimes, the easiest place to hide is directly in front of you."

"Was that your husband with you at the Eclipse?" he asked.

"No, that was my secret service partner," she replied, laughing.

Ronnie paused. Now for the awkward bits. Cameron hesitated before stammering, "About the um, the um—"

Sydney's grin widened as she watched him flush even darker. "You mean the awkward parts in the bedroom?" she teased. Cameron squirmed uncomfortably, his eyes focused on his feet.

"Surveillance is invasive. It must be to find evidence. It turns normal day life into a reality show," she explained. "You don't need to feel embarrassed. We're professionals—we know what to watch closely and when to respect a subject's privacy. People are people. They do the same things. Nothing you did stood out any different."

Relieved but still uneasy, Cameron glanced toward Mr Abdullah and Major Juma. "Do they know everything?" he whispered. "You know, I mean everything?"

She leant in, whispering in his ear, "We all keep a few secrets to ourselves."

They stood and Sidney announced that she had to go. "It is a real breach of protocol that I meet with you," she admitted. "Mr Abdullah initially refused, but I tend to get my way. I wanted to wish you well. I know a lot about you, Cameron James. You'll do great things. I do believe you have found yourself. Leave Ronnie here. Cherish your friendships—and love her heaps."

She leant forward giving him a kiss on the cheek and turned to leave. Pausing, she reached into her abaya, pulled out an object, and placed it in his open hands, wrapping his fingers around it, and whispered, "Don't stop. Keep it up—it looks great. This is what I use. Goodbye, Ronnie."

As she exited, Cameron opened his fingers to find a silver shaver. His face was burning red, glowing brighter than the lounge lights. He avoided eye contact with Mr Abdullah and Major Juma, dreading their silent amusement.

Despite the very traditional Arabic surrounds, Cameron received a steady supply of alcohol, primarily Bacardi and Coke, along with an occasional glass of Sauvignon Blanc. As the flight time drew closer, Major Juma signaled Cameron to follow him, leading him to the very last *majlis*, tucked away in the back corner of the lounge.

"One more piece of business, Mr Cameron," he said, pulling a folded sheet of paper from his pocket. "I have here a report concerning the Warehouse No.5 fire at the Fruit & Vegetable Market earlier this year. The report notes the specimen examined showed signs of staining, most likely engine oil, but no sign of any fire accelerant."

Cameron stared at Major Juma, confusion fogging his mind. Too much wine, maybe.

"Mr Cameron," Major Juma repeated, a little frustrated that Cameron had not understood the cryptic message. From a small bag, he retrieved the piece of the piano case—well, what remained of it. Cameron had forgotten about it.

"So, my grandfather didn't do it?" he asked.

Major Juma quietly added, "Off the record, and given the circumstances, the lab only conducted limited testing. However, the forensic scientist verbally confirmed that the stain is very old, but most likely human blood. More extensive tests is required to make that conclusion definitive," he paused before continuing. "But in his opinion, it is human blood. It would be highly unlikely that you'd be able to draw any DNA samples from it."

Major Juma handed Cameron the piece of the piano case.

Cameron stared at the fragment for what felt like eternity. "So, he was the killer," he muttered.

"My professional police judgement says this evidence alone cannot lead to a definitive conclusion," Major Juma replied. "But my gut tells me your instincts are likely correct."

Cameron's vision blurred. He found a place to sit.

Breaking the silence, Major Juma continued, "You face a choice. That fragment can remain filed under the file of the Fruit & Vegetable Market fire, leaving the mystery of your two girls simply that, a mystery. Or you can accuse your grandfather of murder, based on evidence that is incomplete or inconclusive. The decision lies with you."

Cameron voice steadied as he responded, "I just exposed a friend, knowing he will rot in jail, because it was the right thing to do. No regrets. If my grandfather committed a heinous crime, he deserves the same. It's the right thing to do."

Major Juma thought long before responding, "Mr Cameron, your so-called friend committed a major crime and will pay the appropriate penalty, based on facts and evidence. As for your grandfather's case, it rests on a 'maybe.' He cannot be held accountable based on speculation alone. Exposing this may only bring grief, pain and misery to those who have already endured enough. Think carefully, Cameron. As a policeman, I must emphasise that the evidence you hold does not meet the threshold for conviction.

Mr Abdullah approached, signalling that it was time to leave. "Enjoy your flight, Mr Cameron," he said. "From this point onward, you're on your own. No backup, no protection. Do stay in close contact with the Embassy and authorities when you get back. Our time together has come to an end."

At the gate, Cameron handed his boarding pass to the flight attendant, "Welcome aboard, Mr James, let me escort you to your first-class suite."

Settling into his seat, Cameron reached for the Australian phone Jacqui had bought him before leaving.

"Is that you, Cameron?" came Jacqui's anxious voice.

"I'm on the plane. I'm coming home," he replied.

"How long for?"

"It's a one-way ticket."

He switched the phone to flight mode.

CHAPTER SEVENTEEN

In the comfort of his first-class seat, he again read his boarding pass—Cameron James. He smiled. *I'll make you proud, Great-Granddad Edmund.* The door of the plane closed. He felt a sense of relief and at peace that the Lebedev affair was over—at peace with his sense of duty. He had done right. Truth must prevail.

After sleeping peacefully for several hours, he refreshed himself with a shower and enjoyed meeting new friends around the bar at the back of the plane. "Hello, I'm Cameron James," he said repeatedly, relishing the introduction every time. He ran a sheep farm on the south-west slopes, while his partner pursued a career as a legal partner in a law firm. Recently, he had completed a trip inspecting alternate breeds of sheep to the Merino, including the French Merino, the Rambouillet, in France.

As his flight neared Australia, his thoughts focused on the words of Major Juma and the choices he must make. He understood what Major Juma said in relation to the determination of guilt. As he processed his thoughts, he realised the same principles applied to forensic accounting—a suspected crime must be validated by evidence. Let that process take its course. He had a duty to expose the truth. He was comfortable with that. He will tell Jacqui the evidence collected thus far and what needed to be done to reach a conclusion. They would do that together.

Cameron's thoughts went back to one of his favourite books, *Kings Row.* He now had a new understanding of Henry Bellamann's book as a deeper commentary on society than he had initially appreciated. He wondered again why Grandma had not wanted him to read it "until he was older." As he recalled the events in *Kings Row,* he pondered upon the secrets hidden behind the lights in a high-rise, the reality behind transactions on an otherwise ordinary invoice and the secrets hidden by his grandfather. Sidney's words kept echoing in his mind: "*The easiest place to hide is directly in front of you."* Cameron now saw things that had been in front of him but had gone unnoticed. He resolved that this must change.

As he walked through the Sydney Airport terminal, a TV news broadcast on a large television screen caught his attention. The words "White Birch" filled the screen. He momentarily stopped to listen. The world's biggest crack down on money laundering had begun. Arrests were happening around the globe. The news story claimed it as "one of the biggest blows to organised crime and a major disruptor to Russian-backed syndicates."

Text crawling across the bottom of the screen read: "*White Birch—Russia's National Tree—a national symbol, fundamental to Russian culture and patriotism ...*" The news presenter listed many countries where arrests had been made, with a map of the world, scattered with red dots. "So far, there have been no links to White Birch in Australia."

Cameron smiled. *Not 'till now.* And walked off.

The Foreign Affairs staff were waiting for him after he cleared customs, escorting him to a hotel in the city. The following morning, he met Foreign Affairs staff and Federal Police officers. He received his new passport and met Daniel Mathias, his case manager—an ex-policeman in his mid-forties. He was no Sidney. Daniel and his team would check in with Cameron regularly for the first few months. Cameron was required to check in every week and immediately report any suspicious activity or visitors on a 1-800 number. No sign of a Major Juma covert phone app. Cameron also sensed there would be no free drinks at the bar.

"Do you have a Sidney working for you?" Cameron asked.

"We do not disclose staff names," replied a rather overweight male agent with thick black framed glasses.

The moment amused Cameron. He welcomed the news that

there would be no surveillance. A representative from Cameron's bank arrived and names of accounts were changed, including credit cards, with increased limits, and a separate account created for his newfound wealth until he could get appropriate financial planning advice. Arrangements were made to transfer his money from his UAE accounts to his new accounts in Australia.

Cameron enjoyed calmy instructing, "I'll keep a couple of hundred thousand in my everyday account, thank you."

A new driver's license had been prepared, and he was being "adjusted" on the electoral roll.

He rented a very smart, top of the range LandCruiser and headed for Harden, enjoying a pleasant and relaxing drive home. He arrived just before 4.00 pm, going directly to the offices of R.S. Forbes Solicitors, smiling at the sight of Jacqueline's car parked outside.

Jacqueline, her father and Mabel warmly greeted him. Mr Forbes eagerly sought updates on Dubai, but Jacqui interrupted, directing Cameron to her office to see her latest research that she completed in his absence. Locking the door behind her, they embraced, her kiss sucked every breath out of him. They began where they left off and were soon both breathing very heavily. They quickly redressed, making themselves presentable to exit the office.

As Jacqui took the handle to open the door, Cameron put his hand on hers. "Jacqui, we need to talk."

"Plenty of time to do business, Cameron. Let's settle in first—"

"Please," Cameron persisted. "Can you come out to Binya now? It's important."

Jacqui's face exposed her concern, "You're getting me worried again, Cameron."

"A lot has happened, and I need to share it with you, now."

"As long as we can continue where we just left off," she added with another kiss. "This house sale settlement must be completed today. How about I join you in an hour or so?"

"That's fine," Cameron accepted. "I'll go and unpack, freshen up and get the smell of sheep in my nostrils."

Cameron drove down the track, parked in the normal spot at the farmhouse and entered the gate. His first project would be building a garage inside the fence line with an automatic door and sensor lighting—a lot of it.

As he entered the gate, the farm truck came bouncing over the paddock from the direction of the creek. He expected to see Young Billy extricate himself from behind the wheel, but to Cameron's surprise, out jumped Gary. He could immediately see a very different Gary. He stood more upright. His body appeared in better tone. His hair was cut. His face alive and full of colour.

"Hi, Boss, I didn't know you were coming back," Gary greeted him. "I didn't recognise the car."

"Let's cut that shit out immediately. We were school mates, remember? It's Cameron. It's always Cameron," Cameron grinned, grabbing Gary's strong hand. "Now, let's try that again: Gidday mate."

They embraced.

"Young Billy around?"

"We don't see him much these days," Gary explained, his eyes shining in the sun. "He wants to, but it's a struggle. Got him milking the cows but most of that I've been throwing away. It's more about finding him something to do."

"Ian's kept me updated. Sounds like you have everything under control—and then some."

"I'm not being critical or nothin' but there was a lot of things that needed doing, Cameron," Gary said as he eyes scanned across the farm. "But there is nothing we can't fix."

"I'm not surprised. Between Young Billy and my grand-mother, I'm amazed it kept ticking at all."

"I've got some ideas—"

"Ian's filled me in a little on that. I'm keen to talk. Been doing a bit of reading myself. Let me get settled for a few days and we will sit down and chat."

"Can I ask one thing?"

"Sure, but I think I know what that is," smiling, Cameron placed his hand on Gary's shoulder. "The answer's yes. Yes, I'm staying. Register me as a sheep farmer."

"Bloody beauty," Gary's grin lit his face, and he stood even more upright.

"And as long as you want to be, you will be part of that."

They embraced again and Gary jumped back in the farm truck and started the engine. "Nice wheels, Boss."

"Lucky what you get on a rental upgrade sometime," Cameron replied. After a pause he added, "This is a better welcome than the last time you greeted me," he said with a grin.

"You saved me, Cameron," he said with tears swelling in his bright eyes.

"Get your arse to work."

As he started to move off, Gary added, "There's a big box in there that arrived by courier a couple of days ago. It is addressed to you. Must have known you were coming back."

Cameron grabbed his belongings from the car and made his way to his great-grandmother's bedroom. Officially now Cameron's room—his four poster-bed. Cameron quickly scanned the room—*nothing is going to change in here.*

He made his way to the living room. In front of the fireplace sat a large black wooden box, obviously very old. Foam blocks had been wrapped around it for protection. Given the recent events, he momentarily hesitated opening a mysterious, unknown box. It was addressed to Cameron Blanche, Binya, Harden. The sender, Heather Gilbert—a name he didn't recognise. Noting the sender's address was Bowral, he sensed a connection with Aunt Agnes.

Cameron removed the plastic packaging and opened the lid. An envelope addressed to him sat on top—inside a letter from Heather Gilbert, who identified herself as Aunt Agnes's grandniece. He opened the letter. It read:

Dear Cameron,

Grandma Agnes asked me to send you this. She said you were overseas but coming home very soon. She said you and a friend, Jacqueline, had visited and that Jacqueline had been back and had asked again (She said you two were going to make a lovely couple). She indicated that you were chasing family history stuff, but she was not too clear as to what specifically. You may have noticed Aunt Agnes is very good for 98 but she is getting frail and her memory fades at times. Anyway, she said you were looking for something, she could not recall specifically what you were looking for, so I decided to send you the whole box.

We stored all of Grandma's things in our shed. Most of it is furniture and household items such as crockery and the like. This box, which was Grandma's original glory box, contains her more personal belongings. I thought it best to send it to you to pick through.

I would be very pleased if you could return it to us when you are finished.

Regards,
Heather

Cameron opened the box and began methodically reviewing every item. It was not just an evidence search. Cameron felt privileged to have this personal insight into Aunt Agnes.

Handmade gifts from grandchildren, birthday cards, newspaper clippings of family and other similar things. As he dug deeper, he found old photos, recognising some pictures of his grandmother, even his mother as a young girl. There were wedding photos and several newspaper notices noting births, deaths and marriages. As he worked his way through the box, the items were obviously getting older and older as he got deeper and deeper. He had nearly reached the bottom where a lot of the contents were in old brown paper bags, some with handwritten notes on the front identifying contents, all in the same handwriting and then some bags with no labels.

He picked up a brown paper bag—nothing written on the outside. He first pulled out a newspaper cutting of the death notice of Cecil Barkley. Second item was the death notice of his grandfather. He felt in again. One more item—an envelope, addressed simply: "To Mr Cecil Barkley." He turned it over. It was sealed, nothing written on the back.

A chill went down his back. He was breathing rapidly. He would often get excited when he discovered something of importance in a spreadsheet, but this feeling was far more intense. He felt everything moving at an accelerated rate.

He got a knife and sliced open the top of the envelope. It contained a single page of very hard to read writing, written with a fountain pen and with little punctuation. He read it slowly, word by word.

Dear Cec,

I am a coward a weak soul who is not worthy to live. From that day I have come to you many times to tell you what happened but have been gutless every time It was me I killed Jane and Kathleen but believe me Cec it was an accident. On that night I was driving into town it was raining hard. As I came down the hill passing the track to the waterworks a thud hit the side of the truck and a bump. I had no idea what it was and stopped. I saw nothing. I stopped and walked back I thought something must have fell off the truck and only then did I see the two girls they had come out the waterworks track and couldn't stop down the hill and ran into the side of the truck. Kathleen had a bad knock to the head and a lot of blood. Jane was lying in the ditch and there was a tyre mark across her dress her eyes stared straight into me but she would not answer she just lay there. That's where I failed as a man I panicked I put them in the box on the truck with their bikes and went into town to tell you or the police or someone. But when I got there I couldn't do it. I went back to the farm and then later back into town to go to the police but saw all the cars at the dance hall. I tried to tell you then but the words wouldn't come out. You know I come over to your place lots of times and every time it was to tell you but every time I couldn't. I went home and drunk until I couldn't remember. I wanted you to know before you died but when I went the hospital they wouldn't let me in. I've written this letter so when you wake you can read it but by then I will be dead. I cannot live with this anymore and I'm not going to have you die before me. I buried them and I have looked after them and attend them all this time. You will find them with God. You are the only friend I have ever had and I failed you. I am a coward gutless person that cannot call myself a man worthy of anything. I swear I did not see them. It was an accident. I feared no one would believe me.

Will

Cameron studied the letter for some time, frozen in the chair. He held the one piece of critical evidence that solved a fifty-year-old mystery—an undelivered letter, waiting all those years to be read. The tragedy of that night and the years following overwhelmed him. He recalled when he and Jacqui had done the ride, how steep that bank was and how slippery it must have been in the rain. Closing his eyes, he vividly envisioned the accident happening. *But why hadn't his grandfather simply reported it? How much grief would have been saved if he had just come forward? How different may things have been? If he had of come forward, would he have been believed? Would he have been punished as a criminal for a crime that was an accident?* More questions kept bombarding Cameron's mind. Questions he had no answers for. He reminded himself to focus.

"The truth," he muttered. "Must stay focused on the truth."

He checked his watch. Jacqui would be arriving any minute. He walked to his bedroom. Passing Grandma's room, he opened the door and entered. "Did you know?" he asked aloud. He doubted it, but if she had, she would have taken the secret to her grave. *To protect her husband,* he thought. In the darkness of the lounge outside his bedroom, he sat with his head resting in his hands. *Sorry, Grandma, it had to come out.*

Hearing the approaching car, he returned to the dining room and sat at the head of the extended dining room table in the very chair his grandfather would have sat on for every meal. At the far end, Aunt Agnes's glory box sat on the floor, with its contents scattered in piles on the table. Jacqui arrived and a few minutes later, he heard the opening of the breezeway door.

"Hello," she called out. "Cameron, you there?"

He didn't respond. He felt sick, knowing the task ahead of him, but his duty remained clear.

She appeared at the door, carrying two bottles of wine. "There you are. It's all very quiet."

He stood, motioning Jacqui to a chair at the table, "Come Jacqui, sit down."

Her expression shifted—her smile faded. Placing the wine bottles on the cupboard beside her, she surveyed the mess of papers on the desk and Cameron's solemn face. He was pale and beads of sweat had formed on his forehead.

"Cameron, you're frightening me. What's going on?"

"Jacqui, I need to tell you something and I will get straight to the point." He took a breath and continued, "There was an accident. My grandfather was driving his truck. Jane and Kathleen were riding their bikes down the waterworks track in the dark. It was raining heavily and they couldn't stop. They were killed."

"What?" her faced twisted, "How do you know this? Are you saying, your grandfather killed Jane and Kathleen? What the hell, Cameron?"

"Jacqui, let me tell you everything."

Jacqui sat in silence and stared straight ahead.

Cameron began. He described how he went in search for a milk can, returned for breakfast and suddenly connected the piano box in the milk shed to the box that had been seen on his grandfather's truck. He explained how he found damaged bike frames and the stain on the bottom of the box. He told her how he had got the stain tested.

"So, you knew this before you went back to Dubai and you didn't tell me?" Her face twisted in emotional pain, her anguish evident.

"It all happened at the same time," he replied. "Just after I found it, I got a phone call to return to Dubai. That had me scared shitless. I was running around organising the farm. I didn't know what I'd found. It took me some time to process it myself. Adding to that, I was very limited about what communications I could make. I was still working it out myself. I had no idea what it meant at first. The shed is full of bikes. They could have been the girls, but I had no way of proving that. The stain in the bottom of the box. Was it blood? I had no proof. I had to find out. It was all conjecture."

"You should have told me," she replied coldly.

Cameron tried to remain calm, "Told you what? I had found some things, but I had no idea what they meant or that I didn't even know if they were connected to the girls? Back in Dubai, I got it tested, and I only got the results of that yesterday, minutes before I got on the plane and frankly, they are not conclusive. And I'm sitting here telling you as soon as I got here."

"You could have, should have, told me what you knew."

"Jacqui, please, just stop for a moment because none of that matters anymore."

"It matters a lot, and you didn't tell me."

Cameron could hear Jacqui's anger.

"Jacqui, it doesn't matter because we have this," he said, pointing to the papers at the end of the table.

"Gary told me it arrived a few days ago. I didn't even know it was here when I saw you this afternoon. It came from Heather Gilbert, Aunt Agnes's grandniece. It's Aunt Agnes's glory box."

He handed Jacqui Heather's letter, which she gave a cursory read.

"I just found this, just before you arrived," he said, reaching out for the brown paper bag he had sitting on the table. He pulled out Jacqui's grandfather's newspaper death notice and handed it to Jacqui. He then handed her his grandfather's death notice. Lastly, he pulled out the envelope and handed it to Jacqui. She scanned the envelope, opened it and read the letter. She sat silent. He didn't know if she was reading it or just staring into space. After some minutes, tears swelled in her eyes, and she placed the letter down on the table.

"So, where are they buried?" she asked. Her eyes staring into space.

"I just read this myself, sitting here waiting for you. I don't know."

More silence. "We don't know it was an accident. He killed them," she said.

Cameron said nothing. Her eyes remained fixed staring directly ahead.

After a long period of silence, she stood up, "I have to go."

"Jacqui, let's work through this together," he said, placing his hand on her shoulder, but she pulled away.

"Space, Cameron. I need space. I need to go," she said, grabbing her bag and keys and leaving.

Cameron felt upset but knew he had at last done the right thing. He sat silently for some time, trying to piece together all the information and how the tragedy had unfolded. He tried to imagine how different the scenario would have been if his grandfather had confessed at the time. He asked himself why no one had pieced it together before now. Why had no one ever read the letter?

A couple of hours passed. He hadn't heard from Jacqui so he rang her number. It went to voicemail. He rang her home and her mother answered—Jacqui had come home briefly, gone to her room, but had left again, not saying where she was going. They had assumed she had returned to Binya.

Not wanting to alarm her, he claimed he could hear the car approaching, so he bid her goodnight and hung up.

A little later, he tried Jacqui's mobile again, but again, it went to voicemail.

He waited.

Later, he went to the kitchen sink and filled the electric jug. As he turned away, his eye caught a flash of light. He peered into the otherwise darkness. There were car headlights shining in the paddock, near the quarry.

"She's found them!" he exclaimed. "Hidden right in front of us. Of course, Sidney."

He rushed out to the rented LandCruiser and drove to the quarry.

Her car was parked on the edge of the quarry wall, positioned so that her headlights illuminated the quarry floor. He parked at the top of what had been the entrance and walked down into the quarry. She sat a few metres up the bank, to her right stood a shovel alongside human bones protruding from a hole she had dug. She made no acknowledgement of his presence, her eyes fixed on the opened, shallow grave.

"How did you know?" he asked.

She sat some time before responding. "You're the one telling me to read the numbers. To look at what is in front of you."

"I didn't know, Jacqui."

"You didn't add it up? What two places did your grandfather forbid you to go? The dairy and the quarry. There were no snakes, Cameron. The quarry hasn't collapsed, Cameron. Your grandfather was telling you a lie all along. You didn't listen or see.

"Where did he go to die Cameron? The quarry paddock. He didn't die of a heart attack. He killed himself—deliberately at this spot—an overdose I bet—no autopsies in those days."

She was right. He recalled Sidney's words: "The safest place to hide is right in front of you." Cameron had failed at the one thing he excelled at, on a matter closest to him.

"How did you know to dig there?" he pointed.

"Oh, Cameron. Where is the forensic accountant now? Where is the person who wonders why birds are circling in a specific area or why a field is dug up when it's the only paddock ploughed? He said in the letter he looked after them, so don't you think there would be a clue, however small?

Cameron's eyes surveyed the quarry in the limited light from the headlights.

"How many trees to do you see? One. And the rocks there weren't as random as the other rocks. Come on, Cameron. It wasn't difficult—if you wanted to find the answer."

He resented the implication that he hadn't wanted to find the answer, but she was right; the answer had always been clearly in front of them all this time.

After some time, Jacqui spoke, "You should have told me, Cameron. You weren't truthful and open. What else haven't you told me?"

Cameron thought deeply. The silence stretched.

"I love you, Jacqui," Cameron replied. "Over the last few weeks in Dubai, I have realised Ronnie is someone I didn't want to be. The two people I care for the most are you and Ian. I've hurt the people I love most. I love you. I've left Ronnie behind in Dubai. I'm Cameron and I want you. I love you."

Her face remained expressionless, and she said nothing.

Neither of them heard it at first—a faint rumble, barely audible. Then, the clatter of rocks. The beaming headlights from both vehicles made it difficult to see the quarry walls. Before they realised, the quarry wall to Jacqui's right, directly under her car, began to slide toward the floor of the quarry, ever so quietly but rapidly gaining momentum. Rocks and dirt streamed past Jacqui, barely a metre away, spilling over the partially opened grave and engulfing Cameron, who stood on the quarry floor.

Blinded by the headlights, Cameron had no idea of the size of the avalanche rushing toward him. At first, it felt like being struck by a wave in the surf, the powerful undercurrent pulling his body into a rip. Within seconds, Cameron was engulfed into a tomb of complete darkness. Initially, he felt no pain, but he couldn't move. He struggled to move his head and hands but couldn't. He could feel the muscles in his limbs tense, but he could not move them. He couldn't even determine where his limbs were in relation to his body. He didn't know if his eyes were open or shut, but dirt scratched his eyeballs—he had an uncontrollable urge to wipe them but couldn't. He tried to inhale, but it was like plastic smothering his face. He opened his mouth, only for it to fill with dirt. He tried to exhale but failed. His lungs began to scream for air. The pain was excruciating as capillaries and alveoli began to explode with the pressure of mounting carbon dioxide, then he began to drown in his blood. His head pounded as his brain begged for oxygen. Then, there was no more. His heart contracted one last time.

On the outside, Jacqui sat stunned. Where Cameron stood only moments ago was now a pile of dirt and rock. Her thoughts drifted to the cultivated soil her father would talk about. The smell lingered in the air. It was exactly the same. Exactly as she remembered it.

EPILOGUE

It was late—the sky black, cloudless and moonless—the Milky Way clearly creasing the heavens above. Cameron often spent evenings on the Binya verandah watching the night sky. His recovery had taken a long time, but his health was slowly improving. From the verandah, he could see car lights parked on the side of the road, near the quarry, which had become a popular night-time gathering spot for the town's youth. He didn't object.

The council had erected a memorial for Jane and Kathleen Barkley on the roadside adjacent to the quarry, including a small parking bay. A sign informed visitors that the quarry was on private property and not accessible, but that hadn't stopped the many visitors. Cameron and Gary often found remnants of campfires at the quarry. Cameron had erected a sign that read "I don't mind you coming, but take your empties," and most people complied. Danger signs were erected around the top of the quarry, but it was safer now that most of the wall had collapsed. Authorities concluded that the weight of the vehicle, parked on the very edge, triggered the collapse.

Nearly a year had passed since Cameron's burial in the landslide. His grandfather had been right about that. The quarry was dangerous. He should not have survived—he was in full cardiac arrest when paramedics arrived. Jacqueline had called 000 immediately and began digging. In her efforts to dig, she inadvertently sliced deep into Cameron's left leg. The presence of blood immediately pinpointed his location, ultimately saving his life.

Paramedics arrived in minutes, by which time she had almost dug him free. They began resuscitation efforts, defibrillating him several times until circulation returned. They intubated him and continued to artificially ventilate his lungs. A rescue helicopter from Canberra, with an emergency physician on board, evacuated him directly to the Canberra Trauma Centre.

Being in the witness protection program, Cameron's entry into the hospital system triggered an immediate notification to the Federal Police. Police and Foreign Affairs staff swarmed the hospital. At one stage, the hospital was placed into lockdown. Confusion heightened when Jacqueline—followed by Cameron's mother, when she arrived from Melbourne—insisted his name was Cameron Blanche, not Cameron James.

Case manager, Daniel Mathias, arrived via Federal Police helicopter from Sydney to take charge. He explained to Jacqueline that Cameron had applied for a legal name change. Authorities soon determined that Cameron's injury resulted from an accident and there was no suggestion of foul play or criminal intervention. The Commonwealth government media machine acted immediately to ensure only the name "Cameron James" appeared in any media, with no reference to his recent arrival from Dubai.

Cameron was the last to know the severity of his condition and his near-death experience. The long, deep cut to his left leg became the physical symbol of his miraculous escape from death. But his traumatised lungs suffered the most life-threatening damage. Doctors kept him in a medically induced coma for ten days. His recovery had been complicated and slow.

His mother and Ian were at Cameron's bedside when he took his first unassisted breath as they delicately eased him off the ventilator. At least that's what they told him—Cameron could not remember the moment. When he finally awoke into a state he could remember, to his surprise, he found Colleen by his bedside. He learnt that she had visited nearly every day, often with Ian. When Cameron first returned home, Colleen fulfilled many of the nursing duties including bathing him daily. Ian and Gary quickly had a shower installed in the bathroom. Colleen still visited nearly every day, providing meals and attending to the housework.

Cameron steadily improved over the year and now lived a reasonably normal life, except for anything too strenuous. Scans had found no neurological deficit, but his lungs would never get back to their pre-injury state.

Harden briefly became the centre of national and international media attention immediately following the discovery of the bodies. At times, the media outnumbered the locals. The dramatic end to the search added to the drama and attention. Cameron monitored most of it through social media and TV news channels. The witness protection program worked over-time to ensure minimal coverage of Cameron. The media focused on Jacqueline Forbes who had found the bodies and solved a fifty-year-old missing persons case, rather than her rescue of Cameron.

The deaths of Kathleen and Jane Barkley fifty years earlier were soon being described as a tragic accident. Response to William White's role in the story was mixed. Initially, the media attacked his cowardness in not coming forward. But while it was commonly agreed he was wrong in not immediately reporting the accident, there was a growing swell of sympathy for the pain and mental anguish he had endured, culminating in his suicide. Two national men's support groups highlighted his case in their promotion of greater need for mental health support for men, particularly rural men.

There was a common sentiment that the whole event not only had seen two girls accidently killed but several lives shattered. One national headline read: "A sad sad affair." The story published William's letter in full.

The funeral didn't take place for some time, until the coroner had released the remains. It was a huge event with media appearing to outnumber the mourners. The police had to restrict attendance in the church using bar coded entry invites issued by the Forbes family. St Paul's Anglican Church was lost in a sea of flower tributes. An attempt to count them stopped when they quickly reached 1,000.

The Prime Minister was asked in a press conference if he would be attending the funeral, to which he replied, "The death of two children is strictly a private family affair." He had previously telephoned Mary Forbes to pass on his condolences and the condolences of the nation soon after the discovery of the remains. The day after the funeral, both the Australian and Sydney Morning Herald newspapers front page was a full-page photo of St Paul's Anglican Church in a sea of flowers, with the hearse barely visible. It had become a symbolic picture of the tragedy.

Jacqui had accompanied Cameron in the helicopter evacuation to the hospital in Canberra and visited him frequently at first. But their relationship had been scarred. Jacqui continued to believe Cameron had not been truthful and had not shared information with her and told Cameron she would always have concerns he was not telling her everything. Cameron felt that she begrudged him for solving her case. She returned to using the name Jacqueline.

Cameron was very disappointed to find out that Jacqueline had kept her own secrets in not sharing that she had pre-signed contract deals for the publication of a book and rights to an overseas television show that specialised in cold case stories. Both swung into action immediately after the bodies were found. With Cameron incapacitated, his mother, Ian and Gary took immediate action to stop media access to Binya. A temporary injunction was enacted until Cameron could make his own decisions. The police assisted by making the whole property a crime scene. When Cameron could, he took legal action to prohibit any entry onto Binya. Nine million dollars gave him a good platform to commence any legal action required. The witness protection program assisted and worked silently to minimise Cameron's exposure. Jacqueline inadvertently assisted with her keenness to promote her solving of the case by focusing the spotlight on her. Cameron controlled entry to the property, which he basically limited to the quarry, and even that was restricted at first. Cameron refused all requests for interview.

When he found out about the media deals, the relationship cooled even further. Cameron's refusal to participate ended it completely. When Cameron attended the funeral, he sat with his mum and Paul, Heidi and Bruce, along with Ian and Colleen, all in the row behind the Forbes family. But the flame that Cameron had for Jacqueline had been extinguished. He felt betrayed by the media deals and questioned her true motives in trying to solve the case.

Mary Forbes demonstrated a lot of strength immediately following the finding of her sisters' remains. She insisted that they be returned to the graves where they had been originally buried by William White. When she proposed this to Cameron, he was shocked and asked why.

"Your great-grandfather bought this place because it was called Binya and believed that was a term for resting place. This has been their resting place for fifty years. And I'd like it to stay that way."

Cameron had no objection, but the local council did and while they initially opposed it, they suddenly changed their minds. When Cameron asked Mary how that had happened, she simply replied, "When the Prime Minister tells you to phone him if there is anything he can do, sometimes he is good at his word."

It was said the funeral procession reached from the church to Binya. An exaggeration most likely but accepted into the folklore. All the flowers from the church were transferred to the site and covered the quarry floor. Mary even had a plaque mounted on a granite rock to mark the place where William White took his own life. The spot became symbolic for men facing mental health anguish.

Mary found peace that her sisters had finally been laid to rest. She felt no anger against William White, but rather pity. Mary hadn't withdrawn into a cocoon as Cameron expected, but rather emerged as a strong woman, active in the church and community, even at one point addressing a national conference on men's mental health in rural settings. At one point during the funeral, she laid her hand on Cameron's and whispered, "It had to come out. All is at rest now." Cameron was so relieved that her fear of finding out that her sisters may have been raped and murdered had not been realised. Mary also shared with Cameron that she was not happy with the media deals Jacqueline had engaged, but said she would not allow that to bring further trauma to the family, though Cameron observed they were never as close as before.

Soon after the discovery, Jacqueline's father was diagnosed with an advanced brain cancer and died a few months later. After his death, R.S. Forbes Solicitors closed and never reopened. Jacqueline got a job in Sydney and rarely visited Harden. Cameron would sit with Mary in church and visit her regularly, but not if Jacqueline was in town. They both agreed that they would not tell Jacqueline that they met regularly. One day, a truck arrived on Binya to deliver the antique office desk from the Forbes office that had been Mr Forbes from his early years as a solicitor. Mary insisted that Cameron take it. He remains unaware if Jacqueline knows its whereabouts.

Cameron's mother, Rosemary, initially took the news of her father's involvement in the death of the sisters very badly. At first, she lived in fear her son would die. At the same time, she was angry with Jacqueline and Cameron for exposing her father as a killer. She declared that she could never enter Harden again.

Maybe it was the national pity, the publicity promoting men's health needs, or, more likely, the positive support from Mary, her closest friend from childhood, that helped Rosemary accept the tragedy for what it was: a terrible, accidental series of events.

Both Mary and Rosemary would often accompany Cameron, Ian, Colleen and the children on picnics to the rock paddock. Gary would sometimes join. Cameron got to know his stepfather Paul a lot better. Paul had stepped up to the plate, taking a lead in a lot of the legal response to Jacqueline's request for access. He became active in supporting the farm, often travelling to Harden, leaving Rosemary at home in Melbourne.

A coroner's inquest was held and concluded that Jane and Kathleen Barkley had been killed in a hit-and-run accident. The report concluded that whilst Mr William White was the driver of the truck, he appeared not to have contributed to the accident, but he had failed to report it, which is a crime in itself. He had committed a number of other crimes as well, including interfering with human remains and not reporting a death. Soon after, the police returned the evidence that they had collected to Cameron, mainly the piano case and the 1954 International truck. Cameron took the piano case to the quarry one night, by himself, and burned it. He was working with a retired mechanical restorer in Cootamundra to restore the International truck.

Aunt Agnes died unaware of the accident or the discovery of the bodies.

Cameron sat on the verandah, sipping red wine. He had a whole new perspective on the concept of the resting place. Not only in regard to Binya but within himself. He found himself stopping at the grave of the bushranger, John Gilbert, just as his father would do, but now with a new appreciation. He even returned with a shovel and whipper snipper to clean the grave site. He smiled to himself when he read an article in the local paper about the mysterious return of the "caretaker of the grave."

Whenever he went to Sydney, he would stop at the Private James Gordon rest area, appreciating that James Gordon was, indeed, at rest. And just maybe, the location symbolised the peace efforts—and those of all the troops—brought to each and every one of us, regardless of where we live.

Today, Cameron signed the purchase papers of Currawong, the neighbouring property, where Jane and Kathleen Barkley had been raised. Mary Forbes had approached Cameron, informing him that the farm had been bequeathed to her on the death of her father, and was, therefore, in her name solely and not tied up in her husband's estate settlement. She had determined a price that she declared not negotiable, which underestimated its net worth considerably, but she refused to negotiate. Cameron didn't hesitate—not because it was a great business opportunity, but because he saw it as the right thing to do and it gave Mary comfort and peace. When he asked Mary if Jacqueline had agreed, she replied that Jacqueline had told her that she didn't want anything to do with it "ever again" and instructed her mother to "do what you like with it."

Mary said she was happy to comply with her wishes.

Gary was moving into the Currawong homestead and would oversee both Binya and Currawong operations from there.

He would have liked to have enjoyed tonight's drink with Ian, but Ian, Peta and Kurt were away this week performing at the Tamworth Musical Festival and receiving much acclaim.

Jacqueline's book, *Before Your Eyes*, had been released a couple of weeks before. It got minimal media coverage and, from what he could gather, had been slow on sales. One review in the Sydney Morning Herald concluded it was a story with minimal content. Cameron agreed, a hit-and-run accident and a tormented soul that lacked the courage to come forward, who died a broken man. That's the story. He had not seen the book for sale in the Harden Newsagent—the public interest appeared to have moved on.

He sipped on his wine and for a moment, in the drifting night air, he got a whiff of the smell from the dairy. It was that familiar smell, exactly as he remembered it.

THE SPIRITS OF THE DEAD

A poem by Kenneth Mackay

Sitting lonely in the silence, come the phantoms of the past,
And across my heated fancy are their shadows swiftly cast,
Till the ghosts of buried mem'ries in the chamber silent tread,
And I seem to hold communion with the spirits of the dead.

While around me in the ether that through ages floats in space
The soft flutter of their pinions seems to cool my tired face,
And the odour of their presence as a subtle incense strong
Steals before my jaded senses like a strain of mellow song;

And I feel sweet spirit fingers lightly press upon my hair,
Till the weary brain, responsive, gladly casts away all care,
E'en as though their unseen watching bore with it a healing balm,
As of old a voice on Galilee gave deep and sudden calm.

Stay awhile, ah, best-loved spirit! Let me feel thou standest by!
Let me feast my eyes a moment where my thoughts forever lie!
And though thou art but a vision, born of dreaming long and deep,
But a mirage of the senses, but a picture dawn by Sleep,

Yet, oh slumber, lock thy chambers, that no other enter in!
Let me welcome back my loved one — pure from earth and earthly sin!
Let me meet my long lost idol freed for aye from death and pain!
Let me see she but remembers! — then I have not dreamed in vain.

Nearing now till I can almost feel her breath upon my cheek,
Though the face seems brighter, fairer, comes the vision that I seek,
And I gladly spring to clasp it — this my love of days now old,
But, alas, as cold as marble is the form my arms enfold;

While a voice, which seems to echo somewhat of a distant day,
Gently whispers, "I may never give you back a love of clay
That amid the dust lies buried with the one you loved so well, —
Never more to hold dominion where a purer theme may dwell.

Oh, cast thou aside the idols which beset an earthly life!
So that when the fight is over — and thou leav'st the weary strife,
I may meet thee at the portals of the realms of endless day:
Then thy hopes will all be garnered — and our love will be for aye."

Source: Kenneth Mackay, *Stirrup Jingles from the Bush and the Turf and Other Rhymes*, Sydney: Edwards, Dunlop & Co., 1887, pages 69-70.

ACKNOWLEDGEMENT

Writing a novel is an immense undertaking, requiring dedication through multiple phases, including creative development, drafting, writing, revising, rewriting, editing and proofreading. What begins as an exciting project soon becomes an all-encompassing pursuit—one that, at times, takes precedence over everything else, often at the expense of family and friends. There are moments when it becomes the overwhelming priority, demanding time and focus above all other responsibilities.

For that, I apologise. I am profoundly grateful to my loving and devoted wife, Karen, whose unwavering support and patience have been invaluable throughout this journey. Her encouragement—both emotional and practical—has been instrumental in bringing this project to completion. I could not have done it without her love and support.

With deep gratitude, I wish to thank the family of the late Mrs Mary McKee for graciously granting permission to feature her painting of *Binya Homestead*, created in the early 1990s, as the cover image of this book. Her work beautifully captures the spirit of place and memory, and it is an honour to share her artistry with readers.

Binya is a fictional story. Cameron, his family, their ancestors, and the events depicted in these pages are imagined. While the novel touches on some historical truths—such as the 1st Light Horse, its early recruits, and the heroics of Kenneth James McKay—its heart lies in storytelling.

Yet Harden-Murrumburrah is not fiction to me. It is a deeply special place—my birthplace and where I spent the earliest years of my life. My mother grew up on *Binya,* and until the family sold the property in the 1990s, it remained a place of wonder and freedom for me. I cherished every chance to explore the dairy and shearing shed and to scramble over the granite rocks. Those moments are forever etched into my heart and soul.

I wish to honour all who have called *Binya* home: the indigenous peoples who originally cared for these lands, the pioneers who ploughed the first fields and raised the first sheep, the owners before my family, those who have cared for it since and those who will follow. I trust *Binya* leaves with each of them, as it did me, a legacy that endures.

ABOUT THE AUTHOR

Neil Kirby holds a Bachelor's degree in Journalism, a Bachelor of Business in Human Resource Development, and a Master of Public Health. With extensive executive leadership experience in ambulance services across Australia and the Middle East, he has also conducted significant research in Canada, focusing on his passion—rural and remote healthcare. As a founding member of the International Roundtable on Community Paramedicine, he has played a pivotal role in advancing pre-hospital care worldwide. In recognition of his contributions to rural and remote service delivery, he was awarded the Australian Government Ambulance Service Medal in 2004.

Born in rural New South Wales, Neil has remained deeply committed to supporting rural and remote communities. He completed his schooling in Warilla, NSW, where his school honours his legacy with an annual award for outstanding school service in his name. Throughout his distinguished career, he has provided operational leadership during major multi-casualty and disaster events while also ensuring healthcare reaches some of Queensland's most isolated communities.

Despite his many achievements, Neil finds his greatest professional fulfillment in the deeply human moments of his work—offering care, compassion and comfort to people in life's most vulnerable and often final moments. These experiences have profoundly shaped his perspective on community, connection and the shared journey of life.

He resides in Queensland, Australia.

www.ingramcontent.com/pod-product-compliance
Lightning Source LLC
Chambersburg PA
CBHW030530190726
48283CB00006B/1845